BEARING THE BLADES

TYGER PRICE

JOY FOR LIFE

Bearing the Blades

Published by Joy for Life LLC
P.O. Box 2042, Idaho Falls, ID 83403
www.tygerprice.com

Printed in the United States of America
ISBN: (Paperback) 979-8-9864696-1-4 ($17.95)
ISBN: (Hardcover) 979-8-9864696-0-7 ($28.95)

Also by Tyger Price

The Blades of Sheorae:

Awaiting the Blades novella
An introduction to the world of Sheorae

Get your Free copy here
www.tygerprice.com

For Mark, my real-life Kendrick.
You fulfill my greatest dreams and make them my reality.
Always.

CONTENTS

FOREWORD

I have spent my lifetime being intrigued by the written word... I suppose it's genetic. My grandfather Ernest Hemingway said that to write, one needs to read and read and read. I believe this to be true. Reading gives you a wealth of information and, in some ways, experiences into worlds you might never have a viewpoint on. Then there are the books that come from one's imagination, with a depth of knowledge about a fantasy world. The writer can create a landscape we can relate to on this mundane human plane. It is an exceptional talent to write an intriguing fantasy novel. It explores a world that feels like an exploration of dreams. That is the power of ***Bearing The Blades.*** It dissects and paints a vision of life in your imagination. The first sentences of this novel had me intrigued immediately.

> *'Flaingoold, general of the hawkmen armies, relished the feel of the writhing form pinned beneath his immense right talon. His piercing golden eyes bore down on his human victim, now greatly wounded and helpless.'*

Immediately my vision and imagination were triggered into a world of bravery, heroics, and an instant belief in a half-man half-hawk. The book's first part introduces you to a sweet young child unable to make sense of the magical gifts she was given that would change her life (and everyone around her) forever. Then she comes of age, after years of training, into the power she was gifted as a mere toddler. ***Bearing the Blades*** is beautifully written. It made me feel that this *fantasy* world could actually exist. It is as though the writer, Tyger Price, (and honestly, could there be a better name for the writer of this book?) had visited my dreams, colorized and enhanced them. I was truly mesmerized by the characters and landscape in this wonderful book. The unrequited love, the longing, the intrigue, and the power that each page invokes is a journey you will want to go on.

I have tremendous respect for Tyger Price and her ability to create characters and creatures that have human abilities without being human at all and then making the human characters like heroes in a dream. Thank you, Tyger, for envisioning a world and making it come to life in my (the reader's) mind.

Like I said, read… and read this book and savor its imaginary world. You will appreciate and love the adventure, and you, like me, will most certainly want more.

Mariel Hemingway

THE BLADES

Flaingoold, general of the hawkmen armies, relished the feel of the writhing form pinned beneath his immense right talon. His piercing golden eyes bore down on his human victim, now greatly wounded and helpless.

"What dost thou think of thy mighty union now, Lord Tonclin, son of Klave?"

To accentuate his meaning, the hawkman brought the anvil of his fist crashing down across the man's face. The once-proud commander's only response was an agonizing groan.

Flaingoold stretched out his mighty gray wings and, throwing back his feather-covered head, let out a screeching laugh. Beating his fists against his bare chest, he reveled at his superiority before leaning back toward his prey.

Just then, the glint of steel caught his eye. He brought his left taloned foot forward, clamping the human's arm to the ground. The shift caused a breathless compression upon his victim, but Flaingoold paid no mind. His eyes were riveted on the ornate sword in the man's hand.

Applying pressure to his victim's arm, Flaingoold reverently pulled the weapon from the trembling fist. Holding it to the waning light peeking over the eastern edge of the ravine, the hawkman stared in awe.

The blade alone was a good three feet of steel that rippled upon itself, even in this lighting, due to the folding and refolding process needed to give it its power and strength. Gold-flame ornamentation decorated up its length where the dual-edge met. The razor-sharp edges winked a deadly gleam. The dual-gripped handle added another ten inches to the sword's length, but still it remained surprisingly well-balanced. The guard curved out and ascended, like bronze flames licking upward to praise the majesty of the blade. A golden drac's head lay in the middle of where the flames began. The dragonesque body twisted its way along the handle, embedding there, so as to provide grip but not discomfort. The eyes winked a menacing ruby red with a fire of their own.

"So, this be the legendary Alitaloas? The Great Blade," he murmured. "The one which, with its mate, unlocks the power to rule all of Sheorae."

The sensation of energy reverberating from the sword coursed through his arm, electrifying his body. Since their rediscovery five years previous, the mighty Blades were all Flaingoold had thought of, along with their destiny to free the land from the dreaded Drokmar, and of his own determination to be the one to bring about said destiny, thus indebting all the Seven Nations' allegiance to himself.

Around the precipice comrade after comrade stood watching, each with one or two human weaklings cowering beneath them.

"Find the dagger and scabbard!" he ordered.

Hungrily, he returned to the great weapon in his hand. The eyes of the dragon called to him. He peered into their depths, and he could see his grand future. He could see himself standing, poised at Dorincia Castle, his mighty wings outstretched, their gray expanse reaching out with their dark, smoky tips brushing both sides of the great throne room that must be there. Then with the mighty Blade gripped in his hand, he would fly off to defeat the villain Drokmar and his hosts from hell.

Of course, his lieutenant general or even his own mate would be there to wield the other blade. He would need their larger size and ferocity for the great battle of the Seven Nations, but he alone would vanquish the demon. He alone would claim Sheorae as his own. Then when they placed the golden crown upon the silver-speckled feathers atop his head, he alone would stand erect, his bare chest full, tail-feathers flared. And all would then proclaim him Flaingoold the Magnificent!

"General!"

Lathan, his Second-in-Command, drew the hawkman from this reverie. Flaingoold turned just in time to catch the scabbard with his spare hand, then seized the flung dagger in his beak. Flaunting his own agility, Flaingoold let out a hearty laugh. His men mimicked their commander's reaction, adding a few cheers of victory. The general then slipped the sword into its nesting place and removed its famed companion from his beak.

Legend referred to this as a dagger, but he was surprised by its size and appearance. Though obviously smaller than the 'Great Blade,' what it lacked in size was made up for in craftsmanship.

Its blade reached two feet in and of itself, elaborately decorated on the bottom four inches with gold and bronze. A mere palm-width across, the hand guard was tipped on either end with small dragon heads. The gleaming sentinels flanked a thumb-sized sapphire centered on the hilt. The handgrip was a gently curving hourglass of ivory, with two opal orbs making the curves. Gold plaited steel tapered down from the hourglass, extending and expanding to encase another large sapphire as the pommel. Still, when Flaingoold gripped the handle, his hand reached past the end.

Fascinated, the hawkman took in the scabbard. It bore no grand embellishment, merely ancient runes, but it was made of a durable material unfamiliar to Flaingoold. An adjustable strap looped around behind, to be worn across the back over one shoulder. On the front was an additional inverted sheath to hold the Dagger, so the Durluki, or Blades Bearer, could easily bear both Blades at once.

Excitement swelled in his chest, for he realized he held his life's ambition in his grasp. With deliberation, he slipped the dagger into the sheath, whispering reverently, "Lorooki."

Clutching the scabbard in his fist, he raised it triumphantly overhead, pumping his mighty wings.

The hawkmen soldiers, who had been anxiously watching, now threw back their heads in piercing screeches. Flaingoold reveled in the cheering. He folded his wings back as the clamor died down. Staring off into the setting splendor of the sun, he again imagined what it would be like when the whole world cheered for him.

"Stealing the Blades," the forgotten Tonclin rasped, dust settling around his broken body, "doesn't make you the Mentaloss!"

Rage riveted the general's golden gaze on his insolent accuser. His wings rising, Flaingoold glared Tonclin into breathless silence. The air thickened for many stifling moments. Then a humorless smile rearranged the hawkman's stony face.

"Perhaps not." The words escaped Flaingoold's beak like bubbling crude oil. He lowered his head slowly and delighted in the fear in his victim's eyes. "But killing thee… *proves* thou are not."

After a menacing pause, he straightened suddenly to cry, "Kill them!"

Flaingoold sneered as bedlam erupted around him. Screeches and guttural whistles mingled with pleading cries. He sent his own claw crashing mercilessly down upon the head beneath him and howled, "Kill them all!"

Looping the strap over his head, between shoulder and wing, Flaingoold situated the scabbard against his chest, out of the way of his wings. Then, turning into the eastern sunset, he took off toward Ithleen, their closest city, some 200 leagues away. He couldn't afford an Alliance Beacon out here in the open so close to the Dead Lands. He would need reinforcements and safety to make the necessary Alliance. His men angled quickly in behind him, forming their customary "V," which granted added lift to those behind, saving energy for the long-distance flight. But he paid them no heed. His goal, now, was Ithleen.

Scenery became nothing to him but a jumbled blur. Power-lust and need for recognition now drove the general on at a breakneck pace. He left Kuroo Ravine and the breathtaking Mataya Falls nestled in the Tamerik Mountains far behind him. Soaring over the beautiful Tranquility Meadow brought no peace. The illuminated horns of the last remaining wild unicorns prancing in the prairie below brought no joy. Even the dark contrast of the dreaded Kyren Forest, fast approaching, to the paler, dusky plain sparked nothing in him. Only pride and greed consumed him now.

Suddenly a cry rang out.

"Dragon Striders!"

Flaingoold spun around. His officers swerved quickly so as not to collide with him.

It was true! Coming up fast, in the last glimpses of sunset, was a band of the great legion known as Dragon Striders—humans who had somehow learned to train dragons to carry them into battle and fight with them. The Striders were usually only armed with swords or whips, but matched with the dragons' size, agility, and fire-spurts, they were a deadly and formidable enemy—one that struck fear in many a battalion.

The general of the hawkmen nation now felt this fear trickle up his own spine. He had only a scouting squad with him of a dozen males and females. The approaching foe's numbers were a mere six or eight. Still, his troops would be hard-pressed to out-maneuver the great dragons, even with his bolder females, in this waning light. He also knew they wouldn't be able to out-distance them for long.

But maybe long enough. He smirked, facing forward once more.

"Make for Kyren Forest!" Flaingoold roared.

Now cursing himself for the reckless pace he had set, the general hoped his tired men could make it deep enough into the forest to take refuge among the trees. The elves, orgrins, and other strange creatures of Kyren Forest could not possibly be more dangerous than the ones pressing in behind them.

The hawkmen had flown high above the wind currents to make faster time, but as the first dotting of forest sped beneath them, they dove for lower skies.

Dragon bellows and human war calls gained sharply behind the frenzied birdmen.

Just a little further. There—where the trees are thickest. Flaingoold begged his depleted strength. But their next dive attempt was intercepted.

A mighty amethyst-colored dragon soared past beneath them, cutting off their escape.

Coming up short, Flaingoold and his men clustered together. The Striders swarmed around them. Though nearly twice the size of a human, the half-hawk, half-human soldiers measured only a fifth of the size of these flying lizards circling in. The general's mind scrambled for an adequate plan for his already worn-out comrades. Tactical procedures were snatched from thought when a ruby-red dragon sent a flaming torpedo streaming toward the cluster.

"Split!" Flaingoold ordered.

Hawkmen spun frantically in either direction. The deadly ribbon scorched its way through their midst.

The Dragon Striders dove in to attack. An all-out dogfight ensued. The mighty whoosh of wings beat the air. Screeches, roars, and cries were heard among steel-on-talon-and-steel clashes and explosive flame bursts.

Flaingoold soared, dove, climbed, and spun, each time barely missing sword, flame, claw, or whip. His men were giving their all, but he had failed them. Their gallant general's only care now was his own precious feathers and keeping the Blades for himself.

He clenched his treasure close to his chest. He sought any means of escape. But every dive for safety resulted in crashing against a blocking dragon, propelling him back into the fight.

Finally, keeping the coveted Blades clutched in his left hand, Flaingoold drew his sword in his right. Renewed adrenaline seeped into his aching wings, and he charged the next dragon to approach.

The Strider, wearing gold banners to match his dragon, easily blocked the attack as he whooshed past. Quickly turning his dragon, the Strider circled back. Then he reined in the mighty beast for hand-to-hand combat with the hawkman general.

Flaingoold let out a roar. He propelled the force of his sword at his opponent, aiming just below the helmet. The Strider met his assault. The clash of steel was deafening. The Strider's fist shot out, crashing against the general's face. The force sent the hawkman careening through the air. His foe laughed and charged. Enflamed, Flaingoold attacked with renewed venom. But as he came up, the Strider rolled his dragon. Mighty claws gashed the general across the leg.

Pain shot through the hawkman's lower body. His right claw hung limp. This injury would make more evasive maneuvers impossible. So, the hawkman attacked his foe head on yet again.

Once close, Flaingoold fought to stay there. He did not want to contend more with the dragon. But this proved to be a little too close. While he blocked a blow with his sword, the Strider's other hand made a grab for the Blades. The hawkman's hand clutching the great scabbard shot up and out, away from his body and away from his adversary's grasp. A superior smile split Flaingoold's face at his opponent's foiled attempt.

But the sting of a whip lashed around the general's wrist. The bite in his flesh caused his grip to wane. Before he could respond, his arm was ripped back, and he was flung backward through the air. The prized scabbard flew from his hand and slipped from around his neck. Flaingoold grabbed for it, but it propelled out of his reach.

The scabbard plummeted and bounced off hawkman and Dragon Strider alike. Each creature grasped the air, trying to claim the Blades.

Lathan, the lieutenant general, was the last diving bullet to come close. His talons grazed the loop of the scabbard before it was enveloped by the trees.

The deafening fight continued above. But, slipping through the timber and careening down rocky crags, the sacred Blades finally came to rest in the spiky arms of a wild blackberry bush.

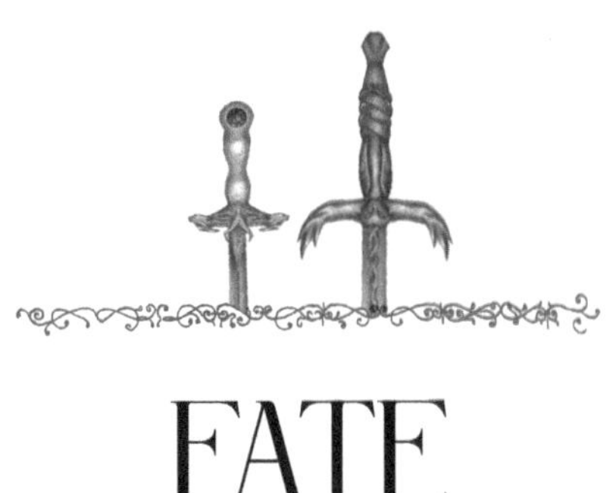

FATE

The resounding crack of the immense golden doors being flung wide echoed through the Great Hall of the Elvin Sanctuary in Tymalia. The shimmering pools of color that were the walls of the oval-shaped room refused to absorb the sound until it bounced off every surface and finally found refuge in the apex of the dome, forty feet above.

Opposite the doors stood a raised platform. There, five grand chairs were situated, each intricately decorated with carvings depicting the designated domains of the five Lords of the Elves, who occupied them. The Lord who graced the centermost, more richly decorated chair had sprung from his seat at the intrusion and stood poised at the top of the steps which ran the entire half-circle of the dais.

Recognition turned to irritation as the lone figure from the doorway advanced into the stately elf-man's sight. His chestnut eyes narrowed with annoyance.

"Memsy! You can't just come barging in here!" boomed the Lord from his lofty perch.

But Memsy the Sorci never faltered her determined step across the glassy floor.

"This is a private meeting of the Elfin High Council," he continued with authority. "The public meetings are held at the quarter moon, as you well know!"

Still, the slender, silver-haired woman did not stop her stride until the skirts of her long, burr-speckled, brown dress brushed the bottom of the five steps. She dipped into their customary bow, but the mischievous grin on her face belied the respect it should have demonstrated.

"My deepest condolences to the High Council… and their great patriarch." Her satiny voice danced over them. Her smile deepened, and laughter filled her eyes as the patriarch stiffened in response to her mocking tone.

Slowly, his gaze raked over the presumptuous female before him. The point of her ears stuck out through her long, straight tresses: the only physical feature distinguishing the magical race of elves from humans. Her hair was brushed back from her face, revealing a silver swirling emblem on her forehead that matched his own. It resembled an elegant letter "S" dancing its way through a figure eight—the symbol of the sorci—the scholars and most gifted of the elves.

"You can't be here," the patriarch reiterated, folding his arms across his silken amber robes.

"Now, Daerlot, dear. Don't try being pushy. It doesn't fit you," Memsy countered, resting her hands on her hips, eyes gleaming.

Indignation flamed his face. He did not appreciate this blatant disregard for his authority, especially in the presence of the High Council. He could feel the four pairs of eyes upon him, and it gnawed at him.

"I told you. You can't be here," he railed, pointing a finger toward the exit behind the intruder. "Now, get out or I'll have to…"

"And I've told *you*, little brother—" Memsy folded her arms in front of her with a scowling smirk, pinning her eyes upon him, "—just because you are fifty-six years younger than me, doesn't mean I can't still lick you in a fight!"

Daerlot could only sputter, thinking of no rebuttal to his sister's audacity. But on hearing muffled chuckles from the high councilmen behind him, his posture became rigid. His face reddening, he thundered, "Guards!"

Memsy's hands dropped to her side and her face became dumbfounded. But she recovered quickly, raising her chin with dignity, her eyes never leaving the patriarch's.

"I have found the Blades," she stated evenly.

The crystal-coved hall fell completely silent. The guards ceased their advance. Not a sound was to be heard. It seemed even the walls were holding their breath in astonishment. All eyes were sealed on her. Awe mingled with surprise.

Apart from gifts for seeing past, present, or future, the sorcis were the scholars of legends. Being a sorci himself, Daerlot knew the prophecies. He knew this prophecy particularly. He understood the gravity of this development. More than anyone—other than Memsy herself, he knew what it meant for Sheorae. And he knew what it meant for her.

"But the Blades," Daerlot said, barely finding his voice, "were never meant to come to the elves."

Memsy released a short sigh and closed her eyes. When she finally opened them, sadness etched her features, and a skim of tears brimmed her eyes.

"They did not come to me, Dala." The endearing nickname in the midst of such grand company bespoke the grief now apparent on her face.

The patriarch's brow furrowed as he tried to discern her meaning. After a moment, Memsy sniffed to stifle a sob and then turned back toward the grand entrance.

"Adianna," she called gently.

"Adi…" Daerlot's breath caught in his throat.

A long mass of auburn locks framing the round face of a child poked out from around one great golden door. Large, emerald eyes peered across the formidable expanse of the Great Hall, wide with apprehension. Shyly, the head retreated a little.

Memsy advanced a few steps toward the child, and bending over, she extended her hand, as if enticing a timid animal to approach. Then she gently spoke, "Adianna, my love. Come to Memsy."

Thus invited, a smile spread over the little face. Relieved of fear, the child emerged through the door. Dressed in simple peasant's garb of a mouse-brown smock and white apron, she was little more than four.

Her approach to her precious Memsy was greatly hampered by a long, burnish-red scabbard she had partially slung over her shoulder. Her hands were wrapped around the large, golden handle of a mighty sword encased within that scabbard which was dragging along behind her. Still this burden could not hinder her smile.

Daerlot could sense the array of emotions emanating from all in the room as they watched the child toddle toward his sister, but none was so profound as his own shock and panic.

When the girl reached her side, Memsy lovingly ran her hand over the reddish-brown curls and smiled at her warmly. Heaving a deeper sigh than before, the sorci turned back to the platform, keeping her hand on the child's shoulder.

"My Lords," Memsy announced dolefully. "This is the legendary Durluki." She then gazed back down, smiling sadly at the bright, trusting face, and mused, "The Blades Bearer."

At first, no one could speak... or even breathe. But then, the room seemed to explode in a riot of voices. Disbelief, incomprehension, even dismay echoed on every side. Even the guards were voicing their disbelieving opinions.

But Daerlot forced all this out of his consciousness. Instead, he focused on projecting his thoughts to his sister.

Mems, how can this be possible? he pleaded.

Her forlorn eyes met his. *I don't know. But it is true. She found them while we were picking berries. And now... she bears the mark.*

They both looked at the lovely child they cherished, who somehow had the fate of their world in her hands. Adianna had slipped behind Memsy's skirt trying to hide from the clamoring voices. Now her wide eyes peered from her hiding place at the loud, angry-sounding argument spilling forth around her.

Oh, Dala, the woman's thoughts pleaded. Her eyes, brimming with tears, searched his face for answers. She unconsciously removed her hand from the child and wrapped her arms around herself, the way she always did when faced with a problem she couldn't find a safe answer for. *What will become of her? Evil seekers are all around us. They hunt for the Blades even now. They will hunt HER!* Tears spilled from her grief-stricken eyes. *She's just a baby, Dala. What can we do?*

Daerlot's gaze again fell to the child. Protectiveness warred with uncertainty and incredulousness.

How can this be? She, of all people, should have been safe from all this horror, at least for now. He just couldn't wrap his mind around how this could be possible. How could a child wield a sword she couldn't even pick up and use it to procure the freedom of nations?

Shadows of the past merged with thoughts of the future, and he struggled to tell them apart. Nothing made sense. Slowly, he pursed his lips and released a sigh.

When the great patriarch began descending the steps, the Hall fell silent again. Daerlot came to a stop in front of the child where she still hid behind his sister. He squatted to be more her size and called to her, "Adianna, precious."

His gentle voice invited her to peek around Memsy's skirts.

"Dala?" her sweet voice questioned.

"Yes, Precious." He smiled, outstretching his arms. "Come to Dala."

The radiant smile returned as the child emerged from her hiding place and ran to his embrace. She dropped her burden to hang from her neck, and she threw her arms around him. The hilt of the sword pinned under his ribs as she squeezed tightly. Then she pulled back, relieving some of the pressure. Her burden forgotten, she placed her hands on his cheeks as concern creased her brow.

"Oh, Dala," the child said, her lips poking out in a pout. "I see so much fighting and lots of scary monsters!"

A grin split his face. He placed his hands on her tiny hips, twisting her from side to side. "You are tapping my sight again, you little minx," he said playfully.

Her pout turned to a grin. Her eyes twinkled with mischief.

Daerlot quelled the visions he was receiving. He dared not let the child see the carnage which might lie in wait for her.

As she is still so young, she does not know, yet, how best to use her powers. He stared proudly at the little imp, who had so quickly become such a large piece of his heart. *But she will learn.*

His thoughts were interrupted by one of the councilmen behind him.

"Who is she?!"

Relyat, the tall, lanky Lord and Keeper of Animals who had vacated the throne to the right of Daerlot's, demanded, "Where did she come from?"

Heaving a sigh, Daerlot stood and turned, instinctively pulling the child to his side in the same protective manner his sister had done.

"My fellow lords," their patriarch announced in deep, authoritative tones. "This child is Adianna. A woodcutter's daughter from the southwest edge of Kyren Forest. Her parents have just recently given her to the sorci, Memsy, to rear."

"Why?" blurted out Gushmere, the Keeper of Earth, who stood beside Relyat. His face flamed as red as his wavy hair when all eyes turned to him. He then sputtered, "I mean… that is to say… why would mortals give their child to an elf… that is?"

Memsy stepped forward at this time to lovingly pet the child's hair. Though she kept her eyes on the girl, she answered in quiet wonder, "Her parents feared her."

Daerlot did not turn, but he tilted his head to Memsy, feeling her amazement. His lips pressed together a moment, as he silently chastised the woodcutter for his stupidity once again. Then he clarified to those present, by adding, "She possesses the powers of the ganji."

Muffled gasps were heard from the guards behind them. The four high councilmen merely clustered together, each murmuring among themselves.

Finally, Dosumay, Lady Keeper of Water, glided out of the circle, her wispy, blonde hair flowing around her. Gracefully extending an accusing finger toward the child, she demanded in lilting tones that washed away any harshness she may have intended, "Does she bear the mark of the Durluki?"

The quiet glimmer of hope to spread across the faces of those before him was swiftly dashed as Memsy said, "Yes, my lady. It appeared within moments after she found the Blades."

As proof, Memsy scrunched down by the child and gently pulled the right side of Adianna's collar away to lay bare her shoulder. There, found on the smooth skin where the child's collarbone tucked into the hollow of her shoulder, was a small golden emblem of a drac—with its long neck and tail curved back around an inverted sapphire teardrop nestled between its wings.

Gushmere, who was rather portly for an elf because of his dwarf ancestry, excitedly popped down each step to get a closer look.

"May I?" he gushed, extending both hands at the same time.

Instantly, Adianna backed away. Memsy caught her around the waist while Daerlot turned with them, a hand on the girl's back.

"It's okay, child. It will be alright," Memsy reassured.

Adianna's large, green eyes searched the sorci's frantically. "Will it burn?" she whispered timidly. The child's gaze darted apprehensively to the strange man with red, wobbling cheeks.

"No, dear," Memsy smiled, as Adianna's pleading eyes returned to her. She then added, nodding to the man in question, "He is an elf. His touch will not harm you."

The child looked to Daerlot, seeming to need more assurance. Emerald eyes, so full of trust, pulled at his heartstrings. He gave her a small smile, then nodded slightly.

This was all the encouragement she needed. The girl squared her shoulders, held her head and gaze erect, and took a dignified step toward Lord Gushmere.

The elf excitedly poked his hand into his vest pocket hidden among his ruddy-colored robes. Pulling out a pair of spectacles, he skittered over to kneel in front of the little girl.

Perching the spectacles upon the tip of his nose, Gushmere eagerly ran the pad of his finger over the mark. Then he scratched gently at the sides of it with his fingernail, but the emblem did not move or curl. It stayed fixed as a natural extension of her skin, like a birthmark.

Gushmere remained in awe for several moments, but then an odd look slowly reshaped his face. Daerlot became nervous, watching the Keeper of Earth's gaze seem to be uncontrollably drawn to the golden hilt tucked under the girl's arm. The gold sparkled from the scabbard slung around the child's neck, calling to him, inviting him to see what his future could be. Gushmere's hand crept slowly toward it, like an obdurate craving drew him. But before he could touch it, Adianna wrapped both arms around the scabbard, swinging it out of his reach. So abrupt was her motion, the Blades slapped angrily against Memsy's heels, causing the woman to flinch.

The man stared wide-eyed for a moment before his body convulsed with a shiver. Then with understanding in his voice, Gushmere consoled, "Okay, child. It's alright."

He backed away before attempting to stand, hands raised, conceding to her unchallenged right. "That's as it should be."

Lord Gushmere gave Memsy, then Daerlot, an apologetic look before stepping over to the rise of the dais.

He tucked his glasses back into their pocket with a thoughtful look, then announced with both authority and awe, "It is the true mark of the Blade Bearer. All is as the scrolls prophesied."

More muttering erupted among the remaining three lords on the stand. Daerlot's mind raced through all he could remember from the Blades Scrolls. He searched his recollection for some catch, some loophold, some… hope. Straying across a thought, he nearly yelled at the shortest of the elves on the dais, "Meiron!"

The abruptness of his call startled everyone, even himself, but it got the desired man's attention.

"Yes, my lord." The short, spindly man stepped forward, eager to do another's bidding.

"Didn't the Scrolls mention something about maturity or—" Daerlot waved his hand absently in the air, "—age of something or other?"

Meiron's pale brow furrowed in contemplation. He propped his elbow on top of his arm against his chest as he tapped his thumb absently against his pursed lips.

Daerlot could feel his sister's curious gaze moving between the concentrating elf and himself. He remained focused on the slight little man, urging him to find the detail that eluded him. It might be their only hope.

Everyone waited with bated breath. The silence was again palpable. Everyone's eyes were trained on the studious yet jovial Keeper of Flora and Fauna as he wracked his mind for the answer. Finally, Meiron's face brightened.

"Yeees," he breathed out slowly. His voice became stronger with conviction, as he continued, "Yes! In the first part of the second scroll."

Meiron's hand flew out, jabbing the air in the patriarch's direction. Then the elf slapped his knee and, chuckling, turned to the others as if a punchline had just been realized. His expression dropped, though, upon seeing he was alone in finding the humor. Clearing his throat, he turned back to Daerlot.

Then in low, flowing tones, from memory, Meiron quoted:

"The Durluki, though strong and brave,
Must gain age of awareness, before lives to save,
And monumental task fulfill,
Reach a maturity of mind over will.
Then, with Mentaloss, the two unite,
Taking upon them our perilous plight.
A pure pact to never thwart nor cease,
An eternal alliance to gain our peace."

Meiron's voice faded into silence. No one spoke, all pensively contemplating the new meaning behind these ancient words.

Age of awareness? The words tumbled over and over in the patriarch's brain. *Maturity of mind? The mind is awareness. So, could maturity be an age? The age of maturity? Mind over will. Could she have until the age of maturity, and then…?*

Suddenly, a vision sprang upon his mind, cutting off his previous thought. He could feel the subtle change of his eyes from their usual russet to the smoky hue they became when his prophetic sight took over. Slowly he closed his eyes, so as not to inhibit the flow of the vision coming upon him. Time, events, years passed before him. He took it all in, breathed in the heady, intoxicating rush of it all. He remained still, even after the vision faded, etching every detail to memory, searching for any hidden meanings.

Only the feel of a tiny hand tugging at his robe brought Daerlot out of his reverie.

"Dala." Adianna's concerned eyes drew his. "Is you alwight?"

Daerlot smiled despite himself. "Yes, my love." He gently cupped her soft little chin in his hand. A peace settled in his mind and soul. "Everything is going to be alright."

His sister's gaze and thoughts sought his. He merely smiled at her. Then, taking Adianna with him, he ascended the steps of the platform. The swords the child carried thunked off every step. Memsy and Gushmere trailed close behind. The other three lords parted when their patriarch attained the top step, granting him passage.

Daerlot proceeded to his throne in the center, which was embedded with emblems of all five realm holdings of the elves: earth, water, plant life, animals, and fire. Then, scooping the child up, he placed her, standing upon his vacated seat. Backing away a few steps, he raised an outstretched hand, acknowledging the young girl.

"Lords and Ladies," he said, "the fate of our world rests in these tiny hands."

The statement hung in the air for a moment before he continued.

"But… she will be granted time to grow, in both mind and body. As Meiron has recited, she must reach the 'age of awareness and maturity' before even an alliance can be made. It will be up to *us* to help her in this.

"There are many paths lying within this prophetic destiny of which we know not, but of this one thing we have the ability to know, to mold and to harbor in safety until the time is right. We now share a sacred honor. For it is given to us to bear the safety and the tutelage of the one who is chosen to save us. What a blessing and a great responsibility to be ours. There is, at last, hope for the future. For the true Durluki has been found!"

And with that, the patriarch, the great elfin leader, took Adianna's small hand in his and went down on one knee in front of her. He winked at her quickly, then bowed his head in homage.

The other lords stared in awe, casting a hesitant glance at each other. Then finally, after gathering their wits, the Keepers followed suit. The patriarch grinned to himself as they each bowed beside him in front of this petite soul, who was destined to be the savior of all Sheorae.

Adianna's eyebrows were raised so high they were hidden in her hair when Daerlot peeked at her. When her surprised eyes locked on his, he winked at her again.

Adianna snatched her hand from Daerlot's to hide her giggle. He smiled back at her, and despite the child's efforts, her laughter trickled forth.

Slowly, the patriarch rose to join his sister. The other lords awkwardly rose as well. Then, they gathered around the occupied throne, smiling encouragingly, introducing themselves and asking questions all at the same time.

Daerlot smiled as he watched Adianna's eyes dance due to all the fawning she received.

"But Dala," Memsy pleaded as soon as he came to put his arm around her. She leaned in close to him, her eyes still on her baby girl. "What is going to happen? What will become of her?"

He gave her shoulder a squeeze and consoled, "That is not all for us to know at this time." He looked down at her tortured expression. "Maybe not ever."

Seeing her frown, he continued, "But I do know we can keep her safe. At least until she is old enough for the Mentaloss to come and this destined alliance to take place." She seemed unconvinced, still observing the child with concern.

Gently, he pulled on her chin until she begrudgingly turned her head to face him. The corners of his mouth dipped deep into his cheeks as he pursed his lips with empathy. Worry and anxiety were lining her face, making her look older than usual, though still nowhere near the 782 years she boasted.

"Tomorrow we will gather your things," he promised with conviction. "And the two of you will move inside the safety of Tymalia. We can keep the Blades safely hidden here until it is time for her quest to begin."

Memsy turned away disbelieving, but he caught her chin again with his fingers and turned her back.

"You will raise her, just as you planned," he assured her. "She will be the child you always wanted to have… if things had only been different."

He glanced over to where their little auburn-haired imp was already winning the hearts of the Keepers of Sheorae. "You will have the help of the entire Elfin Council to teach her along the way. And when the age of maturity approaches, she will be trained in the ways of the Ancient Scrolls until the Mentaloss comes."

The look on Memsy's face told him she still did not believe it would be that simple. That it couldn't be as happy as it sounded for whatever length of time. Not for her. Daerlot gathered her in a reassuring embrace.

"Don't worry, my dear sister," he said, rubbing her back. "Everything will be fine."

He placed a confirming kiss in his sister's soft, silver hair. But as he looked over her head to the laughing child still perched upon his chair, a shiver of apprehension skittered down his spine, and he wondered, *Would it?*

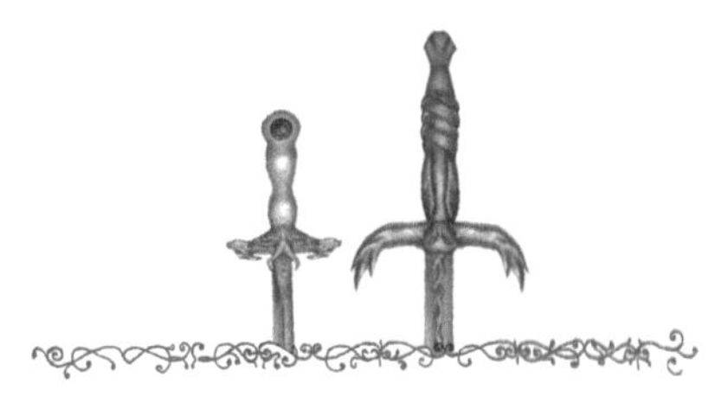

INTRUDERS

W*hat a peaceful day*, thought Adianna, as she gazed at the lush green canopy above her. She reclined against the gnarled roots of a great elm tree with her hands tucked beneath mounds of auburn hair.

"Yes, peace," she said. A smile settled on her face, and she closed her eyes.

Her lessons with the Elfin High Councilors were long and intensive now that she was eighteen. The warrior training was fun, but the constant lessons in the Scrolls were growing monotonous. She already knew them backward and forward. Why did she have to keep going over them?

These lessons, on top of her regular duties at home, usually consumed most of her days. So, the young woman relished days like today.

With Tarron, her best friend and usual sparring partner, off negotiating water privileges to the Dead Lands, the councilmen were alternately filling in on her weapons training. The portly Gushmere always gave her a good workout. Even though he didn't move fast, he was solid as the earth and strong as an earthquake. She could whack away at him for hours and get nowhere in defeating him.

Relyat was a deceiving opponent. Though tall and lanky looking, he had speed and agility to rival any cheetah. But like that impressive feline, the elf could only go for short bursts at a time. In between these, sparring with him was really rather boring.

Dosumay was a formidable partner. Her movements were slow, fluid, and usually predictable. But she had the ability to broaden her fighting range, so while Adianna came in with a frontal attack, Dosumay would swoop in from behind, making contact. And when she did, it was with the force of the ocean—of this, the girl was certain. Adianna was glad Dosumay had bowed out of the rotation this time, due to her despair in still being unable to get water to the lands surrounding Drokmar's hold.

But today the lot fell to Meiron. The studious little botanist, though very familiar with the elements of fighting, was not well versed in application. She still had to laugh at the astonishment he showed when she had swiped his feet out from under him for the third time in the first half hour and dangled her blade in front of his beak-like nose. Needless to say, class was dismissed early, and her time was now her own until evening.

Adianna felt a growing need to savor these moments recently. She was increasingly aware peace would be something dearly precious and perhaps unattainable for her all too soon. She knew her journey was nigh at hand. Before long, hunters of all kinds would stalk her every movement. She had seen it, through Memsy's visions. Her beloved Memsy did not possess the more far-reaching and continuous clairvoyance that Uncle Daerlot did. Still, as a sorci, Memsy could occasionally see into the future. It was on one such occasion, when the woman tossed in fitful sleep, Adianna had caught a glimpse of what could lie in store for her. Yes, soon it would begin. She knew it.

Her own nightmares had begun again as well. They started when she was about fourteen and only came occasionally, at first, maybe once every year or so. They would last for only a few days then disperse. They were coming more often now. She didn't know whether it had anything to do with Drokmar's band of dalphene becoming bolder or not, but the nightmares came three or four times a year now, for longer periods of time. This last invasion of her dreams had already gone on for nearly a fortnight.

They were always the same type of dream. Fighting, despair. Everyone depending on her. Being unable to conquer, and the fate of her world choking in the evil grasp of a monster.

She opened her eyes again, willing those scenes to creep back into the shadows of her mind where they belonged.

No, for now—peace. Tranquil and serene, she told herself. All those sad and perilous thoughts must be pushed aside. She must savor 'the now.'

Pulling on all her senses, Adianna absorbed the forest around her. Overhead the trees groaned at the wind whipping through their branches. Their far-reaching arms stretched and swayed in a dance as old as time itself. The air was moist as the afternoon sun strove in a futile attempt to dry out the ground hiding beneath the leafy canopy. The damp, humid fragrance of moss filled her head. How she loved being in these woods.

Just then a flash of movement caught her eye. There to the left, Adianna spied a squirrel bounding into the small clearing. The small reddish-brown creature scampered toward the elm where she sat. But upon spotting the girl, the squirrel stopped short.

"Hello, little one," Adianna said softly. She came up onto her elbow, shifting slowly toward the intruder.

The squirrel's bushy brown tail began to flip backward and forward, sending the black-tipped fur fluffing about. But still, it did not run. It stayed hunkered down, ready to bolt, and shifted to stare, twisting its head from side to side to scrutinize her with each of its large black eyes.

"*Naa nuw tat tu lacmar,*" Adianna cooed the elvish words she had learned and perfected under Relyat's tutelage. They served to calm and greet the woodland animals and other creatures of Sheorae.

The squirrel's tail quit flicking. Curious now, it sat back on its haunches, shifting its head to get a better look.

Smiling and keeping eye contact, Adianna slipped her free hand into the open food pouch sitting beside the bow and quiver she always carried when alone. Then she gingerly extended her hand to reveal some dried fig pieces and a few seeds.

"*Na tut swee tu*?" she offered.

The fluffy squirrel crept toward her, tentatively extending its front paws a step, and bringing its hind feet to meet them. After a wary pause, it would repeat the motion. Adianna maneuvered to lean over the low, gnarled root which separated them as the squirrel approached. When within reach, the squirrel wiggled its black nose around to sniff the hand and food intently.

"*Tat tu lacmar,*" she soothed again. Using the root as a prop, she extended her left hand in front of the right before repeating her offer.

"*Na tut swee tu.*"

Her appealing tone and friendly gesture seemed enough invitation for the little critter. The squirrel climbed into her palm and stuck its forelegs on her other hand to sniff more earnestly at the proffered food.

Adianna smoothly sat up, keeping her hands uneven but still together, so as not to disrupt her new friend.

The tickle of the squirrel's whiskers was pleasant as it sniffed around, deciding which morsel to take first. Picking up a fig in its mouth, it transferred the morsel to its hand-like paws and sat back on its haunches to enjoy it. Its hind claws were little prickles in her hand. And the way it turned the fig around in its paws after every nibble was intriguing. But what kept Adianna's attention was the tingling warmth creeping up her arms since they first touched. This happened whenever she came in contact with any animate creature. With each creature having its own degree of heat and dazzle of energy, often the sensation still fascinated her.

The warmth flowed within her and quickly reverberated through her chest, where it began to swirl rapidly. The spinning increased and increased. She closed her eyes as faster and faster it went. The intoxicating movement tingled her senses into full awareness. The vortex compressed, spinning faster and faster, until finally, it climaxed in an explosion of heat and light that shot out through her every limb.

The squirrel paused momentarily, for its companion's response to this phenomenon was a slight intake of breath behind closed eyes. Then, flicking its tail dismissively, it resumed its munching.

Adianna opened her eyes, peering around her with new awareness. She noted her peripheral vision was wider and more in focus. The scratching and creaking of the trees became more pronounced, and she could detect more scents floating in the breeze.

Giving a slight giggle, she went back to observing her companion. She could now smell its musky male scent. The fur covering his chest had the same black color which adorned the tips along his tail. The rest of him was a reddish-brown blending well with the early fall colors of the forest. His claws were narrow fingernails protruding from each little digit.

She could smell no fear emanating from him, so she relaxed again against the elm, watching him with continued interest. They stayed, contentedly thus, until the squirrel picked up the last seed and proceeded to devour it. Then Adianna noticed the sharpened angle of the light peeking through the trees.

"Sorry, little one." Adianna sighed as her companion finished its snack and sniffed hungrily over her palm for more. "I suppose I should be getting ba—"

As one, their heads sprang up. Their bodies tensed, keenly aware of some intrusion, some kind of faint rustling movement from in front of them. Then all was quiet, yet the tension remained. The squirrel's tail resumed its previous spastic twitching forward and back, and its ears flicked to the front and sides seeking out any sound. His head was turned so one eye could stare intently in the same direction in which the woman looked.

They simultaneously heard an indistinct brushing of leaves. Instantly, Adianna turned her hands to the elm. The squirrel hopped from her hand and ran straight up the tree. Then, snatching her bow and quiver, she sprang to her feet. She slung the weapons over her head. Once they were settled on her back, she flipped her long skirt over her arm. Then, looking up the elm where her friend had gone, she quickly followed it straight up the tree.

Adianna's fingers and the toes of her soft, doe-hide shoes clung effortlessly to the tree bark in her assent, like invisible claws. She scampered noiselessly up to a thick limb some forty feet from the ground. Then, clinging with those invisible claws, she swung around the tree, placing its trunk between herself and the origin of the sound. From there, she paused to gain first sight of the approaching danger.

Her wait was not long. Presently, a pair of orgrins entered the small clearing.

Adianna had never understood how these huge, lumbering beasts could move so silently through the brush. Their enormous bulk, with the look and texture of craggy rock, was characteristic of the ogres they derived from, and ogres themselves were never quiet in motion. Indeed, they shook the very earth at a leisurely pace, and their love of smashing things made sneaking near-impossible.

No, Adianna reasoned the orgrins must get their stealth from the goblins, which the ogres had been crossed with by the ancient oracles. The goblins, being purely nocturnal creatures, were quite deadly in their stealth. They were ruthless and vindictive creatures, whose main purpose in life was to feed. The ogre genes made the orgrins mobile during the day, with nearly impenetrable skin. But they were still left with the wide, gaping mouths and razor-sharp teeth from the goblins, along with their cheery dispositions. Adianna had been instructed never to cross an orgrin in a foul mood. Nor one who was hungry!

This pair of orgrins halted shortly into the clearing. The one in front began sniffing purposefully at the air.

"What is it, Donk?" the one from behind queried, his voice a low rumble, like a distant rockslide.

The one called Donk didn't answer but continued sniffing and smelling the air high, from right to left. Then, lower, from left to right. On the third sweep, it stopped and peered straight ahead. Its face split into a sickening leer. Its bottom jaw protruded, baring a line of spiky, orange teeth, as it grunted with satisfaction.

"Human."

The other added its own sadistic chuckle, but before it could say anything, a third orgrin pushed past, barreling into the clearing.

Adianna snatched back behind the tree, her heart skittering in its attempt to keep beating. She inhaled deeply to calm herself but didn't dare to let it out. Slowly, she peeked out again.

"Humans?" this new one grunted with menacing glee. It now licked its paper-thin chops, looking around excitedly. This one was smaller than the other two, with its arms swinging like a gorilla. But Adianna could tell it was still around eight feet in height.

"Aaah, Lug!" moaned the one who was pushed aside, annoyance evident on its face. "Get on home?"

The shorter one, Lug, stopped its excited prancing to turn and snort at the other in response.

"Don't have ta," he said, snorting again. "Ma said I's to keep yous all outta trouble."

"But you's the one's what's always gittin' us inta troubles, troll!" the offended one retorted. When all he got was another snort in reply, he added, "Ain't I's right, Donk?"

Donk was crouched, continuing his sniffing while the other two argued. Not looking at his brothers, but in the direction of the elm, he stated, "Zog's right. Go home!"

Lug's standoffish response was cut off when Donk pointed a craggy finger and slipped past him.

The brothers watched Donk approach the elm. His wide nostrils quivered as he continuously sampled the air. Then, reaching the base of the tree, he snatched up Adianna's food pouch. The woman cringed inwardly for foolishly leaving it behind. With bated breath, she waited for Donk's next move.

He sniffed at it intently, turning it over and over in his three-fingered hands. His face broke once more into a sickening grin. A puce trickle of saliva oozed between his jagged teeth and over his scant lip.

"It's young." Donk snorted a chuckle.

The others gathered around him. Lug made a snatch for the pouch, but Zog shoved him aside. A loud crack, like two boulders colliding, sounded sharply in the clearing as the smaller orgrin rammed Zog out of the way before his fingers could brush the leather fringe.

"Quii—eeet!" Donk hissed and planted his huge hand in Lug's face, giving him a disgusted shove. At the same time, he caught the younger one's foot with his, sending Lug careening backward.

Adianna cringed again, waiting for the impending crash, but in vain. The smaller orgrin's stealthy agility took over, and the huge creature rolled backward noiselessly and was on his feet again in a low crouch before the girl could blink. Indignantly, he snorted at his brother.

But that one didn't even notice for Donk was scanning the ground by where the pouch had been. He placed his hand on the indention in the moss where Adianna had rested just moments before.

The young woman inched around the trunk to get a better look.

"Still warm," Donk's raspy, cavernous voice chuckled again, more saliva oozing over his chin.

The others mingled their hungry mirth with his, and their shifty gazes scanned the surrounding clearing. A wet smacking noise escaped Zog's mouth, which made Adianna shudder, and she clung tighter to the rough bark. Donk now resumed his sniffing with gusto. Then, jumping up, he lashed out his thick arm and pelted Zog square in the chest.

"The scent's mingled with rodent! Spread out and find it!" Donk barked.

Adianna slipped back behind the tree, listening to their every move. Fortunately, they wandered out into the clearing away from her. Their movements weren't very audible, but she could tell the location of each by their sniffing and snorting. Also, she could hear the occasional slobbering of anticipation, which sent an eerie dread trickling down her spine.

Then prickles on her neck alerted Adianna to one of the orgrins rounding the edge of the tree. She dared not look. Though she was far enough off the ground to be out of their reach, orgrins were strong enough to shake, if not fell, a tree and knock her out of it. The fall alone could be deadly, not to mention what awaited her on the ground. With all her training, she was still no match for three hungry orgrins, even if she touched one. So instead, she clenched her eyes shut.

Slowly she tensed every muscle. Her nails were now digging into the bark to which she clung.

"Sniff, sniff, sniff, sniiiffff," could be heard below her. "Sniff, sniff, sniff."

One of her nightmares flashed into her mind of being hunted, cornered. She couldn't breathe. She couldn't move for fear of being caught.

Oh, please, she silently pleaded to that Great Being said to be creator of all. *If there is, indeed, a purpose for my life... please, don't let them find me.*

"Sniff, sniff, snort. Snniiiiiffff."

Lidded darkness was slowly creeping in on her. Panic squeezed the air from her lungs.

"I have it!"

Adianna's blood ran cold. It sounded like Lug—right below her. An enormous lump thunked in the pit of her stomach.

The other two orgrins joined Lug, mingling their snorting with his.

"He's right! It's human!" Zog responded.

Oh, please, she pleaded again, a tear slipping down her cheek. Her muscles began to tremble and quake.

"Let's get it," Zog growled with a snort. "Quickly! This way!"

Adianna's eyes flew open when she heard them slip off into the forest to the northwest. She glanced down disbelieving, but indeed, they were gone. There was no sign of them. Their slobbering had dissipated, leaving no trace of their departure.

Releasing the death-grip she had on the tree, she nearly collapsed on the limb just beneath her. Pushing a few strands of hair away from her face, she then dropped her hand to her chest. She chuckled softly. She felt her heart pounding twice as fast; her lungs screamed at her for being neglected. Her gaze impulsively rose above the trees.

"Thank you!" she breathed aloud with a smile.

Adianna looked around below. The orgrins were still nowhere in sight. *Where did they go?* she wondered.

Spotting where they had been, she visually followed their tracks, which disappeared away from the waning sun. *Why would they...?*

Adianna's breath caught. *The road to the village!*

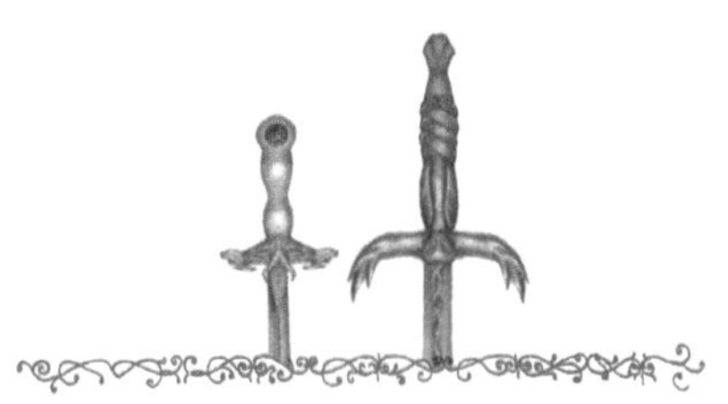

FOREST ATTACK

Twirling her skirt back around her arm, she took off along the limb on all fours. Her fingers and toes were once more clinging to the bark as she went. Coming near the end of the limb where it dipped with every move, Adianna stretched out her body and then sprang into the air. With leaves whipping past her face, she adjusted her body midair so as to squarely land on the approaching branch of the next tree. Landing lightly and with ease, she scampered across the widespread arms of the new tree.

Jumping from tree to tree, she covered ground quickly. Still, she knew the orgrins would move faster. And they had a head start.

I only hope no one is on the path.

This thought was soon dashed as, seconds later, the distant sound of fighting reached her ears. Quickening her pace, she darted through the treetops. With each new branch, the scuffling increased. She could make out an occasional crack of boulders colliding and the chinking of steel ricocheting off rock. Then, closer, grunts of exerted orgrins mingled with exclamations of a male voice.

She was nearly there when she noticed she was getting heavier on the branches. Then her grip began to slip.

"Come on! Just a little longer," she pleaded. She could see the break in the trees, heralding the path laying just beyond.

She could also see some of the battle occurring here and there. Flashes of color and movement. But little more. She scampered more heavily through another wide tree, the branches bowing and creaking in protest.

There was a clearing off the bend in the path ahead, and she could see one of the orgrins down. This surprised her, as it was not an easy feat, due to their size and strength. The other two were being pummeled haphazardly by the sword of a man with a black hooded cloak. Deep rumbling growls warned her of the orgrins' rising anger. Not a good sign.

One more tree and she could be in range. But to the tree in question, she could see the distance was great. That would not be safe with her waning abilities. She gauged it as she approached, calculating how far out to jump and where best to land.

This is it, she told herself, psyching herself up for the challenge. *Let's do it!*

Into the air, she leapt. But as her toes left the branch, she felt the abilities leave her. She could no longer steer in the air. And she knew she would no longer be light, nor have grip when she landed. There was no way for her to reach the chosen branch. She was falling too quickly. Frantically, she grabbed at branches whipping past her fingertips, until finally, she grasped one. Her fall slowed, and she could maneuver a little. But not enough. Adianna plunged through the leaves, clinging to the protesting branch in her hands. She felt her feet touch a limb. But her thin shoes could gain no grip, and she skidded along its bark. She was not stopping. Not even slowing down.

A strangled cry escaped her when the objecting branch ripped from her hands, flipping back violently. Still, she gave it no heed, for the distance between her and the great trunk of the tree was quickly narrowing. As crash or fall were her only options now, Adianna prepared herself for the inevitable. She cringed. *Here it comes!*

Thwack!

The full length of her torso collided with the mighty tree, flinging her arms around it with the impact. Air whooshed from her lungs, and though she tried to keep her head back to avoid collision, a spot above her right eyebrow smarted something awful. Stunned slightly from the blow, she clung to the trunk, fully aware she was still a good fifteen feet up.

Gathering her wits, she settled her feet and slowly released the brittle bark beneath her fingers. Orienting herself to her surroundings again, she turned to where the fight was taking place. Apparently the raucous she'd made had gained the orgrins' attention, for all three were now peering into the trees in her direction to see what had caused the noise.

The stranger took advantage of this. He brought his broad sword crashing down on the shoulder of the closest offender. Zog let out a howl. Even though the blow hadn't penetrated his hard, thick skin, it had been knowledgeably issued, resulting in the temporary paralysis of the creature's right arm.

But the mortal didn't stop. He quickly advanced on the next. This one Adianna recognized as Donk, and he had turned in response to his brother's yowl. Donk lumberingly acquired a tree branch for a weapon to appease his mounting rage.

Adianna maneuvered to a limb closer to the fight. Crouching, she settled her dress back into place, then pulled the bow off her shoulder. From there, she watched, fascinated. First of all, she had never seen an orgrin in actual combat before. She had never understood how a creature with such stealthy running could be so burdensome in battle. She had secretly assumed it was just a training excuse Gushmere had used for her to acquire a more perfected technique. But now, she could see firsthand the bulky thickness of their arms and waist made agility from those joints nearly impossible.

But she was also mesmerized by the stranger. His strong sideways stance spoke volumes as he deflected a blow from the creature's club. Then with a sleek spin to the side, with both hands, the man brought his sword around, and pulling with all his might, he flipped the feet out from under his enemy.

Seeing Zog spinning round and round, beating himself in the arm, trying to revive feeling, and Lug rolling on the ground striving to regain his feet, and Donk's wide swings with his tree-club being repeatedly deflected, Adianna was awestruck and stayed her hand from her quiver. This stranger obviously knew what he was doing and could do it well. Adianna watched, enthralled.

Finally, Lug was on his feet. With a vengeful bellow, he charged the human. Adianna's breath caught, but when the orgrin dove for him, the dark stranger jumped at the last minute. Landing on the back of his enemy's neck, the man ran up the monster's spine. Pushing off the creature's rump, he flipped through the air, konking Donk on the back of the head with the flat of his sword, then landed nimbly behind the two in a crouch. Donk went sprawling thunderously over Lug's head and crashed in a heap on the ground. The stranger stood slowly, eyeing the protesting heap.

Zog, on seeing his comrades being thus defeated, abandoned his attempt to regain feeling to his arm. He raised his good arm to use as a club. From behind the stranger, a growl escaped the haggard creature as he propelled his bulk across the clearing toward its target.

Sweeping an arrow from her quiver, Adianna touched it to her bow. The man flipped off his hood and spun to face the roaring orgrin. He braced himself for another assault, but she quickly took aim.

Adianna knew the skin of the orgrin was as hard as a thick layer of rock except under its arms. There, not only was the skin penetrable, but the heart and lungs were measurably unprotected. Thus, orgrins seldom raised their arms, even in defense. Apparently Zog's paralysis and outrage had over-shadowed his judgment of concealing this vulnerability.

Adianna instantly muttered the elfish incantation for swift and true flight, but just as she let the arrow fly, an unexplained darkness engulfed her outer vision. So real and intense was the clutch of it, it made her flinch when the string left her fingers and twanged into place.

The arrow whizzed through the air and sank into the fleshy bicep of the orgrin's arm. A painful injury, but far from fatal.

Fighting against the darkness threatening her, Adianna focused on the creature crumpling to his knees.

Just as quickly as it came, the darkness dissipated. Now she was aware of the man seeking her out. Dark hair, in wavy disarray, framed his handsome face. Strong chiseled features were softened by a boyish appeal, like he enjoyed laughing despite the hard set of his mouth. His piercing blue eyes scanned the curtain of forest, struggling to penetrate it. She held her breath, but instinctively, those sapphire orbs found her. His jaw slackened with surprise, but his gaze held hers.

She, too, remained rapt, fending off the darkness and fighting the intensity of his gaze. An instinctive sense of danger pressed upon her senses. Still, she was transfixed by those eyes.

The low groans of the beaten orgrins were forgotten as the stranger took a step toward her. But before he could take another, out of nowhere, a powerful green blast came careening through the clearing! It hit the man squarely, flinging him backward through the air.

UNEXPECTED

A shocked gasp stuck in Adianna's throat while she watched, helplessly, as the man sailed over the pile of downed orgrins and landed behind them where the clearing was again being claimed by the forest. She was only barely aware that Zog and the others were now prone and motionless on the ground, the reverberations of the blast having barreled over them in its path of destruction. Her eyes were still riveted on the crumpled heap of the stranger lying defenseless just beyond them. Dismay clutched her very being. Her senses slowly numbed to all else.

She could not look away. Approaching danger screamed at her awareness. But still she stared, watching intently for some breathing, some movement, some sign to say he would be alright… that he would live. Suddenly this was the most important desire she had within her.

Slowly, the faint sound of footsteps crept into her consciousness. Shaking her head to clear it, Adianna pulled her gaze from the prone warrior and turned to the sound.

A dark figure materialized around the bend of the road and glided into the clearing. Shrouded in a deep burgundy cloak lined with hunter green and gold embroidery, the apparition floated toward the clearing's center. With each step, a pale green dress hem could be seen through the part in the cloak.

Coming to a halt just a few yards from the now quiet, stony beasts, two slender arms emerged from the cloak and removed the hood. A fountain of golden curls spilled forth, cascading down the intruder's back. The late afternoon sun, filtering through the trees, set the swirling mass aglow. Still the forest shadows left a faint mint hue adorning the locks. The face enveloped by those curls was as delicate as porcelain. No flaw nor blemish. And strikingly beautiful.

But the eyes... their glassy golden aura spoke evil to Adianna's whole being.

A dull moan came from the prostrate stranger who lay helplessly fixed before those eyes. Adianna started to look over at the man but stopped. The cloaked woman raised an arm in his direction. The dainty fingers tickled the air for a moment then suddenly went rigid. Instantly an iridescent flash sprang forth. A single bolt of lightning shot between the orgrins toward the unconscious man, sending his body into a spasm of convulsions. Dazed, Adianna could only stare in horror at the quivering body. Yet another spurt of electricity gripped him, snaking its way around the man's body. A gleeful bubble of laughter exploded through the trees.

The unholy sound, in the sight of so much pain, snapped something within Adianna, and she sprang into action. Flinging her hand over her shoulder, she snatched an arrow. A habitual stream of motion had her nocked and ready to aim. But there she froze.

The cloaked woman had swiftly turned her head to Adianna in the same moment. Those golden eyes, with vertical, cat-like pupils, now bore into hers.

Still and breathless, the two women assessed each other. A carnal hostility, very real and tangible, lurked within that stare, each one sizing up the other. Slowly a smile crept across the porcelain face. Adianna could detect a subtle dare creep into the glint of the other woman's eyes. But the spell was too gripping for the girl to react in any way, until one golden eye dipped into a wink.

Then, instantly the hold was broken. The arrow flew.

In a millisecond, the cloak flew up, covering the figure from view, then the whole figure crumpled to the ground, the arrow whizzing past unaffected. In the next instant, when the cloak hit the earth, the heap exploded into green flame. Just as suddenly, a long, flying, snake-like creature shot upward out of the midst of the flames.

Slack-jawed, Adianna watched the sea-green serpent slither an ascent toward the treetops, pumping its great, silent wings. Two partly webbed foreclaws tucked tightly to its glistening scales were barely visible as it twisted through an opening in the canopy. Then it was gone. The creature's fading laughter trickled back through the thick air.

Unaware she had been holding her breath, Adianna released a strangled sigh. Raising a hand to her chest, she crumpled to a heap on the branch and slumped back against the trunk of the tree. Air seemed sweet now, and she savored it rushing into her lungs.

Still astounded, her eyes strayed again to the small patch of sky framed by an array of leaves. The encroaching darkness within her, the gripping sense of danger had left with the shape-shifting creature. All that was left behind was an uneasy peace.

Could that have been...?

The green flame on the ground died down to a smolder. *It must have been!* A scorched diamond in the dirt was the only proof of the strange encounter. That and the destruction it left...

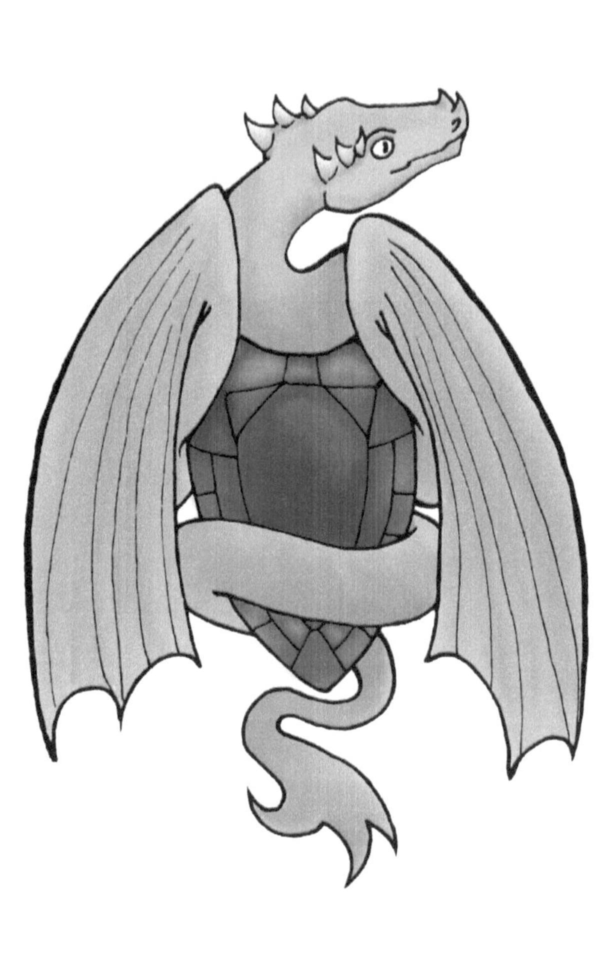

HEALING WOUNDS

The stranger!

A strangling fear gripped Adianna, seeing once more the cloaked heap of man lying unnaturally contorted on the ground across the clearing. There was no movement; no life was visible.

In a panic, Adianna quickly slung her bow over her shoulder. Wrapping her hands around the branch on which she sat, she swung nimbly off, and then from limb to limb until she landed gently in a crouch.

She wanted to barrel headlong across the expanse, but the sight of the unconscious orgrins reminded her of the lingering dangers. Glancing first at the opening in the treetops, then at the smoldering diamond, she stepped cautiously into the open. Uncertain as to the effect the blast had on the orgrins, Adianna did not abandon care in her approach. She wished she could keep more to the trees, but knowing it would take too long, she gave them a moderate berth and tiptoed silently past the motionless rock-men.

Her goal came into view. His back was toward her as she approached, and she quickened her pace. Despite the black cloak, she could discern his body curled on its side, his knees and head bending toward each other.

She noticed, too, his broad shoulders tapering to a lean waist and his head covered in dark brown waves. Most everything else was covered by the coarse black fabric.

Coming around him, she surveyed his form for any obvious damage. She pulled back the cloak, gently, exposing a white cotton shirt and brown breeches. His handsome face was contorted in a grimace, like a little boy with a skinned-up knee. Pity stirred within her.

She shot a glance at the orgrins, then rubbed her hands on her hips a couple times, figuring what to do first. Kneeling close to him, she gave the man a gentle shove, moving him onto his back. Quickly, she flinched away. Just that small amount of contact sent heat, strength, and waning adrenaline coursing up her arms plus scorched the palms of her hands as if she had been shoving at a fresh warming stone.

With him on his back, Adianna took inventory of his outward condition, blowing absently on her hands to cool them. The shallow rise and fall of his chest, covered in a worn but clean squire's shirt, quieted the biggest fear she had.

"You're alive!" she breathed. The gravity of relief that washed over her was overpowering. Her eyes fell shut, staying the unexplained tears springing forth to moisten her lashes. An emotional lump swelled at the back of her throat and pushed behind her nose and cheekbones. Pulling her lips between her teeth, she bit down, annoyed at this unprecedented reaction.

Taking a deep breath, she slowly opened her eyes again. But upon seeing his pained face, her own face contorted, and she had to look away.

She took another calming breath. Then she pursed her lips.

You're being ridiculous! You don't even know him.

Quit being such a sissy girl! This last thought sounded more like her cousin, Tarron, taunting her. He always knew how to get her back up so she would get the hard stuff done—just to spite him.

But it was enough, for she turned back to the stranger. Looking over his body with a clinical eye, she took account.

"His torso seems to lie flat on the ground," she said aloud, as if Tarron or Daerlot or one of her other tutors were there behind her taking notes.

"So, I don't think there is damage to his back." Remembering how high and far he had flipped through the air, this was a relief.

Then looking over his home-spun pants, she noted his powerful legs. Though they were at a relaxed bend, they were straight.

"No apparent broken leg bones," she checked off.

Coming back to his torso, Adianna glanced at the arm farthest from her, where it had fallen when she had rolled him over. Out away from his body, it made him look more exposed and helpless. Still, it appeared straight.

"Check," she said aloud.

The rise and fall of his broad chest was shallow but regular, and surprisingly unlabored. She absently gave a nod, silently checking off another point.

His neck was straight, his collarbones gently curved. His shoulders were powerful, even in repose. Then she came to the arm closest to where she was kneeling. It was then she perceived the blotch of red seeping through his baggy white sleeve. She had not noticed it before, since he had been lying on this arm when she approached, and it had become partly covered by her dress when she had knelt. Quickly moving out of the way, she could tell his forearm laid at an odd angle. With the obvious break, she marveled at his sword still being clenched in his fist.

A new wave of pity for this broken warrior enfolded her, and she choked down an unexplained sob. She noted her hands were shaking as she moved to untangle his weapon—whether from emotion or from fear of the anticipated pain shortly coming for both of them—she couldn't tell. She hesitantly folded her hands around his fingers, and, cringing from the burning sensation, awaited the rush.

Like a torrent held back by a broken dam, the sensation came crashing forth. Adianna gasped. The heat of it was so intense. She nearly released her hold, desiring to stop the assault on her faculties, but she knew she could not help him without touching him. It couldn't be helped.

The wave began to churn and spin deep within her. Growing dizzy, she closed her eyes. The heat was becoming unbearable under her hands. In her chest. Whirling and whirling, the sensations spun to a fevered pitch.

Spinning and spinning, and then exploding into a blast of light, bright and brilliant, streaked with shades of lavender and blue.

Dazed and breathless, Adianna fell back on her heels, her hands slipping from the stranger. She put a shaking hand to her chest to calm her panting breath. She gazed at the man in amazement, and she marveled at the intensity of this new experience.

His head was back, slightly exposing his neck, his Adam's apple not overly prominent. His face was square and turned away from her. His chin, strong yet not roughly chiseled, showed the speckled shadow of a beard unhappily held at bay.

Placing her knuckles on the ground on either side of his injured arm, she leaned forward to see his face more squarely. She pulled his chin gently toward her. Her powers recognized the feel of him, so there wasn't a repeat of her staggering experience just moments before. Still an intense warmth radiated from his skin to hers, then back to his again as if it were at work doing something, not merely warning her from the contact.

Her gaze searched his face. *As handsome as any elf,* she decided.

High cheekbones lent him a noble air. His forehead showed signs of laugh lines abandoned to give way to scowls, and she wondered at what had made such a drastic change.

It was then she noticed the dark splotches on the side of his forehead close to the hairline. Leaning further, she moved to better investigate. Brushing aside the soft locks, she found a jagged gash about three inches long. Fresh blood matted the hair around the wound, but surprisingly, the clearer, yellowish plasma was already oozing slowly from the injury itself.

Gingerly, she felt around with her fingertips, inspecting the gash, trying to ignore the intensity of the heat caused by the touch.

"Gratefully, it isn't too deep," she said softly. "It must have happened after he landed."

This thought was confirmed as she inspected the ground where his head had been when she came upon him and found a craggy rock protruding out of the hard dirt. It was smeared red with his blood.

She thought back to how his body had thrashed around in the electrically induced seizure. Agonizing in the memory, Adianna didn't notice the wound closing until it literally moved beneath her fingers. Flinching back, her gaze became glued to the gash. It was closing up! Right before her eyes.

Though much slower now her hand was removed. Mouth gaping in wonder, she gently pushed the blood-wet hair out of the way and watched. Very, very slowly, but definitely, the ragged edges were moving across the wound to meet each other.

In awe, she found his face. "You're a healer!" she breathed.

A giddy excitement shot through her, and she gently placed her hand over the wound. The heat returned, growing steadily. Adianna drew her bottom lip between her teeth, biting back the searing pain, pushing it from her mind. Instead, she closed her eyes and focused on the pulsing wound beneath her palm. She could feel the gash closing faster as the heat increased.

When all was still and the heat had receded some, she opened her eyes, anxious to see the result. There, where the ugly gash had been, was now only a jagged red line. This, too, she figured, would lighten and disappear in a day or two, as his body continued to heal itself.

"Unbelievable." She sighed, deeming this the neatest thing she had ever witnessed. She absently waved her scorched hand in the air, trying to cool it, still watching the healing injury.

Suddenly, something brushed Adianna's ribs, making her jump and spin away. The man's good hand slowly sank to his chest. She quickly relaxed and reined in her accelerated heart rate.

The stranger's eyes fluttered, trying to seek her out. He licked his lips and swallowed hard between shallow gasps. Thinking he meant to speak, she neared with an encouraging smile.

Despite a few feeble attempts, he finally got out the word, "Sword."

A soft smile spread across her face as Adianna reassured him, "Your sword is right here."

She retrieved it from where it lay by his broken arm and passed it to the hand he struggled to raise. His grip tightened around the handle, but the only movement of the heavy blade was from the rise and fall of his shallow breath.

The weakened man began to struggle in an attempt to rise with little success. Adianna instinctively placed her hands on his shoulders to restrain his movement and keep him still, but when her hands came in contact with him, it was like touching the rocks lining a fire pit. She flinched back again. All the same, he laid his head back down. His lashes fluttered, eyes searching upward, though seeing little.

"My... hand... won't work," he said in strangled breaths.

"Shhh. I know. I know," she soothed, brushing a few dark curls away from his forehead. His gaze found hers, and she looked into its blue depth, remembering the power his eyes had held over her earlier. Now they carried a pained glaze which hazed around the edges. He struggled to stay conscious and alert, but the tortured look on his face and his shallow breathing now suggested some internal damage.

Still, she promised him softly, "I'll take care of it," before turning her attention to his arm.

Carefully, she unfastened the cuff of his shirt. It opened wide, but she chose to rip the sleeve rather than chance rolling it up and disturbing the arm.

"Oh, my," Adianna breathed once the material was out of the way.

The forearm turned grotesquely away from her, even though his arm rested close to her knees. Seeing both bones were broken was unmistakable; the forearm appeared to have an elbow of its own. And about a hands-width from the actual elbow, where its copy bent, blood was oozing around a piece of sharp, white bone protruding from the flesh.

Panic lurched within her. Her hand flew to cover her mouth. Not to stay any nausea, but to strangle a cry from coming forth. The stranger didn't notice, as he was still struggling to move his head around, searching, taking in his surroundings.

Adianna frantically searched her memory, not for medical procedure, but for an inkling of how to best enhance this healer's abilities. She vaguely remembered Relyat saying as long as a healer did not lose large amounts of blood, they could not die from wounds. Fortunately, his blood loss, thus far, had been minimal. Considering all he had undergone, this was an appreciated miracle.

I guess I should first set the bones and close up the wound, she told herself.

She nibbled at her lip as she reached forward. Her eyebrows knit together, and her eyes scrunched. She inwardly cringed, anticipating the burning awaiting her touch that couldn't be helped. Gingerly, she placed a hand on either side of the break. She clenched her teeth as the searing white heat leapt up her arms. She felt as gently as possible with her thumbs, focusing to find the space between the two bones. Barely managing to block out her pain, she was about to push the bones back into place, but she felt fingers brush the back of her arm.

Startled, she released her grasp, flinging her hands into the air. The stranger had raised his head slightly, and his haggard eyes were instantly powerful and bore into hers.

"Are you... safe?" he breathed with great effort.

A piece of Adianna's heart melted for this courageous and gallant warrior. She couldn't resist brushing her fingertips along his cheek. The pain of the touch meant nothing; the press of tears was too prominent as she smiled warmly into his earnest expression.

"Yes," she whispered, her voice trembling. "All is well."

He rested his head back and closed his eyes. He turned ever so slightly into the warmth of her fingers.

Thinking him slipping into sleep, Adianna gave his cheek one final stroke. Then she turned back to the unpleasant task awaiting her.

Repositioning her hands as before, she gave another fleeting glance at the peaceful face. Her jaw set tight, she offered him a silent apology. Then looking determinedly at the wound, she clenched her teeth, steeling her courage. Slowly, but forcibly, she pried the bones toward their proper places.

She felt his body grow rigid beside her. A low growl escaped his lips as the piece of bone slipped back inside. She could only imagine the pain being caused by the jagged radius and ulna bones ripping their way back home. Adianna barely flinched as the man came up, half-sitting, grasping her upper arm in his viselike grip. His crying growl told her he didn't mean to hurt her; still she released her grasp. Mouth agape, his eyes searching through her unseeingly, he was looking for the balm needed to hold back the agony.

I will give it to you, she thought, as an idea came to her. Her gaze penetrating his, she softly chanted, "*Po sec mearo-ket ta no-fypho Leashi donnso meashra lyso. Bi yon meash lup.*"

The mystic words hung in the air, echoing between them as if down a long, narrow corridor. Her gaze stayed locked with his, but she was aware of tingling sparks dancing around the edges of their stare.

Slowly, his grasp waned. His gaze dipped once, twice, three times—and he lay back again. He settled softly into a peaceful sleep. Still, it wasn't until she heard his breathing level off to a low, deep rhythm that she turned back to setting the fissures.

Now without fear of disturbing his slumber, she pressed the bones back into place. Somehow with using his abilities, Adianna could see, in her minds' eye, the edges of the bones within his body. Thus, she was able to line the breaks exactly. Then, encircling the break with her hands, she closed her eyes and focused all her thoughts and energy to that spot. She could feel the puncture wound closing, could visualize the outer edges of the bones fusing together. Then, finally, she couldn't withstand the intense heat any longer and let go.

She fell back, panting for breath. Her crumpled hands trembled in agony, and she couldn't bite back the sobbing any longer. She pulled her knees to her chest, wrapping her arms around them, her hands sticking out like mangled claws. With the exhale of each strangled sob, she sent cooling air blowing over her blazing hands.

As the pain abated, she was able to quiet her crying. A subtle breeze stirred through the clearing, quelling the pain further. Slowly, her breathing became deeper and more even, and she laid her forehead against her knees. She sat silently, awaiting the chill to course through her arms announcing it to be over; the burning was done. She focused on her breathing and the light breeze. When the chill came, so did relief and a release that left her whole, as if nothing had happened.

Her eyes had drifted shut with this release. When she raised her head, she opened them with a sigh. Now she could return her focus to the stranger and tend to his safe keeping.

Knowing the bones in his arm could still be easily rebroken, she scanned the area for something to use as a splint. Seeing a branch near the edge of the trees off to her right, she went to fetch it. She broke it across her knee to make two pieces short enough to fit between his wrist and elbow. Then, snatching up another branch, she repeated the process before returning to her patient.

She ripped the brown hem from the front of her skirt. Situating the sticks at four points around the fracture, she lashed it all together with her hem. She then sat back to eye her handy work. After a careful once-over, she felt confident the bones would remain stable regardless of how they might be inadvertently bumped.

Finishing the final knot, Adianna froze. A low rumble could be heard off to her left. It was short at first, but each time it repeated, it became longer and louder though it was always close.

Rising, she cautiously stepped around the stranger and followed the sound in the direction of the orgrins. Straining to hear, she crept right up to the mound of rock creatures. Realization dawned and mirth bubbled inside her. Zog, the one she had winged with her arrow, must have been knocked unconscious by the blast and sleep had overtaken him, for now… he snored.

A giggle escaped Adianna's lips, but she pressed her fingers against them to suppress it. She couldn't afford to wake them, and she was not certain as to the enduring effects of the blast.

The Blast! Remembering the vicious attacker, she looked to the scorched diamond-shape in the weeds a few yards beyond the orgrins. A faint trail of smoke ascended from the blackened ground. Her gaze followed it toward the trees. As she peered at the patch of sky where the flying serpent had disappeared, the girl got the eerie sensation of being watched. Eyes riveted to that patch of blue, she slowly shook her head. "We have to get away from this place."

She turned away from the canopy and quickly returned to the wounded man. As she looked over his large bulk, her shoulders sagged a little. An aching fear clutched her heart for she knew what she had to do.

If only I had my cloak with me! She thought of the shamere-mail cloak she had left back home. The metal had been discovered by the dwarves centuries ago and was the only material to keep the burning from reaching her skin. But it couldn't be helped. Absently, she rubbed her hands over her hips again, while accessing her next move.

"Well." She sighed, straightening erect again. "I certainly hope you are as strong as you look." She removed her bow and quiver and slung them over her left arm. She then pulled on the man's good arm until he was in a sitting position. Her breath hissed as she drew in air between her clenched teeth. "Because…"

She leaned down, pulling his arm over her head and placing her right shoulder against his midriff. Fire burned through her hand and shoulder. "I'm going to need…" Lifting with her legs, she staggered under the extra weight. The intense heat was near crippling. "All the help… I can get!"

The sound of his sword falling to the ground caught her attention. Her eyes rolled heavenward. She allowed herself a soft groan before scrunching down to pick up the weapon.

Straightening again, she heaved another sigh. Then she gritted her teeth against the burning. Rounding the snoring orgrins and giving the treetops a final glance, she trotted off toward home.

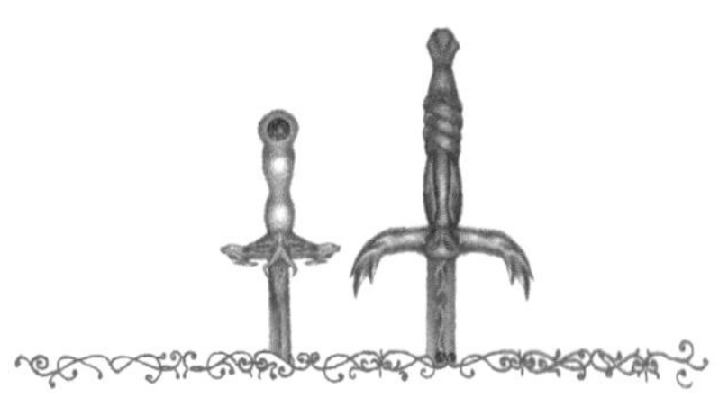

THE STRANGER

I*'m completely surrounded!*

Sweat rolled down his face. It hurt to move. Everywhere he looked, there were orgrins. They were closing in on him, licking their chops as if he were a roasted pig at a family gathering.

How am I ever going to get out of this one? He frantically searched for some means of escape. He could find none.

His body tensed, preparing to fight. He hurt everywhere, some places more than others.

The enemy was prepared. They would finish him quickly.

This is it!

He readied himself, watching them approach, their craggy hands outstretched. Putrid, green saliva oozed between their jagged razor teeth.

But just as they were about to attack, they stopped. A sound distracted his assailants, coming from somewhere behind them. The clinking of metal pots and the clunking of clay bowls.

Orgrins don't use cookware.

He and the attackers turned to see what was making the sound. Between the monstrous creatures, he could see a young woman. Though her hair was pulled back with a tie, several auburn curls fell forward into her face, and she had the most alluring emerald eyes. The lovely apparition was cleaning off a slab table. Behind her stood a large cooking hearth.

Blinking through the haze, Kendrick struggled to focus on the sound. Slowly, the orgrins disappeared. The girl disappeared. In their place, arching over the top of him, was the simple ceiling of a bedding cubicle.

He then became aware of his prostrate condition, of a soft feather pillow beneath his head, a restrictive wrap around his left arm and, tucked under his chin, the clammy feel of damp blankets surrounding his bare chest.

Where am I?

He lolled his head to the side. A small window from somewhere beyond the head of the bed was bathing the room in a soft post-dawn light. A simple wooden chair stood close to the bed, facing him, as if someone had recently occupied it to observe him. The only other furniture in the room was a bureau built into the wall facing the window just past the end of the bed. It was wide, with wooden handled drawers curving out toward the center of the room. On top of the bureau, nestled in the high-arching space cut into the wall above it, was a cheery arrangement of wildflowers as well as a high shelf harboring a few leather-bound books.

Across the room from where he lay, a tall oval door stood ajar, exposing another room equally furnished in its simplicity just beyond. From his vantage point, the outer room held an open fireplace used for cooking with the slab table he recognized from his dream sitting before it. Two carved wooden chairs sat at either end of the sturdy table. The tantalizing scent of cinnamon mingling with cooked apples drifted in from that room, as did the sounds from his dream.

Someone's in there! The heavy stone of apprehension squashed the hunger pangs kindling in the pit of his stomach. *But friend or foe?*

Alert now, he raised his head quickly. This minor movement sent the room spinning around him. Through pinched eyelids, and with his jaw clenched against the pain, he scanned the room again. Finally, he spotted what he sought. Beside the small vase of flowers, his sword rested beneath a stack of clothes on the bureau.

Tightening his abdominals in an attempt to sit sent pain coursing through his body. Originating in his chest and spreading out were millions of tiny needles viciously pricking their way in all directions, trying to free themselves from his body. Impulsively, he tried to stifle the sensation within him by bringing up his constricted hand peeking out from beneath the covers. But as he brushed his arm against the heavy coverlet, a different pain exploded upon his senses.

Groaning, he laid his arm back down. The excruciating sensation numbed his fingers, and he grimaced at the splint encompassing his throbbing limb.

"Broken!" he growled in frustration, plopping his head back onto the pillow. His breathing was haggard as he fought the pain.

Before he could dwell further on his condition, Kendrick became acutely aware of the sudden silence that had settled in the next room. His gaze flew to the door. The apprehension settled in his very center now, and his muscles tensed despite the pain. He prepared for the unknown.

A fluffy-looking shadow appeared just outside the door. Shrouded in darkness from the lighting behind it, its silhouette was the only discernible identification. Before he could make out what it was, it disappeared again.

With his body still tense, he listened with his whole being. *What was it and where did it go?*

The soft sound of a door opening was heard, then an urgent voice.

"Memsy! Come! He's awake!"

The voice was young and feminine. The enticing thought of the woman in his dream flashed through his mind. He could remember, vividly, those dazzling green eyes set in a heart-shaped face. But rapid footsteps invaded his awareness, and he pushed that thought aside.

Kendrick tried to shift to allow an easier use of his good arm for defense, but this merely resulted in pain marring his vision. Helplessly, his head plopped back onto the pillow again. The footfalls reached the door just as his vision cleared.

What he saw surprised him. There, standing in the doorway, was a tall, stately woman with no resemblance to the girl from his dream. Thick, silver hair spilled over this woman's shoulders in sleek rivers that reached past her waist. She moved slowly now, stepping just inside the door and bowing. The tips of her ears peeked out through the semi-translucent hair, but it was the silver swirling emblem now rippling on her smooth forehead that held his gaze.

"A sorci?" he said, his voice cracking from lack of use. "I'm impressed."

A slow smile crossed the woman's lips as she inclined her head to him again. "As am I… Master Healer," she stated, searching his face.

Kendrick blanched inwardly. It was an unspoken rule by those striving to survive in Sheorae to not volunteer personal information, even as trivial as names, let alone secret particulars. Drokmar's special band of mercenaries, called the dalphene, needed to know very little about anyone to hunt them down and take their life in their attempt to build a massive reserve army. No, the dalphene merely had to catch and kill someone in a treacherous act or a selfish endeavor to have claim on one's soul. These claimed souls, along with any other wicked souls past, were then Drokmar's as soon as those ridiculous Blades were found and a new alliance made. Then the souls were resurrected into the hated rectors, the most ruthless killing machines alive. Worse even than the goblins.

But since it had been nearly fourteen years since the last alliance, Drokmar's minions were getting more selective—seeking out special qualities or abilities. So, this stranger knowing of his healing powers made him more than a little nervous, even if she *was* an elf.

Uncomfortable now under her probing gaze, Kendrick fidgeted, attempting to cover his awkwardness by trying to prop himself with his good arm. Little movement was accomplished before he winced from the pain.

He let out a humorless laugh. "I seem in very poor shape, indeed, to be a healer, m'lady," he said, trying to sound as doubtful as possible.

One eyebrow rose as a cynical smile settled on the sorci's face. "If you were not a healer, you would be dead," she replied. Her low melodious voice belied the gravity of the statement.

Feeling trapped, Kendrick could do nothing but stare at her as she approached and sat in the chair beside the bed. Her hazel-green eyes never left his. Their golden wheat color, rimmed with a lively green, was so keen and aware, he knew instantly they missed nothing. A tightening clogged his throat, and he struggled for what to do next.

Finally, squinting one eye in a dubious look, he queried, "Dead? From a broken arm and a few bangs and bruises?"

The sorci's smile broadened as a snuffy little chuckle escaped her. For just a moment, he thought he saw the honey-colored center of her eyes flash a smoky gray, but it shifted back so quickly he wasn't sure it really happened. But there had been a subtle change in her smile.

"Actually," she stated matter-of-factly. "The bones in your arm are already set and healing nicely. Your body should complete the process in, I'd say, less than a week. The bang on your forehead," she flicked a finger in that direction, "has sealed and is doing well. You'll not even see a scar in a day or two. A few ribs were broken but are mending quickly. And then there's the angry bruise you received to your right knee which has already begun to yellow. So, all in all, you'll be fit to fly in a few days."

Kendrick was dumbfounded. He glanced at his knee, and just bending it slightly under the blankets, he knew she was right about the bruise.

But yellowing, already?

His good hand rose to his head. It took him a bit of feeling around just to find the injury she had alluded to, but there it was. The smooth ridge in his skin was no longer tender, but judging from the size and shape, it had to have been pretty bad. Merely taking a deep breath confirmed to him about his ribs. Still, he reached across, fingering them gently. He attempted to twist—to feel the extent of the internal damage and healing—but the movement again flooded his senses with those same prickles as before, hinting at high voltage electric shock recently.

This is insane! With injuries such as these, the rate of recovery has to be some three times faster than my normal accelerated rate. Unless of course... but I couldn't have been out that long. Could I?

Puzzling this all over in his head, he didn't notice the woman's intense stare, probing and searching.

Finally, she broke the silence by plopping the palms of her hands down on her thighs. "Well, you must be hungry. I shall leave you to your thoughts, Master Healer, and we shall bring you some broth to nourish you and ease some of your pain."

She stood then, turning to the door. But before she could slip through it, Kendrick called out.

"Hey! I mean, pardon me, but… how long have I been here?" He gave a casual sweep of the room and wished his voice hadn't sounded so bewildered.

The sorci turned to him, resting her hand on the doorknob. The hint of a smile pulled at the corners of her mouth as she appraised him.

"You have been with us not yet a full day, young sir."

Amazement flooded Kendrick's thinking. So much so he did not hear the door latch click.

Adianna cracked open the door to peek in. The man reclining on her bed appeared deep in thought and a little perplexed. Her heart quickened upon seeing him. Adianna took a deep breath then ducked into the room, keeping her head down. She balanced the tray on one arm and closed the door quietly. The man still hadn't seemed to notice her. So, she tucked some of her hair behind her ear, chastising herself for vainly removing the tie, and stepped forward.

He started when she placed the tray containing a bowl of casimine broth and a dish of sayflower biscuits with fresh apple butter onto the chair by the bed.

"Oh… thank you," he stammered. He fidgeted, then winced. He growled softly under his breath.

"Could you—oh." He paused when he caught sight of her. "You aren't the sorci?"

His recognition was so disconcerting all she could muster as a response was a shake of the head. She had the sudden thought to introduce herself, but Adianna quelled it quickly. It was safer not to know too much about strangers or for them not to know too much about you. So she stood there, nervously biting her bottom lip.

His appraising look took in the length of her, and she felt her cheeks flame. Slowly, the corners of his mouth raised approvingly.

Her stomach tightened, and she pushed down a saucy retort that would wipe that impertinent look off his face.

"Might I please beg your assistance, Miss, in helping me to sit so I might sample the delicious-looking treats you have placed before me?"

At first, Adianna was a bit miffed. From the look he had been giving her, she felt his words had a facetious double meaning. She opened her mouth to give him the mild tongue-lashing she felt he deserved, but then her eyes widened with panic.

She hadn't expected any contact with him. She had left her shamere gloves hanging on the hook by the front door next to her cloak. Her memory was all too clear of the last contact she had with him. Her use of his powers had been the only thing to keep her alive in her attempt to get him back to the village, and she had just been able to get back on her feet a few hours previous as it was. Now, her jaw slackened as she peered pleadingly at the closed door.

The man seemed to find her reaction comical, for she could hear him chuckle under his breath. His gaze was merrily running over her when she turned back to him. His taunting behavior irked her. She instantly squared her shoulders, wanting again to put him in his place. But then she remembered he was their guest, so she turned for the door.

"I'll just go get…" she began, giving him a reproving glance over her shoulder.

"No, it's alright." The toying gleam left his face at the sight of her actually moving to leave. "Come here. We can manage," he urged, a bit more adamantly, waving her closer. Unfortunately, he waved with the hand that was closest to her, the broken one, and he winced with the pain of it.

Upon seeing him in pain, her resolve slipped. She had seen his handsome face in too much pain in the last sixteen hours, and her motherly instincts nagged at her defenses.

Adianna sent another frantic look to the door, suddenly willing it to open with Memsy's miraculous arrival.

"Come on," he said impatiently.

She eyed him abruptly, but at seeing him glancing frustratedly down at his prostrate body, her flared temper cooled. *This must be so hard for him.*

Apprehensively, she approached. She cleared her throat, carefully pulling the chair out of the way to stall for time. The comforting smell of the broth and the bready biscuits filled her senses, mingling with the scent of cinnamon and apples.

Slowly, she took a deep breath, bracing herself for what was to come. He was awkwardly maneuvering his good arm into place, trying to get it into a position to shift most of his weight himself, but the grimace on his face told her it wasn't easy. She pulled the side of her lip between her teeth, then slowly placed her hands under his arms.

Instantly, the contact with his bare skin burned. It was quickly followed by the sensation of light flooding up from the encounter. She grimaced faintly and tried not to focus on the pain or the swirling display going on inside her body. She struggled to concentrate on getting the task over and done. But as his strength burst forth through her limbs, she marveled at how strong the stranger was, even when injured. She lifted his upper body without any fuss, causing his own push off of the bed to send him flopping against the pillows propped against the wall.

His head came up so hastily his shocked face was just inches from hers. This caught Adianna off guard, and she released him abruptly, stepping back in a rush. Her cheeks colored at the dumbfounded look he gave her. She could tell he was amazed by her uncharacteristic display of strength. His brows puckered, and she squirmed under his scrutiny. She dipped her head shyly. Seeing the forgotten tray, she retrieved it as a means of distraction. Without looking up, she settled it on his lap.

Uncertain now whether to leave or stay, she hung back against the bureau. She straightened the already tidy items found there, attempting to distract her mind from dwelling on the occupant of the bed. She failed miserably. The sound of him sipping broth made her smile and relax a little. But when there was nothing else for her to do but stare at him, she attempted to leave.

"So, Miss."

Adianna turned back at the sound of his deep, rich voice. She found his incredible blue eyes upon her.

"Where exactly are we? Are we still in Kyren Forest?"

She opened her mouth to answer, but he went on.

"And you. Who are you? You obviously aren't an elf. But your eyes..."

Adianna froze. His soup forgotten, he stared at her. Her breath caught. She forced herself to meet his gaze though she desperately wanted to look anywhere else.

How much does he remember?

"They seem so familiar."

"No," she answered too quickly. "I mean, yes. I mean..."

Answers were swimming around in her head tumbling one over the other. Adianna closed her eyes to regroup and stop her stammering. Her palms pressed together. Her fingers pinched her bottom lip, and she tried to decide which question to answer first. She figured she'd start with the safest.

"Yes, you are still in the forest." Her hands sliced forward in a decisive manner. She opened her eyes to look at him. Then, with a smile, she added, "You are in Tymalia."

"Tymalia?" the stranger interjected, his eyes bugging out a little. He dribbled soup from his spoon in the process.

"Yes," she said more slowly, watching him brush absently at the wet droplets trickling down his bare chest. He was staring into space, somewhat astonished, so she went on. "You are in the house of Memsy, the Sorci." *Elves were safe,* she told herself. *They were meant to be neutral in the conflict... at least until I came.* "She went to get her brother, the patriarch. That is why she had me bring..."

"The patriarch! Of the elves?" This time broth splattered all over the tray in his lap. "Blast!"

Wide-eyed, Adianna jumped forward to be of assistance, but she was too late. The man reflexively grabbed with his injured hand. His growl echoed in the room when his broken arm came in contact with the tray. The broth went flying all over his face and chest while biscuits hit the far wall of the sleeping cubicle.

Trying hard not to laugh in the face of his aggravation, Adianna bit down on both her lips at the same time. She piled the fallen dishes quickly on the tray. Then placing it on the chair, she offered the end of her apron to the soaking-wet young man.

Reaching across himself with his good hand, he yanked the edge of the apron from her in frustration. This quick movement brought Adianna nearly falling into his lap.

Trying to prevent a collision with his injured arm, she grabbed for his pillow but fell on his shoulder, her other hand landing on the bed by his hip. The burning of contact was instantaneous. Then, through the pain, she could hear the man sputtering.

Snatching her hand from him, she shoved at the hair that fell in her face.

"Are you alright?" she queried, thankful her voice sounded concerned—not in pain.

He sputtered again, but merriment was in his eyes. "I'm fine. But I found myself with a mouthful of curls when I was vying to dry my face."

Adianna impulsively flipped her hair over her shoulder out of the way. "I'm so sorry, sir," she muttered, staring apologetically at him.

A new burning was creeping through her now, this time from her cheeks, as she took note of how close their faces were. His eyes caressed the slope of her neck then flit to her lips. Adianna knew she must be blushing all over, for the heat of it permeated over every inch of her body.

Breathe! Her lips parted, but the effort only made her think of how close his lips were and not of the much-needed oxygen.

Mentally, she shook herself. Then frantically pushing herself back, she clawed at the knot of her apron. Freeing it, she handed the whole thing over to him. He took the proffered material and dabbed distractedly at his face. He seemed to be enjoying himself. His mischievous blue eyes danced happily and were perusing her up and down with renewed interest. She quickly looked away.

Seeing the dishes, she leaned over him, keeping adequate distance, to gather the fallen biscuits. Flinging them on top of the dishes, she said, "I'll just go get you some more."

She propped the tray on her hip and scurried to the door. Just before she could leave, he called out, “Wait, Miss.”

She turned back to him.

He blotted at his chest with the apron. “How long have I really been in legendary Tymalia?”

Adianna scrunched her eyebrows a little at his sarcastic tone. “We arrived in the early evening yesterday.”

“We!”

She could tell by the shock on his face now would be the best time to leave, so she ducked out before he could further pummel her with questions.

TRIVIA BEFORE SECRETS

Adianna closed the door with a smile. Turning into the main room, she came face to face with Memsy and Daerlot. The dishes rattled on the tray at her abrupt stop. Sobering quickly, she stammered, "There you are."

Memsy arched an eyebrow, but her gaze was cheerful. "Is our guest finished already?" she queried.

Adianna looked at the empty dishes and scattered, untouched food. She could feel both her mother's and her uncle's eyes upon her.

"No, Mems. The gentleman had… a little accident. I was just going to get him some more."

Dala's eyes spoke of merriment despite his brows being knitted together. "Did you tell him anything yet, my dear?"

Mm, Adianna loved her uncle's voice. It always had a way of soothing her no matter his expression.

"Not about the attack, Dala. I just told him where he was and when he came."

Memsy looked to Daerlot. "Apparently the healer is curious about his accelerated recovery. He asked me of the length of his stay, as well. We will most likely be confronted with that question, brother, in one form or another."

"Yes," he replied, his thoughtful gaze resting on Adianna. Though his hair was shifting from blond to silver, bespeaking age, his skin retained a tight, youthful glow. Still, his eyes hid the shadows of many years. She felt like fidgeting under his scrutiny, but his expression cleared, revealing his usual happy self.

"Don't worry, my dear." He stepped past Memsy to pat Adianna on the arm in a reassuring manner. "All will be well. Trivia before secrets. Right?"

He smiled at her, then moved to the door.

She stopped him with her hand on his arm. "He is expecting you. And with a lot of questions, no doubt." A small, knowing smile touched her lips.

Daerlot patted her hand with his and returned her smile. "That is good. Maybe we shall get some answers, as well." He nodded at the items in her hands. "Bring that in as soon as you can. This all may concern you more than we know."

He winked at her and was opening the door before Adianna could use his power to understand what he meant. The two elves retreated into the other room.

Adianna was glad she hadn't thrown out the wash water. She hurried to the basin and frantically washed the tray and dishes. She didn't want to miss anything; her curiosity was piqued. Refilling the dishes with warm broth and fresh biscuits, she didn't care about the noise the utensils made. Within a minute or two, she was back at the door, turning the knob.

"In all my traveling," the stranger was saying with cheerful amazement, "I don't think I have ever even come close to finding Tymalia, and here I am. Brought by a mere gir—" He stopped mid-sentence when he saw Adianna enter.

Everyone turned to her. She swallowed hard and plunged into the room. She placed the tray on the man's lap in silence. Then she moved around behind Daerlot to linger by the bureau, hoping to find out more about this intriguing man.

Daerlot stepped aside to block Adianna from the man's gaze, which was riveted on her.

"We wish to welcome you to Tymalia…for the time being," the patriarch stated. "And hope your stay and recovery with us will be pleasant."

The patriarch then pulled the chair over in front of him and motioned for Memsy to have a seat. Adianna knew they were setting themselves up for an unfair advantage. With Memsy situated to easily pick up the man's thoughts and Dala in proximity to receive visions of past and future, the stranger didn't stand a chance of getting anything by them. She knew these were necessary precautions for the safety of the village, but this time, Adianna felt it was too much invasion of his privacy. Still, she was too interested to know what they would find out to say anything.

"Now, Master Healer," Daerlot began when Memsy was settled. "What is it you remember?"

Adianna started at the bluntness of the question. Dala was typically urbane to a fault. Slowly, she peeked around him and listened for what the stranger would say.

He, too, seemed surprised by the abrupt inquiry but recovered quickly.

"Not much really, my Lord—Daerlot, was it?" the man conceded, his voice thick, contemplating. At the elf's nod, he continued, "I was coming through the woods from the east, and I was suddenly attacked by orgrins. Three of them, if I remember correctly."

Daerlot shifted his weight into Adianna's view of the man, so she had to move as well. The man was deep in thought.

"I believe I got one… no, two down. Then there was a shout. I turned, and the third had been shot with an arrow under the arm. I was scanning the edge of the forest when a green haze took over everything. Then all went black."

The man looked at Daerlot, shaking his head. In this movement, he caught sight of Adianna watching him. His eyes narrowed slightly as if sifting through memory, then grew wide with recognition. Adianna's sharp intake of breath was almost painful in her chest. Her eyes widened, too, as she wondered again how much he remembered. The man raised his hand to point in her direction and was about to say something, but Daerlot cut him off.

"And why would a dalphene be after you?"

The man stopped as if struck. He could do naught but stare at the patriarch, mouth gaping.

Silence stretched on between them, until finally the man found his voice. "Dalphene? I'm not sure I know what you're talking about."

Daerlot shifted his stance again, this time bringing himself to his full height, by which Adianna knew he was getting upset but was trying to contain it.

"You have had more than your share of experience with the dalphene, so I think you know exactly what I'm talking about, human," her uncle responded.

Adianna drew her lips into her mouth. She could feel the tension mounting. *What is Dala talking about? What is he seeing?*

Still, she kept her gaze on the man. His eyes seemed those of a caged animal at first—intense, fearful, yet ready to spring. But slowly he narrowed them. They grew very calm, merely waiting with only the slightest hint of challenge.

"Very well, Healer. We will play it your way, for now." Dala's consent dripped with irritation. "It was a dalphene who attacked you after the orgrins. You were hit both with pulses and with blasts, and it nearly took your life… but didn't."

The man stared, all haughtiness gone. Intensity mingled with shock. She could see his chest rising and falling more rapidly now.

"If the dalphene wanted your soul for your healing abilities, it would have been swift and painless and over before you knew what hit you. This one hit you—again, and again, and again. Then left you alive."

The man's jaw shifted tightly as Daerlot continued. "A very vindictive thing, too, she seemed. Isn't that what you said, my dear?"

Her uncle turned abruptly to her, pinning her with the question. Taken aback, her mouth flew open, but nothing escaped. Distress settled in at the sudden spotlight.

"She?" The man enunciated the word. He sat staring intently at her. His azure eyes bore into her, demanding a response. She could feel Dala's upon her, too.

"Y-yes." She fumbled for her voice and ducked her head to avoid looking at either of them. "At least she acted amused."

"Amused!" the man erupted, causing him to bump his arm again. His features contorted, and he plopped back against the pillow. Teeth clenched tight, he thumped his head once against the wall of the cubicle and pounded his good fist against the mattress. The healer's breath came out in sporadic puffs through his nostrils, yet he seemed focused on settling the pain.

"Well," Adianna tried again, when his breathing was more even, struggling to not let his outburst affect her. "I mean… she seemed to take pleasure in the attack."

The healer pinned her with a look of venom. "Took pleasure in charging my body full of electricity and blasting me who knows how many times?" The man's rage was tangible and directed squarely at her.

Adianna's own temper flared in the face of his. Memsy could tell, for she was moving quickly to intercept, but it was too late.

"Don't blame me!" Adianna barked, taking a step toward the insufferable man and brushing Memsy's hands aside. "I didn't do it!"

The man's anger stopped short like water had been doused on him. His burning eyes cleared and seemed to refocus, as if seeing her for the first time since her previous statement. "Of-of course not," he stammered, ducking his head a little. "My apologies."

Adianna merely crossed her arms with a huff. Her temper couldn't be cooled so easily. She pinned him with her gaze, trying to rein in her anger.

"Could you describe the dalphene?" the man asked softly. His gaze penitently searched hers. The rich blue captivated her into thinking any moment clouds might go floating past in their beckoning depths.

Realizing she was about to sigh, she bit the side of her lower lip. Then, forcing herself to look down, Adianna pushed a lock of hair behind her ear, trying to concentrate.

"She was young. Of course, she was young!" She chided herself. *Their aging is frozen when made a dalphene! And no one old was accepted by the serpent.* "And she had blond hair. Very curly and lovely. Her face… was absolutely beautiful. Like porcelain. And her eyes! They were golden in color, more cat-like than human. And full of malice."

"Malice!" the healer snorted. His temper spiked again, for his nostrils flared, and both fists were clenched despite the pain it must have caused. His jaw tightened as he glared at the coverlet. Suddenly, he glared at her.

"And you? Why didn't you shoot her like you did the orgrin? It was you who shot him, correct?" he accused. "So why didn't you shoot her, too?"

Adianna was caught off guard for a moment, her arms dropping to her side. Daerlot moved to come to her aid, but she quickly countered on the ungrateful cur.

"I tried to, you buffoon!"

His eyes widened under the attack.

"But she transformed and flew off." She flung her hand in the air, then pointed a finger at the stupefied man on the bed. "Besides, your little fits of temper don't change the fact you are avoiding the questions you've been asked. Do they?"

She crossed her arms defiantly, daring him to challenge her. He stared back. The two glared each other down, and she prepared for a fight. But, surprisingly, one corner of his mouth came up. Next, the other. Then he chuckled softly, shaking his head from side to side.

"No," he said, never taking his eyes off her. "No, they don't."

He ducked his head sheepishly. With his good hand, he rubbed his chin, his eyes alone looking up, tentatively, a couple times. He glanced from Adianna to the patriarch, then back again.

Finally, he shrugged, flopping his hand back down.

"Actually," he said, looking at Daerlot. "I don't know what the dalphene want with me. I have noticed a few dogging my trail for the past couple months, but I have no clue why. I try to keep my nose clean, if you know what I mean. I avoid confrontations with Drokmar's soldiers whenever possible. I don't care about his plans so long as he leaves me out of them. Besides, I've heard the Blades have been lost for years."

Daerlot and Memsy exchanged subtle glances. Adianna just swallowed hard.

But the man failed to notice, staring down at his broken arm. "So, I don't know what they would want with me. But I am surprised to find out this particular dalphene was a woman," the healer mused, rubbing his chin again.

"All the others have been men, and they have all kept their distance. But…" He shrugged again and smiled. "'Tis no never-mind. All will avail itself in time, right?"

The patriarch matched his quirky little smile and stated just as jovially, "Or you'll be dead."

The man's grin vanished.

Dala turned then to the ladies and heaved a sigh. "This will suffice for now. Come, my loves, there are things to attend to. And you, little one, will have lessons at the usual time tomorrow."

He tapped Adianna on the tip of her nose, then hooked his arm with hers to turn her to the door. She could feel Daerlot keeping her powers firmly at bay, allowing her no access to his clairvoyant ability. Adianna couldn't help a little pout.

"Now let's leave the gentleman to his food and his healing."

To the healer, he muttered, "Good day, sir. We will speak again."

Then Daerlot ushered Memsy and the bewildered Adianna from the room.

Blast! Kendrick punched the coverlet after his visitors left. *What does she want with me now? Am I ever going to be rid of that she-devil?*

DARK GAMES AFOOT

A shrouded figure ghosted along the long, torch-lit hallway. Her burgundy cloak skimmed along the dark, uneven floor without so much as a whisper. The torch light played dazzling tricks, lighting the golden tresses about her shoulders with shades of red and orange. The walls of the corridor were a wide arch of rough-hewn igneous rock over her head, and they twinkled in the torchlight. But her eyes were focused straight ahead. She knew her way well.

As she came around a sharp corner, two hulking monsters guarding a door came to strict attention.

"Mistress Seymira!?" a voice rumbled deep and low despite the obvious surprise. Both of the rectors' faces were anxious. The face of the one who had spoken was pallid, beyond the norm, and he seemed to be gulping down on his fear.

She pinned each rector in turn with a scathing glare and took pleasure in seeing them slink back ever so slightly from her petulance.

She found it hard to believe she used to be terrified of these unearthly creatures, their mere existence a freak of nature and treacherously dark magic. The shape of them could have been strikingly attractive with their chiseled muscles rippling out of their large humanish forms, if it were not for the ashy, pasty color of their skin and constant look of decay. With black mold crawling from every crease and crevice of their bodies, and the very aura and stench of death itself, these creatures could strike fear in even the stoutest of hearts. Which was good because that was their purpose.

The rectors were a sinister creation made from the resurrected souls of beings who had died while involved in treachery of some form, from the simplest selfish act of lying or stealing to the more nefarious crimes of murder and betrayal. With each alliance of the Blades, those dastardly souls, regardless of gender or species, came back to life in various designs of the forms standing before her. Like the dalphene, they could only be killed by piercing their heart or removing their head. Each rector hungered for little more than to fulfill their master's bidding. Especially if that bidding included exacting vengeance or extirpating entire villages if need be.

Yes, she used to be horrified at the very thought of these ruthless killing machines, but now they cowered before her! She reigned over them, and they feared her wrath.

The sheer pleasure of this thought incited Seymira now, sending an addicting ripple of lust for power oozing through her veins. Her life was filled with such moments now, and she smiled to herself as one of the fearsome rectors scrambled to open the door for her. The other stepped around to remove her cloak. She wrinkled her nose at the putrid smell assailing her senses with the creature's hands so near.

She smoothed out the line of her very form-fitting, mint-colored dress and was grateful Lord Drokmar kept only the cleanest minions to work in the palace. The more time elapsing between alliances, the stronger, the more ruthless, and the more skilled a rector became. But without the rejuvenating effects of an alliance beacon, the demons continued to decay. With nearly fourteen years of corrosion, the legions of rectors were becoming rank and repugnant, many losing thick patches of skin, exposing caustic and blackened tissue beneath.

But each and every one of those thousands knew her, cowered before her, and clambered to perform her every whim. She could go nearly anywhere in Sheorae and be treated with the respect that comes from power. Or she could shape-shift and become any female she chose, to toy with anyone's life she wished. For a purpose or just for fun. And to top it off, the future ruler of all Sheorae had picked *her* to stand at his side.

Indeed, she had everything she ever wanted now. Well, except for one thing. Her thoughts skittered to the episode the other day in Kyren Forest. Seymira's teeth clenched tightly. Pushing it from her mind, she stalked through the open doors into the throne room of Drokmar's fortress.

But in her fourth step, Seymira halted.

The room was large with high ceilings and great double doors opening onto large balconies facing east over Sheorae. The vast stone floor was a black and gray checkerboard leading to the high pedestal where an ornate dual throne was perched. It was across this game board a dark and painful game was now being played.

Seymira knew instantly what was happening, and a black hole opened within her chest while a knot tightened and gripped in the pit of her stomach.

Two rectors were standing silently, with a slender, middle-aged man held tightly between them. The man's eyes were wide with fear, yet he trembled in silence. Sweat slid down his upturned face into his hair.

In front of the quivering man stood her lord and master, the great Drokmar. Drokmar's hand, palm out and fingers spread, was outstretched toward the man now struggling to not cower before him. With his eyes closed, her master's handsome face looked peaceful, giving no hint at the agony he was about to inflict.

Seymira was aware of other dalphene ambling about over to the right, callously betting on how the poor man would fare, but she appraised their master silently. She always found his tall, regal frame magnificent, with a leonine grace, discernable now, even as he slowly breathed in and out. His black hair was cropped short along his neck in the back but longer on top so it fell across his forehead when his head was tilted down like now. With his shortened hair, his ancestry was easily denoted by the points of his ears.

From her vantage, she could see most of his face. The strong lines of his cheeks. His dark mustache curving out over the corners of his mouth. His trimmed beard descended from the center third of his bottom lip to spread over his chin and halfway up the edge of his jaw. She loved the way it spiked up slightly at the tips toward his mustache. It made him look like he was smiling even when he was concentrating heavily, like he was now, or it added a sinister facet to his deadly glare. She also loved his wide yet full lips and the stately arch of his eyebrows.

Indeed, a most darkly handsome face.

Just then Drokmar opened his eyes, fastening his gaze on the human held before him. With his extended hand, he motioned the nervous man forward.

The hulking brutes guided the man closer, patches of their black corroded muscles peeking through the pallor of their skin. The restrained man's eyes widened, and Seymira could hear his exaggerated gulp from across the forty feet separating them.

Seymira's breathing accelerated in time with the applicant's, remembering vividly when it was her standing, shaking, before the master.

It wasn't often Drokmar took on more members of his dalphene. Her own induction two years prior was the most recent, until now.

The applicants were always informed beforehand of what to expect—the risk, the pain. They always had their choice in the matter. The process bound them to the master but to choose it of their own free will? This made that bond more potent, the claimant's abilities stronger, the flow of power—irresistible. She prided herself in the fact that Lord Drokmar himself identified her bond to him to be the most potent of all the dalphene. It had set her above the rest, despite the fact she was the only female out of the present twelve… or because of it. She prided herself on that as well.

But even though she had come to it willingly, her heart had still pounded, and her muscles had tightened involuntarily. She had stayed perfectly still, though, through it all. So still. She had focused on the master and what it would mean to stand with him—stand beside him. What it would mean for him… and for her.

But apparently this applicant didn't have the same focus, for as Lord Drokmar pulled out a small dagger, the man panicked. She didn't have to see his face to know. The tightening of the rectors' grip and the growing strain with which he resisted made it evident.

Drokmar motioned at his two minions again. Instantly, the sound of shredding material filled the room, and the man's shirt was stripped open to his waist, exposing the olive skin of his chest. A strangled cry escaped the victim. He crumpled to his knees but leaned his head back, willing his body away from what awaited him.

The dark figure before him took a slow, but deliberate, step forward. Drokmar's eyes were keen and burning with a light of their own. Seymira watched him slowly bring the blade across the palm of his own hand. A deep crimson line showed the weapon's path, oozing her master's life force.

It seemed everyone in the room was mesmerized by the ghastly display—rector, human, and dalphene alike, so none but Seymira seemed to notice the blade in Drokmar's hand getting closer to the man's chest.

Suddenly a gasp was heard, but before the applicant could even flinch, Drokmar's hand shot out with lightning speed. An agonizing cry filled the recesses of the great throne room.

Seymira didn't need to see the man's wound. She knew what it looked like. Her hand instinctively moved to settle over her heart. Her fingers absently traced the crescent-shaped scar that rose against the thin fabric of her dress. Still her eyes never left the scene before her.

The rectors forced the man to bend backward, giving their master access to the wound. Drokmar stood over the suffering man and squeezed his injured hand in a tight fist. Seymira watched as seven drops of the thick blood slipped effortlessly through the air and into the now visible wound.

Seymira clenched her teeth firmly, preparing herself for what would come next. She knew she did not want to watch, but she could not look away.

Drokmar raised the blade and ran his breath across it. Within seconds, the rancid smell of sizzling blood made her nostrils twitch and flare. The master's eyes took on an eerie hue of lifeless black. He opened his mouth, and his once perfect teeth were now sharp, jaggedly formed replicas. Puce saliva seeped over the serrated knives that lined his widening mouth. The handsome face contorted into something sinister and menacing. He brought the blade back to his mouth and ran his tongue across the shaft of it. Green slime clung to the knife in its wake.

The man was trembling again as all watched the weapon get closer and closer to him. With a flick of the wrist, Drokmar had the gooey edge of the steel flat against the gaping wound.

Seymira flinched back a step at the blood-curdling scream. Her hand clenched into a fist over her heart, remembering the feel of goblin acid searing her skin closed. The smell of scorched flesh invaded her senses. She knew it was a necessary part of the process, to keep the master's blood from escaping, but it was so brutal she didn't know if she could stand it. What was left of the human inside her struggled to drag her from the room, but she had to stay or the respect she claimed would drop a notch. She had to watch the remainder of the conversion procedure.

With the wound sealed, her master flipped the small dagger, catching it easily, and brought the pommel down gently against the man's chest. A pulse of electricity surged through Drokmar's hand, through the knife handle like a ground wire, and into the man's quivering body.

Seymira reacted to this last shriek with a sharp intake of breath. Her eyelids dipped for a brief moment upon seeing the man lose consciousness, and she let her jaw relax. It was over. The incubation period would now commence, and if he survived, they would have a new member to their mighty dalphene within the week.

She couldn't help a condescending smile though, watching the rectors drag his vapid body away. He had resisted, shied away. *She* had suffered in silence and was now highly favored by the master. This one would be little more than a mercenary or a messenger.

Too bad, she thought. *I liked Vo Shen.*

"Ahhh, my pet."

The deep voice of her master brought Seymira back to the darkly handsome personage before her. His face had resumed its dashing features, with all the engaging charm of a god. The delight she saw in his midnight eyes held her, imprisoned her. He made her feel so craved. The promise of a place by his side when he conquered Sheorae was almost as appealing as just being by his side.

"Come." He beckoned to her, having slid the dagger into its sheath and passed it off to an attendant. An alluring smile played across his face, and he invited her to join him.

She came willingly, placing her delicate fingers in his hand. It was smooth and flawless, with no hint of the injury that had marred it only moments before. His fingers closed around hers, and he drew her hand to his face.

"I'm so glad to have you home at last." His voice was seductive as his lips brushed the back of her hand.

He pulled her closer and directed her toward one of the great balconies. They stepped out on the large half-circle protruding from the massive tower high above the hold and became surrounded with stars. The black sky was dotted with them, and they invited the couple's gaze. But the twinkling diamonds could not keep Seymira from savoring the fantastic view.

The world stretched before her in a great panorama of undulating shadows. The reflected sky bounced off Tyronda Sea in the distance, several leagues away. She could just make out the spiky towers of Dorincia Castle silhouetted by the mirrored lights on the sea. The majestic peaks of the Tamerik Mountains were farther off to the right, shielding Tranquility Meadow beyond. And over to the left, across the barren Dead Lands where the rectors were reborn, lay Leorae.

It had once been her home, had once been her whole world, and the limit to her dreams. But now—beholding all the splendor before her—those aspirations seemed paltry in comparison.

Seymira breathed in the heady night air. A superior smirk transformed her features. No, it could *all* be hers!

Just then Drokmar turned to her with a slow sigh. "Well, little one." The light from the throne room lit his features. The sultry smile he gave her warmed her to the core. "You have been abusing my powers again."

The seductive tone belied the accusation and warning in his statement. Goosebumps rose under the finger he trailed down the side of her arm, and sudden panic gripped her.

"What do you mean, Master?" Seymira asked, her voice hesitant.

A soft, humorless chuckle rumbled low in his chest. He watched his fingers trace random lines on the back of her hand.

"You know exactly what I mean, Pet." His grip on her hand tightened as he went on. "I know when you use my power, and I know how." He brought his steely eyes to hers, holding her imprisoned. "And I can feel your emotions when you do it, so I also know why. So do not play coy with me."

Pain shot up her arm the instant his hand clamped around hers. She bit down on her lip as her bones creaked in the vise of his grip.

"It would not be in your best interest to use my power for your petty grievances. Not if you value your life here."

Drokmar's eyes narrowed, increasing the force of his stare. Still, he released her hand.

Seymira instantly swallowed the lump forming in her throat. Flexing her fingers, she couldn't pull her gaze away. The look in his eyes was so intense she could feel terror clenching like a fist in her stomach. She knew what happened to anyone who crossed this ruthless being.

Penitently, she stepped closer.

"I'm so sorry, my lord." She reached out to him and tried to steady the shaking in her voice as she continued, "I don't know what came over me. A stray human vendetta. I'm so very sorry. It will never happen again. I promise. I swear to you, my lord. I..."

"Shh, shh, shh." One of Drokmar's fingers came down upon Seymira's satin lips, halting her hysterics. His eyes were now scorching orbs raking over her face, intense yet inviting. She could not resist the lure she saw there.

"There is no need for that, my pet." He brushed his knuckles along her cheek in a calming manner. His touch made her insides molten rock.

He brought his other hand to cradle her face, holding her ever so gently despite the power and the strength she knew lurked just beneath the surface.

"I have plans for you, little one. Soon the world will be mine for the taking. I will make the future glorious. You like the sound of that, don't you, my sweet?"

He had slowly been pulling her face closer and closer to his as he spoke, so now he was just a few heartbeats away. She strived to concentrate. To formulate a coherent thought.

Ever so slowly, she watched one of his eyebrows ascend higher, accentuating the question. She searched frantically for her voice. It cracked on the first attempt, so she nodded her head.

"Yes!" she managed breathlessly.

An enchanting smile spread across his face. "Good," he murmured, deliberately enunciating each sound.

She could feel his warm breath against her mouth.

His eyes lowered to her lips, open and waiting. Drokmar slid the hand cradling her chin slowly around to the back of her neck, leaving a path of fire in its wake.

The dalphene could hear her heart fluttering, keeping time with that of a hummingbird's wings. But it changed in an instant.

The hand behind her head suddenly clamped a fistful of her hair in its iron grip.

"Because if your plans differ from mine…" His voice was hard with malice as he forced her head back.

She saw a white flash dart across his eyes and instantly the crescent scar over her heart pulsed a wave of stinging current through her body. A soft cry of pain escaped her quivering lips.

Still, his expression remained calm. He traced a finger along her exposed throat. So tender compared to the ruthless grip still holding her head wrenched back.

He brought his gaze back up to hers. Fearful and panicked, she stared into his eyes—so full of rancor, and dread consumed her. His next statement cut like ice in the dead of winter.

"I would have to take your head—myself!"

TYMALIA

Adianna tried to tag along with Daerlot and Memsy after leaving the healer's room. She wanted to know what Memsy was able to pull from his thoughts. What he was hiding? And what Dala was keeping secret? But Memsy had confined her to house duties while they went and collaborated without her.

So there she was, sweeping and cleaning while the most interesting thing to happen in Tymalia in her lifetime was being discussed without her.

Adianna swished the broom with a huff. A plume of dust billowed into the air like a volcano spewing forth ash. The dust particles attacked her nostrils, irritating their delicate tissues. She rubbed at it, but it was no use. She sneezed. Then sneezed again. And again.

Adianna rubbed under her nose with the edge of her finger, blinking rapidly to hold in what moisture she could, but it did nothing to quell her frustration. She grabbed the broom in a strangling grip. She was about to resume the daunting task when she heard a call from the healer's room.

"Excuse me? Hello?"

Adianna dropped the broom and scrambled to the door, nearly knocking over a chair as she went. She brushed her hands over her hair and dress, then went in.

Upon opening the door, she stopped short and gaped. Abruptly, she averted her gaze, her cheeks flaming. The man was sitting on the edge of the bed wearing nothing but the coverlet draped across his lap. His shirt hung around his neck like a yoke.

"Oh, it's you." The awkwardness of the situation was evident in his voice. Clearing his throat, he plunged on.

"Would you be so kind as to help me with my clothes?" he asked, sounding exasperated, but annoyance entered his tone as he added, "I can't seem to do it without bumping this blasted arm!"

"I, um, yes, sir." She stepped toward him, trying to keep her eyes on his bare feet. But she couldn't help looking at him when she was close enough to assist. She held his sleeves out for him to easily slide his arms through. She tried to focus on the faint scars slicing over his collarbone, but unbidden, her gaze swept over his broad chest. The muscles, well-developed, moved effortlessly to his bidding, then strained teasingly at the material when she pulled the shirt over them.

"Now if you would be so kind as to hold the trousers open for me," he stated, his voice a bit huskier than before. "I'll hold the blanket in place and step into them."

Adianna's face was on fire, but she knelt in front of him and helped guide his feet through the pantlegs. She kept her head down at the level of her hands, about a foot above ground, eyes glued on the floor as he stood. She carefully pulled the breeches up, trying to avoid any embarrassing or burning contact. But when the material caught at his upper thighs, her thumbs brushed along his skin. She flinched away. The heat searing her thumbs was belittled by the flame on her face at the thought of the hard sinew covered by smooth skin.

"I think I can manage the fastenings," he stated with a sniff of amusement. "We wouldn't want to meddle with your delicate faculties more than absolutely necessary."

Adianna looked at him, horrified. There was a lopsided yet devilish grin on his face. She backed away, and he propped the blanket against himself with his splint. His gaze pinned her as he jerked his trousers up the rest of the way.

When he turned from her, awkwardly balancing most of his weight on one foot, her hands flew to her cheeks, and she spun around. Mortified, she tried desperately to think of something else. Anything else. She grasped at the first coherent thought to enter her mind. Clearing her throat, she asked, "What are you doing up?"

"I'm going out!"

She could tell by the distant sound of his voice he hadn't turned back yet, so neither did she.

"I'm not one to stay abed longer than absolutely needed, especially on a day like this. There!"

Adianna looked over cautiously. With a flare of conquest, he turned a striking smile to her. He had his arms spread out wide in victory of his little accomplishment. At that moment, despite his very manly features, he looked like a triumphant toddler, and she couldn't help but smile at him.

He sat back on the edge of the bed, and she watched him pull on one of his boots. As he slipped into the other boot, he stated, "It looks like a beautiful day out. Want to join me?"

The surprise must have been evident on her face for Adianna was aware of her wide eyes and her arched eyebrows.

"I..." She looked out the window. The sun-kissed leaves beyond barely rustled. The sky was clear and blue. It looked lovely.

"Alright," she decided, resolutely. She looked back at him and wanted to melt at the smile lighting his face. Her legs felt weak. Still, she forced her mind to work.

"Let me just grab—"

She didn't finish but ducked out of the room. She dashed to the front door of the cottage she and Memsy shared. There, on a hook to the side of the door, she snatched up a glimmering pair of delicate mail gloves and the matching cloak beneath. She paused, glancing again at the weather outside through the front room window, then peered at the shamere cloak.

She could hear his uneven approach through the adjoining room.

The gloves should be enough. He seems to be getting around alright and shouldn't need much help. She put the cloak back on the hook and pulled the gloves on, sliding them up past her elbows.

The healer had just entered the room as she settled her sleeves over the cool, metal gloves. She grabbed the door latch and swung it wide.

"Afraid of getting our hands dirty, are we?"

He smirked as he limped forward.

The corners of Adianna's mouth indented deep into her cheeks, but she said nothing, waiting patiently at the door. He hobbled past her with a quirky smile on his face. She fought back a half-smile of her own and followed him into the bright sunshine.

Adianna closed the front door quietly behind her then leaned against it to savor the view. The dazzling sun was spreading its adoration onto everything in its reach. She could not remember ever seeing the world look clearer and more beautiful.

Beyond the door of the cottage lay a quaint little flower garden, one of the few in Tymalia, and Adianna was proud of it. The foliage around the cottage was a patchwork of rich velvet in varying shades of green. Snapdragons and chrysanthemums nestled in here and there. An arched arbor stretched over the break in a short hedge surrounding the yard. A swath of the village Commons was just visible at the far end of the path beyond the hedge. The Commons was beginning to be populated with the people she knew and loved, cherished and adored.

A sad pain pricked at her heart. There was so much she loved about this elfin sanctuary. The thought of someday leaving—someday soon—left her aching. Would she be strong enough to leave when the time came?

She eyed the stranger standing before her. The man had paused a short distance from the door, his eyes adjusting to the brilliant light. Breathing deeply, he had his face upturned, his expression joyous. His glittering eyes matched the azure sky above. His rich, chocolate hair took on burnished highlights in the sun.

The white shirt she had helped him into was a tighter style than the squire shirt he'd worn when she had brought him here, and it stretched against the muscles of his upper chest and shoulders. It would have hung loosely from there, had it not been for the belt slung around his lean hips. Surprisingly, the belt held his sheathed sword. She could see the tip of it peeking from behind his brown breeches.

With one brow high, Adianna eyed the man. It was then he chose to look her way.

"What?" he asked, a quizzical half-smile on his face.

Adianna pushed away from the door taking casual steps toward him and indicated the sword. "You expecting trouble?" she queried dubiously.

"What?" He glanced in the direction she specified. "Oh."

She heard him chuckle, and he slapped his hand down on the silver and bronze hilt.

"No, I just…" He shrugged, looking back at her. He appeared to be searching for an adequate excuse. Finally, he gave her an embarrassed half smile and shrugged again. "Old habits, I guess."

He rolled his eyes before going on. "Not that it would do either one of us much good." He extended his arm, the white wrapping explanation enough.

Adianna was about to give him an uplifting remark, but he went on, asking, "By the way, who did the handy work?"

Caught with her mouth open, she looked at the arm stretched toward her. "I believe Daerlot did that one."

She remembered Dala had given the healer his name, so she didn't have to be concerned with using it around him. But the man's expression changed at this information. He looked a little nervous, anxious even. It made her wonder just how much he knew about the patriarch's abilities and how much was speculation due to rumors.

Rapidly, the man turned away from her to look around. She followed his gaze to the right, across the fifty-some yards separating them from the next cottage. Then she watched him stare straight ahead for a bit. Then his perplexed gaze shifted to the left toward the dwelling at a similar distance in that direction.

With his brow puckered, he gave her a quick glance. Then he hobbled past the edge of the house, stepping beyond the flower garden. The man looked as if he were trying to get his bearings and seemed very uncertain of where he wanted to go.

Finally, he turned a flabbergasted face to her and said, "I have no idea where I am, nor can I make hide nor hair of which direction to go." He slapped his good hand softly against his thigh and asked, "Would you be so kind as to show me about your village, m'lady?"

With a smile, Adianna stepped forward. "Where is it you would like to go or see?"

"I am at your disposal, madam," he said with an exaggerated flourish of the hand, like sweeping off a hat into a gallant bow. "I will go where you lead."

She suppressed a chuckle. He wobbled a little in his showy display, keeping most of his weight on his left leg. Suddenly, she felt a little giddy. She felt sure it was because she was about to escort this dashing young man around the inner recesses of Tymalia, something she had never before been able to share with another human being. That had to be what the butterflies within her meant.

"Then shall we start with the grounds or the Commons?" she asked.

"I'm not sure I follow," he replied, looking slightly perplexed.

"Here, let me show you."

She stepped his way, past the edge of the cottage. To the rear of the dwelling stood a thin grove of trees which stretched in meandering bulges toward the neighboring dwelling.

"The grounds of Tymalia are laid out in a large oval shape. There are two rows, if you will, of dwellings with acreage behind them," she said, directing his gaze.

She swiveled around to point in the opposite direction at the gently winding path stretched out in front of the cottage. "All the dwellings face the Commons area at the center of the village. This is the source of Tymalia's concealment. See how there are clusters of trees everywhere?"

She barely waited for his nod. "They represent the forest and the plant world in the village. This constant plant life, as opposed to the inconstant agriculture, which is harvested, then replanted, provides homes for the animal life."

At that moment, as if on cue, a cottontail rabbit hopped out of the trees to cross the path. Adianna chuckled, knowing the animals in the village were excellent listeners. Flicking her eyes to the stranger, she could see his resulting smile at the irony of the creature's appearance. When he met her gaze, she swallowed hard and looked away.

Clearing her throat, she scooped up a handful of rich black earth. The moist dirt molded effortlessly in her fist. She extended her hand to the healer's view, brushing the contoured clump with her thumb, causing it to crumble slightly.

"The soil is some of the best in Sheorae," she stated with the pride she knew Gushmere shared. Then, brushing the dirt slowly from her hands, she pointed to the north-east again.

"In the Commons stands a bubbling fountain as well as a blazing hearth pedestal, resulting in each of the elfin domains being represented: earth, flora, creature, fire, and water. This is what keeps Tymalia safe and hidden from the outside world. All are alive and moving which can give the village the ability to move, making it a constant safe haven—even from Drokmar, if he were so inclined to find us."

Adianna saw the surprise in the man's stare. She could well imagine his shock at her bold statement. Nothing, these days, seemed safe from Drokmar's ever-tightening grasp. But it was true.

"Not that the Serpent has any need to come after the elves, of course," she added, trying not to sound nervous. "They are neutral in the conflict. The only possible threat the elves hold is knowledge."

And me, she thought, swallowing hard. Quickly, she turned to the man beside her.

"Anyway!" Her voice cracked, but she stepped toward the wide path. "As I said, all dwellings face the Commons. Each family is responsible for the land directly behind their home. About three acres apiece."

Adianna swung her arms away from her hips in both directions, pointing to the small fields on either side of the path. She could hear the awkward progress coming from behind her, so she knew he followed. She swept her gaze across the corn stretching off to the left and the wheat over to the right.

"Three acres doesn't sound like enough to feed a family," the man stated from behind her. "Is there more to your family than you and the sorci?"

"Just Mems—just my mother and me. My uncle lives with his family by the Sanctuary."

"Your mother?" The healer had come abreast of her but halted sharply. The startled look on his face left her slightly unnerved. Had she said too much?

"But you aren't an elf." It wasn't a question.

Adianna could feel her ears flaming where they should have been pointed if she *had* been an elf.

"No, I'm not," she confirmed, but offered no more. Adianna raised her chin and walked on, eyeing him askance.

He hobbled along with her. "But how…?" he asked, somewhat bewildered.

She halted to face him. He stopped, too.

She started to formulate a reply. One that would not give too much away. Yet unexpectedly, in the presence of this human, long buried memories came clawing to the surface. All the circumstances that had led to her residing with Memsy, the impact discovering the Blades had on her life, and the fact her real parents had never once tried to come see her, filled her with grief. She could not answer. Such a simple question, yet she could not answer.

She suddenly felt heavy. She could not look him in the face. She could feel his eyes upon her, expectant, but she could not look at him.

"I…" What could she tell him? She couldn't tell him anything. Even if it were safe, she couldn't find words. The pain was too alive suddenly, but why—she didn't know. She couldn't deal with this now. She wanted to physically leave it behind.

She turned, but before she could take more than a step, the man took her hand in his. Slowly, she turned to the warmth seeping in through the shamere mail. His large hands enfolded hers. She thought she should probably pull away, but there was something in the gentleness that soothed the encroaching agony.

"I'm sorry." His voice was a soft velvet blanket smoothing over her sorrow.

Her eyes sought his. They, too, were warm and inviting.

"I should never have asked such a personal question. Forgive me?"

The empathy in his words touched her deeper than anyone's ever had, aside from her elfin family. It felt so sincere. She gazed back at their entwined hands.

The stranger brought his hand to his chest, pulling her hand along with it. With a small smile, he said, "I would get down on one knee to beg forgiveness properly, but I fear I would topple us both."

Adianna laughed, and the man's smile broadened.

"Shall we?" The healer nodded toward the path.

She grinned, and they continued, silently taking in the sunlight and greenery. Adianna wondered if she should say something, but there was no discomfort in the silence. Like a quiet moment between friends.

She was curious as to what he was thinking though. They were just coming between the cottages of the inner row of the village, and the Commons opened before them. The stranger's step slowed to a halt. His features took on a mixture of amazement and appreciation.

Adianna looked out over the Commons and tried to see it with new eyes. She knew it to be nearly 300 yards from the western tip to the other, just beyond the Sanctuary, though with that great building looming at the far end, the space seemed dwarfed somewhat. This end was littered with covered stalls spaced far enough from each other as to diminish the sense of encumbering the open feel. Each stand had various produce and other goods.

Automatically, she looked to the second one from this end of the third row. The eggs, garlic, and herbs she had laid out earlier were barely picked over, but she knew that would change the closer it got to the supper hour.

Beyond the exchange market stood three giant verda trees in a row cutting across the Commons. The limbs of these mighty trees had been cut very high up so as not to impede the open, airy feel. Still the upper branches stretched out and overlapped each other, creating a patchwork canopy over the stalls.

From the row of verda trees, a beautiful stretch of lush, green lawn spanned a field of several hundred feet before three more centennials reached for the sky. She had always loved the elfin magic that allowed the brilliant sun to shine on the field despite the wide-spreading branches. Several of the village children were now engaged in their playful games as ferrets darted in and out of their frolicking. Adianna remembered many happy times on that field, from games to festivals to just larking about between studies.

Beyond the second row of giant trees, the walls of the Sanctuary were visible, though the verdas currently obscured the size of said building from view.

Adianna had looked upon this every day for most of her life, so it was difficult to determine what her reaction would be to behold it for the very first time. Still, one thing she had always loved about the Commons, and the village, too, was how clean and fresh everything appeared. There were no brambles or dead grasses covering the ground as in other parts of the forest. Everything was trimmed and lush… as if the village was a hidden garden, tucked away from the world.

Other than that, she couldn't see anything much standing out. She had been to the village of Fal Dura across Kyren Forest, nestled on the banks of the Fal Reche River, several times in her life. It being a human village, it seemed a likely basis of comparison. Even with this comparison though, she couldn't see anything so different in Tymalia's nature to warrant such a look of surprise from the healer as she now beheld. For the first time in her life, Adianna questioned whether Tymalia had influenced Fal Dura. Or had the humans actually influenced the elves?

The healer trudged forward a step or two, pulling her mind from this quandary. He now wore a quizzical look, and Adianna followed his gaze to the stalls scattered before them. Before she could guess what puzzled him, he turned to her.

"Where are the people to man the stalls?"

Adianna's mouth opened to issue a response as she looked back to the stands in question. There were a few she-elves in amid the fair, who occasionally picked up a clove of garlic or a few turnips or the like. She did not see any men, so she offered, "The men are usually in their fields or out in the forest doing the various tasks entrusted to their lineage. Don't the women usually do the cooking?"

The man's head dipped to the side, and his eyebrow quirked. "Yes, of course, the women usually do the cooking. I was referring to the merchants."

Adianna felt he was laughing at her, yet for what she did not know.

"This is the market, is it not?" At her nod, he continued, "Then where is everyone? The buyers, the sellers… the money changers."

"Oh, money." She chuckled at the notion. "We don't use money."

"Then you barter?"

Her eyebrows knit together. "Sometimes with Fal Dura, but we don't need to here."

The man crossed his arms awkwardly in front of his chest, careful not to bump the splint. The look on his face was a mixture of interest and puzzlement. "Then what is your method of exchange?"

Adianna was vaguely aware of the tightening furrow of her brow, though she couldn't understand the perplexity on the healer's face. "Everyone contributes to the welfare of the village."

"I can see that, but where are the people selling their contributions?" He spoke as if to a child, his hand extended toward the Commons.

She arched a brow. The challenge pricked her nature, but she drew in a calming breath before proceeding slow enough for him to comprehend. "I told you—we do not sell. We do not barter."

She folded her arms across her chest and leaned forward at the waist, hoping the movement would help her words enter his thick head. "There is no need for that here. Everyone contributes. Everyone has their needs met. Everyone prospers."

She gestured back toward home, then out to the Commons. "We all grow or produce the needs of the village. We keep what we need for our families and bring the remainder to the Commons for the others." Her arm swept out, encompassing the village, and she repeated, "Everyone contributes. Everyone prospers."

The healer tipped his head back slightly and eyed her with an inscrutable look. "You're serious."

It was again a statement, not a question, though Adianna could not fathom why either one would be necessary. "Why is it so hard to believe?"

"Because, my dear, people simply do not deal so fairly with each other, nor with such consideration."

The sad understanding pressed in on her, and she sighed. "No... people don't." Her eyes met his. Slowly she added, "But elves do."

They strolled on in silence, each deep in their own thoughts. They crossed the market, then followed the curve of the Commons. Adianna let the healer stay on the inside so he could see everything better and had less distance to walk, she told herself. But as they strolled, she found herself quite content to run her gaze over him more than the scenery. She, too, found she was very much liking what she was seeing. Never in her life had she ever met someone as intriguing to consider or appealing to behold. Yes, elves were lovely creatures, both male and female, but this man...

She quickly looked away when he caught her looking at him. Her cheeks flamed, and she felt grateful he wasn't an elf who could hear thoughts. He didn't say anything, but his quirky half-smile reappeared. Her cheeks burned all the more. Still, she was growing fond of that smile, the way it defined his high cheekbones and made his eyes dance mischievously. The look suited him.

Just coming around the first row of verda trees, Adianna heard a low hiss, almost a snarl. The Healer's hand went to his sword. Adianna knew exactly when he realized his wrong move by the sharp intake of breath and the muffled groan. Fortunately, she knew the culprit, and so reached out her hand to stay his tension.

With her gloved hand on the man's arm, she turned to the source of the problem. A face was peeking out from around the great tree. The face was lizardish in shape and design yet had an eagle beak to finish out the scaly snout. The advantage of his long sapphire neck left his body hidden behind the tree. Its large ears ended in fur that matched his scales, yet they laid back against his head in his discontent.

"Now, Puffin," she cooed, stepping forward around the tree. "Is that any way to treat our guest?"

With a snort and a puff of smoke, the creature turned and flew away.

They came beyond the verda trees in time to see a pot-bellied creature with wings decidedly smaller than was needed for extended flight—especially for such a rotund body, some three feet tall and seven feet long.

"What is it... exactly?" the Healer asked, looking somewhat perplexed.

"He's a pygmy dragon."

"That's a pygmy?" Wonder was evident in his voice.

Adianna stared after the retreating ridged back; the gold arrowhead tail tip flicked dismissively. She thought back, trying to recollect seeing pygmies for the first time but was at a loss. Puffin and his brood had been a part of her life as far back as she could remember. So, she had to imagine what it must be like for the Healer to see one for the first time.

"They are a cross between a drac and a griffin, right?" the man inquired, still gawking after the dragon.

"Yes," she answered. "They have the dragonish shape from the drac, though the gryphon lends it the shape of its head and feet. And the belly, of course. I am afraid no self-respecting drac would be seen with a potbelly." Adianna chuckled.

The healer smiled but still did not take his eyes off the pygmy dragon, so Adianna continued. "Drokmar hunted the pygmies to near extinction. My mother and I adore them, so we keep the last three safely here." She pointed to where the dragon in question had landed. "Puffin here is my favorite."

The healer continued to watch the dragon with a very thoughtful expression on his face. After a few moments, he started walking again alongside Adianna. She peeked occasionally over at the healer, but his expression stayed thoughtful, until he happened to glance over and catch her watching him. The corner of his mouth worked up. "You know, he called me a rogue."

Adianna gave him a questioning look.

The healer tapped his temple. "One of the quirks of being a healer." He motioned to where the pygmy had retreated. "I can hear dragon talk. Apparently even of types I have never seen before."

Adianna nodded. They walked in silence for a short way. Then she glanced sideways at him. "And are you?"

The healer's brow furrowed as he came to a stop. "Am I what?"

Adianna looked askance at him, with a twinkle in her eye, trying to hide a smile, "A rogue?"

He chuckled, glancing at the ground at nothing in particular. Then he looked up innocently. "No, ma'am."

She arched an eyebrow at him.

His smile widened. "At least not today."

He gestured in the direction they had been heading. She resumed their walk without even trying to hide her grin.

The meadow was lovely and calm as they walked on in silence. Suddenly, back from the far corner, came a childish squeal followed by a high-pitched roar. They turned just in time to see a boy and Puffin tumbling and rolling across the ground.

Adianna put her hands on her hips. "Oh, that little rascal. He is always pouncing on Puffin when he's not looking."

"Don't get too frustrated by it. From the sounds of it, Puffin adores it *and* the children."

She considered this, her eyebrows high on her forehead. Several more elvin children came over to join in the fun. Some were hollering, encouraging the boy, while others were on Puffin's side. Adianna couldn't help but nod her consent and smile.

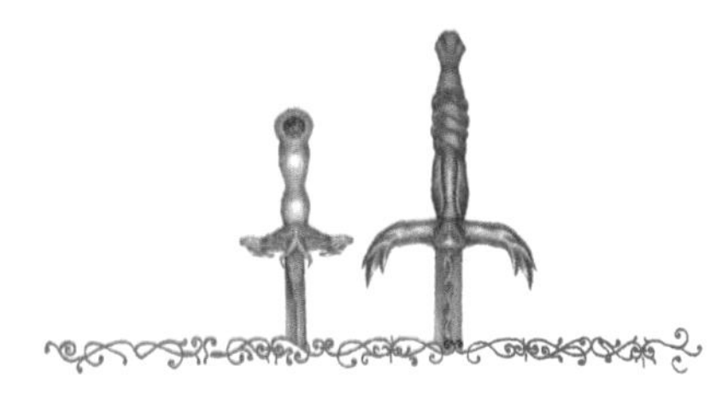

SANCTUARY

Once they passed the second row of verda trees, the healer stopped midstride. Adianna smiled and looked up at the grandeur of the Sanctuary. It was rectangle-shaped with the short ends at the front and back and the sides long. Across the front were three square-shaped turrets, one at each corner and one in the middle, rising skyward and spired off to a point high above the roof of the building. Matching spires crossed the back of the Sanctuary, though shorter than the front ones. These turrets, six in all, rose higher than even the giant verda trees standing sentinel before them. Tall slender windows were spaced evenly along each side. The whole building was made from granite sprinkled with crystal deposits, making it shimmer all over.

Pride swelled Adianna's heart at the awe on the healer's face. She loved this building and had spent many, many hours of her life learning and training within its walls.

"Each of the spires represent the elements of nature within our world. The three in the back represent the earth, vegetation, and animal life. These front corners represent fire and water. There before the fire spire is a hearth pedestal granting fire to the whole village. And before this one is the communal well where we all gather water. Except for those who are keepers of water, who materialize their own, as with the spark for the fire keepers. That center spire represents the keepers themselves and contains the door. The hall, itself, is used for important gatherings. It is where the Great Elvin Council meets, and it also houses the archives where all the chronicles of Sheorae are kept. Most of the elves of Sheorae spend at least a little time every day studying in the archives."

As if right on cue, an Elvish woman came out the front door.

"Good evening," Adianna called, pausing before using her aunt's name. "Dear auntie. How are you today?"

"Very well, my beloved niece." Daerlot's wife, Senith, smiled warmly at Adianna and appraised the gentleman at her side.

"I see our visitor is mending quickly," she said, continuing to the hearth pedestal.

The healer bowed, raising two fingers to his forehead as if touching the brim of an imaginary hat. "Yes, I thank you, m'lady. Your lovely niece...?" He indicated Adianna with a questioning look between the both of them. At Senith's nod, he continued, "Has been kind enough to show me around your magnificent village."

Senith smiled but said nothing more. She simply proceeded to gather spark.

"Is Dala working late?" Adianna knew Senith was a water keeper and did not require use of the well, but with Daerlot being a fire keeper, she was curious.

Senith's face closed off all expression. "Yes, he has some studying to do." She pulled out a second flint stick from her pocket. "Dear old... Gushy is with him, so I am taking spark to his wife."

Adianna smiled at her aunt's use of the nickname she, herself, had given Gushmere—which he detested.

Senith gathered the spark and nodded to Adianna. "Good day to you, my darling. And to you, visitor."

They said farewell and watched Senith round the far side of the Sanctuary. Adianna smiled at the healer, and they resumed walking, each in their own thoughts.

Toward the back of the Sanctuary, soil and minerals mounded against this corner spire. Specks of crystals appeared to topple right from the granite building across the ground. The path became uneven with ripples, as if this earth also longed to frolic over the mound.

Coming around the corner, the healer was so intent on the flora and fauna on display that he failed to watch his footing. He gave a sharp intake of breath, then hopped in a tiny circle on his good leg.

Adianna took hold of his arm to steady him. "Are you okay?"

"Yes!" he growled out through clenched teeth. He gingerly stepped forward but could not hide the limp.

Concerned, Adianna kept a hand on his upper arm. "Let's cut through here."

She crossed in front of him and gestured toward the grove of trees clustered around the far corner of the Sanctuary. They stepped off the path onto the cushy grass.

"Watch your step," she urged.

The earth converged with grass at the center of the building. Trees and brush sprang up in random clumps, and small critters scurried in all directions.

They cut straight through the grove, skimming the corner of the building, and coming along the side. He seemed to be moving better, but just as they emerged from the trees, the healer again stepped wrong on his injured leg. He let out a painful groan and toppled toward Adianna. She reached out to help him, but he rammed into her, knocking her off balance. Her back hit the granite wall with a thud.

The healer's hands flew out to catch himself. They smacked against the wall on either side of Adianna's head. An excruciating growl escaped through his clenched teeth. He slammed down onto his elbows to relieve the jab to his broken arm, forcing his forehead right against hers.

Adianna instantly pressed her hands against his chest to prop him away from her enough to stop the singeing across her brow.

Another guttural growl broke free from the man. His eyes were clamped shut, and his mouth contorted. His breathing was ragged and uneven. She opened her mouth to speak, but he groaned again and reflectively pounded his good fist against the wall beside her head.

She waited until his breathing became less strained, the creases around his eyes less profound.

"Are you okay?" she whispered.

Slowly he leaned his head up, taking in a long, deep breath before opening his eyes.

They automatically met hers, their faces just inches away from each other. The concern she felt was drowned out by something new. Something she had never experienced before. It was warm. She felt like she was melting from the inside out. *Is it his breathing*? she wondered as she felt its warmth brush against her cheek. *Or could it be his eyes smoldering into mine?* She was also acutely aware of the rest of his hard, muscular body so very close. This new awareness spread through her body as his eyes dipped to her lips. Breathlessly, she couldn't help but look at his as well. Soft and full and invitingly open.

He didn't move. Neither did she. She didn't dare. She didn't dare to breathe, though her lips parted to allow air in that wouldn't come.

Still, she could not pull her eyes from his lips, for they were now moving ever so slowly toward hers.

She should say something. Do something. Anything. But she couldn't even breathe; how could she possibly move? His lips were just a breath away.

"My niece?"

The healer's lips stopped. They closed, then pressed together. A ragged breath flowed through his nostrils, pelting her cheek, then he pulled away.

"My niece! Is everything well?"

Adianna blinked rapidly at the face above hers, trying to get her brain to function. Finally, she pulled her eyes away from his. Senith was standing in a doorway with Gushmere's wife. Despite the embarrassment at being caught in such an intimate-feeling situation, Adianna stifled a laugh at the expressions of near horror and great interest respectively on the two women's faces. Still, she had to quell the disappointment at being interrupted and thus never knowing what would have happened.

Adianna hollered over in a breathless croak, "Yes, Auntie. Thank you."

With the spell now broken, she looked back at the healer, remembering her previous concern. "Are you okay?"

It was hard to read his eyes. She saw frustration, surprise, and… something else she couldn't quite name. Longing, maybe? She looked away, surprised at her wishful thinking.

"I'll be fine," he answered at length, his voice low and husky. He cleared his throat. "Though I suppose now we are even."

Adianna was perplexed. The mirth on his face was unmistakable but unreadable.

"Even?" she queried; her brow puckered.

"Of course," he said, pushing away from the wall, his eyes never leaving hers. He teetered before getting his balance. Then that mischievous smirk returned. "Now we have both fallen on each other!'

The laughter bubbled inside her, and as she let it go, a great grin spread over his face. It nearly took her breath away.

"Yes," she countered with a coy little smile. "But if you will recall, it was *your* fault—both times."

The gentleman slapped his palm to his midsection and grimaced in feigned assault, which only made her giggle all the more.

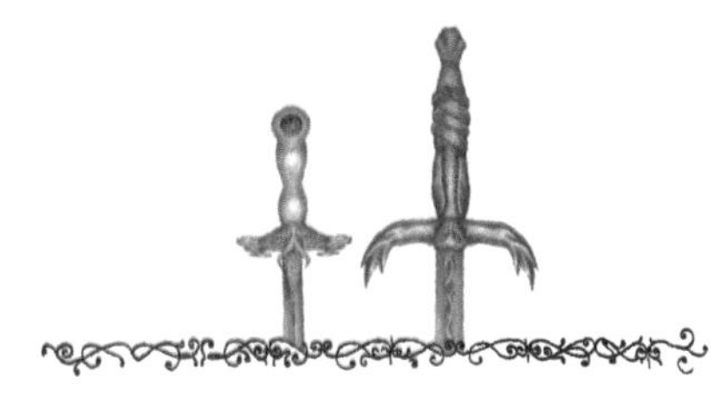

SOMETHING DIFFERENT

The sun was getting low in the eastern sky when they reached the cottage. Kendrick was feeling better as far as prickles and aches went but was also feeling run down. Still, he had been thoroughly enjoying his time with Adlanna. He had overheard the pygmy dragon refer to her name, and even though he couldn't really use it, it was nice to know. He kept trying to make her laugh all the rest of the way back. He loved hearing her laugh.

He had them both laughing when they came through the cottage door. His mirth stifled though when he saw the pair of sorcis watching them from the main room just beyond.

Memsy seemed pleasantly surprised to see them together. The patriarch not so much. He seemed rather tense and irritated. Kendrick could literally feel the older man's growing angst. Before he could make any sense of it, Memsy bubbled forth.

"So, there you two are. We were wondering where you had run off to."

"Yes, I was showing our Master Healer around the village as he was feeling up for a bit of an excursion," Adianna explained.

"Fabulous," Memsy responded, rubbing her hands together with delight.

"And did you enjoy your little trip?" Daerlot inquired with a cold tone.

But his wording proved their undoing. Adianna and Kendrick cast one look at each other and burst into fits of laughter. This unfortunately made the older gentleman's face even stormier.

Kendrick struggled to suppress his mirth, but the older man's face made it near impossible. He coughed and cleared his throat trying to gain composure. Still, it was Adianna who was able to speak first.

"Actually, our healer took a tumble and nearly took us both out."

The humor was not lost on Memsy, and she joined in the gaiety. Seeing her eyes dance set Kendrick to laughing again. Still, one glance at the patriarch, and he stifled his laugh, pressing his lips together.

"Well, healer," Daerlot cut in, pointedly leaving off the 'Master' title the female used. "You must be getting tired."

Kendrick was well aware it sounded more like a command than an observation.

"Actually, I am feeling a tad fatigued," he agreed slowly. Then he turned his back on the patriarch's condescending gaze to face Adianna. He took one of her hands into his.

"Thank you for the walk, my dear," he said, staring deep in her emerald eyes. He stood, tracing a nondescript pattern on the back of her glove momentarily. Then he brushed his lips across it. The strange metal felt cool against his lips, but he never released her gaze. "It was very… enlightening."

He couldn't help letting one corner of his mouth lift into a crooked smile, which deepened as color touched her cheeks. He hoped her mind was on the same event that filled his thoughts right now.

"Niece," the patriarch's cool voice cut in, again. "Don't you have some chores to do? I'm sure the healer would like to go lie down."

Kendrick didn't need to look to know the expression on the other man's face was not pleasant. And when he turned, he found the elfin lord fuming.

The girl's mother was a different matter. She stood, sorci emblem rippling, looking rather intrigued at some thought. She did glance at her brother, but rolling her eyes, she returned to the younger couple with a smile.

"Yes, my love. We don't want the chickens to get fussy." She handed Adianna a basket. "Gather the eggs for tomorrow's market, then bring the water. I'll get supper ready."

Kendrick stepped aside, for she sent the younger woman shooing past him toward the door. "We'll fetch you some water."

Eyebrows high, Memsy looked as if she were eyeing him over a pair of spectacles. "I'm sure you will want to wash after spending so long in bed. And I'm sure you will want to do it before you join us to eat."

It might have been a better attempt at a scold if she hadn't winked at him.

"Thank you, madam." He smiled and gave a small bow. "You are very kind and gracious."

The sorci opened the door to shuffle the younger woman through. Adianna seemed reluctant to leave but finally flashed him a quick smile before ducking out.

With Adianna gone, the air in the little cottage became inimical. Kendrick didn't look over at the other male in the room. There was no need. Instead, he watched Memsy step to the cold hearth. She seemed oblivious to the tension exuding off her brother. Instead, she went about preparing: gathering pots for water, pans for cooking. With those in place, she bent to the fire start under the cooking grate. She turned her hand, palm up, to tickle the air. Instantly, a small flame appeared suspended in the air just above her palm. At her tiny blow, the flame jumped across, lighting the wood for the stove.

Kendrick's eyes lit up. He always knew the elves to be the keepers of the elements within nature, and he knew they could call forth those elements at will. But he had never actually seen a fire keeper call forth fire.

But on the irritated patriarch, Kendrick's delight fell flat. This elf merely pinned him with a calculating gaze.

Kendrick sighed and touched his finger to his brow in salute. "Thank you for your hospitality, m'lord. I am much obliged."

The elf's gaze was hard and wary. "You're most welcome, sir," he cited, going through the formal pleasantries with polished finesse. "We hope your stay is pleasant and your healing—quick."

"You are most kind, m'lord." With hooded lids, Kendrick gave a small, deliberate bow, acknowledging the patriarch's point was received.

The elf folded his arms in front of him, setting his jaw in a hard line. Kendrick felt the seed of rebellion stir in his belly but turned to the room he had been in before.

Once behind the closed door, Kendrick raked his fingers through his hair. *What was that elf's problem?* Kendrick thought back over his stay thus far in Tymalia, searching for anything he might have done or said to warrant the patriarch's reaction. But he came up blank. *It could just be a daddy-daughter thing,* Kendrick thought to himself, but from the look on the elf's face, it was something much more.

Kendrick pulled the single chair over below the lone round window. He tried to distract himself from the feisty father-figure in the other room, so he thought of Adianna. Rolling through the day in his mind, he had to admit to himself that unless someone were shooting daggers at him with their eyes, he thought of little else but the charming young woman. That flyaway mass of soft fiery hair. Those captivating emerald eyes. The way she bit her lip while deliberating what action to take. She laughed easily, joked easily. And though timid at times, she carried a quiet confidence which intrigued him. Yes, he thought of her a lot—when people weren't glaring at him.

This made him think of the pygmy dragon, Puffin. On their first meeting, Puffin had called him a rogue. And then from across the meadow, the creature had glared and said not only would he be watching him but assured Kendrick he would not be the only one. The dragon's eyes had narrowed, but Kendrick had recognized the species' attempt at a smile, and it wasn't a happy one.

Kendrick felt a renewal of the disquiet the dragon had instilled in him, even now in the privacy of this room. He twirled the gold band on his middle finger. He felt vulnerable. Exposed.

He glared at the door while kicking off his boots. The thunk of each one seemed too loud. He was starting to get agitated.

It is just this place, he tried to tell himself, jumping to his feet. He limped the length of the room, then turned and limped back.

It's too quiet here.

It was true. Even outside, with trees and people around, it was too quiet. Like they could read his thoughts. Hear his mind.

Maybe they can!

This thought stopped him dead in his tracks. He turned to the door.

This place is crawling with sorcis! He knew some sorcis could see the past and the future and who knew what else. Could they see his? Could they probe his mind and see his life laid bare for their scrutiny? Is that why the patriarch was so inhospitable all of a sudden?

The thought made a shiver trickle down his spine. *No! That can't be*, he tried to convince himself. The old man was just being overly cautious of a stranger around his—niece? *But why was she his niece*? *Why was she even here*? He had never heard of elves taking in humans. Ever. But here she was. And the two sorcis had evidently claimed her as their own. It would thus stand to reason the patriarch would be excessively protective, like any father figure would be. It was just understandable. Right?

Kendrick was not convinced. He would have to be more guarded with his thoughts, just in case. Still, he had to get his mind off this topic, or it would drive him mad. He spied the three leather-bound books on the built-in shelf across the room.

Quickly, he lumbered over to the bureau and snatched one of the books off the shelf. He began thumbing through the large leather-bound book. It didn't take long for him to become distracted. Not that the content intrigued him as much as it grabbed his attention. Even though he had hoped for something other than cooking recipes or whatever else women would have on their shelves, he never expected this.

Flipping through the pages, illustrations of every species in Sheorae were whizzing past. As he slowed the pages, he was amazed to see the humans, animals, and beings were depicted in various attack formations.

At this, Kendrick slapped the book closed to peered at the cover. The weathered tome held no inscription, but on the spine was the title. There in bold black letters, it read *Creature Combat.* His mouth drooped open, and his brow furrowed in consternation.

Instantly, he examined the other two volumes on the shelf. The one lighter-colored book was entitled *Weapons and Warnings*, and the other, older, more battered book was called *The Art of Diplomacy.*

In disbelief, he inspected the book in his hands again, wondering if it were an illusion. Still dumbfounded, he peered at the door. He could not fathom why books such as these would even be in the home of two single women, let alone on the personal shelf in one of their rooms.

Carefully, he thought through what he remembered of the exterior dimensions of the cottage, but even with his sketchy reckoning, there was just no possibility of this being a guest room. The structure was not big enough.

He hadn't really thought about whose room he had taken over for his stay. It hadn't even occurred to him that he was taking someone's room. But now that he really thought it through, it was obviously apparent—he was in one of the women's rooms. But which would possibly have a reason for books such as these?

He thought of the lovely young woman, Adianna. Her soft, gentle features. The lips so ready to smile or laugh. Her alluring eyes. No, she would have no need for harsh, worldly books such as these.

Then his mind wandered to the other option. Sorcis were noted to be the scholars of the elves. Thus, Memsy could have reason to study such things, he supposed. Yet it was perplexing that these particular topics were kept here and not in the archives spoken of in the Sanctuary rather than some softer, less meaty subjects. And more curious still that the older would relinquish her room rather than the younger. Typically, with other cultures, the younger members were expected to forfeit their bed for company. But who was to judge the inner workings of the near-immortal mind?

Kendrick sighed and was about to slide the volume back into place on the shelf when he heard a soft rap on the door.

"Come in," he called, tilting his head to see who would come through. He was delighted to see wavy auburn hair surrounding a smiling face.

Adianna stepped into the room, her hands loaded. In her arms she carried a tray holding a basin with a pitcher sloshing water. On one side of the basin sat a large sea sponge; on the other was a shaving blade and small hand mirror.

As she took the items over to set on the chair he had moved under the window, he let his gaze roam over her form. She was decidedly beautiful. Slender and attractive. But he had known many of those in his life. Yet, this one was different somehow. True, she was active and lively. Lighthearted. But there was something more. Nothing like any of the women he had ever known. Save perhaps one.

Abruptly, he shoved that thought aside, burying it deep down where it should stay. He focused on the girl in front of him to regain his train of thought.

Adianna was just lowering the tray to the chair. He watched her curiously as she lowered and lifted with her legs. No, she wasn't like the others. With one exception, the women he had known had all been either snobs and social-climbers or small village wall flowers. He'd had a wide range try to snare him in one way or another. But in the end, they all wanted *from* him or refused to stand supportively beside him.

Adianna seemed different. She was easy to talk to, quick-witted, and good humored. And she seldom stumbled when he baited her! He smiled to himself thinking of earlier, the many laughs they had shared in so short a time.

He was still smiling when she turned to face him. She ducked her head, a delightful pink touching her cheeks.

He, self-consciously, cleared his throat, then remembered he was still holding the book in his hand.

Searching for words, he stammered, "I was just admiring the unique collection of books here."

Adianna met his gaze, but her blushing only deepened.

"They're just a few Dala gave me long ago." She attempted to be flippant about it, but the slight ringing of her hands showed she was still uncomfortable.

"These are yours?" Kendrick wished his voice didn't sound so surprised. He stared at the volume in his hands, abashed they really belonged to her. He slid the book back into place.

He regarded her in a new light as he crossed the room toward her. She was still flustered about something. Her eyes would meet his, then quickly dart away. When he was nearly to her, she ducked around him and skittered over to the bureau. He let her pass but kept his gaze upon her while moving the loaded chair to the side of the bed. She was trying hard not to notice him at all. She straightened the three books into perfect order, then toyed with the flowers in the vase.

He settled himself onto the bed, a leg on either side of the make-shift table.

"Thank you for this," he said, pointing a hand at the supplies before him.

Her hand paused on the bureau drawer she was about to pull out to give him a sweet 'you're welcome.' He was surprised that, despite the previous unease in the room, she smiled brightly at him.

She turned back to the dresser and rummaged around in one of the drawers.

He gripped the handle of the pitcher and poured the water, careful not to slosh. Still, his mind was on her.

He compared her with the many other girls he had seen throughout his travels all over Sheorae. Many of them started out looking convincing, as though they were someone different, but they all turned out to be the same. They just had different packaging. *Would this one prove different?*

"Dinner will be ready in about half an hour," she offered, a folded garment in her hand. "Is there anything you need help with before I go?"

Kendrick struggled to keep a straight face. "Of course!"

Adianna stepped closer, her expression questioning.

Looking as despicable as possible, Kendrick said, "I think I should need help bathing."

His eyes held hers, gauging her reaction closely. Yet it was difficult for Kendrick to keep up the façade as he watched the range of emotions cross her face in rapid succession. Especially in her eyes. First, they widened slightly when she halted, her mouth sagged open. That was quickly replaced by them narrowing, the left eye ticking narrower still. Then an eyebrow arched cockily as she placed her hands on her hips. *What is she going to do?* He gave in to a lopsided grin.

She sauntered lazily over until she stood directly in front of him and leaned over the basin until her face was mere inches away from his. She smiled sweetly at him and batted her eyelashes. "Well, since today you are not a rogue, that means you are a big boy and can handle it yourself."

Then she flicked her finger right in the middle of his forehead.

"Ow!" he blurted and blinked. Rubbing his forehead, he smiled and watched her scamper from the room, her laughter trailing behind. She paused at the doorway, merriment dancing in her eyes.

"Dinner," she stated pointedly. "Half an hour."

"Yes, ma'am," he responded, still rubbing his forehead.

Her laughter continued long after she had closed the door.

A worthy opponent. He grinned and nodded appreciatively at the closed panel. *Maybe she is different after all.*

LEAVING TYMALIA

Adianna tried to stifle the elation she felt surge forth as soon as Daerlot dismissed her from lessons. She failed. Even Dala's apparent annoyance at her rush to be gone couldn't quell it. His brusque behavior could not kill her good mood.

He did manage half a smile as she planted a kiss on his cheek.

"Farewell, Dala," she chimed, heading swiftly for the door.

"Farewell, dear one. Bring me a few juicy ones," he called as she ran down the hall.

She smiled softly to herself, slowing once she reached the Commons. She couldn't blame Daerlot for being annoyed. She hadn't been much of a student today. No, as soon as Memsy had informed her at dinner the night before that berries were on and she would be getting out of lessons early, she had been overjoyed. Lessons were droning on these days at a monotonous pace, and these breaks in the monotony three days in a row were exciting beyond belief.

It had become even more exciting when Memsy had asked the healer if he would like to join her.

"The walking seems to be doing your injuries some good," Memsy had said, her eyes dancing between him and Adianna, a peculiar smile on her face.

Adianna still could not believe what all happened then.

She had just stared at the healer, wide-eyed, somehow forgetting to breathe. Freshly pressed and clean shaven as he was, he was dazzling. More spectacular than any man she had ever seen—regardless of species. His dark hair, still damp from washing, waved around his face and glistened in the firelight.

He had stared at Memsy for a moment, reading her face, then had turned to her. His blue gaze roamed over her face a while, then a soft smile came to his lips.

"Would you mind too much if I hobble along with you?"

His deep voice washed over her, and, at first, she couldn't focus on his question. She was using all her concentration to pull the much-needed oxygen in and out of her lungs at a seemingly regular pace.

"I... uh," she began, but at the shaky sound of her voice she stopped, instantly appalled.

Adianna! She scolded herself. *You sound like an idiot!*

With great effort, she looked at her plate. Striving for a nonchalant shrug, she grappled for control of her voice enough to answer.

"Sure. No problem. I mean, if you want."

She gave another lopsided shrug but made the mistake of looking at him. His softly probing eyes were still upon her. She felt her heart accelerate at the subtle change of his smile.

Can he hear my heart? she wondered, with dismay. *Is it giving me away?*

He leaned forward against the table, resting his chin in his hand. He gazed intently at her, and his voice was low as he coaxed, "Are you sure I won't slow you down?"

Then Adianna recognized that playful glint around his eyes and mouth.

He's toying with me again!

Without thinking about it, she rolled her eyes, spell broken.

"Well, I don't know," she said, feigning thoughtfulness, scrunching her nose. "You are pretty helpless."

She heard Memsy gasp, but plunged on, leaning back in her chair.

She flung her hand in his direction. "I mean, I'll probably have to carry your bucket, as well as my own."

The healer mimicked her recline with a chuckle. His amused eyes never left her face.

"Probably," he conceded.

"And," she added, leaning forward again abruptly, "we will be going beyond the village borders. Who knows what could be out there on the prowl… or the hunt?"

She scrunched her eyes, trying hard not to smile.

He, too, leaned forward then, eyebrows raised. "Oh, most assuredly."

Then his brow knit in a piteous expression. "But you will protect me, won't you?"

Adianna pressed her lips together firmly, cutting off the giggle striving to burst at his pitiful face.

She sighed, her brow high. "I'll try, but you're just so darn helpless. I don't know if I can protect you and the berries both."

The healer was struggling hard then, too, to keep up his alleged pleading.

"What if I promised to carry my own bucket?" he implored, reaching across the table to take her hand.

Adianna had flinched away instinctively from his touch, but then had slowly leaned back out of his reach as a cover-up.

"I guess," she sluggishly conceded, trying to stay calm, seeing his uncertain expression.

She remembered, now, wanting to tease him more, desiring to wipe that look from his face. She had shaken her finger at him then.

"But we have to come home with some," she had chided mockingly. "So, you don't get to eat them all!"

Her heart warmed as she remembered the conceding smile return to his face while she snatched her plate and his and headed to the wash pot.

Now, as she approached the cottage, her stomach fluttered to the beat of a hundred butterfly wings. She tried to convince herself it was her continued freedom from lessons which had her elated, but she knew better. She couldn't wait to spend the afternoon with this stranger who had so quickly taken control of her faculties and made her long to be with him.

She wished she had the nerve to ask him about himself. What was his name? Where was he from? Was he spoken for?

But all of these questions were strictly taboo. She knew she wouldn't ask, and he wouldn't offer.

At least the typical reason why this personal information wasn't shared did not apply here. He was definitely not a dalphene. But who was he?

She skittered excitedly into the cottage. He was sitting at the table, waiting, but jumped up as soon as she came through the door. Did she dare hope he was as eager as she?

"Your mother is over at your aunt's. She said we could go on without her."

Buckets already in hand, he passed one to her. She took it, carefully avoiding contact with his skin.

"Fabulous!" she chimed and turned back to the door she had just come through.

On the way out, she snatched her cloak and gloves. She could feel his gaze upon her as she settled the shimmering metal cloak over her shoulders and slid the cool gloves into place. She met his quizzical gaze, silently, after he had closed the door.

She knew what he must be thinking. *The day was wonderfully warm out, and here she was getting all done up for winter.* Well, he had her there. She couldn't explain it to him. She wasn't to let anyone know about her powers or the results of having them. And she couldn't even explain exactly why.

Cursed evil! It had made her life full of secrets, and at times, she really detested it. *Times like this when a gorgeous man is staring at me like I have lost my mind!*

But she put on an overly exuberant smile and urged, "Are you ready?"

Subtly, his expression changed to coincide with hers, and he gave her a quick nod. So, with that, she skipped off through the gate and headed north.

Kendrick shuffled along behind Adianna between a potato field and raspberry patch. They were just reaching the northeast edge of Tymalia when she began looking around in earnest. Then, at the end of the field where the ground was turned back over to the forest, the young woman raised her hand to halt him. She hopped over a couple of squat potato plants toward a group of trees. Before Kendrick could ask what she was about, she jumped from the edge of the potato patch to hide among the trees. She then tentatively peeked out beyond the trees toward him and looked all around in the direction of the village.

"Okay. It's all clear," the girl replied.

Kendrick could feel his brow scrunching up for he truly didn't know what to think of her actions. He stepped gingerly past the bushes onto the forest floor. But when he had stepped beyond her, Adianna hopped back toward the potato plants.

"M'lady?" he queried, glancing in her direction, but she had disappeared.

Kendrick whirled around and found the entire village was gone. He tottered back but to no avail. All he saw in every direction was forest.

He thought he could just make out the trill of the young woman's laughter, but he could not determine from which direction it came. Then, clear as day, he heard her voice coming from near the clump of trees.

"Over here."

He limped that direction, dodging bramble and stubbing his toe on a rock. But when he reached the trees, she was still nowhere in sight.

Then, like a ghostly apparition, her arm appeared out of nowhere, sunlight reflecting off the mail glove across her upturned palm.

"Here. Take my hand."

The smile he could hear in her voice dissolved any nervousness he felt about what he was seeing. His hand closed around her glove, and she instantly appeared before him. She then pulled him closer. Within the motion of stepping forward, the whole of Tymalia appeared behind her. The potato field, the raspberry patch, the cottages, even the Sanctuary towering beyond that.

"Whoa!" he breathed.

Dawning tickled his understanding, and he tilted back toward the trees, still keeping hold of her hand. When he shifted to his back foot, everything disappeared except for the hand he clung to. He then stepped forward into the domesticated terrain of the village and stepped out again.

"This is amazing." And he tried it two more times, despite the young woman's laughter.

Finally, he hopped forward to come to a standstill by the woman. In his joviality, he looked down at her, only to realize she was very close and her upturned smile very appealing. Flashes of the incident the day before played through his mind. His eyes were drawn to her lips. He couldn't help but wonder just how heavenly they might taste. Her smile relaxed under the weight of his gaze. He could hear her breath stagger in, pause, and slowly tumble out, telling him she was affected by their nearness as well. That just made the siren's call of her rosy lips that much more enticing. He could not resist lowering his to them ever so slowly. He pulled softly on her hand, drawing her gently toward him. Still, he could not take his eyes off her lips until his own were so close the nearness impeded his view. Her shallow breath tickled his lips, and he made the mistake of looking into her eyes. Her eyelids were dipped so low. Her eyes spoke desire through her lashes.

That was his undoing. His hot breath left him in a sigh, and he moved to close the distance.

Suddenly, within a hair's breadth, she jerked back a step, pushing off his chest with her other hand. At the same time, the buckets thunked to the ground. Her eyes were wide and wild, searching his. Her mouth fell open, but no breath escaped. She just stared at him.

Kendrick held his breath, waiting for her reaction. He had wanted to kiss her so badly, wanted to still. But he could no longer tell what she wanted. He couldn't read her face like he had so many times before. She seemed stunned, maybe even a little fearful. He wished again, for probably the hundredth time in the last two days, he could read her thoughts.

She slowly looked at her hand still resting on his chest, blinking repeatedly, though her eyes stayed wide.

He raised his free hand in an attempt to lift her chin and speak to her. Before he could touch her soft skin, her hand moved from his chest to pull his hand gently down. Now holding both of his hands averted from her, she looked up and half-smiled.

"Shall we go pick those berries now?"

Her gaze was soft, but he sensed a slight pleading within their depths.

He released his breath with a gentle smile. "That would be lovely." His voice was husky even to his own ears. He cleared his throat and scooped up the buckets. "Lead the way, m'lady."

Adianna ducked her head, and she pulled her hair behind her ear. He could see her trying to hide a little smile while she stepped past him into the forest. Seeing this made his smile broaden, and he fell in line behind her.

The forest was lovely this morning. The trees high above filtered splashes of sunlight through their leaves and outstretched branches. The air was fresh and moist and vibrant for this late in the fall. Peace radiated around them while they meandered along an animal trail. It was hard to believe this was Kyren Forest where dangers lurked at every turn. No, indeed, it felt the perfect place for a midmorning sojourn.

Kendrick's knee was doing much better, despite him aggravating it the day before. His healing seemed to have resumed its normal rate since awakening yesterday. He dared not think about what mystical powers the elves could have used to heighten his abilities. He just delighted in his renewed mobility. Before leaving the cottage, he had pressed on the bruise, getting just the slightest twinge as a response. Now it hardly pained him, and though he favored that leg, he kept pace with the lithe young woman in front of him.

They soon reached a low butte. Right in front of them was a somewhat noticeable trail where the rocks had been smoothed by continuous use, which extended over the crest.

Kendrick presented his hand to the young woman to assist her initial assent. She offered a shy but appreciative smile and grasped his hand gently. The metal of her gloves was cool and smooth against his skin. He wondered about their necessity. It was quite a warm day, even among the trees. There had to be some other reason, but what he didn't know.

The gloves and cloak both appeared to be made of some kind of metal, which was ridiculous for a woman her age. Still there were those telltale books in her room. He already knew he wasn't dealing with the typical female.

The shiny silver color suggested either the obvious silver or possibly steel or shamere. With what she had shown him of the elfin way of life, garments of any kind made from silver seemed too frivolous. With the way the cloak swished about her, he knew it was too light to be steel. So that left only shamere.

What he knew of shamere was sketchy at best. He knew it was a metal discovered by the dwarves long before they left Sheorae a millennium and a half ago. It had been one of their secret mixtures, and therefore, very rare. Kendrick had seen the precious metal used in Leorae, the human capital city, at the dragon training center there. A number of the caregivers had worn vests or tunics made from shamere, as it repelled heat, even at very high degrees. *But why would she need to repel heat?*

A slow smile spread across his face as he remembered the incident of just a few moments previous. He didn't know about her, but he definitely felt the heat of the moment.

Unbidden, his mind strayed to their walk the day before, when he had fallen into her. The pain of it had hurt like the dickens, and he had cussed himself for being so careless in his footing. But then he had looked into her eyes and all that had faded away. All he had been aware of, at that moment, was her lovely, upturned face and the warmth radiating from her body. It seemed all he had to do was look into her eyes and he was hooked—both yesterday and today. They had called to him, beckoning him to come closer into those emerald depths—so innocent, so naïve. And then there were her lips. He had never felt such a draw to kiss anyone in his life, staring down at those soft, rosy lips.

A subtle scratching noise brought Kendrick's mind back to their surroundings. His steps slowed, and he listened intently. Adianna made an odd twittering sound, then smiled back at him over her shoulder. Still, he listened. Then a slight scraping was heard again off to the left of the path. Quickly, he searched the trees on that side up ahead. Indeed, there were several scratch marks in the bark from the sharpening of tusks.

He stopped in his tracks. Yet Adianna moved on. There was no time for pleasantries; he called out to her. "Adianna. Wait!"

Just then there came a low snort.

Instantly Kendrick leapt forward and caught Adianna around the waist. He pulled her off the trail toward a clump of trees. Despite her surprise, he pulled her around and stuffed her between the trees, then shielded her with his body.

"What...?"

He cut off her question with a sharp shush, bringing his finger to his mouth. "It's a braidoc."

He was just leaning back to peek around the tree shielding them when something hit him hard in the side. Instantly, he was propelled backward fifteen feet, smacking hard into the trunk of a tree. He hit his head, then crumpled to the ground.

Kendrick tried to quickly push himself up, but the pain in his side made him collapse again. He pushed off with his good arm, and he rolled. There he halted. He was face-to-face with a mouthful of long crooked teeth flanked by two sharp, curving tusks.

BEASTS, BERRIES, & BIRDS

A low, gurgling growl rumbled through the huge mouthful of teeth. Then a snort erupted from the black nostrils within the large furry head, which sent hot air blasting into Kendrick's face.

"Whoa, Groozer! Stop!"

Adianna hopped forward and grabbed the beast around his thick neck, pulling the massive head to the side. "No, Groozer, he's a friend. We must be nice."

At this, the creature turned back to look at him, and Kendrick could have sworn it wrinkled its nose at him before huffing a very slobbery puff of air in his direction.

The girl made the same twittering noise she had made before.

"Come on, old boy," Adianna said and tugged at his neck a couple of times to get him moving.

Kendrick wasn't sure which to be more amazed at—the girl's bravery and skill at taming a braidoc or the fact the creature was actually listening to her.

Kendrick got a good view of the beast as it sauntered away. It was three-feet tall at its massive shoulders with a thick, bushy head. The healer jerked his leg back, so the creature didn't nick him with the tusks curving from the side of its mouth.

Adianna leaned over Groozer's long back, patting the animal, and asked intently, "Are you okay? What were you trying to do?"

The creature flicked its long, club-like tail in his direction. Kendrick instantly ducked to narrowly avoid his head being smacked by the anvil ball at the end of it before the animal snorted off into the forest. The dodge sent pain shooting through his side, and Kendrick grabbed his ribs. He held his breath against the pain. Gingerly, he fingered around before answering through clenched teeth, "I was trying to protect you."

"No." Adianna squatted by him, a dubious look on her face. "That's what he was trying to do."

Kendrick huffed, but the sarcastic attempt at a laugh simply brought more pain to his side. "Of course he was," he grumbled.

"How bad is it?"

Still propped on his elbow, he finished the examination of his side, then the back of his head. "I'd say a slight concussion and about three or four cracked ribs."

At her concerned expression, he continued gallantly, "Never fear, my dear. All should be mended well enough by this evening." Then he flashed her what he hoped was a brilliant smile.

One of Adianna's eyebrows arched high on her forehead. But presently, she stood, then extended her hand to him. "Can I help you up?"

Kendrick was doubtful her delicate hand and petite frame would be much help in getting him to his feet, yet he would chance the difficulty in rising in the hopes of seeing her smile by his acceptance of her generosity.

When he took her hand, her grip was firm. Then she pulled his bulk up effortlessly from the ground. The surprise must have been evident on his face, because her eyes got big as if she had somehow made a mistake. She stared at him, pulling both of her lips between her teeth. Next her gaze skittered past one side of him then the other. Finally, she looked back at him and plastered on a tense smile.

"Shall we?"

Kendrick could feel a pucker between his eyebrows, but he gave a slow nod.

At that, she turned, scooped up the buckets, and hustled back onto the path.

He felt the corner of his mouth dip deep into his cheek as he followed her through the trees. This girl was just one mystery after another. *Will I ever get answers? Or just more questions?*

She continued in the lead up a hill. This gave Kendrick the chance to hang back a ways and let his gaze roam over her. Wavy hair, the color of an autumn sunset, fell to her waist. Even with the cloak, he could not mistake her slender, well-proportioned figure. She was amazing to look at, but nothing in her frame bespoke the brute strength it took to pull him to his feet one-handed with so little effort. It just didn't make sense. That wasn't the only thing to not make sense, either.

The elves didn't take anyone into their confidences anymore, let alone outside their ranks. Yet here was a human not only among them but beloved as one of their own.

Then there was the girl herself. He was still amazed at how easy it was to be around this little minx, how easy she was to talk to and tease. And yet she was a woman! Most definitely a woman. But women weren't chums. They weren't one of the good old boys. Many had little on their mind other than day-to-day living or landing a husband. Most couldn't even be trusted. Mostly they were a needed but blasted nuisance.

Then along comes this little vixen, and now the rules seem to have changed before his eyes! He had not allowed himself to be swayed by a pretty face since… well… for a very long time. And he had never felt so drawn to kiss *anyone* so soon or so intently.

I'm sure it must have surprised her as much as me. She is such a young, quiet, little thing, he mused, watching her descend the other side of the hill, the buckets swinging from her hands at each step. *In close proximity, at least.*

A quirky smile spread his lips as he chuckled beneath his breath. He would have happily laughed out loud at the memory of her many snappy comebacks to his baiting her last night. Each time he had taunted her, using age-old antics which would set any other woman either fuming or blushing for cover, she had been nearly as quick to blow him off with some tease in return.

No, she is definitely not like the girls I'm used to.

What a relief! And so intriguing.

He came to the base of the rocks where she was waiting for him with a smile.

"You alright?" she asked cheerily.

"Doing great!" he exclaimed, then grimaced when the effort pierced his side with pain. "At least, if I don't breathe deeply. Lead on."

He brushed his hand in a little bow, toward the thin worn path wandering off through the trees to the left. She smiled at him but floated off into the forest ahead of them.

Here there was barely a path visible, and it meandered in and out of the trees for a little way further before coming to a steep natural wall jutting up over their heads. They followed along the outcropping until they came to an abrupt break in the formation. This narrow intrusion was a mere two to three feet across, then the wall continued to curve off to the west.

He followed Adianna, stepping into the meager crag. The escarpment, though not very tall, was deeper than he would have thought.

As he emerged through the narrow ravine, he was surprised to find himself standing in a berry patch. He knew blackberries grew wild in many places throughout Kyren Forest, but apparently the elves of Tymalia cultivated their own, for this was by far the largest patch he had seen anywhere.

Big, bulging blackberry bushes with their prickly arms extending in all directions were staggered throughout the large open space created by the rock wall. The projection of boulders, where it was just taller than himself behind him, extended in either direction and looped around to complete an oval. The walls dipped nearly to ground level at the sides, then jutted up to a ridge over twice as high before them.

The sun was beginning to reflect its heat off the tall ridge in front of him as it continued its arch to its zenith.

The bushes were well groomed, and Kendrick could hear the soft trickle of water from the escarpment at the back of the berry patch. But as he looked closer, he could see there were only a few berries on each bush ready for picking. Most were in need of several more days of ripening.

Confused, the healer wandered around wondering why the sorci had sent them. She had said the berries were ready.

Just then, glancing over, Kendrick noticed Adianna still walking purposefully through the patch toward the ridge. She was happily looking up while she approached it.

He followed her gaze to the high rocks above. There, about three-fourths of the way up the ridge, was a ledge jutting out. The back of the ledge made a dent in the rocky face of the cliff wall. This made the ledge a good five feet deep and just more than that wide. And right in the center of it was a lush, beautiful bush dotted heavily with deep, purplish-black berries.

The girl stopped a few feet from the rock wall, still in sight of the polka-dotted bush. A look of sheer joy danced across her face. Kendrick enjoyed the delight playing on her delicate features, but seeing her standing there, he became aware of how tiny she seemed compared to the height of the ledge.

"Wait a minute," he stated, stepping closer to her.

She turned her smile on him.

"Just how do you propose we get *those* berries?"

Honey brown eyebrows came together over emerald eyes in a puzzled expression. "How do you think?" she retorted softly. She handed him her bucket, then reached down to remove one of her shoes.

Kendrick felt his mouth bob open, and he just stared at her in amazement. Grown women didn't climb cliffs. Not that he had anything against it. On the contrary. Yet the women he had known did little other than the typical daily grind—if that. Climbing rocks was unheard of after about eight or nine years of age and frowned upon even then. He just couldn't believe it.

After removing the other shoe, she glanced back at him. He could only imagine what she saw.

"Oh, I know." She retrieved her bucket, sliding the handle to the crook of her left arm, and proceeded to remove her gloves. "Your arm and ribs." She guessed wrong. "Don't worry! You can stay down here and pick the few available on these, and I'll go up and get the rest."

Then with him still gaping after her, she tucked her gloves into the belt cinching her tiny waist and turned with a smile toward the rock face.

She pushed her cloak over her shoulders, so it hung straight back from her neck. Then she grabbed hold of the wall with her right hand. Despite watching her in wonder and a sense of awe, he was not prepared for her next move.

Before grabbing hold with her other hand, she hiked up the hem of her dress to above her knee. She then positioned her dainty foot nearly waist-high on the rocks.

He knew he should probably look away. It was likely she was only used to coming alone or with other females, and that made her forget propriety. But he couldn't resist staring at the curve of that creamy calf. His mind wondered at the feel of that soft, rosy-white skin before she hoisted herself up the rock wall.

Clinging to the rocks with her left hand, she flicked her skirt back out of the way to free her right leg for the climb. His eyes nearly bugged out of his head as the smooth, pale skin of her lower thigh became visible.

Quickly, he turned away, snatching at the closest berries to him. Ignoring the sting of the thorns, he tugged at the berries, not caring whether they were ripe or not. An uncharacteristic wave of embarrassment warred with the rebellious side of his nature. Finally, the wild side won out, and he peeked back toward the woman.

Completely oblivious, she continued her assent of the rock face. She was about halfway up now, making steady progress. Occasionally she flipped her dress out of the way from hampering her toes in finding proper holds on the cliff wall. Her bucket slid from shoulder to elbow in her assent.

"You," Kendrick began, more in awe than in accusation, "are not like other women." Then he cringed, scolding himself for just blurting it out, afraid the blatant statement might offend her.

But the young woman's laughter bouncing off the rocks soothed his self-chastisement. Then he heard her reply, "You have no idea!"

Before he could stop himself, he again blurted the first thing to pop into his head. "Not even the elf women I have seen or met climbed cliffs."

"Maybe they did," she teased. "You just didn't see it."

He chuckled slightly at the thought.

"No, I don't think so," he mused, staring at his hands fumbling with the handle of his bucket. "Most of the women I've known—elf or not—were either overworked or too stuffy and refined." He looked over at her then, instantly aware of the potential insult of his words.

With her feet planted, and hanging on with the hand that had just reached the ledge, Adianna turned to him. She let her other arm dangle toward him. The bucket slid down it rapidly, but just as it was about to fall from her hand, she caught it in her graceful fingers.

She pinned him with a quizzical gaze and asked, "You think I lack refinement?"

Kendrick took a step toward her, appalled he'd made such a blunder. His mouth popped open, and he instinctively moved to apologize. But then he caught the mischievous glint in her eyes. Her mouth curved up in response to his discomfort.

Seeing her teasing him while hanging from a stone wall, he couldn't help smiling fondly back at her.

"No," he said, his eyes roaming over her delicate features. "*They* lacked life."

She gazed back at him, and her smile slowly faded. He could see a small line appear between her brows, and he wondered what she was thinking.

She said nothing more. Instead, she swung her bucket up to the ledge and shimmied up the rest of the way.

He went back to gathering berries, trying desperately to figure out something to say. He kept glancing up at her. She seemed to be focused on her work, but occasionally, he would catch her peeking his way before pushing her hair over her shoulder and resuming her work.

When she wasn't looking at him, he had the chance to take in the geography surrounding them. He noticed how the ridge arched from the dip at each side of the berry patch, coming to a wide, rounded peak above the ledge where the woman's berry bush grew.

Just then a smile stretched his face. Stepping slowly toward a low edge of the patch, he called out, "So how does such a splendid berry bush come to grow way up there?"

She did not glance over at him. She kept her eyes on her task, but a sweet smile crossed her lips. Then she stepped in front of the bush, putting her back to him. He watched her heave a sigh.

Perfect! he thought and slipped over the lip of the low, natural wall. He moved as quickly but quietly as he could while listening to her tale.

"Memsy and I planted it here when I was about five," she began. "I picked the spot myself." Her voice took on a soft, dreamy tone, apparently lost in memory. "She said we could plant it anywhere I wanted, because it was all for me and me alone."

Kendrick paused, curious why such a thing was possible in a community such as the one she described yesterday. Still, he dared not question, or he'd give himself away.

Fortunately, she continued on her own.

"See, when I came to live in Tymalia, minor adjustments were made in the community structure, as happens whenever any member is added or removed from the village.

"Dala… I mean the patriarch, took everything into account. Down to the particulars of my diet, comparing the nutrients my body needed to that of the others. It was decided an added allotment would be granted to me alone for those nutritional differences. More grains, vegetables, and fruits; less meat, eggs, etc."

Kendrick halted as his foot slipped on a rock. He listened with all his frame, but she kept talking, so he continued.

"One of the necessary additions was more fresh berries, and I suppose blackberries had just become a symbol for me by then."

He could hear her voice below him now. Could hear the hint of amusement in it, as he peered over the top edge of the ridge. "And why is that?" he asked with a grin, which broadened at her surprise. *Mission accomplished.*

"How'd you get up there?" she asked, smiling at him, her eyes dancing.

"Oh," he shrugged, poking a thumb back over his shoulder. "Just the refined boring way."

He beamed down at her. Her responding laughter bounded off the rocks.

He glanced at her nearly full bucket. "If you're about done, you're welcome to come up and join me," he invited.

She smiled brightly. "I'll be right there."

He gingerly sat at the edge, his legs dangling over, and placed his scantily filled bucket next to him. Leaning over, he watched her purple-stained fingers hastily skim over the bush below. Her fingers flew, snatching up the succulent berries with both hands and plopping them into the bucket sitting between her knees.

Finally, she stood, hefting the loaded bucket in her hand. Crossing to the north side of the ledge, the beauty placed her toes on the lip of a crag and pushed herself up to grab another crag a couple feet to the left of where his feet dangled.

"Here." She beamed, swinging her weighted bucket up toward him. He carefully braced his splinted arm along the landing, keeping his upper arm close to his chest to support his battered ribs, and retrieved it from her. Then he struggled to keep his eyes averted as she proceeded to climb.

When she was very near the top, he brought his leg over along the ledge for balance and offered her his good hand to help her the rest of the way.

For just a second, she eyed his hand, but then she flashed him a smile, saying, "Thanks, but I have it."

At first, he was a little miffed at the rejection, but felt the wisdom in it when he pushed off, side aching, to regain a seated position.

Within seconds, she was settled on the ledge by him, adjusting her skirt and cloak about her. She slid her gloves back into place over her purple-stained hands. Then she snatched up her bucket. Plucking a fat, juicy-looking berry half the size of her thumb, she held it within inches of his mouth.

"Here!" she offered, proudly. "The best in Sheorae."

He chuckled, and with a big grin, leaned forward for her to deposit the tasty morsel on his tongue. The tangy sweetness burst in his mouth and trickled down his throat. Then he met her expectant expression.

"What do you think?" she queried, flashing him a bright smile. She leaned closer, waiting for his answer.

He thought he could detect a slight challenge for him to deny her declaration. Never one to turn down a challenge, he slowly leaned closer to her. The closer he got, the wider her eyes became. He wondered if she feared—or hoped—he meant to steal a kiss. As tempting as it was, he dodged to swipe two more berries.

"I think you're right," he said with a crooked smile, popping one of them into his mouth.

He gazed deep into her expressive green eyes and offered her the other berry. She paused, looking at the proffered morsel. She leaned further forward, catching it between her teeth, then wrapped her lips around it after she had pulled back. He watched her mouth curve into an appreciative smile.

"Very desirable," he breathed low.

He became aware that the slight rise and fall of her chest moved a little more rapidly. But he never looked away from her engaging, emerald eyes. He felt a pull, drawing him into their liquid-jewel depths. Instinctively, he brought his hand up, oblivious to the awkwardness the bandaged splint provided. He moved slowly, not wanting to startle her, but he longed to feel the smooth skin of her pinking cheek. Her round lips parted in response to this action, and his eyes were drawn to their fullness.

Suddenly, she turned away, just as his fingers were about to caress her skin. She snatched up her brimming bucket.

"Feel free to eat as many as you would like, then," she stated, wedging the container between them. She offered him an awkward smile. "Compliments of the one 'human only' bush in Tymalia."

He studied her profile briefly, as she looked out over the view before them. She peeked at him askance, but his eyes were still upon her, causing her throat and cheeks to flame. *It just makes her even more lovely*, he thought.

But he was feeling like a cad. Pulling his eyes away, he scolded himself for being so bold with her. He had blatantly tried to kiss her twice, and it wasn't even noon. *When did I become such a scoundrel?*

Chuckling to lighten the mood, he reached into the proffered bucket. "Why, thank you, m'lady. I'll do my best to eat as many as I possibly can." And with a crooked smile, he pinched several plump berries lightly between his fingers. He dropped them into the cup of the other hand. Popping a couple into his mouth, he arched an eyebrow at the girl's amused face.

In that moment, her responsive giggles floated around the crest of the ravine. He shouldn't delight in the sound of her laughter as much as he did, but he couldn't help it. The enchanting sound of it, the way her eyes crinkled around the edges, the rosy tone of her cheeks, they all were endearing themselves to him at an alarming rate.

He tipped the bucket in her direction and lifted a quizzical brow. She accepted the quiet offer, pulling a small handful of the juicy bunches.

They sat there on the ridge, savoring the sweet berries and admiring the view in contented silence. He enjoyed the fact she didn't feel it necessary to fill the space with mindless prattle. They could just enjoy being with each other.

He looked out over the view from their raised vantage. Kendrick realized there were trees on the ridge behind them, keeping the location of the bushes protected from any flying passers-by. Still, they also got the elevated advantage of looking out over the small makeshift valley.

He had always loved this type of view, being above the stress and turmoil of the world. It had always brought him peace at times when little else did. Now, with this amazing creature beside him, the peace was almost tangible for him. He couldn't remember being this content in years.

Just then a couple of swallows darted out of the lower hemlocks. The pair whizzed around in a happy dance below the higher canopy. Presently, the dance slowed to gentle meandering together through the air.

"You know," Adianna whispered a little wistfully. She continued when Kendrick turned to her. "I've always envied birds."

Kendrick smiled at the childlike innocence of the statement. "Really?" he replied, encouragingly.

"Obviously, the ability to fly has natural appeal," she quipped offhandedly.

That brought to his mind the thrill and rush he had felt of soaring through the clouds. "Most definitely," he commented, a gentle smile tainting his voice. He watched the swallows swoop and dive among the trees.

"But with birds… and I guess it is with any animal, I suppose, but—they are what they are." Her voice was very low and thoughtful in its musing.

He waited for her to elaborate, without looking her way.

After a moment, she continued, "There are no expectations… to be something more. Something they're not… or don't want to be."

This caught Kendrick by surprise. He looked at her profile. *What are they wanting you to be?* He rummaged through possibilities, none of them really seeming horrible enough to match such a long face.

Still, he could sympathize. He knew exactly what she meant. At least nothing she faced could be so terrible and life-altering as what his family had expected of him. What he had left them over. What could quite possibly keep him from ever going home again.

He shook off the memories and sorrow that threatened to pounce on him. Instead, he focused on her. He put his hand over the gloves clenched in her lap. The tension she tried to hide everywhere else was evident there. He plied one of her hands into his and held it tightly. He didn't really know what to say with her looking at him so keenly. Finally, he simply gave an understanding smile and looked back out over the view.

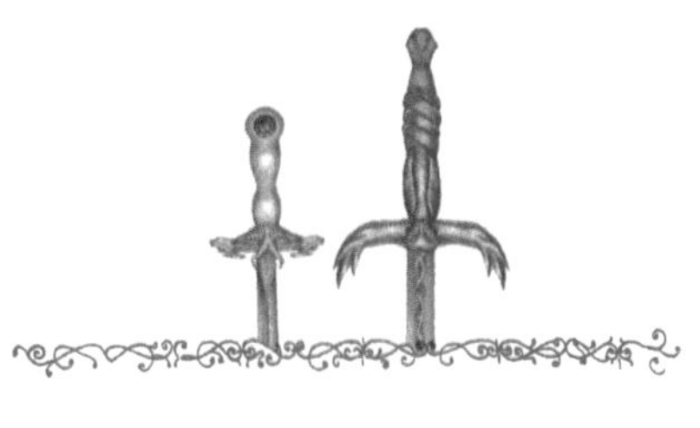

TAG

"You know, m'lady," the healer enquired.

Adianna paused in her stride. They had done little talking since they left the ledge and now were just emerging through the illusion shield surrounding the patchwork of farmland within the village. Her companion had not released her hand once. "What's that?"

She felt his thumb draw little circles on the back of her glove.

"Thanks to our friend—Groozer, was it?—I have already called you by your name. Might I beg the privilege of calling you Adianna?"

A thrill zinged through her, but she was not sure whether it was from his question or from hearing her name coming from his lips. She felt her cheeks flame to life. Regardless of the reasoning, the ecstasy far outweighed any need for caution, so she nodded her approval.

She was just about to ask him for his name in return when she noticed some village children sneaking around the edge of the cottage up ahead. Brydon was in the lead, hunched over to duck behind a large piling of firewood. Following the boy's line of sight, Adianna spotted Puffin grazing on turnips in the small field off to their left. The little dragon was facing away from them and therefore couldn't see the approaching doom.

Adianna growled under her breath, propping her unheld hand onto her hip, her bucket resting heavily against her thigh.

"What's the matter?" the healer asked, concerned.

"That boy," Adianna moaned another growl and jutted her chin toward the children.

He glanced in the direction she indicated, but she didn't wait for his reaction.

"I'm going to stop this, before that poor dragon gets hurt," she said, pulling up her skirt to run over to do just that.

"No, wait!"

Before she could take a step, the healer pulled her hand close to his chest to halt her advance. His blue eyes were dancing, still gazing off toward the children and their prey, when she raised a questioning look to him.

"Puff knows they're coming," he whispered with a smile.

Adianna's forehead creased, but she didn't have time to comment.

"Come on." He released her hand, wrapped his arm around her cloaked waist, and gently guided her off the path.

They stepped quickly between the rows of browning potato plants toward a clump of aspens nestled a short distance from the trail. Concealed now behind the trees, the man deposited his bucket on the ground and snatched hers as well. With his hand on her back, he urged her closer to the far side of the trees, and they both peeked round. Adianna leaned over, giving the man a higher angle. Still, she cast him a questioning look before focusing back on the scene before them.

The children had made considerable progress, though they had been sneaking from tree to bush with only the mildest of shushes. Puffin seemed to be eating his turnips aimlessly, completely oblivious to the encroaching danger.

Finally, Brydon broke ahead of the others, waving them to back off. The dragon lowered his head about to take another mouthful of the crunchy white bulbs he had pulled up, when the boy took off running straight for the dragon.

Adianna was about to cry a warning when she caught a peculiar pull at the corner of the dragon's mouth, like he was hiding a smile. His eyelids lowered, and he seemed to focus on something other than the vegetables before him.

The boy reached full speed, and within several feet of the dragon, he leapt into the air with a mighty roar. But as soon as Brydon left the ground, so did the pygmy. Spread-eagle and no time to react, the boy soared through the air and landed flat on his face in the upturned dirt.

Adianna's hands clamped over her mouth to quell her laughter, but it was no use. The look of Brydon coming up sputtering and spitting, with clods of moist soil sticking to his face and the roaring chuckles of the healer behind her, she fought in vain.

Even Puffin snickered heartily as he swooped through the air just above the squealing children. He took another turn above them, and the kids danced with their hands outstretched, reaching and cheering.

Just then the dragon swooped toward Brydon. His feet barely touched the ground as Puffin grabbed a mouthful of the boy's trousers and hauled him into the air by the seat of his pants. The guffawing healer stepped out from behind the trees. Puffin was now darting over the children with Brydon's flailing arms and legs skimming just above their reach.

Adianna picked her way out of the potato patch to join the healer. Brydon's hollers for help all but drowned out the snickering whistles of the pygmy. She noticed other elves rounding the sides of the houses to see what all the commotion was about.

Just then, Puffin veered toward her and the healer. Brydon's limbs drug dust-plumed lines in the dirt when the dragon dipped to eye level. Instinctively, Adianna flinched back, but she perceived the healer stood his ground, chortling merrily. Still the pygmy approached fast. At the last minute, Puffin shot straight up over their heads.

Brydon let out a cry, for suddenly he was falling through the air. Adianna gasped. But at just the right moment, the healer stepped forward and deftly caught the flailing boy.

How he caught the boy without hurting his injured arm or side, she couldn't tell. Still, it was with a mighty guffaw he looked down at the stunned boy in his arms.

"Let this be a lesson to you, lad!" the man quipped. "Dragons always know more than you think. And they know how to take advantage of it."

Puffin landed gently on the ground in front of the man and let out a screeching, guttural sound which mingled with the man's laughter.

Brydon's face turned beet red, and he glared at the gloating dragon. Then, kicking his feet high over the man's arm, Brydon scrambled free and hit the ground running.

"I'll get you, you piggy pup!"

Adianna could hear the teasing in Brydon's voice, and she laughed as Puffin squeaked a cry before turning to lumber away on all fours. The other children cheered while watching Brydon give chase.

The romp quickly turned into a game when Brydon got close enough to slap the pygmy on the rump. The animal instantly turned his long neck to shoot forth his head to tag the retreating boy with his snout. Brydon skittered to a halt so abruptly, trying to change directions, that his feet slid out from under him, and he landed in the dirt once again. The dragon chortled his delight and continued in his original direction.

Laughter exploded all around Adianna from children and man alike. Tears were squeezing out of her scrunched eyes, and she had to hold her sides, she was laughing so hard.

"Oh, yeah?" Brydon hollered at the faces of his unruly audience. Squeals and shouts erupted as he scrambled to his feet again to chase after anyone nearby.

"You're it, Kimblin!" he cried, slapping his hand on the shoulder of a dark-haired boy close by. Then Brydon skedaddled in the opposite direction, while the boy who was it craned his face, looking for a target.

Adianna's laughter slowed, and she delightedly watched the children at play. Kimblin was still running after anyone who got close to him. Finally, he touched his hand on the back of a tiny little girl.

"There, Tanny! You're it!"

The little three-year-old squealed with delight as she turned to chase after everyone. Tanny's silver hair, which reminded Adianna so much of Memsy's, streamed out behind her while she gave chase. Adianna noticed all the children darted at a much slower pace with the little girl running around giggling gleefully.

Just then Adianna felt hands settle gently on her shoulders.

"They're having a great time, aren't they?" The healer's deep voice sounded close by her ear.

Adianna's heart started. She expected his all-seeing eyes to be upon her. Instead, he watched the children, a huge smile on his face.

This close, Adianna could tell just how much taller he was than she and see the thick lashes framing his azure eyes. She could also smell the warm, fresh scent of him. Her heartbeat quickened, and she ran her gaze along the strong line of his jaw. Despite the shamere cloak, she was still keenly aware of the length of his body behind her, and she longed to lean into it.

He was so close yet unaware of the effect he was having on her. His eyes were still settled on the merry romp.

"Oh, look! Look!" he said suddenly.

Adianna turned the direction his hand indicated.

"The little one tagged somebody."

Adianna tried not to think of his face, now right by hers. So close that if she were to turn her head, she would feel the searing sensation of his skin along her lips. Instead, she focused on the scene before them.

Tanny had tagged Lecter, one of the oldest boys in the group, over on the far side of the field. Lecter was now chasing back after the little girl, hunched over, his arms dangling. He looked like a hunchback chasing away onlookers. The little girl's squeals of delight could be heard over her assailant's hooting and snorting.

Just then, Tanny came running past Puffin, and the dragon grabbed a mouthful of the little girl's bodice. The pygmy turned quickly with the girl's dress in his mouth. Just as Tanny clamped her arms and legs around Puffin's long neck, he took off, leaving the snorting boy behind.

The dragon's leap into the air landed just a short distance from where Adianna stood, and he set the gleeful child onto the ground once again. Tinkling peals of laughter erupted from the child. She staggered back from the dragon. Once she gained her bearings, she leapt forward, flinging her arms around the dragon's neck.

"Oh, fank you, Puffin!" she exclaimed, kissing him on the side of his face.

Adianna smiled despite herself at the adorable child. Tanny then turned to her excitedly.

"Miss Annie! Miss Annie! Did you see me? I fwewed!"

Adianna bent to stroke the little girl's arm. "I did, Tanny! That was amazing!" Her smile was nearly as huge as the child's.

The little girl took a step closer, sheer delight on her small face. "You seed me fwy, too, huh, Mister Sir?" Tanny coaxed the healer, grinning triumphantly.

"Indeed, I did, Miss," the man said, squatting before the expectant child. Adianna's mouth dipped open as the big, burly warrior stroked the little girl's cheek affectionately, while still keeping his other hand on her own shoulder.

"In fact," he went on. "I would say you were a natural-born Dragon Strider."

At the man's nodded bow, Tanny giggled with delight. Adianna was mesmerized by this man. The man winked at the little girl, which sent her into more giggling hysterics.

Adianna realized she was still gaping at him when his eyes met hers. Startled, she stood abruptly. But his response to catching her gawking was an intriguing raise of one eyebrow. He pinned her with that gaze and came up slowly. She really wanted to look away, but she couldn't.

Saved by the child, Adianna felt Tanny grab her hand. Pulling on her, the girl cried, "Come, Miss Annie! You twy."

Caught off guard by the request, Adianna coughed slightly. She tried to ignore the healer's hearty guffaw and the dragon's nervous squawk. Instead, she scooped up the handle of her abandoned bucket.

"Actually," she said to the little girl. "I need to be getting to Miss Memsy. So why don't you take these..." Adianna placed a handful of berries into Tanny's cupped hands. "And go back to playing with the others. Alright?"

The girl smacked her little lips a few times, as if she were already tasting the yummy treat. "Oh, fank you, Miss Annie!" She beamed and went running toward the others with Puffin close behind.

"Miss Annie?" the healer asked inquisitively.

Adianna blushed. "That's just what my cousin calls me when we are away from the village—Annie. Some of the others have picked it up."

He scooped up his lighter bucket and nestled it in the crook of his arm above his splint, then reached for hers. He gripped the handle, pinning a few of her fingers in the process. She tugged slightly, but his fingers squeezed in response.

Eyebrows high, she made the mistake of looking at his face. His luscious eyes were upon her: smoldering pools of liquid blue topaz.

"I think I prefer Adianna," he whispered.

She felt color flood her cheeks, but she could not look away. Those sparkling pools called to her like the sirens of the Tyronda Sea. She felt his thumb stroking small circles along her metal glove. Still, she could not look away. A subtle change moved the muscles around his mouth like a smile was about to creep forth.

"Shall we?" he asked.

Air rushed in through her open mouth from the breath she didn't realize she was holding. "Yes." She nodded, looking away.

This time he let her pull her hand free.

CLASH

The clash of steel echoed around the yard and vibrated up Daerlot's arm. Dripping with sweat, he pressed back against the attacking blade with his own. What used to be an easy defense now required quite an exertion of energy. Slowly, he inched the swords farther away from his body. His breath burst forth in spurts between his teeth, but he was making ground.

With a sudden dip, then shove, he broke free, sending his opponent stumbling backward. Daerlot swung low at the unsteady, retreating legs. Before his blade could make contact, his target was gone. His adversary's agile body flipped backward out of reach.

Daerlot attacked. His competitor parried. Then it was Daerlot's turn to turn aside and dodge. Clang, clang, clang—the sounds of assault rang out while the two continued the onslaught with each other.

Then the patriarch countered a downward slice from his foe. Daerlot shot his weapon upward, thus propelling the rival away. But the elf's adversary followed through with the motion, spinning low. The enemy came fully around so quickly Daerlot could not react fast enough. Before he knew what was happening, the tip of a sword touched dead center on his chest.

The patriarch froze, his weapon suspended above his head. He grimaced, and a low growl rumbled in his chest, making his opponent giggle.

Daerlot huffed, then taking a step backward, brought his sword through at an angle. The momentum of the motion sent both contenders twirling. While the elf whipped around, he raised his weapon to the ready. When he came to a stop, his sword rested against Adianna's neck. Sadly, hers hovered a hair's breadth away from his own throat.

Staring at each other, the two panted. Then a smile crept across Adianna's face.

Suddenly Daerlot saw not his worthy opponent but the little girl who held his heart in her hand. He could not resist smiling back.

She was dressed in the traditional feminine warrior garb of the elves. Light and form-fitting, the hunter-green dress was elaborately embroidered around the edges with burgundy and silver threading. The skirt was loose and brushed her lower thighs a few inches above her knees. The cap sleeves barely topped her shoulders, and the bodice was plated with a low waist that dipped to a 'V' in the front and back. Arm shields encircled her forearms. Her feet were clad in high-cut boots reaching over her calves.

Head to toe, she looked the formidable warrior they had trained her to be. Still, with her cheeks flushed from the exertion of their sparring, and her eyes bright with the triumph of a tie, he saw only the sweet child he loved.

How did this all happen so fast? Where is my little girl?

Adianna's elation waned, and concern touched her face, making him realize he had been frowning. Daerlot quickly brightened. Flexing his wrist, he pulled the sword away and released his pose.

"Well done, my dear," he said, though the enthusiasm sounded off, even to his ears.

"Is everything alright, Dala?" she asked, the worry evident.

"All is well. Though I fear you are getting too good for this old elf."

Her laughter filled the distance between them.

Before she could respond, the healer came around the corner of the cottage. Daerlot stiffened. He locked eyes with the man, bringing him up short. But their agitated interlude was short-lived, for soon, the healer's gaze was drawn to Adianna.

Daerlot's tension intensified while he watched the healer's response play from surprise to appraisal then to something akin to deep admiration. To this, a blush dusted the girl's cheeks. The elf's jaw set tight.

He pinned the younger man with a glance, then took Adianna's sword.

"May we help you, healer?" he asked, pointedly leaving off the 'Master' again.

The man blinked abruptly and looked back to Daerlot. He hesitated a second, and the patriarch felt he was being sized up. Then the healer replied, "Actually, I heard the sparring and weaponry going on. I came to see if I could step in for a round or two."

The man's hungry eyes turned appreciatively back to Adianna. "I'd like to have a go… to see how well I'm healing up."

Daerlot's smile at the man was strained. He switched both swords to his right hand and wrapped his arm around his niece.

"I'm afraid we were just finishing up Adianna's training for the day," he said as he moved her away from the man and toward the back door of the cottage. "She needs to change and be heading home for her evening chores."

He pushed Adianna further toward the door. Then he turned back to the young man and challenged, "You can have a go at me if you would like."

The healer appraised the elder. His gaze shifted to the girl slipping through the door. A small smile spread across the young man's face and got bigger as he turned back to Daerlot.

"If you don't mind. I think I would like that. A lot."

Daerlot smiled also. He flipped one of the swords, then caught it by the flat of the blade. The man took the handle extended to him.

"What are you doing?" Relyat, who had been sitting in on the training, whispered low when Daerlot came near. "We want him to get better, remember? So he will leave."

Daerlot pulled his gloves more snuggly about his hands. He watched the healer weigh out the sword, then shift it back and forth between his hands, testing the balance and maneuverability around his splint.

"Indeed, we do." Daerlot raised an eyebrow to Relyat. "But what could one good romp do?"

"You *could* kill him," Relyat scoffed.

"Perhaps." A small twinge of delight sprang up at the idea. "But then he would be gone, now wouldn't he?"

"Daerlot, I…"

"Tut tut tut. I'll behave." The patriarch patted his old friend on the arm to reassure him, though he couldn't keep the smile from his face.

The healer was now shifting his stance and deeply stretching the left side of his core. Then his sword sliced in a circle on the left, next on his right. The man seemed to be in good form.

That is good. Then I won't have to be too *gentle with him.*

Daerlot took his stance and brought the sword in a slow sweep back then arched up, so the blade was poised over his head.

"Shall we begin?"

The man grinned, shifted one foot back, and nodded.

At his nod, the elf attacked. His weapon sliced across, clashing into the blocking sword, barely missing the man's nose. Then Daerlot repeated this motion and hammered downward. The man barely had time to block, yet the elf pounded down over and over on the blade poised over the man's head. The healer's footing slipped, and he went down on one knee. At that, the elder swung his sword around the other direction, bringing it up under the blocking weapon.

Steel grated against steel when Daerlot forced their weapons around, twirling a circular motion between them. He completed the circle with enough force to send the younger man scrambling to stay upright.

The patriarch could hear Relyat's groan behind him, but he paid it no mind. He kept his eyes trained on his prey, now stumbling to get up.

The man came to his feet and backed away. He hopped from one foot to another eyeing his opponent closely. When he saw Daerlot was allowing him to recover for a moment, the healer shrugged and loosened his neck up a little before stepping cautiously nearer to battle again.

The elf smiled. He lunged forward. The man was more prepared this time, though, and they parried and countered several times before the upstart backed away to circle the arena.

Each watched the other closely. Daerlot was aware of the man's strength and skill. The man was agile and quick on his feet. Daerlot knew he had only been able to down him because his quick attack had caught him off guard. But he knew the man to be a warrior despite his denials and evasions. He knew too many things about this man. He had to stay wary.

"I wonder, my lord. Why do you allow the girl to stay here when you dislike humans so?" the healer asked. Just then he sprang forward, his weapon coming crashing down over Daerlot's sudden upward block. Another clash downward, then a stroke from the side. Then the man brought his sword in again from the other side.

Daerlot spun away. He brought his sword across, ricocheting off the man's counterattack. The elf stepped back. They circled each other.

"I have the highest regard for humans, healer," Daerlot said pointedly.

He swept his hands wide in a mock bow. Then he attacked again. Steel clanged. The man skittered to the side, then lunged forward. He flitted to the other side and lunged again.

"Well, you don't like me."

Daerlot plunged his weapon toward the center of the man's chest. The man jumped sideways so the blade could not hit its deadly mark. Still, the sword caught on his shirt, slicing through like butter. The elf backed away.

"You are very observant." He could not keep from smiling.

The man fingered the hole in his shirt.

"Touché," he said, looking back.

Daerlot nodded. But the man matched his smile and his eyelids lowered. His advance was slow and deliberate. Suddenly Daerlot felt like he was being stalked.

The elf barely had time to react. Soon the clattering of swords was near deafening. Without his heightened perception, he feared he would be hard pressed to keep up. As it was, Daerlot didn't have time to think; he could only react, his inborn survival instinct taking over.

His aged arms were beginning to ache, but still the human did not let up. The determination on the man's face told Daerlot the healer had something to prove.

The patriarch found himself grappling to keep his ground. He kept falling further and further back. Now each pounding with the sword vibrated up his arms. He clenched his teeth and searched for an opening. He found none.

A swift blow came in from the side, followed by one careening overhead. With his weapon still high in the air, he sensed an assault coming in from the other side. Daerlot jumped out of the way. Not realizing he had gotten so far over, he ran into the large chopping block used for firewood. He teetered to gain his balance, but before he could, he felt hard steel hook behind his right foot. Next thing he knew, Daerlot was flat on his back in the dust, the tip of a sword dangling in his face.

"Other than besting you on your own ground," the healer said, shaking out his injured arm. He leaned down, propping his foot on the chopping block. "What reason have you to dislike me, your grace?"

The patriarch looked past the deadly weapon in his face to the young man's challenging grin. It was a look very similar to what Daerlot usually received from the young pup whenever the elf tried to steer him away from his growing affection for Adianna. It was a look that made him worry about the safety of his village. And it was a look that brought on his vision, foretelling the man's current path's future. Scenes of a vision, hidden from his sister and niece, but etched in his own mind. Adianna crying inconsolably. His son, Tarron, sheathed in anger. Elves divided in battle. And Memsy… *Oh, my sweet Memsy.*

Emotion stung Daerlot's eyes, and he swallowed the lump forming in his throat before he was overcome to stare at the young upstart. "You will destroy my family."

The gloating drained from the man's face like water through a sieve. Daerlot could not mistake the hurt and anxiety he saw in those blue eyes. The man backed away slowly; then he staggered further, turning. His sword hung down, slicing a small trail in the dirt. He dragged his feet a few paces but stopped. With his shoulders slouched, the victor now looked the defeated.

Daerlot got to his feet and slowly dusted himself off. The silent Relyat looked from him to the human and away. No one said anything.

The patriarch felt the need to go over to the man, to console him, to say something. But before he could reach out to place his hand on the man's shoulder, Adianna came skipping through the door.

She came up short though, looking around. Her gaze lingered on the healer before finding Daerlot's eye.

"What happened?" she asked softly.

Daerlot wanted to speak, to shrug off his guilt somehow. Instead, he just looked over to the man who still had his back to them.

Slowly the man turned to Adianna. He put a smile on his face that didn't reach his eyes.

"All is well," he said gently.

He studied the girl's face for a moment, then looked to Daerlot.

"Thank you for the sparring, your grace. It was… helpful."

The two stared at each other. Though they said nothing, there was an understanding that silently passed between them.

Daerlot pursed his lips, not letting his pity escape, and nodded.

With a heavy sigh, the man extended a hand to Adianna. "Shall I walk you home?"

She responded with a slow smile and stepped over to him.

"Thank you, Dala. I'll see you tomorrow," she said over her shoulder, then nodded to Relyat. "My Lord."

The healer brushed his hand over the back of her cloak but did not make further contact with her. The man braced the sword against the chopping block as he passed. Daerlot watched the man peek back over his shoulder before he led Adianna around the corner. He detected apprehension in the man's glance, then they were gone.

Daerlot's jaw flexed, and he drew in a deep breath. Unhurriedly, he turned to his remaining companion, the air tumbling from his chest.

Relyat's lips were pursed, but his eyes were sad. "You shouldn't have told him anything, Daerlot. He isn't malicious. And his future is not set."

"I know."

He looked back to where the couple had disappeared. A new vision clouded over his mind. The healer was just a boy, clinging to a woman's waist. The boy had his face buried in her skirts, hard sobs racking his body.

Broken tree limbs scattered the ground. The sky was dark behind them. At their feet sat a nest and three baby birds lying lifeless.

A few more scenes flitted into Daerlot's view, but he closed his eyes to them. With head bowed, he whispered again, "I know."

LEAVING

It can't be true! Everything within him screamed it couldn't be true. Not again. He could not possibly be the cause of another family's breakdown. Not when he'd tried so hard. Not when he'd done everything in his power to stay clear of such situations. He could not go through that again.

The old man must be bluffing. *He just doesn't want me around his niece. That has to be it.*

Kendrick glanced over at the beautiful girl walking next to him. He still had his hand poised behind her back, whether to direct her or protect her, he wasn't sure. He let his hand fall to his side. They walked in silence, despite the concerned look on her face. It was evident she had no clue what had transpired while she'd been absent. He was sure she could have heard the clanging of metal while they sparred, but if she had heard what the patriarch had foretold, would she have come with him so willingly?

Just then Adianna caught him watching her. Her eyebrows were scrunched together as she strained to comprehend. Yet she gave him a small smile to comfort his fears.

Kendrick went back to staring at the ground. *This can't be happening.* Not when he finally had feelings for someone kind, someone real. She was too much of what he desired. She was too much of what he had longed for. She was too much of what he dreamed of. And this was just the beginning. They had just barely started getting to know each other, to feel something for each other. Who knew where it might lead? How could some overprotective elf possibly know anything concerning their relationship, which was even so new to them?

No! It cannot possibly be true!

"So," Kendrick blurted out. "Does the patriarch have many daughters?"

Adianna seemed taken aback by the random query. "No... actually, he hasn't any. Just a son who is presently away from the village."

Well, there you go. How can I have any effect on Daerlot's son?

"And how does one become patriarch of the village?"

She seemed even more confused at this new line of questioning, but she answered, "When the previous patriarch passes on, the whole village gathers and votes on a new one."

"And what were your uncle's qualifications that encouraged the whole village to vote him in?"

Her eyebrows rose high on her forehead. "I assume it was because he is kind and compassionate. He views a problem from all angles and points of view as the Council strives for a decision in unison before making any change. Though he is wise, he frequently looks to others for their wisdom on matters, as he knows he is often led by his emotions."

Ah-ha! Now we're getting somewhere.

"And, of course, there is also the fact that he receives frequent visions of the past and future."

Kendrick stopped short, and his heart sank to a deep, dark pit in his stomach.

Well, that is that. I am doomed.

If the patriarch could see the future, it left no room for doubt. A knot quickly built in that swirling pit of fear.

Adianna turned to face him, her concern evident. He wanted so much to reach out and pull her to him. To spend more time with this amazing woman, to see where it might lead, to see if they had a future together. But apparently the only future he could have with her would be to destroy her family. He could not do that to her.

She placed her gloved hand on his arm and rubbed it ever so slightly, the gesture so sweet, so endearing, despite the metal gloves. Those silly gloves that he would never discover why she wore.

He gave her a halfhearted smile and motioned for them to keep walking. Yet he stumbled on in a daze.

A piece of him tried to make himself think he didn't care a flip for the old man and his family, but he knew it to be a lie. Family mattered too much to him for him to flout it—regardless of whose. And even though he didn't know how or why, these elves were definitely Adianna's family. Apparently, her only family. He simply could not do that to her. He cared too much.

Kendrick again let his gaze fall upon this woman next to him. She was so beautiful. So innocent. Yet she had a strength about her he could not deny nor fathom. To look at her made him instantly want to protect her, and yet she trained in species warfare and weaponry. The more pieces he found to her puzzle left him more in awe and realizing there was so much more he wanted to know. He had never, ever met anyone like her, and every fiber of his soul told him he never, ever would find another. Even if he lived for centuries.

"How about, after I get my chores done, I take you beyond the village and teach you how to talk to the braidocs?" Adianna's face beamed.

With her dancing a sidestep next to him, her enthusiasm was contagious. It warmed his heart to know she was trying to cheer him up. But he couldn't allow himself to be drawn in. He had to break ties—and quickly—or he might lose his nerve.

Kendrick saw the pygmies milling near the Sanctuary.

"Actually, I think I'm going to go talk to Puffin for a while."

"I could come with you. I must collect water anyway."

"I... already collected water for you. And gathered your eggs."

At the endearing smile he saw on her face, Kendrick now chastised himself for the service he had performed earlier. He had wanted to do something special for her. Something to make her smile. And doing her chores would allow her to spend more time with him, which was exactly what he had wanted this morning. Now he felt like a cad for leading her on.

"But you run along anyway. I'm sure Memsy has something for you to do. I'm going to be pretty busy after I tell Puffin goodbye."

Adianna stumbled to a halt, her eyes growing wider by the second.

He couldn't meet her gaze.

"Goodbye?"

"Yeah, I need to head out first thing in the morning." He felt like a coward, and his shoulders raised to shield him from the hurt he saw on her face.

"You're leaving? But I… where? When… will you be back?"

He could hear the catch in her voice. He felt like a fist clamped around his throat. He stuffed his hands in his pockets and looked away so he wouldn't reach out for her.

"I… won't be back." At that, Kendrick moped off toward the dragons, leaving his heart behind.

Memsy silently tiptoed into her room. The light from the dying fire in the main room cast her shadow in an unearthly form across the bed. She could just perceive the outline of her daughter under the covers. The girl's breathing was so steady it couldn't be heard.

Good! The nightmares haven't started yet. Maybe they are over for a time. She hoped.

Memsy was often able to stem the onslaught if she could get her thoughts into Adianna's head before they got too bad.

The young woman had started getting nightmares nearly four years previous. They were ever changing but vivid in their devastation. They hadn't figured out any pattern to when or for how long they transpired. Yet they always resulted in the poor girl taking on the Blades quest alone—and failing.

With a sigh, Memsy closed the door. She was so tired from staying up the last two nights until Adianna was asleep, then getting up before she awakened. But it couldn't be helped. Memsy knew she had to keep the girl at bay until she could sort through all she had been taking in about the stranger. Then she could pack it all away into the corners of her mind where Adianna wouldn't be able to reach them, even if the child went probing while Memsy slept.

Yet another sigh passed her lips. She lit a small spark in her hand to see by. Silently, she tottered over to a small table adjacent to the built-in bureau of her room. On the table was a small metal dish. She placed her cupped hand by it, and the cool, yellow-orange flame leapt over to the dish. It burned continuously while the sorci doffed her dress and leggings for a long nightshirt.

While pulling the nightgown into place, Memsy let her mind wander over the events of the past few days. The many walks in the woods she took to keep her thoughts to herself. And the stranger.

She recognized the young man from a vision Daerlot had had many years ago. Her brother adamantly stated this man was not the one, but Memsy knew he was trying to convince himself more than her. She knew Dala was simply scared. So was she; the man would mean Adianna's quest would soon begin. And all the depravities she had wished to spare from the child could now become all too real, especially if it failed.

Tenderly, Memsy took in the mound on the bed. How she longed to stroke those auburn waves hidden somewhere under the quilt. But she couldn't. She had to sort some things out, and she couldn't have the child seeing her thoughts… or her plans.

This stranger. What was Memsy to do about him?

He was becoming genuinely smitten with Adianna to be sure. *Not like the others*, he kept telling himself time and time again. This had worried Memsy at first—after all, who would turn their daughter over to a philandering cur? But the images he conjured were of simpleton country girls, even pampered and papered ladies, all swaggering after *him*.

No, with the obvious disdain he held for those images, she had no doubt he had left them all willingly, with their virtue intact. But would he be so gallant if Adianna were turned over to his care, even for a short while? If not, would his ardor be cooled when the girl screamed in pain at even his gentlest touch?

Memsy shook herself. Leave it to her to waste time with motherly concerns when the fate of the world hung in the balance. What she should be asking herself was if this healer would take on the challenge or desert responsibility? Would he forsake his duty as he had before? Or was he even the one?

Memsy thought of how kind and caring the man had been to Adianna over just the last twenty-four hours alone. Could he really be the shirker Daerlot thought him to be?

Yes, Dala had seen some very disturbing visions since the stranger arrived. But his visions were rather subject to present course and beliefs and had been sporadic in this case. Still, Memsy, more than anyone, knew the visions could be swayed ever so slightly by Daerlot's own prejudices and fears. He wanted to get rid of the young man, to be sure. Yet she was unsure as to whether his motives were to spare Adianna an improper union, which would alert all of Sheorae to her whereabouts, or if he merely desired to keep her their little girl as long as possible.

Memsy really couldn't blame him for that. Adianna had been the breath of spring to their family all these years and had been the fount of her own only true happiness after centuries of loneliness.

At least they didn't have to rely on Darelot's visions alone. But if they did happen to be accurate…

The scenes trickled through her mind, unbidden, until she could take them no more, and she shook her mind free.

With sadness, the sorci reached out to the spark of light still aglow on its perch. The tiny flame leapt to her outstretched hand. With a resigned sigh, she whispered, "We shall see."

With that, she closed her hand around the wee fire, snuffing it. Then she climbed under the covers to claim her few hours of sleep.

Before even getting settled, Memsy realized something was wrong. There was no warmth coming from anywhere on the bed. Instinctively, she felt for her daughter and found only pillows.

Memsy bolted upright in the bed. She splayed her right hand open, igniting flame. Holding the blaze aloft, she searched frantically with her other hand. But the sleeping mound of her daughter truly was a decoy of pillows.

She flung the blankets from her and sprang from the bed. Flinging the door open, she searched every nook and cranny of the front room.

Where could she possibly be at this time of night?

Memsy stilled the panic trying to creep up her throat. *No, she has to be here somewhere. But where?*

Memsy closed her eyes and began to reach out with her mind. No thoughts could be heard. Just quiet sobbing and the sensation of pain. Panic again lurched within her.

It's coming from this way. Memsy stepped purposefully to Adianna's room, now occupied by the stranger.

She saw the door was cracked open. Ever so gently, she pushed on it. She held the flame alongside the wall of the room she occupied and quietly peeked within.

That room was bathed in soft moonlight teaming through the window. A covered shape slept within the shadows of the large bed built into the opposite wall. And there on the floor next to the bed sat Adianna, her shoulders hunched, her body quietly swaying. She had one hand clamped over her mouth. The other hid under the covers touching the sleeping shadow.

"Adianna!"

Not caring if she woke the stranger, Memsy pushed through the door, throwing the flame from her hand behind her to the hearth of the front room. The fire blazed to life in the hearth, illuminating the bedroom through the doorway. Memsy was on her knees next to Adianna's quaking form. She brushed the mass of hair aside to find the girl's tear-streaked face frozen in pain. The girl's eyes flew open at being touched, yet, despite the panic, they seemed glassy and unseeing.

"Oh, my baby." Memsy took the heart-shaped face in her hands. "What are you doing?"

Adianna pulled her trembling hand from her mouth, her eyes closed again. "It's almost done." She got out through clenched teeth.

Memsy looked at the girl's hand hidden beneath the quilt and understood. Still, she gently pulled the girl's arm away. She tucked Adianna's head under her chin and gathered the child in her arms. So softly she cradled the quivering form to her chest, shushing and cooing as she had when the girl was teeny. She pressed her cheek against her dear one's head and rocked ever so slightly.

When Adianna's sobs finally quieted, Memsy drew the girl up and guided her into the next room. She pulled the door closed behind them but didn't let it clasp. Then she led them to the settee to sit and hold her.

"Now, my love. What is going on?"

The girl's shoulders quivered a couple times before her soft voice shakily replied, "He's leaving."

Oh, my sweetheart. Memsy's arm around her daughter's shoulders instinctively drew her closer. "Did he say when or why?"

Adianna sniffled and lifted her hand to wipe the back of it against her moist nose. "Tomorrow. First thing. He didn't say why. Just he wasn't coming back."

Memsy noticed her daughter's hand, curled over and red from trying to hasten the stranger's healing. The burns Adianna accrued from contact with males of her species tended to scorch the surface of her skin without going too deep, but the heat often lingered as if it did. Memsy scooped up the girl's hand in hers. She made the gathering symbol in the air above the delicate skin to draw the heat out, then gently blew across it. The smooth hand quivered under the cooling air.

Memsy peeked through her lashes at her daughter's puckered face, her upper lip clenched between her teeth. The elf did not need to read minds to know the agony on her face was more than the pain of her flesh.

"And do you want him to stay?" she urged ever so softly.

Adianna's face crinkled and turned away. But not before Memsy saw the quivering lip and the tears which fell.

Memsy tilted her head to see the girl's face better and asked, "Did you ask him to stay?"

"What's the point?!" Adianna flung her arms out and sprang to her feet, tromping to the middle of the floor, where she spun to attack. "He doesn't want to stay. Dala doesn't want him to stay. He doesn't belong here. Even Puffin wants him to leave. So, what's the point?"

She hugged her arms around herself and turned to stare at the fire. The dancing light illuminated her face. Memsy watched as the girl drew both her lips between her teeth, as she did whenever her heart wanted something other than what her words shared.

Memsy came to her feet and moved to her precious little girl, who was now so much a woman in every way. Her hand skimmed along her daughter's shoulder. "But did *you* ask him to stay?"

Adianna's face turned to the ceiling then flopped to the side. "What's the point, Mother? He doesn't want me."

The crack in her voice was unmistakable.

Memsy gathered the girl's arms in her hands, turning her toward her. She maneuvered her head to catch her daughter's eye. "You don't know that. But what you do know is that you deeply care for this man. Don't you?"

Adianna rolled her eyes to look past the other side of her mother's head and held herself more tightly. "What does it matter?"

Memsy's hands dropped to her sides. "What does it matter? Quite frankly, my dear, it's the only thing that *does* matter."

Adianna turned again to the fire with a scuff of her foot. "But what about the village? He doesn't belong here. And then there's the quest. I mean, eventually that's going to have to start. What will I do with this love then?"

An ancient sadness crept over Memsy's heart. One that few knew besides herself.

She again took her daughter by the arms and turned her to face her. She did not speak until she could look Adianna squarely in the eyes, then pointedly replied, "You take it with you."

She wasn't sure if her daughter caught the gravity of that statement until little ridges formed between her eyebrows, and keeping eye contact, her mouth worked as if many questions came tumbling to her mind at once.

"But Dala doesn't think…"

Memsy threw her hands in the air and turned from her daughter. "Oh, Dala, Shmalla. He doesn't always know the future. Half the time he doesn't even know what he's talking about."

She turned back to Adianna and snapped her fingers. "But I know who does."

She waited until she could see the question on her daughter's face, then she slowly turned her eyes to the far corner of the room. There, in the corner, was a bench covered by folded furs and linens which housed a secret chest.

Adianna had followed her mother's gaze, and now as Memsy peered back at her, the girl's eyes got wide. They turned to Memsy before she moved her head. Her mouth gaped.

"Oh, no. You can't possibly mean…"

But Memsy was already nodding her head to the affirmative. "Absolutely. Puffin and the girls would be able to tell us instantly if a viable Mentaloss were nearby."

"But Mems. But what if it isn't…?"

Memsy shrugged. "Then we'll know that, too."

She looked into her daughter's eyes, pursing her lips against the sadness. She let her palms skim the girl's upper arms before taking her hands into her own. She cupped them between hers, one beneath, the other patting on top. Memsy stared at the delicate fingers she had held so often over the last fourteen years. And before the sense of loss overtook her, she clung to the feeling inside which told her this was the right course of action.

"My dear, sweet, blessed child. You are now a grown woman. You have trained. You have studied. You have matured in all areas necessary for you to take on this quest. Except in matters of the heart. It's the only thing left."

She glanced over at the door to the adjoining room. She patted the girl's hands again, and with a smile, said, "He is an honorable man."

Her voice cracked, and it took a couple swallows before she could continue. "I know what Dala has seen. But I have heard and seen this man's heart. And I know yours."

Her hand cupped Adianna's cheek. She felt a tear escape her lashes and trickle down. Still, she smiled lovingly into the younger woman's eyes. "Love is what makes a True Alliance. No weapons, training, or legions can replace that."

The young woman's eyes searched hers until apprehension was replaced with trust and conviction. Her lips compressed, then she gave Memsy a quick nod.

She patted the girl's arm and smiled. "Okay. You go gather the pygmies, and I will get the Blades."

Then they separated to their tasks.

Kendrick awoke begrudgingly, unwilling to rise through the thick haze which clouded his brain. The fog surrounding his mind seemed denser than normal. Still, he had enjoyed the dream. He had been dreaming of forest nymphs and wood sprites, many with wavy, auburn hair and penetrating green eyes.

Did I really hear dragons roaring?

Forgotten images from his youth of playing outside the walls of the dragon hatchery emerged to mingle with those of the dream. Dainty sprites pulled jewel-colored hatchlings from their shells. His parents called for him to return to his studies. Green-eyed nymphs rode on dragons sporting flowing, burnished locks.

Wait a minute! That's not right.

As if rising out of a mist in the early morning, he became aware of voices from unseen persons in the next room. Though in hushed tones, Kendrick recognized Memsy's voice. "Adianna, you know it is time, child."

Through his sleepiness he heard the young woman respond, the strain of suppressed tears in her voice.

"I knew it would come, but why now? And him?"

Kendrick came to full attention, and he strained to listen more intently.

"We don't even know him. How do we know he will even go?"

Are they talking about me? Go where?

"Don't worry, sweetheart," Memsy soothed. "It is time, and he has come. Dala has said the signs are there. And that one was unmistakable. He has his choice, but he will do this, you will see. And you… sleep, my love. You are ready. You have prepared for this nearly your whole life."

Prepared for what? Kendrick pushed himself up in bed quietly trying to move his ear closer to the door. *What are they talking about? What signs?* So many questions, and every fiber in his body strained to hear some answers.

"Centuries could not prepare me for this," the girl muttered, nearly unheard by Kendrick. "But I don't want to go. Not now. Not like this."

Kendrick could not help his heart being pulled toward her plight. He knew all too well the turmoil that must be boiling within her. He too had been pushed to do things he did not want to do, tasks forced upon him, quests that were not his own, until finally he had walked away from everything. And never looked back.

"My love." The concern in Memsy's voice was compassionate and genuine. "You will not be alone. You know that! This is your destiny. And I will be with you, at least in the beginning."

Kendrick saw a shadow pass by the fire. Ducking back onto the pillow, he feigned sleep, though still labored to hear. All that reached his ears was some inaudible murmurings and a few muffled sobs. Finally, Memsy could be heard again.

"Come, my love," she said. "Let's get you to bed. No more worries tonight. All will be as it should."

Another shadow passed across the doorway. The light extinguished from the room beyond without a sound and was followed shortly after by the soft click of a door shutting. Silence fell over the humble cottage. Bathed in moonlight, Kendrick was left to speculate, while the quiet padding of beasts meandered away outside.

PAYMENT

The next morning dawned bright and brilliant. Light funneling in through the round window could barely be contained in such a tiny bedroom. Birds twittered outside, beaconing him to come and join them. Yet, Kendrick found he was slow of motion and enthusiasm. He knew he must get moving. He needed to be heading out as soon as possible. But... he didn't want to.

He didn't want to leave the peace of this place. He didn't want to leave without unlocking some of the mysteries he had detected. He especially didn't want to leave Adianna—all of which he may never regain the opportunity for again.

Within him, he felt so much heaviness in so many places, it made him feel so very tired. Then there was the event last night. He still wasn't sure who they were talking about or what any of it meant. He just knew they were expecting Adianna to do something she longed to get out of. That made another sensation lurch inside him and settle with a growl in his chest.

So many emotions warring inside. So much still unknown. Would it be too much of a stretch to think these battling emotions could lead to the destruction of yet another family? Another growl escaped him, and he flung back the covers.

Sitting up, Kendrick draped his legs over the side of the bed then strived to stretch away the cares from the night before. Still, his curiosity would not let him shake the feeling they *had* been discussing him—specifically him *doing* something.

He launched himself off the side of the bed. *If they were talking about me, I shall discover what's going on soon enough*, he told himself, trying to dismiss it.

He frowned as he saw his clothes, remembering the previous day. He knew he had hurt Adianna. He had hurt himself in the process. Then he spent the rest of the day avoiding her. Yet trying to gather provisions to supplement the ones that had gone untouched in his pack the last few days while trying to dodge her *and* her uncle had been draining. Then there had been last night.

He jerked on his pants, annoyed his thoughts had whipped back around to that so quickly.

The frown continued while he stuffed his things into his pack and lingered until there was a knock on the door. He tensed at the sound. He had wanted to leave before he had to face Adianna. He cussed her, himself, the whole situation. Propping himself against the wall containing the built-in bed, he folded his arms across his chest and beckoned the visitor to enter.

Memsy peeked her head through the door. This both relieved and surprised him, and he stepped forward to greet her. He seemed to never cease opening to the combination of the genuine smile and curious eyes which she ever wore.

"Good morning," she beamed. "I was hoping you would be up. It is a beautiful day, and I was wondering if you might wish to get out in it?"

"Actually, I was just gathering my things so I may head out within the hour. I have benefited from your hospitality long enough."

She eyed his packed bag on the bed and the sword leaning against it. Yet she gazed back at him with a winning smile. "Travel can always wait when you have nowhere particular to go. Come along. The morning calls to us. Besides, I have something to discuss with you."

Kendrick turned to the window to hood his response, which was both irksome that she somehow knew he had nowhere to go and satisfying since he might get some answers.

"I was hoping to get out into that delicious sunshine," he said, turning back to his hostess and extending his arm to her.

She stepped forward with a brilliant smile, and the two left the room.

Memsy led him to the outskirts of the village, then turned to walk the perimeter. She seemed to know instinctively where the edge of the elvin defenses lay. Yet occasionally, he would sidestep a little too far, and everything elvish would disappear except the arm that clung to his while they walked.

The two of them meandered the border in silence for several minutes. The woman seemed to truly be enjoying the clear, bright morning. He couldn't help smiling along with her. He so often felt such contentment in her presence, and he would miss it.

Memsy turned her gaze to him. "You don't have much contentment anymore now, do you, Master Healer?"

Kendrick stopped abruptly to stare at her. She had used the exact word he had been thinking! Then he noticed the silvery symbol on her forehead was shimmering ever so slightly. He cocked an eyebrow. *I am going to have to watch my thoughts around you, aren't I?*

Memsy flashed another bright smile.

He snickered a bit but continued their sojourn. He should feel exposed under the circumstances—but not with Memsy. He patted his hand over hers still tucked in his arm.

"No. Contentment has been a stranger for me, m'lady."

"It must have been hard—wandering from region to region, always on the move. Never settling down. Never making… connections."

He eyed her askance. *You just described my life these last four years.*

Memsy's pursed mouth dug into her cheeks. She shrugged and conceded, "Sounds lonely."

Unsure whether she was answering his thoughts or merely continuing her own, Kendrick stared quietly forward. What could he say? She was right.

"And where will you go now?"

He drew in a deep breath and let it out very slowly. He let the pause build because he truly didn't know. He had been headed to Lenchur, the goblin region, when he was attacked. The goblins, there on the outskirts, occasionally accepted some of his skills in the fall in exchange for autonomy and lodgings. But there wasn't anywhere he really *had* to be. In the beginning, that had been thrilling—to go where he wanted, when he wanted, with no one having demands on his time. But now...

No response was forthcoming, but it wasn't needed. Memsy patted his bicep knowingly. They continued on in silence.

They curved the western edge of the village and were heading east along the northern ridge when the elf spoke. "I wish to ask a favor of you, young man."

Instantly, Kendrick's curiosity was piqued. He eyed her without turning his head.

Memsy smiled, and it made him wonder how often she manipulated others to get what she wanted.

The experienced woman chuckled but carried on with her train of thought. "Since traveling is what you do, I was wondering if you would accompany my daughter and me to Ooflic?"

That caught him off guard. Why would she want him to accompany them? Wouldn't she know her brother's thoughts and visions, too? Why would she want him to remain with her family if he was destined to destroy it? Plus, he was afraid staying around Adianna would just make it all the harder for both of them when he finally did leave. He had caught the young woman's tortured expression before she hid it behind her hair, when he and Memsy left the cottage. He knew he couldn't be near her and continue to shun her company. It upset him too much to see her hurting. But he couldn't stay. Not with those visions hanging over his every move.

The woman on his arm said nothing, but her deep sigh warned Kendrick she was apprised of his current thoughts. So, she didn't seem surprised when he simply said, "I can't."

"I see," she replied. "But I am afraid it is what I require as payment."

Kendrick halted. He sensed a trap. "Payment for what?"

"The rescue and healing you received after your attack."

Did she just bat her eyes?

"You know as well as I that I would have healed just fine without your help."

"Not if Adianna would have let the dalphene kill you," she countered bluntly, still smiling.

He knew she had him there. Even though he was pretty sure of who the dalphene was *and* what she wanted, he wouldn't put it past her to over-dramatize her petty grievance. And even if she would have left him out there half dead, there were still the orgrins.

He was about to concede, but he glanced sidelong at his companion and caught a smugness creeping into her smile. That brought his chin up a notch or two.

"These are dangerous times, sorci. Two women, of any species, shouldn't be out traveling."

"Precisely why we need an escort, Master Healer." Her eyebrows rose, indicating she thought his statement absurd.

"Now I know where Adianna gets her snarkiness." Why hold back his thoughts when she could hear them anyway?

Memsy just smiled, raising her eyebrows innocently.

"With what your brother thinks of me, why on Sheorae would you want me to join you on a journey?"

A sadness crept into her eyes, but he couldn't tell if it were for her brother or for him. "My brother can only see shadows of what *might* be if present courses are continued. We always have our agency."

He felt relief at this response. *Maybe there was hope for them then—a chance.* But as his thoughts veered to a certain young woman, Memsy's reference to agency irked him.

"What is so important to make you travel so far and in the direction of the Dead Lands?" he asked her, straight-faced again.

"Adianna has business there," was her only reply.

This surprised him, and he didn't try to hide it. "What business could that delightful young thing possibly have in Ooflic?" He chuckled.

She stared flatly into his eyes. "She must marry."

It was like a punch in the gut. "What?" He coughed.

She continued to stare, tight-lipped.

Something began percolating deep in his innards. "To whom?" His voice sounded rough even to himself.

"It has been arranged."

He had never seen her so emotionless. What had percolated threatened to boil over.

"What about agency?" he roared. "Does she even know him?"

Memsy shrugged. "She actually knows very little about him."

She stepped forward then and placed her hand compassionately on his arm. "I understand your concern, but she really comprehends far more of what is to transpire than you realize."

She obviously meant this to reassure him. It did the opposite.

He turned from the sorci. A full-fledged rage rumbled within him. *How could they be doing this to her? Were they heartless? Marrying her off like so much breeding stock! Was it because they were elves and she was human?* But Kendrick knew that wasn't it. He, himself, had been destined for similar arrangements, which was part of why he'd left.

No, it must be some kind of politics, he fumed. His mind raced through all the vermin he had seen use such arrangements to prey on under-privileged beauties and political heiresses. The selfishness exhibited by all involved except the victim. Only this time, his Adianna would be the victim!

His fists clenched. His breath grew hot. Protectiveness mingled with possessiveness rumbled through his core. He didn't know who this man was, but he wanted to kill him. But he had no right. Well, mostly he had no way. No way to get his hands on that sniveling, slimy, no-good… unless…

Kendrick turned swiftly back to the sorci. Her eyes were wide, watching him intently. Her swirling, shimmering emblem had not relaxed.

He didn't even try to mask his determination. Just pinned her with his menacing glare and said, "I'll do it."

THE PARTING CEREMONY

When Kendrick was asked to participate in their sacred Elvin Parting Ceremony, he was honored. But he never expected the turn of events.

Within the hallowed walls of the Sanctuary, at its very epicenter, he now stood inside the Great Hall, which surpassed anything Kendrick had ever seen before. The size, the shape, even the hues of the walls were awe-inspiring. And it seemed as if the massive, domed room had been made first and then the Sanctuary built around it.

But what impressed him more than the room was what filled it. It appeared these elvin ceremonies were a pretty big deal, for the whole village seemed to have come. Even the three pygmy dragons ambled around on the dais across the room from where he stood.

Kendrick folded his arms across his chest. He looked around at the unfamiliar faces. He tucked his hands into his pockets and kicked at the floor with his toe. After a few moments, he settled back into folding his arms once again.

Frequently, he caught sight of the patriarch through the crowd of people milling around between them. To him, it appeared as if Daerlot were pacing like a caged animal. The grand elf recurrently glanced toward the doors, often sending a scathing glare his way.

Good! Kendrick thought. *Let him be mad. I'm not the one who arranged away Adianna's life. You can glare at me all you want! At least I'm trying to protect the trusting young woman! Not using her as a pawn.*

His jaw clenched. *Where is she anyway?*

He returned curious stare after curious stare from the crowd. Kendrick twirled his ring absently around his middle finger.

Presently, a hand came down on his shoulder. He jerked around to see Memsy's beaming face. He opened his mouth to greet her, but then Adianna stepped up just beyond her, and the sorci was forgotten.

Adianna was stunning. Kendrick could not remember seeing anyone who took his breath away. Yet it happened now.

The young woman, her auburn hair softly twisted away from her face with mounds of curls cascading over one shoulder, was adorned in her usual shamere cloak with one side folded back over her other shoulder to reveal a hunter green gown. Though modest in design and sleek in cut, the dress was embellished with intricate embroidery of silver and gold thread. Matching ribbons wove through the twists in her hair. A ring of daisies crowned her head.

She stood with her hands demurely clasped before her. Adianna's gaze timidly searched his face. He wasn't sure just what she saw there, but it was enough to make her blush and look away. It simply made her look that much more desirable.

He started, the forgotten sorci patting his arm.

"I must speak with my brother before we get started. May I leave my daughter here with you?" Memsy looked rather amused waiting for an answer.

Kendrick cleared his throat before trusting his voice. "Yes, of course."

She nodded, still eyeing him with amusement. "It will just be a moment. When I motion for you, bring her forward so you both stand before Daerlot for the ceremony. Alright?"

He agreed, then watched Memsy reach over to cup a hand along Adianna's face. The uncertainty in the young woman's eyes warred with the tenderness and trust she could not hide. Memsy's thumb caressed her daughter's cheek. Then she turned.

"I'll just be a moment. Watch for my cue."

The lovely woman at his side watched her mother walk away. Or was she avoiding looking at him? Regardless of the reason, Adianna's gaze was distinctly directed away from him.

"You look very beautiful," he offered, trying to encourage those emerald eyes to rest upon him again. Which they did—wide and beguiling. Another blush touched her cheeks.

"Thank you," she whispered but quickly averted her gaze.

Kendrick smiled in response. His mood uplifted, he turned once more to survey the room, looking for some way to engage her in conversation.

"This ceremony must be pretty important around here for everyone to show up like this."

Adianna turned to him rather perplexed. "But of course… Isn't it everywhere?"

Kendrick shrugged. "No, not really. It just happens and people move on with their lives."

Across the spacious room, he caught sight of Memsy and Daerlot in a rather heated discussion. Daerlot was leaning down into Memsy's face to where they were nearly nose to nose. She, in turn, was jabbing a finger into his chest.

"But in Fal Dura when people have gotten…"

"Whoa!" Kendrick blurted out, reaching for Adianna's arm. "Did you see that?"

"What?" Adianna sounded even more puzzled than before. Still, she looked in the direction he indicated.

"The sorci was standing there with her arms folded glaring up at your uncle, when all of a sudden, a pulse of energy came from her forehead and smacked him in the face!"

Now the patriarch stumbled back, blinking, stunned, shaking his head. Memsy pointed at him again and said something undetectable across the noisy hall.

Kendrick chuckled, folding his arms in front of him. *That should serve him!* Kendrick figured Memsy was just as indignant about this whole situation as he was.

The sorci gave Daerlot one last scathing glare, jabbing her finger at him once more. She let her threat sink in but a moment, then turned to the congregation. Beaming a brilliant smile, she raised her hands high in the air, and with a flick of her wrists, signaled everyone to take their places. A hush fell across the enormous room, and the crowd parted.

Memsy's gaze then landed upon Kendrick. With a nod, she motioned him forward.

Kendrick held out his arm to Adianna. She stood there, nibbling her bottom lip. Her eyes searched his, unsure.

Don't worry, my dear. I will protect you. There is nothing to fear.

Kendrick conveyed this with a smile. He gave her a quick wink, extending his arm closer.

Adianna searched his face. His heart expanded upon seeing the look of trust dawning there. She squared her shoulders, put her arm upon his, and smiled.

As they came forward, Kendrick noticed Memsy had stepped back, and Daerlot stood alone at the end of the aisle made by the parted crowd. The dragons now stood sentinel on the dais behind him. Each dragon was animated, their thoughts a jumble and a whirlwind of incoherent excitement. But there was no mistake about the patriarch's feelings. If looks could kill, Kendrick knew he'd have already suffered a thousand brutal deaths by now. So, what the dignified elfin leader did next caught him by complete surprise.

Daerlot took a deep breath, closed his eyes, and lifted his face to the heavens. After Kendrick and Adianna had taken but a few steps, the patriarch began bellowing out a beautiful yet mournful chant that reverberated through the entire hall.

Kendrick's jaw fell slack. Never in his life had he heard such a beautiful male voice raised in song. Though the words were in elvish, the immense love and the anguish of parting were unmistakable in the somber melody.

Awestruck, he glanced to Adianna. She, too, was gaping wide-eyed and slack-jawed at her uncle, but the look of shock on her face was unambiguous.

This took him by surprise. But searching the faces of the audience, the perplexing looks were nearly unanimous.

What is going on here?

Daerlot still had his face raised, eyes closed, but a look of peace had come over him. His hands were elevated from the emotion of the song he sang.

When Kendrick and Adianna came to a stop before him, the patriarch slowly opened his eyes. He gazed with love upon his niece, the emotion seeping into the music. He reached for her, to which she let go of Kendrick's arm. Her hand extended to her uncle, and he made a loop around it in the air, before taking her hand in his.

He repeated the gesture with Kendrick's proffered hand before nestling Adianna's within it—all while continuing the mournful song.

He made a small figure eight in the air above their joined hands. Then he cupped their clasped hands and spoke clearly and distinctly in Elvish so all could hear and understand—save Kendrick.

Finally, Daerlot looked to Kendrick and Adianna, in turn, then stepped back, releasing their joined hands. He continued spouting on in Elvish, so Kendrick watched Adianna. His gaze drew hers. What he saw in that heart-shaped face was uncertainty, surely. But something else. Hope?

Suddenly Kendrick's breath halted. Among the gibberish of Elvin words, he somehow picked out two. Words he had come to know in his childhood from those who would come to visit his father. His head snapped to Memsy. The words he recognized were 'husband' and 'wife.'

"Wife?"

But before his temper had time to ignite, the patriarch boomed out, "Great be the union as we join Mentaloss and Durluki for the good of all Sheorae."

Kendrick snapped back to the patriarch. Indignation flared with a vengeance. But he had no more time to react, for a light glowed around him and the girl then shot skyward. Unseen trumpets blared. The sound reverberated off every surface within the domed space. Elves and humans alike covered their ears, cowering from the deafening sound. Before it subsided, the three pigmy dragons settled back on their haunches, extended their wings, and roared to the heavens.

By the time the ear-splitting noise dwindled, Kendrick's indignation had reached a frenzying heat.

"What in Sheorae is going on here?!" he demanded, his voice thunderous.

He looked from Memsy to Daerlot and accused, "What have you done?"

They both gave him no expression nor answer. His searching led him to look to Adianna.

She met his glare, unflinching yet confused. Those emerald eyes were wide, mystified, and fixed on him. Slowly she pulled from behind her what had been concealed under her cloak. With both hands, she presented to him the very things which had truly destroyed his family. The very things which kept him in hiding for four years. The cursed things which had taken his father from him, his brother, his life.

The Blades of Sheorae.

Kendrick flinched back as if zapped. His arm raised in defense. "Get those things away from me!"

"But they are yours to wield, Mentaloss," Adianna said, moving in closer.

Kendrick snarled in her face. "I said, get those things away from me! I am not the Mentaloss!"

He turned on Memsy and Daerlot, pointing back at the cursed object. "Do you have any idea what you have done?" he demanded. "Those things are a curse! They bring death and destruction to anyone stupid enough to touch them, let alone attempt to do any good with them. Pride and greed follow in their wake. It's just another trick the fairies left behind to torment our world and keep our nations at war with each other. Nothing good will ever come of them!"

"Actually," a short elf from the crowd blurted in, raising his hand. "The fairies had nothing to do with them. They were elfin made from dwarven skill passed down through generations of an elfin line after the dwarves left…"

The elf's voice trailed off, realizing his impropriety.

"So, you're all in cahoots? All of you!" Kendrick flung a gesture to include the whole room. "You are all a part of this depravity."

A hand touched his back. He spun away from it, defensive.

"Please, Master Healer," Memsy consoled, but Kendrick would have none of it.

"And you!" Kendrick accused. "You told me she was to be married off."

"And she was… to you."

Kendrick growled. "You said it was arranged."

"And it was." Memsy gestured to her brother. "We arranged the whole ceremony very impromptu."

"Of all the incorrigible, the most conniving, the most deceitful tangle of ogre dung I have even been made a part of!" He railed in her face.

He wanted to scream at her, to rage at everyone there for their betrayal, their trickery. But Daerlot stepped forward to his sister's defense. He was about to spout something, yet something in Kendrick's eyes stopped him. Kendrick could feel the anger pulsing off himself in time with the beat of his rapid heart. He knew from past experience, when in this state, none dared to molest nor make afraid.

But through the tumultuous rage, a timid voice cut through.

"You didn't tell him?" Adianna questioned. "Any of it?"

Memsy merely looked at her hands. Daerlot looked away.

Kendrick fought the tiny relief springing within him at learning that this young enchantress at least had nothing to do with the deception. *Still, it doesn't matter! They all tricked me—into the two things I swore never to meddle with again.*

He turned his anger onto the great patriarch.

"You deceived us both!" he hurled at the stately man standing like a youth caught with a box of matches. But not for long. Kendrick saw the patriarch's indignation flare of its own accord, and he prepared for a fight. Yet what flared in the older gentleman was cut off by a deep, heavy sigh.

Kendrick turned to it. Adianna stepped forward. She squared her shoulders and locked eyes on him with determination and purpose, despite Kendrick's rage.

"I am sorry, Mentaloss—" she addressed him, dipping her head in a slight bow in conjunction with the title, "—for the deception that brought you to this moment. But you have been chosen in this quest to free Sheorae from the hated evil which binds her. Make no mistake about that. We both have."

"This is insane!" Kendrick roared. "I am not the Mentaloss! And you..." He flipped his hand in the young woman's direction. "You cannot possibly be the Durluki. Durluki are men. Do you have any idea what they've gotten us into?"

But Daerlot stepped forward to intercept Kendrick's advance on Adianna. "Master Healer," he said, resting his hand on the angry man's arm.

Kendrick halted in his progress, more by the ancient's tone than his grasp.

"It is the thoughts of men," the patriarch continued, pulling Kendrick around to face him, "who have deemed the role to men alone. But in reality, it is the Blades themselves who do the choosing. Adianna was chosen many years before this day. It is her destiny... as it is now yours."

"You are mad!" Kendrick yanked his arm free from the elfin leader, backing away from them both. "Locked away in your sanctuary for centuries may have kept you from the corruption and carnage which has befallen Sheorae because of those blasted Blades, but you cannot turn a blind eye to this. Those Blades will destroy our world, mark my words."

"But the prophecy..." Adianna stepped toward him, a whimsical smile on her face. "The prophecy speaks only of goodness being the result. Surely, we will face hardships, but if we keep the end in mind..."

"There has been no good!" Kendrick barked, his arm slicing through the air. "Only evil and despair surround those things." He pointed at the Blades in her hands before turning away.

"But..."

Kendrick saw the patriarch step forward and cut off whatever more the girl was going to say. Daerlot rested his hand on Kendrick's shoulder as his voice soothed. "I know you have seen and been through much, Healer. I, myself, have seen this evil that has spread over our land. For many years before you were even born, I have seen it. But I know what lies ahead for us all if this evil is not done away with and done quickly. This journey, which is now before you, is our only hope. The only way for it all to end. Don't you think we owe it to our fathers and their fathers who died in vain?"

Kendrick turned to face this wise ancient. Images and memories started swimming through his mind. So many things he had been trying so hard to forget. He remembered his brother, his father. Men he had looked up to. Men he would have done anything for.

"Don't we owe it to our families to do all we can to make this world safe for them again?"

Families? That thought brought Kendrick crashing back. The flames flared within him. "*You* said I would destroy your family!" Kendrick boomed in retort.

Beyond Daerlot's shoulder, Memsy's face scrunched, but Kendrick's venom was loosed once again.

"You didn't want me to have her." He pointed back toward Adianna. "You didn't want me near her. You did anything and everything you could think of to keep me away from her! You've lied about her future. You've lied about *my* future!"

Kendrick stalked the patriarch, preparing to pounce. The elf squared his shoulders, even though he instinctively took a step backward.

"The conniving it took to lure me here to take on this quest…" The words fell out of his mouth like pieces of festering bone picked loose from his teeth. "That treachery is bad enough. But then, despite all your glares and your lies, you shackle her to me without even the slightest hint of her being a delusional child with aspirations to free the world from the greatest evil she has *never* even seen!"

The crowd gasped behind him, but he didn't care. Their murmurings did not reach his consciousness. He was fuming. He wanted answers, and this old man who got him into it wasn't talking. He just stared forlornly past him.

Kendrick's gaze skipped to Memsy. She was close to tears. But her beseeching eyes were not on him.

Kendrick turned, following her gaze. His rage was doused in an instant. There before him, the girl he had been yelling about stood erect, her head held high. A stately woman now, with dignity and pride, but with glistening emerald eyes.

"Master Mentaloss," she said icily, sinking into a low curtsy. "We will leave within the hour. When you have concluded your temper tantrum, you may meet us out front." Thus dismissed, she nodded to Memsy. "Mother."

He heard her choke on a sob as she turned, tucking the scabbard into the crook of her arm. The sorci fell into step beside her daughter, and they stalked to the great doors. Memsy leaned in to say something to Adianna, but the young woman shook her head and walked on.

Defeated, Kendrick watched her trembling yet majestic march all the way down the corridor and out of sight.

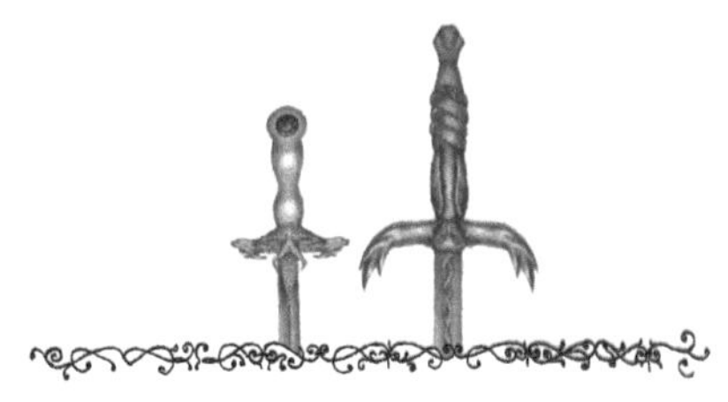

THE JOURNEY BEGINS

The ignominy Adianna had felt over the last quarter-hour had flared into lividity. The whiny warrior came out to the village meadow, followed by Daerlot, shortly after she and Memsy had arrived.

The healer's head slumped forward. He hesitated to meet her eye.

Good! Let him suffer his own *dose of the humiliation he met out to me in front of nearly everyone I've ever known.*

She picked up a travel pack and flipped the top open. She rummaged through it, checking the contents, not really seeing anything. She slapped the flap back into place and yanked the tie harder than was necessary. Flopping it down, she picked up the next pack to repeat the same busy work.

Every once in a while, the healer would glance her way, but she pretended not to notice. How she loathed the man right now!

All his pretty words. All his sentiment and flattery. Apparently, he really is the scoundrel he bantered about being. We should have just let him go!

Why was I so excited just an hour ago? The insufferable man! And he isn't really that good looking after all. I mean who really likes that strong build? That tanned skin? The dimples he cannot hide, even when he's angry? The way his hair tumbles into his eyes as he talks...

When he again looked her way, she realized she was staring at him. Adianna mentally shook herself. *Insufferable man!*

She snapped open the clasp of her cloak and let it fall to the ground. Grabbing the Blades, she looped the holster over her shoulder and into place between her shoulder blades. She fastened the cloak back on, making her cargo nearly imperceptible.

When she glanced again, the Healer's eyes were upon her. The embarrassment he showed earlier melted away even as she watched his jaw work, suppressing some pent-up emotion.

Finally, he could keep it in no longer. He spun around to lash out another tirade at Dala.

"You do realize we are sunk before we begin, don't you? A Union Beacon can be seen and heard for miles! Blade Hunters from all around Sheorae are already assembling and will be here before nightfall—prepared for battle! How am I supposed to protect them?"

Daerlot opened his mouth to respond, but Adianna was quicker.

"I don't need your protection, Healer! I just need you to quit whining and get a move on."

The healer countered on her. "Oh, really? And what of your mother?"

That hit a nerve, which apparently, he could detect.

"You see!" He pointed at her. "None of this was thought through, and now—we all may die."

Adianna spun away from him, folding her arms across her chest. "Insufferable man," she muttered again under her breath.

Memsy stepped past Adianna to intercede. "Actually, Master Healer, since the beacon ignited within the Sanctuary, the magic of Tymalia has displaced its effects. The beacon refracted through each of the pillars, creating not one, but six columns of light, each one illuminating anywhere from thirty to a hundred miles beyond the outskirts of the village in all directions. And most of the trumpeting was channeled underground. So, our whereabouts cannot be pinpointed or even triangulated without great difficulty."

"What?" the healer responded crisply, but before Memsy could explain again, he cut her off. "You know what? It doesn't matter! We have to get moving. And on foot!"

He snatched up his pack and gear, and even though he grumbled under his breath, Adianna heard him plainly say, "Traipsing off to my doom with a bunch of women." He cinched his sword into place. "Well, they better not slow me down."

Adianna's breath halted for just a moment before it seethed out in fumes. If only she could use a jauquist's abilities right then to bore a hole through his middle with her eyes. She took a few calculating steps toward him, planning how best to end his wretched life. She could feel Memsy's eyes on her, almost hear the pleading thoughts in her head to stay calm, but Adianna did not even look her way.

Suddenly a thought came to her. A pleasant smile slowly crossed her face, and it pleased her to see a subtle nervousness settle into the healer's eyes.

Without warning, Adianna twittered a particular whistle. Her smile broadened at the perplexed look on the healer's face.

Just then a beautiful doe emerged from between two cottages nearby and approached her.

"Oh, Adianna," Memsy breathed, disappointment unmistakable in her voice.

But Adianna ignored her, and she stroked the sleek creature's coat. A sinister smile spread over her face as the animal's warmth crept up her arm and tumbled around the core of her being. She closed her eyes when its spinning intensified. The explosion within created only a minor intake of breath, one barely noticeable to the one observing her with mounting reservation.

Adianna smiled sweetly at her animal friend. She placed a farewell kiss upon the doe's muzzle and said, "Good-bye, my dear friend. And thank you."

She flung a withering glance in the healer's direction. Then she gathered up her pack, smiling innocently at Memsy. "Let's go," she grinned.

Heaving a heavy sigh, the older woman bent to pick up her pack and shook her head sadly. Memsy took Adianna's sack, too, and settled it on her other shoulder. Then the young maiden swung the elder one onto her back. Settling Memsy's legs comfortably around her middle, she turned to their onlooker.

She nearly laughed at the bewilderment etched on his face, and with a smirk said, "Try to keep up."

Adianna then bounded off in the opposite direction of the animal she mimicked.

Clinging to the girl's back, Memsy hollered over her shoulder, "Meet us at Warm Springs eight miles from here on the northwest side of the butte."

The dumbfounded healer was soon left far behind.

Warm Springs was a particularly pleasing oasis. Though small as springs go—the waterway it created being only a small stream reaching a mere ten feet at its widest—it had two distinct defining characteristics. The first was the fact its crystal-clear waters burbled right out of a mountainside tumbling and splashing their way over rock and crag to create an aesthetically beautiful waterfall, the likes of which were mostly unknown in Sheorae since the spring resided so far from the road through Kyren Forest. The second characteristic being the fact this freshwater spring stayed the same temperature year-round. A thawing fifty-five degrees in the winter and a numbing fifty-five degrees in summer.

It was at this beautiful spring Memsy now lounged against a rock. Her face tilted to soak in the sun, while her feet dangled in the cool water. Relaxed and calm. Trying to suppress a small smile. For Adianna was pacing like a prowling wild cat.

"I mean, can you believe the audacity of that man? Carrying on and behaving like a spoiled child!"

"We did trick him into this whole ordeal," Memsy pointed out.

Adianna turned briskly. “But that was you and Dala. What does it have to do with me? I had nothing to do with the deception, and yet, he was just as petty and insulting to me as he was to everybody.”

The young woman folded her arms in front of her and began pacing again. Her shoulders rose higher and higher, as if to shield her from the painful memories. “Insufferable man!”

“Yes. You’ve said that.” Memsy lifted a foot out of the water and wiggled her dripping toes. “Repeatedly.”

The sorci smiled at her toes before plopping them back beneath the ripples.

“It’s as true now as it ever was. I mean, the shamelessness of the man to stand there and berate and badger us about slowing him down, when here we sit waiting for over an hour *on him*!”

Allowing the humor to show in her face, Memsy accused, “But you cheated.”

Adianna wrinkled her nose, showing she knew full well she had. “He deserved it,” she pouted.

“I suppose he did, really,” Memsy replied thoughtfully. A slow smile inched across her face. “Did you catch the look of bafflement upon his face when you bounded away, carrying me and all our provisions?”

A brazen smile appeared on the girl’s face, and her laughter bubbled forth like a spring of its own. “It was rather priceless, I must say.”

Adianna stilled. A sadness crept in. Her crossed arms began to enfold her like a shield, and she turned pleading eyes to her mother.

What are we going to do, Mother? She pleaded, knowing full well Memsy could hear her thoughts. *He doesn’t love me. He’s not the one. And now I have caught him and me up in this death wish of confusion and magic... And I don’t know what to do.*

Memsy stood to enfold her little one. She enveloped the child in her arms, though the child was as tall as she. She felt the slight tremors that shook those young shoulders.

“It’s okay, my love,” she soothed and gently stroked the maiden’s back. “It will all work out. You will see.”

Adianna sniffled. "But how can you be sure? We put our lives in a dragon's confirmation."

Memsy pulled back, rubbing the maiden's arms. She sought the girl's gaze, then smiled. "I'll take the confirmation of a dragon over my brother's visions any day."

That made Adianna chuckle despite herself. But slowly, her face crumpled again. "But how can you be sure?"

"We cannot be sure of anything in this life, other than one day it will eventually end." Smiling, Memsy stroked her arms again. "All we can do is have faith. *And* to accept what joy we can from each given moment."

What if there isn't any joy to accept? Adianna sulked.

"There is always joy to be had, my love. You simply have to look around and find it."

Memsy stroked her daughter's cheek, coaxing a smile from her with one of her own. It was an unconvincing smile, but it was a start. The girl then stepped back to gaze around them.

I can always find joy if I simply look for it, Memsy heard Adianna consider. *Well, the spring here is lovely. And the gurgle of the water is both soothing and rejuvenating.* She closed her eyes to savor the peace.

Suddenly, the sound of tromping and stomping reached them from the way they had arrived. Memsy saw Adianna glare in the direction of its origin. *Insufferable man! If he is* so *worried about our safety, then why is he making such an infernal racket?*

She folded her arms in front of her and continued to scowl. *Joy. I'm supposed to be finding joy in every moment I can. But how am I supposed to do that with an oaf like him in tow?*

Then Memsy heard her daughter have an idea. An idea, which, when she heard it come through the maiden's thoughts, made even her choke back a chuckle.

Oh, Adianna. Sadly, you are definitely my *daughter,* she thought. At the girl's responding smile, she sat down to await the healer's arrival.

PRANKS & PRICKS

"Insufferable women!" Kendrick grumbled for the fiftieth time, just as his toe caught on a root causing him to stumble.

It had been hours since he left Tymalia. Hours since they had left him behind. Hours he had filled with grumbling, griping, and moaning about his lot. He had cursed the elves, cussed the sorcis, and complained of a certain long-haired minx. He had bemoaned and vexed so long he was sick of it.

Now, he had finally found the butte and was following its edge around the northern curve. Knowing he would soon catch up with the pesky women, he tried to view his predicament with a clearer mind. After all, there were worse things than being married to a beauty. One with an intriguing mind, a delightful personality, and the ability to set his blood boiling—both in angst and desire.

Drawing in a deep breath, he let this new thought percolate a little. Scenes of the multiple times he had found himself craving to kiss that enticing little mouth of hers played through his mind. Time after time, the desire and the opportunity arose, and though decorum required she pull away, she never seemed unwilling. Hadn't he desired, just the day before, to have the opportunity to woo her himself? To have time with her before she was married off to some scoundrel? There could definitely be an upside now that he found himself to be that scoundrel.

Kendrick felt his eyebrows arc high on his forehead at this tantalizing prospect. He slowly smiled. *Yes. This situation could definitely have potential.*

He could tell by the sheer rock wall to his left that the butte took a dip inward just ahead, so he pushed on through the undergrowth. In a few steps, he pulled back some branches and stopped.

A delightful oasis opened before him. A small expanse of ferns glided forward from where he stood to the edge of a babbling stream. The stream flowed off to his right to be lost in the depths of the forest. Beyond the stream was a grassy knoll.

He stepped between the bushes, out from under the trees. Among the ferns, he was able to see a shimmering pool as well as the origin of the stream. There, in the jog of the butte, the rock wall slanted upward from the water's edge to about halfway up the cliff. Right where the sheer wall and the slant met, fresh water gurgled forth right out of the side of the mountain. Water tumbled over the rockslide to the pool below, feeding mosses and watercress and other greenery on its way down. It was a beautiful sight to behold.

And there, on the other side of the pool, dipping her toes in the cool water, sat the sorci. She hailed him to join her with a big smile on her face.

He meandered downstream a bit, to where the banks narrowed, and skipped across. He scanned the clearing, taking in the natural beauty. His gaze skimmed over both sides of the pool. He even looked up the cliff and above a small outcropping of rock ledge to the right. But Adianna was nowhere in sight.

He settled in next to his new mother-in-law. He guessed that's what she was now. Her eyes danced, and she patted his leg.

"I'm glad you finally made it!" She beamed.

Even Kendrick had to chuckle at her enthusiasm. "How long have you been waiting?"

Memsy wrinkled her nose and shrugged. "Only about an hour or two, is all."

"Or two?" He sounded dubious. "How on Sheorae could you have moved so quickly?"

Kendrick felt something plink off his shoulder. He brushed at it but kept his focus on his companion.

Her chin tilted up, and her smile broadened. "Oh, we have our ways. Plus, we know the forest."

"You certainly must." He brushed at the top of his head where he felt something. "You made some serious time!"

He leaned back on his hands, stretching his legs out in front of him, and gazed around the clearing. Something bounced off his shoulder again. He looked over where it landed on the ground. A tiny acorn? He glanced overhead but found no oak tree, nor any other kind of tree above him. He shrugged inwardly and went back to taking in the splendor of the glade.

Admiration for his surroundings filled his soul. "This sure is a lovely place. I didn't even know it was here." He brushed at something flicking off his neck.

"Most people don't." Memsy leaned toward him then back. Next she sighed, looking over the small dell. The ferns waved gently on the breeze. The gurgle of the waterfall was light and soothing.

"This is one of my favorite places," she confided. "I used to bring Adianna here all the time when she was little. She loved to frolic and play in the stream. And she learned to swim right here in this pool."

Kendrick smiled softly at the woman's reminiscing. He was also somewhat impressed—few human women learned to swim. He swatted at something in his hair but felt nothing.

"Since the water stays the same temperature year-round from this glorious spring, we often come out here to bathe throughout the fall instead of boiling water at home." Memsy leaned toward him as if to share a secret, though her voice didn't change. "Adianna often sneaked away just to go skinny-dipping, until her cousins found out."

They both shared a laugh. Though the older woman wrinkled her nose and looked over his shoulder when something bounced off her head as well. Kendrick looked up, but only saw the rocks jutting out from the sheer cliff wall.

"So where is the little minx?" He smacked at his neck when something pelted him a little harder.

"Oh, she left."

Kendrick's head snapped around, and he gawked at the older woman. "What?"

Memsy nodded, looking a little too innocent. "Yes. She got tired of waiting, so she left."

Kendrick sprang to his feet. "Of all the… And you let her go?"

Her shoulders and eyebrows both rose high simultaneously. The emblem on her forehead rippled and glowed.

A growl rumbled from deep inside him. "Doesn't she realize we're being hunted? Of all the idiotic, pigheaded, insufferable…"

Just then something splatted against the side of his face just below his ear. Memsy stared at him, her eyes wide, her mouth a tall oval. Instinctively, he reached up. His fingers made contact with something moist and gooey. He scraped it off slowly and raised his fingers to his nose. One sniff informed him of exactly what it was.

Someone started laughing up in the trees behind him. Ominously, Kendrick turned his glare at the trees, wiping his hand on the grass.

There, perched on a low branch of an oak several yards away, snickered Adianna.

"You little vixen!" he growled.

She wrinkled her nose at him. "Serves you right."

Without another word, she scooped up her things, including weapons, which were hidden behind the tree, then swung nimbly to the ground. She made it appear so effortless, even with her arms full, that Kendrick momentarily forgot he was cursing her.

She sauntered toward him, keeping unabashed eye contact. She plopped her pile of mail, bow and quiver, as well as sheathed Blades on the grass near him. Then with a smirk, she brushed past him to wash her hands in the water.

Kendrick took a step toward her. "Of all the childish…"

"You would know all about childish, wouldn't you?" she shot back at him over her shoulder. "The way you've been ranting and carrying on all day. I haven't seen such a fit thrown since Puffin ate all of Rachele's sweets at the spring festival. And she's five!"

He saw motion out of the corner of his eye, and his head snapped around to Memsy. She had covered her mouth with her hand. Her laughter was not hidden in her eyes though. Still her emblem rippled and swirled.

He swung his head back to Adianna. She stood, flicking water off her hands, and leveled a challenging gaze on him. He'd accept that challenge.

"I'll have you know, there's been quite a lot thrust upon me this morning. And all I was anticipating was taking a couple women traipsing through the woods to Ooflic. That was all I signed up for. Now I have a wife. I have a quest. I have all of Sheorae resting on my shoulders, and all of Sheorae hunting me down! Then on top of it all off, I have you making childish pranks!"

He flicked his clean hand in her direction, then ran it through his hair. He growled at her but spun away and plopped back on the ground.

"Yes," Adianna moaned. "We all know about your harrowing plight." She turned from him and raised her hands to the sky. "We all know of how the moons and the stars are all aligning against the piteous healer. And how the world should moan and mourn the wretched loss of freedom of our wandering rebel."

She turned back to him, her arms akimbo. "No matter that the whole world is enslaved. That the lives of innocent people are extinguished every day due to the whims of villains and the corruption of the elite. No… we all must listen to you and your rantings."

Kendrick's hands clenched into the ground, ripping grass by the roots. Wrath quaked within him. His nostrils flared, releasing fumes of the flames writhing inside. Every muscle tensed, and his jaw worked intently. *You go too far, woman!*

Before he could make a move on any of his suddenly menacing thoughts, Memsy sprang to her feet. She went straight to her daughter, though her wide eyes repeatedly darted his way. She turned the younger woman and nudged her in the direction of the packs. She then stammered with a nervous chuckle, "Now, dear, I do believe you should settle down and let your husband eat his meal so we can get moving soon."

Adianna resisted a little, then stumbled when Memsy gave her a decided shove. The elder then passed her and stooped to rifle through an open pack. But the younger woman stopped indignantly.

"And *I believe—*" her hands were back on her hips, "—my so-called husband should stop whining and just accept what has fallen to him." She turned back to him. "Regardless of how."

"Do you want to know what I believe?" The healer jumped up, flinging grass everywhere while stepping menacingly toward the young woman.

She crossed her arms defiantly, pinning him with her gaze. "Not particularly."

His lips pursed as his jaw clenched. He glared at her, mentally visualizing what it would be like to wring her little neck.

"I do, Master Healer," came Memsy's voice from behind him.

Anger and annoyance rippled inside him, for he continued to glower at the younger woman. Still, the edge of the affront melted away somewhat when the sorci placed her hand on his arm.

"Won't you tell me what you believe?" she said in a soothing voice.

Memsy's face was both repentant and encouraging, urging him to drop his defenses. He could feel she had a deeper meaning and desire than some flippant rebuttal, and so he could do naught but stare into her calming eyes for a moment or two.

"Alright," he said, his voice measured. He placed his hand on hers, inclining his head toward her. "I believe danger is descending upon us from all sides. I believe those cursed Blades are a magnet for war, not peace. And unless we get rid of the blasted things, we will die just as surely as everyone else embedded with the delusion that anything good could come from them."

He turned at the younger woman's scoff. "And," he said pointedly, his brow darkening over hard eyes, "I believe in marrying for *love,* not convenience."

He missed any change in Adianna's demeanor, for he turned back to Memsy. "I believe love and marriage are a union for the eternities. I believe in growing old with the woman I love, cherishing her above the moons, and wishing to never leave her side. That is what I believe! My mother…"

His voice caught slightly, just at mentioning her. Still, he swallowed the pain and guilt, lifting his chin a notch. "My mother taught me this."

He turned abruptly on Adianna, pinning her with an accusing glare. Anger and loss warred within him, and he struggled to keep a restraint on both. "My mother was robbed of this because of the very things you so eagerly strap to your back! So, forgive me for not being overjoyed at the prospect of running headlong to our graves."

He looked down and twirled the gold band he wore on the middle finger of his right hand. He dug absently in the dirt with the toe of his boot. "I wanted more for the love of my life than fighting and misery."

All was quiet in the glade, save water tumbling over rock.

Kendrick continued to work at that ring until finally, he felt the sorci's hand on his arm once again.

The sadness in the sorci's face spoke of the empathy she was feeling. Pity was mingled there; he could not look upon it. So, he turned back to the woman he must now call his wife.

There she stood, her eyebrows knit together in puzzlement. She stared at him, or more accurately, through him, her mouth slack.

Finally, her eyes focused in on him. "Then… why are you here?"

Her whispered question hit him with the force of an anvil. Looking at her lovely features and her soft, fragile body, he knew the answer. It burned within him with a fire he could not fathom, and he knew this little imp had somehow nettled her way beyond all his defenses, and now, he would do anything to protect her. But he'd be dorshed if he would let her know!

He faced her head on, his arms crossed in front of him, and dared her to challenge what he was about to say.

"Because I live up to my responsibilities, no matter how they are put upon me!"

Kendrick quelled the memories leaping forward, challenging his lie. She did not know his past, nor was it likely she ever would. They would most likely be either killed within the next few days or those infernal Blades would be stripped from them by some greedy sop and leave them nothing to do but part company. A tight constricting in his chest told him just how devastating a thought that was.

All of a sudden, he wanted to commit every line of Adianna's face to memory. She stood there, her eyes downcast, blinking rapidly. Slowly her bottom lip slipped into her mouth. As she worried on that lip and her shoulders slumped infinitesimally, he realized he'd hurt her feelings. He felt his manner softening despite his harsh stance.

"Adianna, I'm sorry, I…" He took a step toward her, his hand reaching out to her. But he stopped short when she shied away from his touch. She instantly snatched up her cloak. The silvery mail glistened, picking up the light surrounding them and bouncing off in dazzling array. She held it protectively in front of her and yet looked at him with a certain degree of longing in her eyes.

Still, her defensive manner cut Kendrick to the quick. He dropped his hands, and his apologetic words died in his throat. His fingers balled into tight fists. His gaze grew severe.

With his voice hard as ice, he gave her a stiff bow. "My apologies, madam."

He pivoted, snatching up his pack, and retreated to the opposite side of the glen.

Adianna moved to say something as he skipped over the bubbling water but stopped. He fought himself over wondering what it could have been she was going to say, but he forced himself not to look her way. Thus, the space between them grew beyond the distance of the glade.

DRAGON STRIDER

Suddenly, Kendrick's head shot up, and the quiet was ripped asunder with a volley of high-pitched roars from overhead.

"Striders," he breathed.

Pulling his gear along with him, he leaped back across the stream and sprinted for Adianna. She had just settled the Blades and her cloak into place and was reaching for her packs. He hurled his things toward the overhang in the rock wall, then grabbed hold of one woman's arm in each hand. Adianna let out a small cry; still both women struggled to scoop up their things as he dragged them to the butte wall.

Pulling both of the women in close, Kendrick scanned the sky. Intent on spying the mighty beasts first, he failed to notice the struggle going on beside him. He wanted to spot the approaching dragons before their heat sensors or enhanced sense of smell could pinpoint them.

"Please release me." Adianna's voice was halted. She seemed to fight for breath enough to speak.

Kendrick paid her little heed, for he could now hear the swoosh of mighty wings. He instinctively scrunched back from the edge, his fingers digging unconsciously deeper into the flesh of the two women's arms. Ignoring them, he sought to catch the first glimpse.

They are so close, and there are many of them. Adrenaline mingled with the fear of discovery.

"Healer. Let go of her arm," Memsy's voice was low, but the command was unmistakable.

He glanced at the sorci, surprised with the sudden demand, when immediate danger was fast approaching. Around her eyes were creases of sympathetic pain, but she did not look at him. She was looking at the woman on his other side.

Just then, the clearing around the spring darkened with great shadows speeding across overhead. Kendrick reacted instantly. He shoved the women back still farther against the protective rock, yet he strained his face forward, bedazzled by the majesty of the creatures soaring above.

Simultaneously the two women reacted. Memsy pawed at Kendrick's arm, a pleading in her voice as she again insisted that he let the girl go.

At the same time, Adianna pulled sharply away from his side. The crag in the rock face was barely big enough for the three of them to fit in side by side, so when she drew away, she had to move toward the opening, toward the clearing, toward being spotted.

Kendrick responsively tried to snatch her back to safety, but the movement increased the intensity of her resistance.

"Let. Me. Go!" she yelled. With one great yank, Adianna wrenched her bare forearm free from his grasp. The force of her movement sent her spinning into the clearing.

A mighty screech rang out above them. Panic washed over Kendrick. He thrust his hand out to her.

"Woman!" he hissed between tight lips. "Get back here."

The girl's brows were pulled down low over her defiant green eyes. Accusation evident on her face, she backed away, holding her arm.

"Halt!" a voice boomed above her.

The whoosh of powerful wings sounded, and Adianna looked up in time to back out of the way quickly. Kendrick's heart clenched as a huge sapphire-colored beast descended into the small clearing. Great wings covered with glistening ruby scales blotted out all traces of the sky, slowing the mighty creature. It softly, but powerfully, landed on the ground between him and his bride.

The shimmering iridescence of the gem-colored scales covering the formidable species had always fascinated him, the way they absorbed the light and cast it out again in luminescent color like individual prisms. Scales of various sizes covered every inch of the incredible creature, from large ones crisscrossing the underbelly from chin to tip of tail to the miniscule facets glistening across each strong wing. He loved the way the tip of their snouts curved over in beak-like fashion. The way the three thorny spikes fanned out behind their eyes, the outer two curving away from the center, spreading like silver-tipped claws protecting the back of its head.

But he recognized this dragon's distinguishing marks, the silver dots running down its chest and muscular flanks. He knew the contrasting streak of red which ran along each powerful leg. And he knew this particular dragon by its sturdy claws, by the five-fingered fore-claws instead of four. Instinctively, he pressed further against the rocks behind him, willing himself not to be seen.

But the dragon's innate sense of smell was not interested in him at the moment. It was trained on the woman. Remembering the magical baggage she bore, Kendrick held his breath.

Adianna stood in front of the imposing beast, wary but unintimidated. The creature sniffed at her actively. Every muscle within him tensed.

We are lost before we even got started, Kendrick agonized silently. He knew by now the magic was talking to the beast. The same magic that governed this world and all the magical creatures in it was harbored in those cursed Blades, and it spoke to dragons. It drew them like a canine hunter rooting out game for its master. That was why the humans had formed their alliance with the great beasts in the first place. And now all was lost.

He brushed aside the sudden feeling of disappointment and listened intently to hear the dragon's thoughts.

The creature sniffed around the young woman, who stood perfectly still. Kendrick heard Adianna greet the beast in the elvish custom. The dragon's response to this was a narrowing of its eyes, which studied her purposefully.

"What is it, boy?"

A sudden irritation at the forgotten rider flickered inside Kendrick but did not draw his attention from the dragon. He willed all his healer senses to feel out what the dragon was feeling, what it was thinking.

The creature snorted in response to the armor-clad man on its back but continued its appraisal of the woman. Finally, it raised its mighty head.

'At last!' was the only thought Kendrick registered from the magical giant. Then it inclined its majestic head in reverence toward the young beauty facing it. Bewilderment filled Kendrick's very soul, and he watched the young woman return the gesture. Never had he seen a dragon respond like this to anyone baring the Blades.

Could it be? Kendrick wondered, looking over his young travel companion. He tried to shake it off. Still, he felt relief flood through him, which mingled with the overpowering elation coming from the great beast before him.

The soldier riding the mighty beast, upon seeing no sign from the dragon of finding what they sought, turned his attention elsewhere. Jabbing his drawn sword in their direction, the Strider hollered at Kendrick and Memsy, "Show yourselves!"

Memsy gingerly took a step forward, but Kendrick held back. Finally, he, too, moved forward, realizing the futility of the situation. He knew that whether or not his looks gave him away, his scent surely would.

The sapphire dragon wheeled its head around to face him. He came to the dragon, his arms out from his sides, palms forward in presentation. Instantly, the great beast sniffed at him. He could tell when recognition dawned on the creature, for it began shifting its mighty shoulders playfully. A deep throaty purr rumbled deep inside its massive body, and it nudged excitedly at his hand.

A dragon never forgets, Kendrick thought with a wry smile.

Concern laced the soldier's response. "What is it, boy?"

At that, the dragon pivoted its head to snort derisively in the face of the soldier. The man jumped back in the riding harness, startled. "What the...?"

Kendrick gave a mirthless chuckle, stepping forward again. "Perhaps the fact *he's* a female has something to do with it, you imbecile," he accused. "Didn't you listen at all in dragon training? When the spear-like scale at the end of the tail is more of a heart shape than an arrowhead, it's an obvious sign of their gender."

To prove the fact, the dragon brought the silver tip of her tail in front of the sputtering man's face for closer scrutiny.

"But I suppose you were probably sick the multiple days they taught that at the Academy."

The soldier yanked the helmet from his head, fuming. He jabbed his sword at the healer though his hand shook with emotion.

"Who are you? And what is your business here?" the man demanded, his voice tight.

A smile touched Kendrick's lips at the soldier's anger. The dragon stretched her head back to him. He ran his hand over the creature's proffered muzzle. The deep rumble returned.

Ah, Master, the purring beast spoke to his mind. *Happy greeting, dearest one. Shyra will rejoice at the knowledge you are still among the living.*

One side of Kendrick's mouth dipped deep into his cheek as old memories tried to press in on him. How could he convey his forlorn regrets to this majestic creature he knew so well?

"Answer me, man!" the irate soldier demanded.

Across the breadth of the dragon Adianna stared wide-eyed at him. If he wasn't so intent on keeping the past in the past, he might have chuckled at the look on her face.

He returned his attention to petting the formidable dragon. "No one of consequence, my friend," he said, matter-of-factly.

He continued stroking the creature, but Kendrick felt a subtle probing of his mind coming from somewhere behind him. Anxiously, he scrambled to tuck the last of his flooding memories back into their vault before Memsy could discern too much.

"I don't believe you, *friend*," the soldier stated pointedly, the truth of it apparent in his voice. "Now, I demand you tell me who you are and what you are about."

Kendrick looked at the youth, amused. He knew he should play it safe, but the challenge was too good to pass up. He arched a questioning eyebrow, still cradling the dragon's head in his hands, and tested, "Or what?"

The dare settled in the space separating them. For several moments, moving water was the only sound. The young soldier seemed taken aback at first. Kendrick simply watched. He calmly ran his hand over the pacified dragon's head and delighted in seeing the temperature rise on the other man's face. The youth's eyes narrowed, and his lips pulled back over clenched teeth. Then in abrupt, jerky motions, the soldier rammed the sword back into its sheath. Reaching down, he yanked the whip from the latch on his belt. He unraveled the weapon with an angry snap.

Kendrick felt the dragon stiffen, though she kept her head in his hands. Her ears, nestled behind the spiky frills behind her eyes, turned down ominously. But Kendrick kept his eyes trained on the over-zealous punk seated on her back.

He felt a hand on his arm and Memsy's voice was low and concerned behind him. "Healer, maybe we should…"

"Retreat, madam. All is well." He kept his voice calm and cool but did not release the younger man's gaze.

The strider, little more than a youth, seemed to be expecting some sort of great reaction to his grand display of weaponry. Upon finding none, trepidation and ambiguity worked behind the soldier's eyes. The seconds ticked by with only the splash of water breaking the silence.

Kendrick saw the soldier's decision before he made the move. The whip lashed out. A resounding crack popped just inches from the healer's shoulder when he ducked quickly out of harm's way. The women shrieked. The dragon wheeled her head with an angry roar, her wings tensing and a swirl of dust swooping through the glade.

Still, the strider was unrelenting. The markings of pricked male pride were etched on his face, and he was going for another display of superiority. But this time, as the serpentine weapon lashed out, Kendrick snapped up his gauntlet-covered hand at exactly the right place and time. The tip of the whip wrapped around the leather glove in an instant. He quickly clamped his grasp around the weapon and jerked it free from the astonished man's hand.

The great beast now thrashed her claws against the soft turf. Enraged guttural screeches ripped from her throat, filling the glade. She careened her head around to glare menacingly at her rider. Agitated threads of smoke swirled up from her nostrils.

Sheer terror etched the strider's features, and he gawked helplessly in the face of the furious dragon. The frightened man snatched several times at his sword, trying to unsheathe it, but was unsuccessful. When the imposing beast snapped her angry jaws just inches from his face, the once-arrogant soldier let out a shrill shriek.

"Shh, Tylin. Shh." Kendrick stepped forward soothingly, his hands stretched above his head. "Calm down, girl."

He began stroking gently against the irritated creature's neck and taunt, quivering haunches. The luminescent scales shivered in response to his peaceful caress. Slowly, the screeching subsided.

Tylin, the dragon, turned a questioning look on Kendrick. Content with the nod that he was fine, she craned her head around to the insolent youth on her back. She snorted a puff of smoke at him, then dropped her head back into Kendrick's calming hands. The purring of a contented house pet rumbled again in her throat.

Shock, mingled with great unease, was embedded on the Strider's face. A subtle smile spread across Kendrick's lips. He knew they never covered *that* in Academy.

Suddenly the sky above was filled with the whoosh and screeching of dragons bent on protecting their own. Kendrick clenched his teeth to suppress a curse.

How are we going to get out of this one?

Kendrick felt a hand skim over his shirt sleeve. To his surprise, Adianna had come to stand beside him. He could see the uncertainty in her eyes though it was well masked on her face.

"Who goes there?" a voice boomed overhead.

Kendrick tensed, recognition flooding him again. He gave Tylin's head a little shove, and the beast pulled away, shifting her stance. He drew his hood up to conceal his features then bowed before the mighty flyers hovering above them.

The young strider riding Tylin was still teetering on the borders of shock and seemed unable to form an articulate answer. So, Kendrick endeavored to offer one.

"Just a poor traveler, my lord," he said, altering his voice slightly. He stretched out his hands in submission, and he continued to bow. "Journeying with my wife and her mother to Ooflic by the Tamerik Mountains."

The young soldier astride the grounded dragon suddenly chimed in, "Don't believe him, Master Sergeant!"

Kendrick's teeth clenched together, mentally cursing himself for being so foolhardy as to toy with the young upstart. It would be their ruin.

"How so, Strider?" the sergeant queried from overhead.

"Because, sir, he… he…" the young fool stared at Kendrick but appeared to be unable to explain without disclosing the Rules of Engagement he, himself, was guilty of violating.

Kendrick's gaze bored into the young strider's, for he knew he had him. One corner of the healer's mouth pulled back into a quirky challenge.

"Come, soldier. He what?" The master sergeant's voice tightened slightly, impatience evident.

"He… uhh," the young man floundered, before declaring, "he bewitched my mount!"

Both man and beast snorted, and Kendrick met Tylin's eyes. The whoosh of wings overhead was mingled with snickers by the surrounding striders.

"Don't be absurd, man!" The dolt's superior scoffed, though his voice was laced with mirth. "Dragons can't be bewitched. They are of the same magic."

The young strider fumed, his face beet red. The muscles of his jaw worked viciously. Still, he glared at Kendrick. The healer felt a little pity for the arrogant upstart, but not much.

"Now what is really going on here?" His irritation was evident, and the master sergeant's gruff voice silenced the chortling.

Kendrick's mouth twitched to the side. The moment of truth had arrived, and the truth would end everything! But before he could formulate the words that would seal their fate, a feminine voice rang above the din.

"Sergeant." Memsy stepped out from under the outcropping of rocks. The hood of her cloak was pulled low on her forehead as she looked to the sky. "My son-in-law tells the truth. We are journeying to Ooflic from Neashen to visit my sister there. We needed to fill our water bladders, so we ventured from the main road to this spring."

The older woman gestured to the water spilling forth from the butte wall. She then directed her hand to the steaming young man on the dragon. "This soldier descended upon us as your forces passed overhead, and his bullying has not been appreciated."

She folded her arms in front of her, pinning the young man with her gaze.

"Airman Penchian?" the officer scolded.

"But, sir, my dragon!" Penchian countered.

But the officer cut him off. "Did she alert you to their having possession of the Blades or not?" he demanded.

The boy's mouth bobbed up and down, searching for an answer that would keep him out of trouble.

"Airman!" the man shouted. Irritation was rising in the commander's voice. The hovering dragons and riders also showed signs of impatience.

Finally, the lad answered to the negative in a tight, military voice. His eyes pelted Kendrick with venom so tangible they were daggers thrown just barely missing the mark.

The commanding officer turned to Memsy. "I am, indeed, sorry, madam, for any abuse you have suffered due to my soldier's impertinence. I assure you he will be dealt with."

"Thank you." Memsy inclined her head to the Master Sergeant.

He touched his finger to his brow in tight salute. "Good journey to you, madam. Sir. M'lady. Good day."

He nodded to Kendrick and Adianna. Then, his voice turned hard. "Airman Penchian! To the sky!"

"Yes, sir!" The red-faced young man tightened the reins around his fist. Giving Kendrick one last death glare, the boy kicked his heels into his dragon's haunches.

The mighty Tylin shifted onto her hind legs but did not take off before inclining her head to the couple facing her in a reverent bow.

"We'll meet again, Master," the promise flowed confidently from dragon to man, but she did not wait for a response.

A great gust of air whirled around Kendrick, threatening to blow off his hood as massive wings pumped hard once, and the beast leapt into the air. He clutched at the coarse material, keeping the hood in place, yet allowing him to watch the shimmering creature's ascent.

The troop of dragons with their riders moved on. Though they were no longer in view, Kendrick kept his face upturned, listening fully to their departure.

As one, Memsy and Adianna turned to him.

"You were a strider?" Memsy queried but was followed immediately by Adianna's question.

"Who's Shyra?"

Kendrick was not prepared to answer questions. Though the sorci sounded enthralled, Adianna pinned him with a look that was far less impressed. She crossed her arms, looking rather hostile. So frazzled, he didn't even think to wonder how she got the name; he merely blurted out, "Shyra's a dragon, and, yes, as a healer, I would naturally have my share of interaction with dragons."

"Naturally!" Memsy gushed. Her hands flew in the air and flopped back against her thighs in exaggerated display.

The younger woman still had him pinioned with her intent gaze. Slowly one dainty eyebrow arced high. "Naturally."

The statement fell flat. Yet her demeanor issued a challenge.

But Kendrick had dared too much for one day.

"We need to get moving. That hunting party is only the first. More will be close behind." A frail hedge, yes, but he proceeded to gather their belongings.

He fastened his sword into place. He scooped up pack straps and flung them over his shoulder. Snatching up the shamere gloves off the grass, he brought them to Adianna. She was still eyeing him inscrutably. The gloves hung suspended between them for several moments while she observed him. Kendrick met her stare. He waited, hoping to make peace, but also hoping his secrets weren't as obvious as they felt.

Her observation of him continued. He didn't know what she saw. He wished he didn't know what she was looking for. Wished even more he didn't have to hide it.

Memsy had gathered the rest of their things and had come to stand next to him. Still Adianna stared at him.

Finally, she collected the proffered gloves. "Thank you," she said softly.

As the cool mail slipped over his fingers, Kendrick noticed a wide welt encircling Adianna's forearm. The angry band was red and blistering. Sudden concern came to him.

"Are you alright?" The shamere had just slipped off his fingertips when he reached for her, so the mail caught between his hand and hers.

She recoiled, and her face contorted. But before she could answer, Memsy stepped forward.

"I have salve here in this pack for that."

Adianna's eyes darted to Kendrick's, but she turned away quickly and submitted herself to her mother's ministerings.

No wonder she pulled so violently out of my grasp with a lesion such as that, Kendrick mused.

He touched his wife's cloaked shoulder. She flinched but did not shy away from his touch. She merely looked questioningly into his eyes.

"I'm so very sorry for hurting you." He hoped the regret, as well as the tenderness he now felt, was being conveyed through his voice. He nearly held his breath awaiting her response.

For several seconds, she peered at him, showing no sign of her thoughts. Finally, ever so slightly, her mouth softened. She gave him a tiny nod. The movement was nearly imperceptible, but it was enough to give him hope that peace might transpire between them.

He offered a small smile and a nod of his own, then backed away.

Within minutes, the tiny band were trekking off again—unsure of what awaited them.

SIZZLE

I don't know how much farther I can go!

Adianna's arms hung slack from her shoulders. Her thighs burned, and her back ached. It was getting more and more difficult to put one foot in front of the other. The occasional trip over a tree root was becoming more and more frequent.

They had been pushed northward from the spring to skirt an orgrin scouting party. Plus, they had to follow the tree lines to keep undercover from bands of hawkmen and striders, which they heard arguing and taunting each other overhead. The adrenaline had carried her for quite some distance, as it had them all, but they had covered more miles than was typically prudent for one day, and the wear was beginning to show on all of them.

From the blackness above the canopy and the bioluminescent mosses illuminating their way beneath, the sun had been down for quite some time. She had no way of knowing how far into the night they had been traveling, but her body told her it could not go on much longer.

Stopping for breath, she put her hands on her hips and turned her face to the blocked sky. With her head thus turned, the drizzle that her cloak had shielded her from was evident now. She felt her hair where the moisture accumulated.

"Great! Now it's raining."

Her enthusiasm for continuing further dampened, she hollered out to the man in the lead. "Healer. We can't continue like this any longer."

The man paused and turned around. His drooping eyes proclaimed his own exhaustion, and her hopes of convincing him sputtered to life.

"We've been going on like this all day. The sun has been down for hours. And now it's beginning to rain. We simply must rest."

The man turned his face heavenward and caught rain droplets on his outstretched glove. He squinted through the faint light, looking from her to Memsy. His breathing looked labored; Adianna watched him deliberate. Memsy came to a stop next to her, her breathing also strained.

"I know you want to put as much distance between us and the beacons as possible, but if we don't rest, we will not be able to get anywhere tomorrow. We must take shelter, and we must rest."

She could tell he knew she was right. Still, he paused. Whether from concern or just plain stubbornness, she could not tell. Finally, he conceded, nodding his head.

"We must find a protected location to rest though." He was looking around in all directions as he spoke. "Somewhere out of the elements, but also sheltered from any nosy passersby. The goblins will be coming out to have their go at trying to find those Blades. But they won't be looking with their eyes, they will be hunting by scent."

He gestured for the women to move past him along the trail, and with the other hand, he pointed in the direction of a blacker mass jutting out of the dark forest ahead. Memsy took the lead in the direction he indicated. The three stumbled along for several more minutes in silence.

Upon closer inspection, the mass turned out to be a large thicket of bramble—ideal for animal cover but not much help for people.

Each looked around for a new possible cover. The drizzle was becoming heavier. Randomly in the distance, Adianna could hear faint sizzling and crackling.

"Do you smell that?" the healer inquired, his brow puckered, and his nostrils flared.

Adianna and Memsy both sniffed the breeze. Presently, the faint yet tantalizing aroma of popcorn tickled her senses. Adianna closed her eyes and savored the appealing fragrance.

With a smile on her face, Memsy responded, "It's volt moss."

The older woman sniffed the air until she had pinpointed the direction. "It's coming from that way."

The healer looked in the direction Memsy pointed. Adianna could see his mind working while searching the shadowed horizon. Finally, without turning his head, he arched an eyebrow at Adianna. That mischievous smile, which she had enjoyed seeing so much back in Tymalia, crept across his face, enticing her.

"I have an idea," he announced. Without awaiting her reaction, the healer reached out for her hand.

Adianna scrutinized him, unsure, yet her mouth quirked on one side. He returned her gaze, but instead of issuing a challenge, he jiggled his eyebrows in a playful manner. A soft snort escaped her, yet she slowly took his hand. His gaze on her became softer at her hesitant trust. It didn't take long for the warmth of his grasp to heat the cold metal. Still, he watched her. Slowly, she smiled at him.

When he finally returned her smile, he laced his fingers through hers. Then he loped off, pulling her behind. Adianna had to keep herself from laughing at his exaggerated, high-kneed tromping over branches and grasses. He galloped on, her hand tightly in his. The aromatic scent of popcorn heightened the further they went. Finally, he came to a stop.

"Look." The healer pointed to some trees just ahead. On the north side, the trees were covered by a dark, rich moss. This thick vegetation sizzled and crackled before their eyes each time the rain pelted it.

When her husband moved to pass between these trees, Adianna pulled at his arm. "Be careful. That stuff can zap you from even feet away in this rain."

A great grin split his face. "Exactly!"

Adianna followed the man past the sparking cluster of trees. She watched him closely, not quite sure what he was getting at. He scanned the immediate area, looking from tree to tree. He looked away from the volt moss-covered trees, taking in yet another thicket of brambles. This time, Adianna noticed the brambles had been pushed back on one side from something large that had tried to nestle under it. Possibly a couple braidocs or a greon.

The healer took all this in. He released her hand and began darting around. He spied under the brambles at the dry ground beneath. He pointed from tree to tree around where they stood and ticked off each beyond the small thicket, all the while making little grunts and murmurs to the affirmative.

Finally, he stepped toward her, rubbing his hands together in front of him, a broad smile on his face. "Yes, I think this will do nicely."

Adianna was lost. Memsy looked somewhat impressed and was shaking her head, but Adianna could see the sorci's emblem shimmering, belying the cheat at her understanding.

With her eyebrows high on her forehead, the younger woman shook her head. "Great! Do nicely for what?"

But the man was already pulling his sword and motioning them forward. "Come, come, come. You ladies get bedded down where it's nice and dry, while I set up the perimeter."

Memsy grabbed the pack he slipped off. But Adianna watched the healer proceed to gingerly rub the tip of his outstretched sword against the moss on one tree after another at about knee height. The thick, earthy foliage crackled and hissed at each disturbance. He continued these agitations from a safe reach until he had made a complete circle around their little area. When he moved his weapon tip from the final tree, connecting it to the first, a tiny sizzle leapt from the tip of his sword and followed the exact path it had taken around the thicket and hit the original spot with a spark and fizzle.

The man sauntered over, grinning like a proud toddler. "There! All set."

Adianna was still as baffled as before. "What's all set? I have no idea what you just did."

"I just set up a safety net," he declared, slipping his sword back into his sheath. "Now no one need keep watch. We may all rest peacefully. For nothing will be able to cross that line without us knowing."

Adianna was still perplexed. "Are you sure?"

"Of course." The man ushered her to where Memsy had already laid out blankets under the eve of the thick brambles. His smile was so wide and teethy, it was impossible not to concede. So, Adianna went along with it, even though she had no idea what was going on.

Soon they were all settled in with the healer lying across the opening of their tiny cove. Despite the impending doom pressing in on the travelers from all sides, the trio fell asleep quickly.

Battle raged on around Kendrick. The clang of weapons, the clatter of armor—sounds he was all too familiar with from his past. The typical adrenaline rush. The high alert of his senses. He knew he was dreaming. He was familiar with the varying nightmarish dreams he often had while in Kyren Forest. Dreams of running, being hunted, fighting. But this time, the panic he often felt was amplified whenever anyone came near a certain auburn-haired beauty. There were too many of them. He wouldn't be able to win or escape this time. Worst of all, he couldn't protect her.

Suddenly, a blinding flash penetrated his vision. He sprang upright. Was he still dreaming or awake?

He raised his hand against the light. Screams pierced his consciousness from all sides. He blinked frantically. Anxious motion rolled behind him. Lightning emitted in front of him. The volt moss!

Kendrick jumped to his feet, weapon in hand. He flung the sheath off the sword and turned to where the light and screeching was most prominent.

To the right, the volt moss had two goblins writhing in its lightning tentacles. Electric energy pulsed through their bodies for a couple more seconds before the charge finally subsided.

Kendrick glanced over his shoulder. Memsy had her arm braced in front of her daughter, yet both had their hands clasped firmly over their mouths, their eyes riveted on the wriggling creatures.

Sizzling and crackling continued from the moss and the bodies but soon was drowned out by a raspy voice swearing in Goblinian.

Kendrick gestured for the women to hold their position and stealthily stepped forward. A third goblin, stalagmite weapon bared, came cussing around his fallen comrades. Even in the faint illumination from the ground-bright, he could see the green slime oozing over the creature's paper-thin lips and spewing with its every curse.

Catching the man's motion, the goblin snapped his gaze on Kendrick and charged. Swift and nearly unseen, the black figure flung itself at him. Kendrick barely had time to raise his sword to counter when the stalagmite iron crashed against it. Razor-sharp teeth snapped inches beyond his nose. Putrid breath, foul and decaying, assaulted his senses.

The healer supported his blade with his right hand and pushed the creature away. The goblin stumbled backward. It stepped on and nearly tripped over its fallen brothers. This agitated it even more. Again, it lunged at him. The clang of crashing weapons echoed off the trees.

Kendrick barely had time to counter; the goblin rushed him from the side. His adversary was not very strong, but Kendrick needed all his wits about him to counter the creature's stealth. Turning and twisting, he parried time and time again. Finally, it rushed at him, crashing into his weapon with such force he staggered back. The creature pressed in on him. Its eyes turning red at the anticipation of blood, it licked out its narrow, forked tongue just a breath away from the man's face.

Suddenly, the goblin tensed. A small screech emitted from its throat, and its eyes rolled back in its head. Kendrick straightened, stepping back. As the creature crumpled to the side, he spotted Adianna standing directly behind it, bow at the ready.

Kendrick surveyed the body at his feet, then saw her arrow protruding from both sides. Relief flooded through him. He peered at the woman lowering her weapon, grateful for her clear-headedness. She was so calm, standing there. She attempted a smile at him, and he was struck again with the thought that he could now call this quick-thinking woman his wife.

He released his breath, returning her smile. She was safe. They had survived. All was well.

Suddenly, the air above them filled with the sound of bellowing, like the sky was filled with whale song. Kendrick flinched from the sound, looking up. But what he saw made him groan. There, in the very topmost of the trees were several large pods, each illuminating as the sounds within grew louder.

"Great! Now the moon shairns have stirred."

They watched long, glowing tentacles stretch forth from the round openings in the pods. Some of the tentacles were narrow and straight with thick tips. Others wound around like curled ribbon, each one deadly to the touch. Then the openings were filled with growing bulbous inflations like air squeezing through a chink in a balloon. Each bulb in turn grew larger and larger until a giant jellyfish-like creature popped from each pod. The creatures were ten feet across and mostly flat on top, with multiple tentacles hanging beneath.

The moon shairns floated lightly down from the treetops on the teeniest air currents created between the warmth of the ground and the coolness of the night. Kendrick pulled Adianna back away from the tentacles of one of the shairns descending close in front of them. The moon shairns were seldom aggressive, but even inadvertently brushing up against one of their tentacles could have devastating results.

Out of harm's way, the trio watched the luminescent beasts meander around, their tentacles brushing a mere foot or two above the ground. Their muted moans rose and fell like some haunting ballad.

"They'll be migrating now around the forest due to the electric charge they feel in the air," Kendrick grumbled. "We won't be able to recharge the volt moss until they've all moved completely away, or we'll wind up frying one of them. But we can't go to sleep ourselves, for we will need to be awake to avoid their tentacles. We can't merely get under the bramble, for if they brush up against it, it will work as a conductor and zap anything underneath."

Kendrick glared at the pesky, though beautiful, bioluminescent creatures. "We're not going to be able to get any sleep until they move out."

This time it was Adianna's face glowing with mischief. "I have an idea."

Kendrick continued to sit rigidly, still baffled he had even let her talk him into this. Both of his companions had fallen asleep quickly, lulled easily by the soft moaning bellows of the gentle, glowing herd. He still wasn't convinced of the sanity of his wife's plan. Yet here he was, perched on the back of a giant moon shairn, gliding along twenty feet above the forest floor.

After repeating his own challenge to trust from earlier, Adianna had climbed the nearest tree.

Why is that woman always climbing things? he remembered wondering.

She had respectfully greeted the alpha shairn of the herd. Then she asked to be granted either a right of passage or to hide a pizza—his Elvish was quite rusty.

Dawning fell upon him, and he had flatly refused to take part. Both women had coaxed and assured him that they'd be perfectly safe up top, and that the herd would protect them along with each other should anything arise. He had been far from convinced as he had no desire to be around any conflict that involved the shairns let alone be atop them. But he had finally relented.

He now leaned cautiously over in an attempt to view the slowly passing ground, but Kendrick still wasn't convinced the squishy cap of the moon shairn wouldn't give way to his shifting. He was used to heights. Even used to flying on various creatures of this world. Yet something like this took some getting used to.

Though Adianna was now mostly just a dark outline atop the luminescent beast moseying in front of him, the creature's glow cast a soft light on her peaceful features.

What has fate and this little minx done to my predictable life?

He spotted occasional light gliding over her and looked up. The rain had ceased, and the clouds had departed as quickly as they had come. Now stars glittered beyond the canopy. The smaller of Sheorae's two moons, Syron, was edging along its northeasterly path.

Summoning courage, Kendrick haltingly maneuvered his way into a prostrate position and tucked his hands behind his head. He relaxed by degrees while he gazed into the heavens.

Syron was his favorite moon. The Moon of the Valiant, with its Ring of Fire Crater winking when full or smiling a great Cheshire grin as it was now. He had many happy memories watching its ascent in the southern sky as a child. He had pretended to be the hero of that lunar myth—aspiring to be a great Warrior of Truth, who would vanquish evil and rescue the innocent.

Kendrick smiled sadly at the naïveté of those boyhood imaginings. Still, he let those hopeful musings lull him into a restful sleep.

DISCOVERY

Adianna stretched awake. By the pale gray tint on everything and the dull glow of the moon shairn, she knew it was just before dawn. She felt fully refreshed despite the repeated nightmares. The underlying energy and vibration of the moon shairn during the night-long ride had soothed her weary bones and aching muscles.

Gingerly she sat up and noticed the nocturnal creatures were beginning their ascent to a new drelth of pods high in the trees.

"Mems!" she called. Then she patted the creature beneath her, gathered her things as it moved near a tree branch, and off she sprang. She saw Memsy following suit, so she looked around for the healer.

The moon shairn the healer rode was just rising past her branch. "Healer!"

When he didn't stir, she picked up a pinecone and chucked it out him. "Healer!"

The pinecone bounced off his back, and he jerked awake. His sword came up with him. But when he perceived the situation, he gathered his things and looked to the trees. He stood awkwardly, looking very apprehensive of his footing. Finally, he turned a pleading look to Adianna.

"How do I get down?" he called, eyeing branch after branch moving past just out of reach.

Adianna chuckled. "Give her a pat so she knows you want to get off."

The healer did as instructed, and the great beast floated toward a branch for him to disembark.

Within moments, the trio had reached the ground. The bellowing moans of the moon shairns drew their attention skyward. Somehow the jellylike creatures squeezed through the narrow openings of the pods. Drawing in their tentacles, the glowing creatures' sanctuaries slowly snuffed out. With one last chorus of bellows, the moon shairns bid the world good day, and all went quiet.

The healer grinned around broadly and stretched.

"I feel amazing! That was probably one of the best night's sleeps I've had in a very long time."

With hands clasped high overhead, he stretched first to one side then the other, scanning the forest. Presently, he stood erect and alert.

"No! No, no, no, no," he groaned, turning around repeatedly.

"What's the matter?" Adianna inquired.

The man growled under his breath. Then he smacked his hands against his thighs. "The moon shairns brought us too far south."

He gestured at the craggy hills just now becoming visible in the increasing light of dawn. "Those knolls signify the edge of Lenchur. We're over a day's journey south of where we need to be to cross the Fal Dura Bridge."

Memsy stepped forward consolingly. "All is well, Master Healer. If we are not where we expected to be, then we are not where anyone else expects us to be either."

He looked at her, confused. Then he turned to Adianna, arching an eyebrow in question. She merely shrugged.

He chuckled but spoke to the sorci. "If you say so, madam."

Then he gestured to the northwest, asking, "Shall we?"

The little band stayed vigilantly watchful of shadows and on the lookout for goblins, until the full light of day bathed the forest in its brightness. With the light came the heat, and the moisture from the night before turned the forest into a sauna. Yet on they trudged.

The day was long, and the group said little.

Adianna's mind was a jumble of thoughts throughout the day. She thought of the quest. She thought of the reasons they had to succeed. She thought of the good people of Sheorae. But mostly she thought of the man on whom their world, and her life, now hinged. Occasionally, she was caught looking at him. Occasionally, he was caught looking at her. Each time, she looked away to hide her flaming cheeks.

Through the immense heat of the afternoon, Adianna had shoved the cloak back over her shoulders, so it just barely covered the Blades. She removed her gloves and tucked them into her belt. Sweat made her scalp itch and trickled down between her shoulder blades. Still, on they trudged.

By the time the sun was heavy on the horizon, Memsy remarked that she was beginning to recognize some of where they were.

The healer smiled. Then he shimmied up an enormous log that lay across the trail. Standing on top, he assisted Memsy over. When the older woman was safely across, he reached down to help Adianna next.

She stared at his hand for several heartbeats. She realized her hesitation was evident when she saw his face. His eyebrows were low and puckered, awaiting her decision. Her gaze skidded away.

"I've got it," she asserted and looked frantically for adequate footholds. She found a couple but slipped on her skirt on the third. She banged her knee on a branch and smacked her elbow on the top.

She could hear the healer sigh heavily. She scrambled to the top as he jumped down on the other side. When she came to stand atop the log, he reached up both hands to help her. The gesture was kind, but his gaze was flat.

"No, really. I've got it." She sat down, kicking her skirts out of the way.

"Of course, you do," he muttered. Then he pivoted to the side, out of her way.

She slid down the huge log and landed in a heap at his feet. She could feel a slight bruising to her other knee. She stood slowly, trying not to wince. She brushed off her hands and straightened her skirt before she chanced a look at his face.

He stood as tall as a sentinel and twice as stony. His jaw worked. His nostrils flared. But he did not look at her at all.

Shame flooded Adianna's chest as she hobbled to join her mother. Memsy linked arms with her and gave her a pat. But the older woman said nothing. She merely lent support while the younger woman walked off her injuries.

But presently, all was forgotten, for the forest before them opened up to a small meadow brimming with hundreds of blue and lavender flowers.

"Dandy daisies!" she breathed.

A great smile spread over her face and that of her mother's.

Dandy daisies were her absolute favorite flowers. They grew in clusters, each with soft, delicate daisy-like petals. In the center of this array of petals were tiny puffballs of matching lavender or periwinkle. The air smelled wonderfully of their tantalizing aroma—just the right mixture of orange and vanilla. Adianna inhaled the heavenly scent.

The women took a tentative step forward and revealed another reason why these were her favorite flowers. As soon as their skirts brushed the wild garden, dozens of the teeniest puff balls possible flew into the air. Everywhere skimmed the little puffballs, filling the meadow with the soft sound of humming.

Stepping slowly through the flowers, Adianna held out her hand. The puffballs, no bigger than her fingernail, were tiny birds. One puff for the body, a smaller puff for the head, teeny sleek feathered wings, and a long, slender beak. Several gathered along her hand, their downy softness tickling her skin. Unhurriedly, she drew her hand closer to her face. At this nearness, she could just make out the birds' delicate eyelashes. Dandy birds—the only birds in Sheorae with eyelashes.

Both a periwinkle and lavender dandy bird hummed up into her face. She whispered her usual greeting. The tiny things glided forward and nuzzled their soft heads against her nose. Adianna giggled at the mild tickle.

Yet they quickly dashed away when the healer went tromping past. He was scowling and kicking through the flowers. A short way in front of her, he paused when a dandy bird landed on his arm. He raised it. But instead of inspecting the sweet little thing like Adianna expected, he flicked the bird away.

Adianna's mouth fell open. "How could you?!"

"What?" he countered. "It's just a prick bird."

Incensed, Adianna stormed forward, getting right in his face. "For your information, they are called dandy birds. They are sweet, and soft, and delightful!"

"And drink blood," he concluded for her.

She scoffed back. "They only drink blood during mating season. And that ended months ago."

She swished past him, giving him a dirty glare. "You should be ashamed of yourself."

But before she could go very far, she heard him thunder, "Fabulous!"

She stopped short, turning.

"Not only am I not allowed to help, touch, or even look at my wife," he snarled right in her face, "but now I can't even flick at prick birds!"

He tromped away, throwing his hands in the air. "What else, oh marvelous one, am I not allowed to do? What's next, huh?"

He quickly stomped beyond the flower-strewn meadow, venting the whole way. "I know. My freedom will be forfeit, too. Oh, wait. That's already happened. Let's see. I'm not allowed to go through the woods or anywhere in Sheorae without being hunted. Check. Got that one, too!"

Adianna felt bad. She reached after him. "Healer, wait."

He kept right on stomping and ranting. "How about be allowed to have a say in whether I am married off or to whom? Nope. Not allowed that one either."

She was about to go after him, but then she noticed all the critters—squirrels, chipmunks, hares, even the dandy birds—were scurrying quickly toward her and to the left. Which registered to her that something they feared was before her and to the right. Yet the healer and all his tirade were straight in front of her.

"Healer," she hissed, rushing after him.

He gave no heed. He turned, gestured his hands out wide in a mock bow, and turned back the way he was going. "But what about being allowed to choose whether I take on a mission that will get me killed? No, never that."

"Healer. Be quiet!" She tried again in a pleading whisper.

He went on, louder still. "Never mind I have been traipsing all over this Great Being-forsaken world for years in the attempt of avoiding said mission. No matter I have spent my life trying to protect my loved ones from this very stupidity! Does that matter? No!"

The healer had just reached another small clearing beyond the patch of trees. Adianna made it to the edge of the last tree and skidded to a stop. She thrust her arm out to stop Memsy as well. Nudging her mother back, she put her finger to her lips, before looking to her exposed husband.

"Does anyone think to talk to me? Does anyone think to ask? No! And here I am, traipsing through the woods to my doom!"

"Well, if yous wearen't so noisy, yous doom wouldn't've finds ya so easily."

The voice was deep, gravelly, and familiar. Instantly, giant, three-fingered hands clamped down on the healer. Two orgrins yanked him up into their clutches. He kicked and struggled, but to no avail. Within seconds, he was strung between them, an arm and a leg in each of their hands.

Donk, the alpha of the three orgrins that had attacked the healer just a week before, took a deep sniff of their captive. "'Ere. We's been looking for yous since ya banged us out flat and tooth-picked our brov'er in the sweets."

The younger brother, Lug, gurgled with glee. "Let's eats 'im. … For Zog."

Adianna's eyes were wide when the healer's met hers. His steely gaze fixed on her, his jaw set. Before she could flinch, he flicked his chin in her direction. He wanted her to go?

Adianna's teeth clenched, and her eyes narrowed. Instantly, she turned to Memsy. She flicked the clasp of her cloak and removed both it and the Blades.

"Adianna, I'm not sure…"

Adianna shoved her cloak and all her weapons into her mother's arms. "Insufferable man!"

Her mother's eyes were anxious. Adianna took a deep breath. "Stay here," she instructed and shoved her behind the tree.

Adianna noticed the healer's expression change rapidly from surprise to annoyance then fear when she stepped out from behind the tree and into the clearing. She couldn't even name his next expression as he watched her fling her hands in the air, wailing, and propel herself at the nearest orgrin.

She flung herself at its feet, clinging to its leg, and bawled, "Oh, Mighty Orgins! Please! Please, spare this lowly human!"

Her fake sobs and spurts of breath covered her response to the sensations swirling inside her.

Lug released the arm and leg he held, sending the healer's body crashing into the rocky legs of his brother, and tried to brush her off. "Begone, woman! Before we eats yous, too."

She stretched her arms up at him. "No, please, Great One. He is my husband. Our children. Please. Please, Mighty One, we need him. How will we live?"

Lug looked at his brother, who shook his head. The younger brother then glanced at her like she was some annoying, filthy dog and nudged her with his toe. "Off wiff yous."

His little nudge sent Adianna sprawling on her back. But she scrambled up quickly and went for Donk. He released the healer's leg and shied back a step. The man dangled in the air, hanging by one arm. She flung her arms around this orgrin's leg.

"Then, please, Mighty Orgrin! I beg of you! Grant me privilege to hug their father in a teary goodbye so I may more eloquently portray the story to our children of their father's demise by the great and dreaded orgrins."

Adianna knew, as a subspecies, the orgrins loved any chance at recognition, and to be personified in story, the more elaborate and fearsome the better. So, she was not surprised to see this request was not flatly refused.

She could see Donk's mind working. A grim smile pulled at his scant lips, slowly revealing his jagged, orange teeth. He looked to Lug, who was already smirking his thin chops and chuckling, his gorilla-arms swaying at the motion. Finally, he looked at the man, held high, still dangling by one arm.

With a great smile, Donk dropped the human, who landed in a heap on the ground. "Say 'buh'bye. Then tell story of fearsome Donk and Lug."

Donk shook his leg free from the woman while the man scrambled to his feet.

"Thank you, Great Eminent Ones!" Adianna jumped to her feet and flung herself into the healer's arms, burying her face in his neck.

"What are you doing?" he growled in her ear.

She didn't answer. She just stood rigid in his arms, trembling. Her breath came in one sharp strand. Sensation and burning mingled, sending that same breath out in short, moaning, painful-sounding bursts. This must have startled the healer, for he pushed her back to see her face. But the sensory overload made her head fall back and her eyes roll slightly. Her body fell slack and would have crumpled to the ground had his hands not been clamped around her upper arms.

But the healer gave her a slight shake, and with a sharp squeal, she willed her head to come up right. She bit down against the pain and blinked repeatedly to focus on his face. He looked terrified.

She gave her head a final shake and became aware both orgrins had moved around behind them.

The healer opened his mouth to say more, but she leaned in, pulling his ear down to her. "Just remember to tuck and roll!" she hissed. "Then aim for under the arms if you can!"

He jerked back, a confused look on his face. But before he could respond, she winked at him, confusing him even further. Then she grabbed hold of his belt and shirt front and propelled him like a javelin over the orgrins' heads.

The healer howled as he went sailing through the air but did have the presence of mind to tuck before landing. The orgrins gawked at the man flying overhead, turning away from Adianna. This gave her the opportunity to spin-kick a foot out from under the big one, then jump up and slam all her borrowed orgrin-strength down upon the other's back.

Over the giants' sprawled bodies, she saw the healer spring to his feet, drawing his sword as he spun around. Amazement etched his face upon seeing the prostrate foe.

But Adianna did not wait for him to catch up. She ran over to Donk, who was recovering the fastest, and ran up his back. Her fleet-footedness resulted in monster-stomps across his body, until she leapt into the air, crashed her feet down on his head, and rolled to a stop beside the healer.

On the man's face, she saw bewilderment and admiration. The admiration quickly won out, to the point where Adianna felt her cheeks flame a bright red. Adianna grinned broadly but instinctively looked away, pulling her bottom lip between her teeth.

A gravelly groan emitted from the face-down Lug. Adianna turned, but the healer braced his arm in front of her. He stepped over to the stirring monster. Yet instead of raising its arm to issue a death blow, the healer stepped alongside the orgrin. He measured a distance of a span and a half from the top of the creature's head with his hand, then with both hands brought the hilt of his sword smashing down in that exact spot. Instantly, the creature's body went limp.

The healer spun around to the other orgrin and observed the stunted creature. Apparently deducing Donk, too, was indeed unconscious, he edged back to Adianna's side.

Looking in each other's eyes, they both released a breath she was sure neither one of them knew they were holding. At this, the healer let out a laugh, which she reciprocated.

"That was amazing!" He shook his head. Full of wonder, his eyes never left hers. "*You* were amazing."

Their gazes held, and Adianna felt a wonderful heat smolder to life inside her belly. She could not look away. She dragged in each breath, emotion heavy on her chest. She really did love this man. She loved how he made her feel. How alive she felt when he looked at her that way. She felt so powerful, and yet she knew she could easily melt into his arms. If only…

He stepped forward in that moment and pulled her into his arms. It was so sudden Adianna let out a cry, unprepared for the instant scorching. The healer instantly released her, with his arms poised about her.

"You're hurt!" he insisted.

"No, I'm fine." So instant was the relief from the burning when he released her, it was easy for her to brush aside his concerns.

"Adianna," he rebuked. "You do remember I am a healer. I can help."

His voice was so tender Adianna actually wished he could. Suddenly, Adianna jerked—she felt someone putting something on her shoulders. It was Memsy and her shamere cloak.

"I'm sure it's nothing," the older woman smiled, rubbing her hands up and down her daughter's cloaked arms.

Memsy gave her a knowing nod, and Adianna leaned into the woman's support. The elf then turned her smile to the healer. "I am so grateful you are both safe."

She affectionately grasped her son-in-law's hand while she kept Adianna tucked in her other arm. She smiled once again between the two, then urged, "Now, we really should find shelter."

In unison, the two humans took notice of the encroaching darkness. Shadows had crept in much closer than when they had left the dandy daisies. The ground-bright was beginning to illuminate patches along the forest floor.

"Come." Memsy gave them both a pat. "I know of a place close by."

The pair gathered their forgotten supplies and followed Memsy as she turned directly west. They made their way with haste. Adianna and the healer exchanged glances in the deepening shadows but stayed silent.

Before long, the forest opened to a grove where pine, oak, and ash trees were replaced by fruit and nut trees. Though the signs of neglect were grossly apparent, the design of an orchard was unmistakable.

Adianna slowed, intensely observing the scene around her. Before long, she was sure. "I know this place."

She looked to her mother for an explanation. Memsy merely acquiesced with a smile. The sorci offered her hand, and the two women meandered arm-in-arm further into the orchard. Adianna turned her head every which way, trying to catch the snatches of memory flitting around her consciousness.

Suddenly, Memsy froze. Adianna instinctively searched her face, but her mother stared ahead, eyes wide with dismay. Adianna followed her gaze to see the burnt remains of a small cottage beyond the orchard. Mechanically, she released her mother's arm and stumbled forward, slowly at first, then gaining speed.

"Adianna, wait!"

But Adianna didn't stop. A knowing panic crept into her soul, and she had to see for herself.

"What is it?" she heard the healer question.

But Memsy called again, "Adianna, please! Wait!"

Still, she pressed on, skirting the ash and stone. She veered around the side of the structure. She brushed past the tree swing, with peals of laughter assaulting her from the past. She whipped through the willow limbs hanging down, frantic to escape the tangles on the ground. Finally, she made it to the front of the cottage and froze.

Nearly the whole front of the cottage was burned to rubble.

She was vaguely aware of Memsy's gasp beside her and the healer arriving breathless and confused.

Again, Adianna stumbled forward.

"Adianna." She felt her mother's hold brush on, then off, her arm.

Adianna stepped through what was left of the charred entrance and looked helplessly around. Though most of the back wall was still intact, many of the furnishings were unrecognizable. Foliage and bramble grew up the walls and tangled across the floor, denoting the many years since the destructive fire had taken place. Only a few stones remained standing where she remembered the hearth having been. Little animals peeked out from nests in the jumbled undergrowth. A few charred axes leaned against the back wall.

At the sound of crunching pottery, Adianna whirled around to see the others nearby. She sought out Memsy's face, but the look of bewilderment matched everything she felt.

Finally, her eyes fell upon the doorway to the second room. Dread enveloped her. She stumbled forward, numb.

At first, a toppled bed frame and the shredded remains of a mattress riddled with rodent nests were all she could see past the door. She touched the blackened door, only to jump back as it broke off the hinges and crashed to the floor. There, beyond it, huddled in the corner were two charred human skeletons locked in a last embrace.

An anguished cry strangled in her throat. The healer was at her side in a moment. Again, she was aware of Memsy's gasp. But the young woman staggered forward, tripping over the collapsed door, and crumpled in front of the burned couple.

She reached out to touch the face of one of the long-since-gone faces but stopped mid-air and recoiled, wrapping her arms around herself.

Tears filled her eyes, and she rocked back and forth trying to calm the devastation threatening to consume her.

Softly, she heard the healer inquire, "Who is it? Who lived here?"

The night was quiet. Nothing could be heard beyond those charred walls. Nothing could be heard at all but Adianna's quiet sobs.

Finally, she sucked in a tattered breath and answered his question.

"I did."

ADIANNA'S PAST

Kendrick jerked awake, anxiously searching for clues indicating his whereabouts. There they were. The small fire. The willow. Memsy reclined, eyes closed. The cottage…

He breathed out a sigh and relaxed.

After burying the remains, they had chosen not to camp in the cottage. It offered little protection from hunters, little protection from the young woman's past. Even beneath this giant tree, hidden behind its immense tangle of branches, there was little shield from marauding parties, but it was better than the haunting of memories. Nothing more had been spoken about what happened here, but he had deduced the bodies were Adianna's parents and neither of the women had been aware of their horrific demise.

Now he sat and stared into the small fire but couldn't seem to receive its heat. Thoughts of sleep were gone. No, his thoughts were a mangled hodge-podge of apprehension, concern, and curiosity. Looking past the fire, he found the sleeping form of the one who was the center of all which plagued him.

At present, Adianna laid facing the fire, though he knew with her fitful sleeping that would soon change. She had even more night terrors than he did in these woods. So, Kendrick took this moment to study her features without reservation.

In sleep, she looked so young, innocent, and delicate. And yet somehow, she had taken out two orgrins single-handedly just hours before. If he hadn't been there himself, he wouldn't have believed it. In fact, he *had* been there, and he still wasn't sure what took place.

Who is this woman I have married? What's her story? He peered through the willow limbs at the ruins of the dilapidated cottage. Then he spotted the newly covered graves in the moonlight. *And if these were her parents, then why was she living among the elves?*

Memsy was resting against the trunk of the willow. Even in sleep, her hand stretched out to rest protectively on Adianna's shoulder. Her sorci emblem glistened in the firelight. *Why would an elf raise a human girl?*

Returning his gaze to his wife, all he had were questions. The more he thought, the more questions sprang forth. More questions, but no answers.

She was beautiful, strong, courageous. *How could a woman such as this come from these lowly surroundings?*

His thoughts lingered once again to their skirmish with the orgrins. He had never encountered that, not in all his years of combat. *Where had she learned to fight? The elves? No, she used strength and technique which were decidedly not Human nor Elvin. So, what's going on here?*

"Tell me of your dreams, Master Healer."

Kendrick started. Memsy was observing him, emblem shimmering. She gave the sleeping woman a loving pat, then sat to appraise him more meticulously.

He stared back at her a moment. Her gaze was too knowing; it made him feel so vulnerable. He searched for an evasion, but their seclusion was nearly total, only the valdashorps croaking in the background. Finally, he sighed. He knew she would get her answers whether he verbally told her or not. So, he poured them each a cup of the chamomile and peppermint tea she had made earlier. After handing her a mug, he wrapped his hands around the warm metal of his own and stared into the fire.

"There's not much to tell," he began. "My dreams are rather pleasant... until I enter these woods. But for as long as I can remember, as soon as I come into Kyren Forest, I get similar, if not the same set of dreams. Each is filled with fighting and death and despair. And everything depends on me—yet more often than not, I fail, leaving those I love exposed."

His grip tightened on the steaming mug. To avoid the onslaught of images, he gulped a mouthful of the hot brew. Then he focused on the heat spreading from his throat to his belly.

"How old were you when you began coming through Kyren Forest?" Memsy's gaze was deeply contemplative, like she was putting pieces of a puzzle together.

Kendrick tried to find her answer without allowing specifics of hows, with whoms, or whys to surface for her detection. "I don't know. I guess I was about five, maybe?"

Despite his efforts, a knowing smile settled on her face. Instinctively, he ground his teeth and looked back into the fire. It didn't help.

"Why this sudden interest in my dreams, old one?" he snapped.

Memsy reclined again against the willow. "Because, Master Healer, they match Adianna's nightmares exactly."

Shock stunted all thought, until he felt warm liquid seep through the leg of his pants. He jerked the mug, cursing under his breath and wiping at the wet spot. He set the mug next to him on the ground. He flicked moisture off his fingers and swiped again at his pants, trying to take in this surprising information. He wasn't sure he liked what it could imply since all his nightmares were too often centered around those blasted Blades. He chose to avoid the implication.

"So, I've told you. Now you tell me. What really happened tonight with the orgrins? And what happened here?" He flung a gesture encompassing the cottage and the graves in unison.

Memsy raised her eyebrows, heaving a heavy sigh. He wasn't sure she would give him the answers he sought, until she slowly leaned forward again, rubbing her hands together. She paused a bit before speaking.

"What happened tonight is actually a continuation of what happened to this cottage. As you've probably gathered, this humble abode belonged to Adianna's parents. They had no clue as to the destiny of their precious baby. As you can see, they were simple peasant folk. She was such a beautiful baby. So pleasant and content.

"They occasionally visited me for potions to cure their ills and whatnot. Often, the cure they sought was an herb or root they passed on their way to reach me. I tried to teach them, but they were happy in their ignorance, I suppose. Things were fine until they encountered problems with Adianna's powers."

"Her powers!?" Kendrick started as if he had been hit. "What powers?"

Memsy's gaze penetrated his. Kendrick could almost feel her inside his mind, searching for answers of her own. Quickly, he closed his eyes and shook his head, holding up a hand to ward her off.

"Please don't. Really. You don't need to. Regardless of how it happened…" He finally met her gaze. "She is my wife. I will do nothing to harm her."

His conviction seemed to satisfy the sorci. She smiled. "The Great Being was wise in choosing you. Adianna's fate is safe in your hands, I think."

Her eyebrows went up again, looking over at her sleeping daughter. "Adianna possesses the powers of the ganji."

Again, her words had the effect of him being struck. "Ganji!" he exclaimed. "They really exist?" He peered at the woman he had just pledged to protect with new wonder. "I thought they were just fairy tales."

"Fairies! Those pesky beings! They have had their hand in many a tale, and most of them true!" Memsy chuckled. "But, yes, ganji are real. They are a preordained, elite royal line of fairies within the human nation, and so are very rare. They appear only once every two to three hundred years. I am nearly eight hundred myself and have only heard of three. But they are real. She is living proof. She has the power to absorb the abilities and powers of anyone or anything with which she comes in contact. The longer the contact, the longer and more acute her abilities to use them."

Kendrick looked at his wife, awe-struck. Thoughts began racing through his mind. This explained so many things: how she was able to fight the way she did, why she could run so swiftly even carrying Memsy, even how he had healed so quickly. It was all linked to her.

Then something Memsy said sank in. “You said problems with her powers. What problems?”

A sad smile crossed her face as she turned to the fire again. She grabbed a nearby stick and began to poke at the fire. “They weren’t really problems, per se. You see Adi developed her powers as she developed the ability to walk. Her parents just weren’t prepared for their toddler to pet a cat, then climb a tree and refuse to come down.”

Kendrick couldn’t help snickering at the thought. Memsy laughed as well, her eyes dancing. But Adianna stirred restlessly, so they quieted. When the girl slept soundly again, Memsy continued in a whisper.

“Her parents moved out here, away from questioning observers. I helped them design the orchard, and her father took to woodcutting. Between the two, they were able to trade rather successfully with those moving around the woods or to or from Lenchur.

“Little Adianna was such an appealing child. And she loved to learn. Anything she could get from me, she would desire. I really shouldn’t have taught her how to coax the woodland creatures to her, I suppose.” She heaved a sigh of remorse.

“One day, she charmed a dove out of its nest to perch upon her finger. Her parents were in awe, until little Adianna tried to fly away with it.”

Kendrick’s surprise was heightened when she leaned toward him and added, “She was barely four years old at the time.”

Mind-boggled now, he could do nothing but stare at the woman sleeping so peacefully, the shadows of the fire dancing on her angelic features.

“It was after that when her parents brought her to me,” Memsy continued. “They were too afraid of her to want to learn how to teach her to utilize her powers. They gave her to me. They said they were going to move to Avari. I supposed they didn’t make it out before…

“It was not a week later fate added another burden to this sweet child’s lot. It was then that the Blades came to her.”

“What!” Kendrick gasped.

She nodded. “They must have escaped the hawkmen and striders that had fought overhead the night before. For she found them nestled in a blackberry bush when we went picking that next morning. She acquired the emblem almost instantly, and so we have protected her and prepared her until the day you would come."

Kendrick's brow wrinkled in question. "Emblem?"

"Ah." Memsy appraised him. "You do not know about the emblems. How much *do* you know about the Prophecy?"

A mingle of emotions played through him. He took a deep breath, letting it seethe out between his teeth. Then he recited in monotone from memory like a history lesson. "A Barer and a Wielder must band together, take the Blades to Dorincia Castle on Balcore Island, unite the Seven Nations, then get past Drokmar's horde to insert the Blades into the Unity Thrones, which have been held in his fortress since he stole them after being banished by your kind. The Blades will then dispel the segregating energy brought on by the Fairies' gifts, and the Alliance will then rule Sheorae."

Memsy's evaluating expression was unnerving when next he regarded her. She did not move at all while she beheld him, except when her mouth tipped slightly to the side.

"It makes sense that that would be all you would know of the Prophecy. A to-do list of what needs to happen, instead of knowing the full situation. But the Blades, my boy, have their own path. They were designed to be incorruptible to the pride and greed of any species. That is why they were taken from Drokmar in the beginning. They felt the lust for power building within him, even while he forged them. And they withdrew from his grasp."

Sadness covered the elf's face and laced her voice. Her eyes glistened in the firelight. For a moment, Kendrick wished he were the one with the power to hear thoughts.

Finally, she shook free of her musings. When she spoke, it was with the soft whisper of a storyteller spinning the ancient tales.

"Regardless of the plots or plans of man or beast, the Blades know their fate. They know the reason for which they were made, and they strive in every moment to move along whichever path is available to them to complete their purpose.

"So, is it any wonder after hundreds of years of tumbling from one defective union to another—all founded on injustice of some kind—that the

Blades would pursue a unique path into the arms of an innocent? Or even with someone set vairnbent on avoiding dealings with them completely?"

Their gazes met across the fire. Logically, he knew she was right, yet panic fringed the outer edges.

"No! No, it's not me!" he asserted. "I am not the one, even if she is." He nodded to the sleeping beauty.

"That's not what Puffin said."

Kendrick froze at the dragon's name.

"Of all the people, Master Healer, you would know the link between dragons and the Blades. You would know how all dragons know when a Bearer claims the Blades. How they can sense when a Bearer or Wielder is near, and when the Blades are wielded. How the dragons announce it with a triumphant roar."

Kendrick's eyes narrowed, but he did not meet Memsy's gaze.

"Like the roar that woke you the other night."

His widened eyes trained on Memsy's. She smiled knowingly. Then a tenderness reached out to him through her expression and her voice. "Like the roar you heard the night your brother died. And haven't heard since—until the other night."

Kendrick clenched his teeth, and his mouth became a hard line. He focused narrowed eyes on the dancing flames.

The dark pain of the past slowly enveloped him in agonizing memories. While he brooded the past, Adianna's peaceful face caught his attention. He searched those delicate features. Unbidden, those gruesome recollections scooped her up and enclosed around her. Including her in those images ripped at his heart harder than ever before. It couldn't be possible. His mind strained to reject it, to think of a way out.

"But Mentaloss and Durluki are men! And besides, I have no emblem of which you speak."

Memsy sat motionless, her face solemn. Then she swung her head sadly side to side. "You men. The Blades require an eternal alliance. Do you really think your unions, allegiances, and treaties are eternal? They can be broken in a heartbeat! Just like that!"

She snapped her fingers for emphasis.

She was right. He had seen it. Time after time the loyalties of the nations crumbled. Each side had their own agenda, and when that agenda became unattainable, alliances were dissolved without fail. *So how could an eternal alliance be made*?

Memsy's voice sounded over the flames. "You spoke of just such an eternal union yesterday."

Kendrick scrutinized her face, seeking her meaning.

"Your mother," Memsy whispered.

Kendrick's eyes bulged. Air streamed through his nostrils, filling him to capacity, yet still pulled in the heady drought. His mouth lulled open. He was struck for several moments, air still flooding his system.

When, finally, he could peel his eyes away from Memsy to stare blindly at the fire, his breath escaped him in one hard rush. The release was so distinct a sharp pain pricked his chest. Still, he stared.

Swallowing hard, he pinned Memsy again, hoping he misunderstood, "You're talking about a marriage."

At her nod, he tried again. "You're talking about a man and a woman, bonded together in matrimony, taking on all the evil clutching Sheorae!"

Memsy pursed her lips and looked into the fire.

Kendrick slumped. His wide eyes searched the ground, searched the fire, searched anywhere for a different answer.

"But we're already married, and I still don't have this aforementioned emblem."

The sorci eyed him as if he were a toddler explaining away his hand in the cookie jar.

"Look, Kendrick." She held up her hand before he could interject. "Yes, I know your name. And I believe it is high time your wife should know it, too. But I digress. This marriage is between the two of you. Nothing I, nor Daerlot, or anyone else for that matter, can do will change that. No deception or technicality can make a marriage. That is up to you. Both of you."

He examined Adianna in the flickering glow of the fire.

"And two things, before you start hedging your denials." She had caught him just before he opened his mouth. "First of all, we both know just how unappealing you view entrusting Adianna's fate—or her heart—to another."

Kendrick tilted his head to the side with a half shrug, eyebrows arched high. She had him there.

Memsy smiled knowingly, then looked at her clasped hands. Fingers still clenched, she opened her palms wide like a book. She quirked her mouth to the side before she spoke. “Now, there is one more thing about her ganji powers that you need to know.”

She took in a deep breath and let it out slowly. “In order to preserve what the fairies considered a sacred line, there was a sort of glitch inserted into their DNA.”

She looked at him, apparently seeking his thoughts on this new revelation. But he had none. He was lost.

“You see,” she ventured. “When a ganji comes in contact with a member of the opposite sex… it burns them.”

“What?” Kendrick nearly leapt to his feet; he was so struck by this news. His mouth bobbed open and closed for several seconds before continuing.

“You mean every time I’ve touched her…?”

His roar made Adianna jump in her sleep. Kendrick flinched back, not having meant to disturb her, and was thankful when she settled quickly back down. Memsy, on the other hand, had her bottom lip clamped between bared teeth and was nodding the affirmative.

“You remember that angry welt she had on her arm after the episode with the strider? That was from you holding her back. That is why she ripped from your grasp so violently in the first place. Her cloak and gloves aren’t merely an accessory. They are her protection. It is the only way the contact doesn’t burn.

“She didn’t have them with her the day she found you. It nearly killed her to carry you all the way to the village.”

Kendrick’s eyes riveted on the girl again, and whispered, “She carried me?”

“Yes. Contact burns heal quite quickly under the circumstances. But I’m pretty sure if it weren’t for her absorbing your abilities to heal, she would not have survived.”

Kendrick’s jaw worked. He marveled at this valiant creature who had risked so much for him, yet at the same time shame clawed at his heart. His throat clogged with guilt. The tip of his nose tingled, and he had to blink repeatedly to keep his beautiful wife in focus.

"My son."

Kendrick flinched. Memsy's hand touched his arm. He hadn't even seen her move. But her eyes bespoke such tenderness and compassion.

"Please," she encouraged. "Be gentle with her heart. Far gentler than you are with your own. She cares for you deeply. There just isn't a lot she can do to show it."

She let that sink in, then sighed. "I had hoped the ceremony would solve it, but apparently not."

She gave his arm a pat. "But take heart! There has to be some way around it—or the line would have died out centuries ago."

He gave a mirthless chuckle as she moved off to lie down, her head near her daughter's. She cuddled in her thin blanket and soon was fast asleep. Yet Kendrick had not moved. He did not wake Adianna when it was her turn for watch either. He had far too much to think over.

THE VILLAGE

The next morning, Adianna awoke bright and early. Mainly due to restlessness—her typical nightmares smattered with images of her parents. So, by the time the others began stirring, she was in the orchard surveying the trees for fruits and nuts ready for harvest.

Memsy soon joined in the gleaning. It was nice to have her nearby. Still, Adianna couldn't help casting frequent glances to the two mounds of freshly turned earth.

Swallowing her grief, she encouraged the others, "Let's get heading out. If we get going, we can make Fal Dura before noon."

No one argued. In fact, no one was saying much of anything. Adianna saw the pity in Memsy's eyes, her gaze enfolding her like a comforting and much-needed hug. And the healer. She caught him looking her way often, but he seemed to be deep in thought. *'Tis of little matter. He will never think of me as anything other than a… a what? A swindler, I guess? Someone he was stuck with, yet who always chose to avoid his touch. If only it were true…*

Shaking herself, Adianna realized she had been staring at him. Especially now with him staring back. His bright blue eyes were intrigued, like a puppy seeing a kitten for the first time and trying to decide whether to play with it or eat it.

Ducking her head to hide her warm cheeks, she went back to stuffing her blanket into her pack. Then grabbing the camp pot, she doused the fire with the remaining peppermint and chamomile tea. The cold puce liquid sizzled into a tuft of billowing steam. She dabbed the tip of her finger into the cast iron skillet to test its warmth, then slid her hands into her gloves before snatching it up.

She trudged over to where her husband was sitting and handed him the pan.

"Could you put this in your pack, Healer? Then we should be ready to go."

Seeing him reach for it, she turned so she could walk away as soon as he had it. But instead of feeling him take the proffered skillet, she felt his hand encircle her wrist. She stared at the gentle band of steel in flesh form. She felt the warmth of him through the protective mail.

His eyes were so deep in color this morning, deeper than she had ever seen them. They invited her to be swallowed within their azure depths.

"My name is Kendrick." His voice was a caress.

Adianna felt her cheeks flame, but she couldn't look away. His gaze held her, willing her to say his name.

"Very well… Kendrick."

She smiled shyly. He returned her smile, so warmly, so gently, she nearly did a double take.

Still holding her, he took the pan from her with his other hand.

"Thank you, Adianna."

She examined his face, for she had no idea what he was thanking her for. Still, she stifled a childish giggle. "You're welcome."

He slowly let her hand slide over his until her fingers slipped off the tips of his skin. He still held her gaze while he wrapped the iron skillet and tucked it into the top of the pack at his side.

"Shall we go then?" he queried with a rise of his brow. Glancing around him, he called to Memsy, "Are you ready, Madam?"

Kendrick stood at Memsy's nod then stepped around Adianna. With his back to her, she brought her hand up to her chest, stroking it lightly with her other. But then she shook herself, disgusted by such an adolescent act, and went to join the others.

They set out at a leisurely clip, enjoying the cool morning. Adianna tried not to think about Kendrick, but every time she looked over, he was watching her with that same curious expression on his face. *What is he thinking about, I wonder?*

With difficulty, she brushed it aside, realizing she had no clue how the male mind worked, least of all this peculiarity she must now call husband.

Plodding quietly through the forest, Adianna recognized a clump of trees. She scanned the skies, seeking the approximate time and how long it would take them to cover the remaining two miles.

We should be there well before noon. It will be nice to see Nalora and the others again.

Abruptly, a sound caught her attention about the same time the healer hollered, "Halt!"

He had his head tilted to better hear the sound. Distant pops and an occasional crash of metal rang through the now deathly silent forest.

Adianna turned back the direction she had been facing, for that was where it was coming from. Then a battle cry and a twittering screech rose above the trees. *Fal Dura?*

Quickly, she began walking again. She could hear the others behind her, but her thoughts were on the sounds ahead. The noises grew noticeably louder, so she broke out into a trot, her eyes on the ground while she strained to hear more—yet dreading what the more might hold.

A woman's scream split the air. Instantly, visions of her parents crouched in their burning cottage assailed Adianna's mind. Before she could shake the thought, she was running.

"Adianna, slow down!" Memsy called, some distance behind her.

"It's coming from the village!" Adianna yelled over her shoulder, barely even turning her head.

The realization of what might be happening hit her, but she no longer thought. She simply ran.

"Adianna!"

The healer's barked plea barely reached her over the din. She just kept running.

The sounds of conflict and destruction increased, mingled with the flurry of wings overhead. Glancing up, she saw dozens of hawk-people heading east. A huge flock of large males with a sprinkling of even larger females, all fully armed.

The fact they were flying away from the village didn't compute. Adianna pressed forward, jumping roots and dodging low limbs. Branches cut into her skin. It didn't deter her. Her lungs were dry and burning, straining to pull in enough air to continue. Still, she did not let up. Seeing a break ahead in the trees, she mustered all the energy she had left.

Emerging from the trees, Adianna halted to gain her bearings. From the few meager huts, barely more than squat shacks, she gathered she was at the southern end of the village. She looked closer at what lay around her and saw tattered pole fences surrounding savagely thrashed gardens, plus several pigs—some wildly screaming, others brutally slaughtered and left to rot.

She looked to the sky. She spotted a few straggling hawkmen flying through the air.

"Why hasn't the crying stopped if they've left?"

Unexpectedly, Adianna saw arrows slice the sky, anxious to target the retreating hawkmen. Through the volley of arrows, several ribbons of black smoke laced skyward.

Adianna yanked her bow from her back and grabbed her skirt. She dodged the huts and cottages on the outskirts of the village, angling toward Fal Dura Square and the river. She stalled only long enough to call into the window or door of an occasional burning structure.

Rounding a corner, she ran smack into someone large enough to send her spinning around and landing face down on the ground. She rolled to her side to look up. Her breath caught in her throat.

There, standing above her sneered a rector—Drokmar's nefarious killing machines. Black mold crawled out from every crease of his pallid and chiseled frame. Standing near seven feet tall, he glared down at her.

"Where you think you're going, Missy?" He scowled, his voice gravel.

Without thinking, Adianna made a savage kick for his knee. She heard the crunch of bones, followed by a piercing screech, and the rector toppled to the ground.

Frantically, she scrambled to her feet, snatching a crumbling plank from nearby. She wrapped her hands around the splintering wood and smashed it, bat-style, against the side of the rector's face. His head floundered as if repercussions were physically bouncing around inside his skull. Then he crumpled to the ground and was still.

Knowing he wasn't dead, she did not stop. Adianna grabbed her fallen bow and took off again at a more cautious pace. Guttural laughs were now intermingling among screams and pleas for mercy, making her blood boil.

Just yards from the square, she slammed to a halt against the back of the village icehouse. Leaning her back on the weather-worn slabs, she placed her hand to her chest. Closing her eyes, she willed the rapid rise and fall to slow, but it was like trying to slow a horse in sight of home. The growing smoke stung her already burning lungs.

Cautiously, she crept through the alley between the neighboring buildings and peered around the corner. The lane leading into the square was littered with various debris from houses but appeared deserted. Following the noise and commotion, she leaned farther out from her hiding place. At the end of the lane were dozens of rectors attacking the men of the village. Apparently fighting with whatever they could grab, the villagers brandished wooden pitchforks and shepherd's staffs, axes, and even cast-iron skillets.

Adianna nocked an arrow to her bow. Braced against the wall, she tried to quell her pounding heart.

She looked skyward and breathed, "Okay! One… two…"

Suddenly a crash of splintering wood erupted behind her. Stifling a squeal, she ducked back into the alley. The screams of children and the merciless laughs of rectors begged her to investigate. There were two rectors at the opposite end of the lane. One stood laughing at the shattered door of a small cottage while the other shoved a torch into the thatched roof.

Great flames began licking their way across the top of the cottage, and the second rector joined his companion. While piteous cries were heard from within, the two assailants backed away, each wielding a club and torch, ready to attack anyone who dared to emerge.

Suddenly the shutters of the single window flew open, revealing a young boy. Behind him were several bobbing heads silhouetted by flames and smoke. But before the boy could take advantage of this new escape path, a rector lunged his torch toward the opening. More screams erupted inside the cottage, with the torch coming close enough to singe the dodging boy's head.

Looping her finger around her arrow, Adianna pinned it to the bow and reached for another. With one fluid movement, she ripped a line of fletching from the retrieved projectile with her teeth then fit the arrow to her bow. It would have been a daring sight to behold, except for the fact that the feathers stuck to her lip. Her frustration mounted with the three consecutive tries at spitting it away, until, finally, she swiped at her mouth with her sleeve.

She rolled her eyes; a low growl escaped her throat. But she fitted both arrows in place, tipping her bow sideways. Swiftly, she raised it, chanting quickly in elvish, then let the arrows fly.

Both whizzing darts embedded in the rectors' backs, piercing the heart and lungs simultaneously. Unable to make a sound, the vicious antagonists crumpled lifelessly in the dust.

Adianna peeked toward the square, then dashed from the alley. Swiveling her head looking for enemies, she sprinted for the cottage as inky black smoke billowed out the door. She leaped over the downed rectors, both turning to ash as their misty essence oozed into the ground, to peer through the opening. The room was all shadows and smoke; she couldn't make out a thing.

"William!" she called. "Where are you?"

"Miss Annie?"

The twelve-year-old boy's face emerged from the depths of the inferno smudged with soot and smoke.

"How—?" He coughed.

"No time," Adianna insisted. "Quickly! Grab the children and head for the knoll south of the village!"

"Yes, 'um!"

He disappeared but quickly reappeared with a small, redheaded child clinging to his neck, his hand wrapped around the wrist of a small girl he towed along behind. This coughing child was holding the hand of a small younger brother. At the rear was a young girl of about eight years, holding a crying bundle of blankets to her shoulder. Adianna touched each tear-streaked, sooty-faced child tenderly, steering them toward the woods.

Sniffing back tears of her own, she hollered after William, "Take anyone else you can find with you, and don't leave the knoll until someone comes to get you!"

"Yes, 'um," was William's reply. He then trotted south, looking back often to make sure everyone was keeping up.

Nocking another arrow to her bow, Adianna covered their escape until the children were out of sight. Then, pivoting on her heels, she made her way to Fal Dura Square.

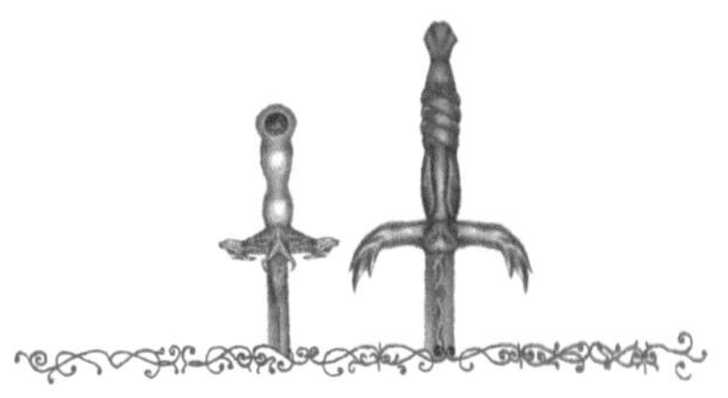

FAL DURA SQUARE

Kendrick pulled Memsy to the side just before pieces of charred roof came crashing to the ground where she stood. The woman gave him an appreciative glance, then he tentatively stepped out from the alley. Suddenly, he jumped back. Grabbing his elfin companion, he pressed them both against the side of the closest hut. Just then several howling rectors ran past. He turned his back to better shield Memsy from view until the noises died away.

Peering around the hut, he checked to see if the way was clear. Through breaks between buildings, he could see those rectors, along with others, running off triumphantly. Screams were mingled with the lamenting cries of vanquished subjects.

"Where is she?" he spat out, in nearly a curse. Kendrick struggled to keep the anxious feeling of dread from assailing him.

He had given chase when Adianna took off. Now his throat and lungs burned from lack. Lack of air. Lack of moisture. All he could pull into them was polluted snatches of smoldered oxygen. But what plagued him most was running straight into a hornets' nest of Blade Hunters, ruthless rectors searching for *them*, and his wife was nowhere to be found.

A hand grasped his forearm gently.

"Don't worry… We'll find her."

Memsy's voice was soothing even though she was struggling for breath herself. Kendrick hadn't realized how tense his body had become until he felt it relax under her reassuring touch. He placed his hand over hers, a corner of his mouth rising into a half smile.

Suddenly war cries rent the air. The clash of steel on wood echoed just around the bend. Quickly, Kendrick pulled back, panicked as to what this might mean.

"Come on," he ordered over his shoulder. Then, he sneaked off in the direction of battle sounds and the rush of water.

Most of the streets of Fal Dura were only packed-earth paths, except for a few lanes, which were merely wider dirt paths. But all these angled toward the Town Square. The Square was actually a large half-circle whose mouth opened onto the Fal Reche River—a large but relatively tame tributary that meandered from the Garren Hills to the southwest of the village and dumped into the Tyronda Sea to the northeast. An aerial view of the village would show it as a sun rising out of the river with its streets as rays fanned out around the orb. Beyond the square was Fal Dura Bridge, the largest of only two bridges to span the river and the only one wide enough to carry wagons. With the main road through Kyren Forest cutting through the center on its way to the bridge, the river and the bridge were the village's lifeblood.

Kendrick tentatively approached the square with Memsy trailing behind him. He slowed his pace, scarcely believing what he saw. Outnumbered, outsized, and barely armed, the people of the village were trying desperately to fight against a whole squadron of rectors.

He hissed out his breath, another battle waging. This one within him.

He fought the urge to plunge into the fray, to aid these people working so urgently to defend their homes and their lives merely because they were in the path of evil.

He pulled his lips back, exposing clenched teeth. He had to do something. But he also had to keep his mother-in-law safe. He had to find his wife amid all this calamity. And he had to make sure the cargo she bore stayed hidden, or she would be lost to him forever.

"What do we do?" Memsy queried, sounding as desperate for action as he.

Just then an elderly townsman trying to protect his wife nearby caught Kendrick's eye. The man wielded a pitchfork against his oversized adversary's club. The woman was clambering behind her husband attempting to block blows with a much too heavy skillet. With one fell swoop, the rector wrenched the weapon from the man's hands and knocked the couple to the ground.

Without another thought, Kendrick darted in, drawing his sword. He struck the first rector he came upon but never took his eyes off the cringing pair. Their executioner brought his club overhead, a menacing gleam in his eye. With a merciless laugh, the rector's club descended.

Kendrick didn't know who was more surprised by the block—the rector or the elderly couple. But Kendrick was relieved he got there in time.

The creature bellowed his outrage. Kendrick spun away from the sidesweep of the club. He followed through, clipping the rector behind the knees with his backswing. The rector toppled to the ground, yowling in pain. Before the healer could finish the assault, the peasant conked the creature on the head with his wife's iron skillet. Their vanquished foe crumpled to the dirt.

The two men grinned broadly at each other.

Just then, the sorci rushed forward to assist the old woman.

"Memsy!" the couple hollered in unison. Their ruddy faces of seventy-some years a piece were aglow with recognition.

The woman pulled Memsy into an embrace. The peasant stepped forward to clap her on the back.

"Jameston. Adora, my dear friends!" Memsy's smile matched theirs. She held their hands tightly.

"Good to have you, old girl!" the man bellowed over the din.

The three barely had time to glance their appreciation to Kendrick before three more rectors converged on them. When Kendrick started swinging, a growl escaped his lips which transformed into a war cry. The fight was on.

Several minutes later, Kendrick glanced around, searching for Memsy. Instead, he spied a youth off to the far-left end of the Square. The young man was fighting valiantly, but he was being overpowered. Just as the thought entered his mind to go to the youth's aid, a familiar figure emerged from a lane near the fight.

"Blast!" Kendrick cursed as he watched Adianna advance into the fray, letting arrows fly as quickly as she could send them. The rectors went down, but so did the youth from a blow from a falling foe.

More rectors converged like plaguing locusts upon seeing their comrades go down. Adianna reached the boy, brandishing her bow like a club, whacking one rector across the chops, then another.

Despite the fear tickling his spine, Kendrick couldn't help but admire the amount of bravado crammed into such a tiny frame. But when Adianna was knocked to the ground next to the youth by a glancing blow, Kendrick's heart plummeted. Swinging and dodging, he frantically made his way through the attacking crowd toward her.

Then, as if in slow motion, five rectors gathered around the fallen pair. He could hear their triumphant laughter and their taunting jeers. Kendrick's heart pounded chaotically. A putrid opponent positioned itself over his wife to administer a fatal blow. Adianna's slender arm went up, her only protection.

I'm not going to make it! He was still several yards away, and the rector was poised with club overhead.

"No!" The cry ripped from Kendrick's chest when the deadly club began its downward swing.

Just then, a volley of rocks began pummeling the attacking rectors. The mini missiles thrashed the poised attacker, halting his assault. Relief flooded through Kendrick, causing a falter in his progress across the square. Several village children, ranging in ages from adolescence to barely more than toddlers, perched on the edge of a nearby porch propelling stones with all their might. Kendrick smiled despite himself.

"Get those brats!" the rector standing over Adianna growled, gesturing with his club.

Kendrick was in motion before Adianna's panicked protest reached him. Other villagers moved instinctively to their aid when several of the fiends stirred to carry out the order against their children. The lead rector raised his club again.

This time the downward swing was stopped by the clash of Kendrick's sword colliding with it. Forcing the club back with the pressure of his own weapon, he allowed his rage to attack the surprised villain. With one powerful swipe of his sword, he split the assailant from ear to hip.

Bringing his sword up quickly, Kendrick blocked a new attack. Just then he heard an arrow whizzing through air, followed by a deadly thunk and a cry. Glancing over, he caught sight of another rector falling at the feet of the screaming children with Adianna's dart through its heart.

Kendrick looked back in time to block the next assault. His current attacker was joined by another who came at him from the side. Faintly aware of more arrows flying, Kendrick kicked the second attacker square in the chest, sending it sprawling backward. Giving a great push upward with his sword, he then drove the first assailant off balance enough to provide a deadly slice removing its head.

Three more converged on him, but before striking, one received an arrow embedded in its skull through the eye socket. When Kendrick looked, Adianna was still poised on the ground by the youth, touching another projectile to her weapon. He turned back to his enemy just in time to deflect another attack. Though keeping his face grim he felt a swelling of pride for this feisty little woman who had his back.

"Get the children out of here!" Kendrick commanded, pushing hard against the two clubs pressing down on him. Flinging the attackers backward, he twisted his head to bark another order. This was halted in mid-thought with another arrow sweeping past, mere inches off the end of his nose, and implanting itself in a rector's chest.

The other rector came at Kendrick, rage in its eyes. He blocked the strike with a jolt. Seeing yet another of the creatures run at Adianna, the warrior walloped his current foe in the nose with his fist. Thus freed, he instantly spun, whipping around backward and catching the passing adversary square in the gut with the broadsword.

Glaring over at Adianna, who had her hand over her mouth, Kendrick yelled, "Woman! Be gone! Get the children! Now!"

"But Mems—" Her response faltered midstream. Her eyes widened, and she moved her hand to point over his shoulder.

Kendrick whirled around, driving his blade up into the midsection of a large assailant nearly to the hilt. Scanning the area quickly, Kendrick used his foot to drag his weapon from the crumpling rector. He caught a glimpse of Memsy, then he turned back to Adianna.

"I'll get the sorci!"

He grabbed the gawking lad his wife had saved by the scruff of the neck and shoved him in the direction he wanted Adianna to go. Grabbing her around the waist, her cloak bulging between them, Kendrick dragged her away from the fighting to the mouth of the nearest lane. He motioned for the kids on the porch to join them and demanded, "Now will you please get these children to safety. And stay hidden!"

He shoved at her shoulder to get her moving, but she resisted, grabbing his hand. Her eyes were a jumbled mess of emotion, but she said nothing.

Despite himself, Kendrick gave her a little smile, nodding ever so slightly. "We'll be fine. Take care, and I'll find you soon. Now go."

He withdrew his hand from her gloved grasp and again tried to nudge her into leaving. This time she balled her fist and placed the flat of her knuckles against his chest.

"*You* take care," she said, pressing her fist into him for emphasis.

His heartbeat pounded against the sweaty linen of his shirt beneath her touch.

"We'll be at the knoll in the forest to the south of the village."

Placing his hand over hers, he tried not to think of what would happen if he could not meet her there. He gave her a half-smile and tipped his chin, motioning for her retreat. "Go," he whispered.

Her eyes glistened, but she turned, shooing the seven children and the lad along in front of her as fast as she could.

Kendrick wanted to watch her go, but the battle demanded his attention. He brought his weapon to the ready and turned in time to block an attacker's club from nestling into his skull. He spun quickly to the right. The unexpected movement sent the rector sprawling. Kendrick completed the turn by planting the hilt of his sword squarely between the creature's shoulder blades. Then, with a sneer, Kendrick tromped off to where he had last seen the sorci.

Where are all these infernal creatures coming from? he wondered as more converged on him. He parried in an instant, then pivoted to deflect another blow. The next rector over-propelled and toppled to its knees beside him. Kendrick brought his hilt crashing down on the foe's head.

Taking on one assailant after another, he made slow progress across the square. But he soon noticed that progress was being made in another way. Glancing around, he saw that though rectors were still scattered throughout the square more than one villager took on each intruder.

"Healer! Watch out!"

Memsy's warning cry infiltrated Kendrick's concentration. Clubbing his current assailant across the jaw with his fist, he searched in her direction. He found her, her eyes wide in alarm and staring past him. He whirled around, preparing his body for anything.

Okay, maybe not that!

Advancing on him rapidly were a dozen rectors, larger than many he had been fighting. His body tensed. With each determined step, they fanned out more and more. Kendrick snatched the crude sword of his last victim. Within seconds, he was completely surrounded.

With a sword wielded in each hand, his gaze darted everywhere, scanning for the first sign of attack.

Several rectors converged on Kendrick at once. He swung first one sword and then the other, deflecting each strike as they came. One rector went down, then another. But soon, they had pressed in on him so much he had no time to react.

Suddenly, one of his swords was knocked from his hand. At the same time, he was whacked behind the knees, which sent him careening to the ground. A rector raised its sword to administer a fatal blow to Kendrick's head, but the healer rolled, taking down two assailants as he went.

Kendrick scrambled to his feet but was tackled by several hard bodies. Flailing, he struggled to keep from getting pinned—but it was no use. Soon, he was stuck with one brute on each limb and a couple more restraining his core. Yet another rector was now positioning itself at his head. Kendrick pulled and thrashed with all his might but to no avail. The fiend raised its enormous, spiked club.

"No!" Memsy cried, trying to break through the fence of rectors encircling him.

Kendrick wished she could be spared seeing his demise. At least Adianna wasn't there.

Kendrick saw the hungry glint in the rector's eye, its muscles poised and ready. A sinister smile crept over its face, and the club arched downward.

INTERCEPT

Suddenly, the air was rent with a booming howl. All the rectors in the square halted, including the one standing over Kendrick. As one, all the assailants turned to the origin of the roar.

Panting for breath, Kendrick made sure the club was not going to lower before he ventured a look. There, looming on the railing of the great bridge that spanned the river, stood the most sinister, barbaric rector Kendrick had ever seen. More height, more muscle, more bulk, more decay, more menacing. The hideous creature leaned, half hanging by one hand gripping high on the main post anchoring the bridge to land, with its eyes trained on him. Even from this distance Kendrick could see the ominous gleam in the rector's eyes.

On the ground, he was flanked by two oversized underlings on each side, standing ramrod straight, eyes forward. These well-trained soldiers wore distinct, high-ranking insignia on their lapels, insignia Kendrick had apprised earlier—noting also that with each increase in rank, the more grotesque the bearer. These were no exception to this rule, and the one on the bridge most assuredly outranked them all.

With all fighting stopped and all eyes on him, the commander grinned at Kendrick, then chortled loudly.

"Finally!" he growled, dipping his knees for emphasis before hopping effortlessly to the ground. "Someone worth killing."

Kendrick shifted his head to appraise this new adversary. The commander advanced, his minions flanking him. Every being in front of him skittered out of his path to where Kendrick now had a full view. The rector's eyes gleamed with blood lust and sport. But there was something familiar in this creature's demeanor, his voice, even his sauntering approach.

Then he saw it.

Where all the other rectors used clubs or swords, this particular brute carried an overly large, fiendish-looking blade, shaped much like a four-foot-long butcher's knife. Its tip curved backward to provide a hook of sorts, morbidly used to cleave his foe from hip to shoulder with a gruesome backswing. The years might have altered the villain's form, but Kendrick knew that weapon. It was the very weapon that revealed the monster's identity. It was that weapon Kendrick had watched helplessly as it had plunged through his father. It was that bloody weapon that the creature stretched forth and pressed under Kendrick's chin.

The healer's teeth clenched; his eyes were steel. The cold metal tilted his face to be inspected by this ghastly rival. The mirth building in the creature's eyes gnawed at him. Instinctively, Kendrick jerked his left arm, trying again to get free, but was still held fast.

The commander guffawed. Snickers followed from the surrounding rectors. Their leader raised his hand, silencing his men. He glanced over at the stripped weapon then stepped forward. The edge of his blade pressed into Kendrick's skin.

Leaning down, his voice low and menacing, he asked, "Where are the Blades?" The sword cut into the healer's throat. "And with whom do you travel?"

Kendrick felt a trickle of blood run down his throat from the bite of the blade, but he didn't feel the sting. Anger boiled inside him. He wanted nothing more than to shred this creature limb from limb.

"You *and* those Blades," Kendrick spat through clenched teeth. "Can go to Vairn!"

The commander pulled back his sword just as a boot landed in Kendrick's midsection. Over his wheezing, he could hear the commander tutting. Next thing he knew, he was yanked from the ground. Strung between two rectors, the healer now found himself facing his opponent. As tall as Kendrick was, the creature still dwarfed him by a head.

With a flick of the commander's finger, Kendrick was stretched to the breaking point.

"Don't make me ask again," the rector growled menacingly.

Kendrick sucked in air, willing his arms to stay in their sockets.

"I don't know where the cursed things are," he gasped through clenched teeth, hoping Adianna was safely hidden somewhere.

The pull on Kendrick's arms eased slightly, only to have his foot kicked out from under him. He landed hard on one knee. His arms were twisted, and his shoulders thrust from behind, forcing him into a bow.

The general heaved an audible sigh. "One more try, mortal. The Blades and your companion."

The tension in the square was palpable. All awaited his reply with bated breath.

Kendrick knew he must die at any moment. Adianna's face flitted into his mind. He would never see her. Never kiss her. But at least she would be safe. Kendrick raised his head and met his assailant's glare.

Unexpectedly, a nearby voice called out. "Please, your Excellency! Wait!"

Kendrick's throat constricted at Memsy's plea. He glanced to where she strained against the restrictive arms of two rectors, barricading her path. A band of cloth was tied about her forehead, hair, and ears, a peasant's garment thrown over her elven garb.

"And who's this old crone?" the commander roared.

"Mems, no! Stay back!" Kendrick hissed.

The commander glanced from him to her, eyeing them warily.

Still, the elf was not deterred. "Please, Great Sir. This man has no knowledge of the Blades. He is merely escorting my daughter and me to Ooflic."

"And why would he do that?"

The rector sounded skeptical. His men scoffed. The commander examined Kendrick's face. Tension on the man's arms increased, urging him to answer.

"This woman is my mother-in-law," Kendrick finally conceded. "Her daughter is my wife."

The rector stared intently. His steely eyes penetrated deep into Kendrick. "Why should I believe you?"

Kendrick said nothing but glared back a challenge.

The commander's eyes narrowed, even though he lowered his weapon. He turned, contemplating, looking at the ground. Suddenly, he swung back to face the healer, the curved tip of his sword slicing right in front of the kneeling man's nose.

"Produce this wife of which you claim, human." The rector brought up the hand that held his weapon across his body, poised to give a fatal swipe. "Or you lose your overconfident life."

Kendrick's jaw worked, wondering how to produce a wife he prayed was far away.

Suddenly, the general bellowed, and his sword dropped to the ground. The hand that held it now had an arrow protruding from either side.

Instantly, Kendrick kicked his raised leg back into one captor's knee. Upon contact, he immediately heard the crunch of bone. The rector to his left released him as it crumpled, roaring.

The healer quickly used the hold of the other rector to launch himself upward, propelling the heel of his hand through that captor's nose. The rector toppled backward. Thus freed, Kendrick scooped up the leader's butcher sword. With it trained on its owner, the surrounding rectors dared not move against him.

Kendrick eyed the commander, now clutching his wrist below the protruding arrow. His teeth were clenched and bared, spittle spewing out with each exhale. The healer stared down the venom assailing him.

The next moment, a knot slammed in the pit of his stomach. A voice rose above the din from the other side of the square.

"I am his wife. Now take your vagabond army and go if you value *your* supercilious life."

Kendrick's arms sagged slightly, for there, standing at the edge of the square, was Adianna, another arrow nocked and ready.

But Kendrick couldn't let his response show. Not with the general's death glare upon him.

The commander broke off the tip of the arrow with his good hand, then pulled it from his flesh. Spitting out his pain, he cast a smoldering glare to Adianna.

Kendrick sensed the rage building in the wounded general. The decay-covered muscles rippled and tensed before his eyes. The rector seethed in every breath.

Kendrick wished he could somehow get between this maniac and his wife, yet he could not move without those eyes pinning him with caged-animal reflexes.

Unsure of which direction the injured creature would launch his attack, Kendrick knew it was imminent. Just then he heard a dull growl building within the adversary.

Since he was facing Adianna when it began, Kendrick meant to move at that moment to cut off the rector's attack. But suddenly a screeching bugle call sounded overhead.

Abruptly, a drac snaked down from the sky into the center of the square. The instant it touched ground, a flurry of jade-colored smoke erupted, revealing a tall, slender man. The grand figure, with his dark hair, olive complexion, and imperial-looking clothing, gazed around pompously, commanding everyone's attention. But Kendrick barely glanced his way, retaining focus on the threat to his wife.

The livid rector hadn't even turned, not caring about what went on behind him. His eyes were riveted on her, and he crept slowly toward her.

Adianna still had her weapon trained on her foe. The two were staring each other down, unmindful of any others.

Kendrick heard the dalphene behind him commanding the rectors to assemble, but he still moved stealthily to intercept.

The other creatures instantly began moving toward the majestic personage who summoned them. All except the general. He continued to press closer to the woman and her bow.

Kendrick dodged around villagers and the assembling rectors. Even though several villagers moved to cut off any rector interference, gaining ground was difficult.

Adianna stared down the advancing beast. Kendrick was only a handful of yards away now from the general. But so was the general—from her.

"Baranof!"

The voice thundered behind Kendrick, causing his foe to pause. The injured creature begrudgingly turned.

"The Great Drokmar wants you to gather your men immediately! We're to attempt a raid on Tymalia by nightfall tomorrow," the pretentious man stated, leaving little room for argument.

Adianna's gaze met Kendrick's for a split second. Yet he quickly beheld the rector again.

At Kendrick, Baranof scowled threateningly. He gave little display of compliance. On the contrary. He seemed intent on murder with little preference for which of the opposing couple he took out.

Finally, the dalphene raised his sparking hand at the rebel and barked his name again—daring him to defy their master.

Baranof's scathing glare landed on Kendrick, who offered him his weapon. The general stalked forward and snatched the sword from his hand.

"We will meet again, mortal," the creature seethed into Kendrick's face.

His hard gaze never flinching, he grinned in return. "Promises, promises."

The muscles of the rector's jaw worked, and Kendrick could tell it took every ounce of willpower the commander had to comply with the messenger's order.

Taking the lead, the beaten rector resentfully commanded his squad to move out. The dalphene crumpled into a cloud of mint-colored smoke, and his snaky drac-form sprang into the sky, leading the way east.

The relief of the villagers was tangible when the army left the square. Many threw down their weapons. Others began congratulating each other, thumping on backs. But Kendrick did not relieve his tense stance until he watched Baranof and his men dissolve from view completely.

Finally, the respite enveloped him when, all around him, people cheered.

FUN & GAMES

For the next quarter-hour, Kendrick did not let Adianna out of his sight. Many of the townsfolk converged on Kendrick, pounding him on the back, shaking his hand vigorously. He tried his best to be gracious and congratulatory amid the revelry. Still, he never left her side, feeling a resolute need to guard this reckless, fool-hardy woman of his.

It seemed everyone in the village knew Memsy and 'Miss Annie,' as they called her. No one knew her true name. But he could plainly see that the entire village adored her. He had been furious with her for disobeying him, and he had planned to give her a piece of his mind when they were finally alone, but his anger melted quickly. For amid the gaiety of these people, she shined.

It was good he had decided not to leave her side because he wouldn't have been able to walk away. Her beauty within beamed more radiantly among these people than even her physical brilliance. He was awed by how much she truly cared for them. And he could tell they felt it, without a doubt.

The news *he* now had claim on her spread quickly. He had never received so many congratulatory slaps on the back, insinuating grins, or wistful sighs in all his life. So, when Adianna remembered the children she had sent to gather beyond the village, he was more than happy to accompany her in retrieving them.

Upon reaching the knoll, his wife let out a whistle. Children of all sizes instantly peeked out from behind nearly every tree, bush, and rock. Cheers filled the small glade, and soon they were swamped.

"Onnie," one towheaded little girl yelled, and she came at a full youthful run right into the woman's outstretched arms.

Kendrick watched amazed, intrigued, and curious at the flying hands of the little girl. When his bride quickly retaliated in like manner, he realized the child was deaf and their gestures and expressions were a language all its own. He heard the whisper from Adianna's mail gloves clinking through the rapid movement of her responses. He was mesmerized and wondered how they could understand any of it.

Several of the children who had gathered around smiled and nodded in agreement as they watched the little pixie's animated face and flying hands apparently tell the story of their daring escape to a thoroughly enthralled Adianna.

"My goodness!" Adianna breathed, folding the little girl in her arms again. Then her gaze encompassed the other children. "You all have been so very brave!"

Kendrick deduced Adianna's movement of forcefully pushing her two fists away from her chest was the sign for brave. Some of the older boys grinned at the compliment and grabbed hold of their vests or suspenders, letting their chests swell.

One such boy, a dark-haired youngster of about twelve years of age, with a toddler clinging to his leg, called out, "I brought all the youngin's I could find, just like you said, Miss Annie." A proud smile creased his face.

"Old Kemp, here." He jabbed his thumb over his shoulder at the short, black-haired boy to his right. "He wanted to stay and fight. But I told him 'We's got our orders! We's to get the little 'uns out of danger an' keep 'um safe till the 'dults shows up sayin' the coast was clear.' I led the way, Miss Annie, just like you told me to."

A crooked smile inched across Kendrick's face at the boy's obvious aim to impress. He could hear the unseen smile in Adianna's voice when she commended him.

"You did an excellent job, Thomas. I am so proud of you. All of you! I am so glad you are all safe."

Just then Kendrick noticed the little deaf girl staring at him wide-eyed. As he returned her gaze, the little pixie swatted at Adianna's shoulder.

"What is it, Nalora?" Adianna signed as she spoke, but the child's eyes never left him.

Adianna put her hands on the girl's hips and swiveled her slightly from side to side. "Nalora?"

Just as Adianna was about to turn to see what the child was staring at, Nalora's lips formed an 'O,' and she brought her thumb up to her chin, wiggling her first finger in his direction.

This time Adianna did turn to him, her brow knit together. When she saw the man standing behind her, a great grin crossed her face.

She chuckled, apparently having forgotten about him. Involuntarily, one of Kendrick's brows went up, and his mouth dug into his cheek on one side.

"Children." Adianna stood, speaking and signing as she stepped closer to him. "This is a Master Healer."

"Kendrick," he corrected, leaning down to shake hands with the little dear. "Her husband."

Adianna's eyes locked with his, a little surprised. He could tell when the memory of this morning dawned on her for she dipped her eyes, her cheeks coloring slightly. He definitely liked it when she blushed.

Her gaze met his again, and a demure smile greeted him.

"Yes, Kendrick."

Such a sense of satisfaction enfolded him at hearing her speak his name he didn't see her fingers flying through spelling it.

Adianna shyly glanced at him but quickly turned back to the children. It made him chuckle.

"He is also a great warrior," she declared.

Kendrick nearly choked on his laugh.

"He is," she went on, enthusiastically. "You should have seen him fight back in the village! He saved Rannen and me, plus took on twelve rectors all by himself!"

Kendrick's mouth popped open. He raised his hand to stop her, but right away he could see the damage had been done. All the boys in the clearing were gawking at him with slack-jawed admiration, and the girls pinned him with dreamy-eyed sighs.

One side of his mouth went up in a nervous sort of smile as he drew his hand back. Self-consciously, he wiggled his fingers at them all.

That was all it took for the crowd to converge on him. Kendrick took an instinctive step backward, but they were too quick. The boys were all talking excitedly at once. The girls simply squealed with delight. He was surrounded with no escape. And above all the voices was the bubbling laughter he loved so well. The laugh he didn't realize he had missed.

As the whole crew tromped through the woods back to the village, Adianna was keenly aware of the healer walking so closely beside her. *Kendrick*, she corrected herself.

Nalora was on her other side, a pudgy, little hand nestled in hers. Trying to focus on something other than him, Adianna began to notice the little six-year-old kept peeking around her to look at the virile young man, too. Glancing at Kendrick without turning her head, she could see he would peer at the child in return. He seemed uncomfortable at first, but then he relaxed, even making a little game out of it, as Nalora ducked into Adianna's skirts, giggling.

Several of the children ran ahead when the village came into view, so when the stragglers, with the young couple bringing up the rear, arrived, they were engulfed with the faster children, who had come to spread the news.

"Master Kendrick! Miss Annie! The village elders declared a celebration tomorrow night!" Thomas, who was one of the foremost descending assailants yelled, "There's gonna be a bonfire, and dancing, and merriment—just like they used to do. There's even going to be some roasted pigs!"

He was nearly breathless with excitement. "The orders are to get all the broken stuff to the town square for the bonfire. I gotta go start on Prowhead Lane!"

Adianna laughed, watching the enthusiastic boy disappear between cottages to get on with the work. Kendrick seemed just as amused with the boy's antics.

With a tug on her hand, Nalora demanded Adianna's attention. The child looked at her with a very quizzical expression, her upturned hand waggling.

"Thomas says there is to be a celebration tomorrow night, with a fire, and food, and dancing." She signed to the child while she spoke, out of habit for those who might be listening.

The little girl started to bounce, her fists clenched in front of her. A squeal escaped her lips. Adianna laughed heartily, turning her head to see if the healer was enjoying the child's excitement as much as she was. His huge grin showed he was indeed.

Eagerly, the little sprite patted at Adianna's skirts. The child's face was very animated as she slapped her fists together then interlocked circles made by her thumb and forefingers several times, ending with her forefinger twirling in a loop away from her lips.

Adianna chuckled again. "Yes," she signed and spoke. "I am sure there will be story-telling."

This was greeted by another squeal of delight. Nalora bounced over in front of Kendrick now. With a heart-winning smile, she tugged on his hand. The man squatted to be more her size, the large smile still in place.

Nalora pointed at him, then swung two fingers over her other palm before pointing to herself.

Adianna stifled a chuckle with a fist to her mouth. She pressed her lips together tightly, trying to keep her smile contained. Kendrick's own smile had faltered slightly, and he turned a perplexed look to her.

Her fist could not hide her laughing eyes though, and they danced at the question on his face. Her voice broke a little with repressed hilarity as she informed him, "She wants to know if you will dance with her at the celebration."

Adianna's suppressed giggle bubbled forth as she watched his eyebrows go up. He then turned a flattered smile to the little towhead girl.

"I would love to," he said slowly and animatedly to her, nodding his head.

This was rewarded with another squeal of joy and a bout of bouncing. Kendrick moved as if to look back at Adianna, but Nalora caught his face in her little hands. She pulled his gaze back to her. The girl then did some more pointing with a few other signs in between.

When she released his face, Kendrick again turned a baffled look to Adianna. This time she let her laughter flow as she repeated the signs. "She said, 'I like you. You're cute.'"

The smile that crossed Kendrick's face took her breath away. He gazed once again at Nalora and replicated the final sign by brushing two fingertips on his chin.

"You're cute, too," he said.

The little girl beamed at him. She clasped her hands together in front of her as she swiveled demurely from side to side. Then she took him totally by surprise by flinging her arms around his neck.

Taken aback, his hands hovered uncertainly over her. Then he gently patted her on the back. When the child pushed away from him, she stood on tiptoes to brush a kiss on his cheek. Then she instantly took off toward the square, her giggling trailing behind her.

The rumble of Kendrick's laughter mingled with Adianna's when he came to stand beside her. She made the enjoyment evident in her eyes, as she pestered, "She is totally smitten with you now."

His face took on a mischievous smirk. "Afraid of a little competition?"

Adianna swallowed hard past the instant lump in her throat. "No, I… I mean… I…"

Oh, I sound like a blithering idiot!

He stepped closer, and she instinctively pulled her cloak around her. Still, he came so close she could feel the warmth of his body even through the shamere mail.

"Will you also dance with me?" his velvet voice washed over her. She could feel the iron band of his arms wrap around her waist, not pulling her toward him, just warding off any escape. She felt tingly all over, and her cheeks flamed. She looked deep into his blue eyes and wondered if she could form any sort of articulate response. Not trusting her voice, she simply nodded.

"Excellent." His breath was hot on her skin. Then, with a crooked smile, he pulled back. "Shall we go assist the others?"

It wasn't till she was out of his arms she realized she had been holding her breath. He held out his hand to her. She placed her silvery-gloved hand in his. Turning toward the square, she hungrily inhaled a lungful, desperate to cool the flame in her cheeks.

Salvaging the village from the attack was going progressively well despite all the damage. Everyone seemed active and energetically involved. Most of the fires had been put out, and the various debris was being piled in the square.

Despite all the work going on around him, Kendrick really focused on little other than Adianna. He still seldom left her side, and when he did, he stayed within sight of her.

She was currently with some other villagers discussing what still needed to be done in that part of the town. Kendrick trailed behind with some other men, testing structure stability. The smell of smoldering wood still stung the nostrils. Memsy, Adianna, and a few of the village elders stopped near the charred skeleton of a large two-story building. Kendrick eyed a nearby hut, noticing the thatch that needed repairing.

Presently, the sound of wood cracking hailed Kendrick's attention. Looking over, he noticed the front wall of that building quivered minutely. Adianna's small group was intent in their conversation. The cracking and snapping became slightly more prominent, and Kendrick could see the wall of the wreckage lean precariously over the group. Over Adianna.

The men glimpsed the danger and backed away. The one known as Ames motioned for Adianna to move back with them, pulling Memsy along. Instead, the young woman turned to look up, just as the burned wall began toppling.

"Look out!" Kendrick yelled, but he was already in motion.

He lunged, catching Adianna around the waist. Tucking her close, he twisted midair and landed hard on his back. In that instant, the building crashed to the ground less than a foot away.

The air left Kendrick's lungs with a whoosh when Adianna landed on top of him, wrapped in his arms. Momentum rolled them, and he heard her groan in protest. When they came to a stop, Kendrick propped himself on one elbow, glancing back at the wreckage behind them. Then he anxiously searched Adianna's face for signs of injury.

"Are you alright?" he asked.

His eyes brushed over her startled face, just inches away. Her breathing was sharp and ragged, matching his. But her eyes were filled only with surprise—no pain, just surprise… and surprisingly beautiful.

With his chest pressing her to the ground and one leg flung over hers, he became distinctly aware of her body, warm and inviting beneath him. He moved his free hand over metal chinking to brush gently along her side, from slender hip to quivering ribs. The feel of his heartbeat pounding in his chest coupled with the sudden tightening in the pit of his stomach.

His gaze brushed over the halo of curls spread wide around her face. The primary shock melted away from those deep emerald orbs looking up at him, to be replaced with something warm and new. His gaze traced the smooth line of her jaw, and he desired to brush his hand over the creamy softness. But before his hand could make contact, cool shamere mail closed over his fingers, reminding him he could look, but not touch.

But the initial disappointment was quelled by the slight catch in her breath. His eyes moved to soft, full lips just inches from his, parted and inviting. His breathing quickened. Oh, if only he could just taste…

"Miss Annie. Master Kendrick. Are you alright?"

At the sound of the villagers' voices, the spell was broken. With a clenched jaw, Kendrick laboriously pulled his hungry mouth away. Still, a satisfied smile crossed his face at Adianna's responsive sigh. *At least I'm not the only one affected by the encounter.*

"Is everyone okay?" came another concerned question.

But before Kendrick could say anything to the group gathered around them, he heard Memsy's smiling voice declare, "They look quite alright to me!"

Pressing his lips together, Kendrick failed in suppressing a chuckle.

"Yes, the fun and games come later, you two! Now is the time to work," one of the villagers guffawed.

An answering laughter erupted around them. The beauty of Adianna's shy smile was heightened by the soft color spreading over her cheeks. How he loved it when she blushed. Still, there was work to do, and he could not possibly woo his wife with a whole village watching.

Kendrick came to his feet and reached back for Adianna. With both hands tucked in his, he pulled her up, giving her arms an abrupt jerk at the top. The sudden movement propelled her forward fast. Wrapping his arms around her waist, he pulled her tight in his embrace, her feet barely brushing the ground. The mail of her cloak bunched against his chest, and he could hear her breath catch, whether from reaction to his touch, the sudden constriction around her lungs, or from mere surprise, he was not sure. A mischievous smile played across his lips, looking into her surprised expression.

"If she would quit distracting me, I could get some work done," Kendrick responded.

Adianna let out a gasp, followed by a playful rap on his shoulder. This made him smile all the more. The merry laughter assailing the couple was rewarded with a beautiful, rosy hue to her cheeks.

Then he said more quietly to the woman in his arms, "Shall we get back to work, or would you rather the fun and games?"

He jiggled his eyebrows roguishly.

Adianna's mouth popped open with a combination of a gasp and a chuckle. She pressed her hands against his chest, pushing off, so he unwillingly set her back on the ground. Still, he kept his hands on her hips, waiting, his eyes searching hers.

Fighting a smile, his wife cocked her head a notch higher, and with a dismissive lift of her eyebrows, turned back to the group of town elders.

Kendrick turned reluctantly back to the task at hand. He was surprised at how much he wished she had chosen to stay with him. *There will be another time.*

Still, as his gaze roamed over her form, the longing for something, anything, from her was irresistible. So why resist it?

"I'll be over here," he called to her, pointing to where he was headed.

The crinkled brow look she gave him bespoke her befuddlement.

So, he continued, "But if you think this is too far away to keep you out of danger, I could come closer."

A hearty chuckle escaped him as he kicked up his heels to avoid the charred piece of rubble she flung at him. Still, it got him the desired reaction, for she could not suppress laughter from bubbling forth. *Ah, sweet music!*

She shook her head at him but returned to her conversation with a smile.

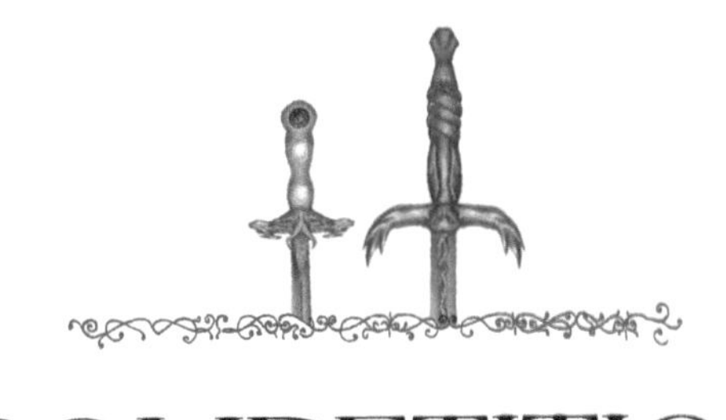

COMPETITION

Adianna couldn't help but notice Kendrick every time he was around. He always seemed to be around. And every time she looked his way, his gaze was upon her or just turning back to her. There was so much warmth in his gaze it radiated across the distance between them and heated her very soul.

Her thoughts returned to his saving her from the toppling building. She could still feel his closeness. Feel the desire radiating from his eyes as they traced her lips. A knot tightened in the pit of her stomach, and her ribs constricted. This was the fourth time he had tried to kiss her, and she could not resist wondering how it would feel. Which would burn her more? His touch or his kiss? The thought was so tantalizing she longed to find out.

"... you will, won't you, Miss Annie?... Annie?"

The words cut into her thoughts. "Pardon me. I'm sorry, what was that?" She tried to focus on Jameston's face, hoping she wasn't blushing too badly.

"I was asking if you and Memsy and your Master Kendrick would stay for the celebration tomorrow, and if you would share the Legend of the Blades with us. You know the story and tell it so well."

It surprised Adianna at how her heart fluttered at hearing the words '*your* Master Kendrick,' and she couldn't help glancing over at him. Of course, his eyes met hers. They were warm and intent on her. Then he smiled at her and gave her a quick wink.

Heat permeated from her cheeks as she ducked her head. Instinctively, she bit at her bottom lip, but the smile crept there, just the same.

Clearing her throat, she responded to Jameston's query. "Yes, we should be able to..."

She glanced back at Kendrick. He had jumped forward to help lift a newly framed wall into place. He had removed his cloak earlier, and sweat was plastering his white shirt to his chest and arms. The muscles strained under the effort, but he seemed unconcerned, his smile full and hearty. Walking his hands down the wood beams, he darted his gaze over to her and caught her looking at him. Somehow his smile got even bigger, but he went back to his task.

"Yes," Adianna mused again, "we would love to stay."

Just then a voice rang out above the hustle and bustle plus the gentle rumble of the river nearby. "She is? Well, where is she? Annie?"

The rush of childhood memories spread over Adianna, and her eyes went wide. She would know that voice anywhere.

"Memsy!" Adianna called. Her mother had been directing the wall raising. Kendrick was just stepping over to her, brushing wood particles from his hands. His head was turned in the direction the voice was coming from, a perplexed look on his face. But Memsy responded to Adianna's call, somewhat wide-eyed and apprehensive.

"It's Tarron! He's here!"

Just as Adianna was about to run off after the voice, its owner came around the corner into the lane.

Tarron, standing at six feet three inches tall, was dressed in the traditional forest hues of elvin traveling garb. His tousled tawny-colored hair, which brushed his collar, and the childish dimples in his cheeks, belied the stately bearing in which he held his lean, muscular body. His smooth skin, typical of the elfish race, was flushed with excitement.

"Adiannie!" he boomed, striding quickly toward her.

A great squeal of delight escaped Adianna, and she flung her arms wide and ran, her cloak flying wildly behind her, into his waiting arms. He lifted her effortlessly, swinging her around in a joyous circle. He buried his face in her hair, inhaling deeply. When they came to a stop, Tarron gave her ear his playful nip before setting her gently on the ground.

With his arms still securely around her slender waist, Adianna looked up at her life-long friend. "I can't believe you are here!" she declared with a joyous smile on her face.

She ruffled her fingers through the locks at the back of his head as she always had. She loved the feel of his silky hair, the way it hung wavy, like hers, and unlike that of most of the elves in Tymalia.

"Me? What about you?" his deep, musical voice merrily chided. "You have never come to Fal Dura without me and a host of other elves in tow." He leaned close, kissed her forehead, and lingered—breathing in the scent of her. Finally, he pulled back, looking into her eyes. "Where is everyone?"

He seemed to want to know, but he never let his gaze leave her face, nor did his arms leave her waist. Her hands slid down his shoulders and rested on the strong bands holding her.

"Memsy is here, of course," she began, her hands patting excitedly on his arms, and a smile upon her face. "And, oh, Tarron! It is so thrilling! It has begun!"

She glanced over to Memsy and Kendrick. What she saw puzzled her, for Kendrick's manner was very heated. His body was tense. His hand was raised to Memsy in an accusatory fashion, and he seemed to be pummeling her with venomous whispers.

Memsy was trying to keep him calm, her hands raised in a conciliating manner, like a lone person trying to calm a riot.

"What has begun, you little minx?" Tarron was asking, giving her body a twisting push to gain her attention.

Adianna returned her gaze to the elf holding her, her brow puckered perplexingly. But her expression quickly cleared as the thought of sharing the news with her best friend brought the excitement back. Giving his arm another pat, she pulled away, saying, "Come here. I'll show you."

Grabbing his hand, she pulled him over to the others, their argument cut short. With their approach, Kendrick turned to face them, crossing his arms in front of him. His face was tight, his body hard as stone. His eyes, cold and piercing, bore through Tarron.

Kendrick's demeanor filled Adianna with apprehension, but looking at Memsy calmed her, for her mother's expression had changed to one of suppressed humor.

"*Ga lay shaloat, na to Memsy.*" Tarron nodded a greeting but quickly eyed the man in front of him. He halted a pace or two away, and something about his shoulders reminded Adianna of the time they had come across a lone orgrin in the forest and suspected there would be a fight.

Positioning herself to the side of each gentleman, she began her introductions. "Kendrick, this is Tarron, my cousin, as well as my oldest and dearest friend."

Tarron dipped his head infinitesimally in greeting, then cocked his chin with a sly smile. Again, Adianna felt her brow pucker in response, baffled, and wondered what was going on without her knowledge.

Turning her attention back to Kendrick, his demeanor had not changed at all: still hard and tense. She rested her hand gently on his arm in an attempt to soothe his hostile behavior, despite the searing pain which surged from the contact. The red, angry light, mingled with streaks of harsh green invading her consciousness, was stunning, but she had no time to dwell on its ambiguous meaning.

"Tarron, this is Kendrick!"

"Her husband!" Kendrick cut in. His hand shot out toward Tarron, though it seemed more in challenge than greeting.

"Her what?!"

Adianna's hand slipped from Kendrick's arm. She cringed at the shock she heard in Tarron's exclamation. He had taken a step back, stunned, and his eyes were fully on her now.

"He's kidding, right?"

Not thinking of what she could say, Adianna gritted her teeth, air hissing out between them. She thought of stalling, but apparently her expression was answer enough.

Tarron pinned Memsy, disbelieving. The older woman pressed her lips together and gave him a slight nod.

"How is this possible?!" Tarron turned on Adianna, railing. "What has gotten into your head? I leave for barely more than a fortnight, and you up and get married! And to a..." He looked over at Kendrick, wrinkling his nose and scrunching his eyes, as if he smelled something disgusting. "... a human?"

Adianna sensed Kendrick move, but she was faster. Her own temper flared, she jumped in between the two, facing the haranguing elf. In her annoyance she brought her fist slamming into Tarron's midsection. The air left his lungs in a gush.

"I'm human, too, you overbearing oaf!" she yelled at him, as he stammered back holding his stomach. "And there's more to it than just getting married. If you would stop acting like the conceited, pointy-eared, pain in the dragon's tail that you are and behave, maybe," she crossed her arms in front of her like a schoolmarm standing over an unruly child, "just maybe, I'll fill you in."

Despite the snickering from who knew how many onlookers, she pinned him with a challenging gaze. The elf braced himself with one hand on his knee, the other still cradling his midsection. He released a long stream of air through the tight 'O' of his mouth.

Adianna thought she heard a muffled chuckle from behind her, but she wasn't sure. Still, it made her realize she had hit Tarron with not only her strength, but Kendrick's, too. A stab of remorse pricked her conscience, but she pushed it down.

"Alright, m'lady." Tarron held the vowels out, like he always did when he was annoyed with her. He straightened stiffly and speared her with a condescending gaze. "Fill away."

It came out as a dare. Adianna's eyes narrowed. Her arms still crossed, she took a step toward him and stated simply, "My quest has begun."

A plethora of emotions crossed Tarron's face. Shock, disbelief, fear, apprehension, loss. His eyes shifted to the man standing behind her. The question was apparent on his face. Adianna imagined Kendrick gave the stunned elf a simple nod, for Tarron's head sunk in defeat.

He stood there, silent for a moment. Then, resolutely, he bobbed his head a couple times before lifting his closed eyes to her. "That's what all the commotion and search parties have been about."

He slowly opened his sad eyes on her. Her agitation melted away. She suddenly felt as forlorn and as tired as he looked. Practically all her life had been preparing to do this. She and Tarron had talked about it, played mock battles about it, and discussed all the ups and downs they could think of about it. And finally, here it was, where nothing was like anything they had ever planned. The unexpected futility of it now washed over her. A single nod was all she could manage.

Lines of worry and despair crinkled Tarron's eyes, and his head tipped back slightly. It would have looked like he was pleading to some unseen being in the sky if it had not been for the clenched tightness of his jaw.

He glanced at Kendrick, then turned a beseeching look on her, and whispered, "Are you sure?"

Tarron raised his hand toward her, an invitation to say 'no.' His imploring eyes tore at Adianna's insides. She could not trust her voice, so she merely nodded again.

His hand dropped limp at his side. Closing his eyes, he drew in a slow, shaky breath. And Adianna held hers. There was so much conflicting energy radiating from him she wasn't sure how to respond, how to help. She had not expected to see him. Not now. Perhaps not ever again. And now her dearest friend seemed to be in a battle all his own.

When Tarron finally opened his eyes, his gaze fell upon Kendrick again. This time there was no plea, no defeat in his look; he just stared at the man for a moment. Adianna had seen him face off a greon before. This didn't seem much different.

Abruptly Tarron's eyes narrowed into a sharp gaze. Before Adianna could wonder what it meant, he turned to her, taking her by the elbow. He glanced around at the various villagers milling around, then leaned down, looking intently into her face.

"This quest is dangerous, Adianna. It will take strength, cunning, and courage. It will take everything you've trained for and more. I know this. *You* know this."

He plopped his hand on her shoulder to emphasize his statement, his mouth cocking into a knowing half-smile. But then the wrinkles appeared again at the corner of his rich, brown eyes. Tarron stared at her as if trying to comprehend something which eluded him. "But, why…"

He licked his lips, trying to find the words. His actions wound her up tight, and she wondered what could be distressing him so. Shifting his weight back and forth on nervous feet, his gaze flicked over to Kendrick before leaning in closer to her. He looked at her again and asked, "Why marriage?"

Adianna's eyes widened slowly. That was the last question she had expected. Her mouth lulled open. She was pricked with the urge to laugh, but the look on Tarron's face was so in earnest, she swallowed the thought quickly.

Then she put some serious thought to his question. Why had they needed to marry? She was stumped. She shrugged, wide-eyed. Her open mouth bobbed in an attempt to conjure an answer to his question. Nothing came. Even 'I don't know' wouldn't form and just came out in a series of 'I… I… I's.'

Finally, she turned to Kendrick, eyebrows raised, searching for some help. Standing with his arm folded across his chest, he had been looking at Tarron with a sly expression like they were playing chess and the man had finally caught the elf in a checkmate. His intense eyes were hooded. Yet his mouth was cocked on one side into a smirk that bespoke of a knowledge of the elf's secrets, which he would use to his advantage.

Slowly the healer shifted his gaze to her. He merely jutted one eyebrow high on his forehead and turned just as slowly to Memsy.

"I've actually wondered that, myself," he said matter-of-factly.

Memsy had been standing a few paces off to their right, cautiously watching the interaction. With the attention now turned to her, she hoisted her chin several notches. Then in a diplomatic tone she stated, unrepentantly, "Plausible deniability."

Adianna scrunched her face, unable to fathom her mother's meaning. She shot a glance over at Kendrick upon hearing a soft snort of air escape him. His lofty look shifted, his jaw set, his lips pursed.

When Adianna looked back at the sorci, she too had transferred her gaze to the scoffing male mortal.

"You reject this excuse, now, Master Healer," Memsy impugned. "But you, yourself, have used it—twice! Once this very day, and it helped to save you *and* the quest."

This response did little to pacify Kendrick. His dubious countenance testified to that. So Memsy went on.

"Also, we felt with Adianna as your *wife*," she stressed the word, "you would be more inclined to shield her from… shall we say," she tipped her head to the side, a slight smile pulling at the corner of her mouth as she watched him, "the wicked wiles of men."

Adianna choked on a cough. "Well," she piped up, slapping her hands together. "That about does it for me!"

She dug the corners of her mouth in deep as she pursed her lips, desperately ready for a change in subject. She looked at Kendrick's calculating expression resting on Memsy and found no help there.

When she turned to Tarron for help, he spoke disbelievingly. "You mean, neither one of you," he pointed back and forth between the couple, "knew why you were being married?"

"Good heavens," Adianna started in a joking manner, poking a thumb over her shoulder at her husband. "Apparently, he didn't even know we were being married until after it was all done."

She tried to chuckle, but it came out strained and put-on. So she cleared her throat, self-consciously. It was hard to read the expression on Tarron's face, but it was intent on the man behind her. The elf sized the man up, lips pursed.

Finally, he broke the stretching silence, a smile upon his face. "I look forward to hearing the story." Tarron stepped to Adianna and slid his hands into her cloak and around her waist. "Later. When there are not so many ears."

Adianna heard a low growl from the healer. But before she could investigate, it was drowned out by a commotion from around the corner at the end of the lane, followed by an impatient, "Where is everybody?"

"Speaking of more ears," Tarron exhaled in defeat. He dropped one hand away from her waist, and with the other, gave her a gentle nudge toward the square.

Turning into the lane came two more elves. Both were of a shorter height than the one standing next to her, but they were of much brawnier build. Their tousled rust-colored hair and smattering of freckles bespoke their dwarf heritage despite the point of their ears.

"Argon! Gaidish!" Adianna squealed, again running with her arms open wide.

The two elves, though keeping openly jovial faces on her, turned their bodies toward each other. Both of them extended an arm out to her. When she was close enough, she leapt into the air, catching each one around the neck with one of her arms. As her legs swung between them, Adianna felt stout bands of iron pushing her through. Then strong hands pushed behind her knees. The whole world flew as she went flipping feet over head backward, her arms the pivoting spindles on two sturdy shoulders. With a final push on her legs, she was flying, touching nothing but air. Nimbly, she landed on her feet facing the brawny duo.

She then clapped, her knees dipped, and she let out a string of gleeful giggles.

"*Ga lay shaloat, na* to you my dear friends," she cheered, jumping up, again placing an arm around each elf's neck. "It is so good," she planted a kiss on one elf's cheek, "to see you!" She then gave a kiss to the other.

Their faces creased in great toothy grins. Their deep dimples made them look like children despite their great size. She could feel their laughter rumble in their large chests. The feeling made her joyfully content with life, and she mingled her laughter with theirs.

Adianna heard Kendrick's exasperated growl from behind her and heard him say, "Oh, what next?"

His irritated tone brought her back to the present, though it didn't deflate her happiness any.

Argon and Gaidish placed her on the ground. She excitedly took a hand in each of hers and pulled them toward the group. Walking backward, she smiled delightedly at each of them.

"This is perfect! The gang's all together. And there is to be a celebration tomorrow! We're staying at the inn. You all simply must stay. Right, Mems?"

Adianna came to a halt beside Tarron and, dropping the newcomers' hands, turned to her mother. But before her gaze found Memsy's, the blond-headed elf claimed her hand, holding it in both of his against his chest.

"Of course, we will stay," he cooed, an overly sweet look on his face.

"Great!" she responded, overjoyed.

Adianna now sought Memsy's face and was slightly confused at what she saw. The sorci was looking toward the ground. Her lips were pulled in, her teeth biting them together tightly, as if she was trying desperately to stifle a smile. As she watched, the elvin woman's gaze darted to the man next to her.

With her brow puckered, Adianna's gaze followed Memsy's to Kendrick. The man paid the sorci no never-mind. His eyes were locked on Adianna. Her breath caught in her throat, for the look he gave her seemed purely livid.

What in the world is wrong with him? she wondered, her eyebrows coming up. She tried to give him a reassuring smile. His only response was a tightening around the mouth as his jaw set. Her smile melted away under the angry heat of his glare.

But then Kendrick stepped forward. "Yes," he said, thumping the length of the hammer he had been holding the whole time into the center of Tarron's chest, and pushing him backward with it. Kendrick stepped in between her and the elf as he continued tightly, "Stay. There is a lot of work to be done."

Kendrick gave the hammer one last shove. Tarron caught the tool before it fell. A cunning smile pulled at the elf's mouth, but the man stalked off.

"Ai," he said softly, watching the man withdraw. "A lot of work."

Perplexed, Adianna looked back and forth from her friend to the man she now called husband, but with each turn she merely became more and more confused.

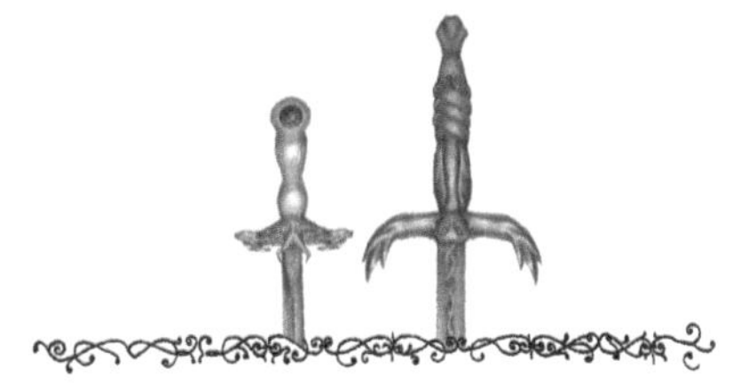

TOO MUCH TO HANDLE

Kendrick scowled, hammering hard at the door he was building. The slabs of wood quivered under every whack. He heard Adianna's laughter ring out. What normally filled him with gladness now consumed him with a bitter jealousy that festered in his chest like acid. He slammed another plank in place.

Glancing over his shoulder, the reason for his anger came into view. The pathetically handsome elf named Tarron was working on replacing the burned planks on the front of a dwelling, just a few feet from Adianna. Though duly attentive to her work on another cottage across the lane from where Kendrick worked, her face glowed, and it galled him to know that blond-headed elf was the reason.

The prancing peacock's arrival was still vividly embedded in his mind. The way he had scooped Adianna up in his arms, nestled his face in her hair, even nibbled her ear. Just the thought stirred the fiery inferno in

Kendrick's stomach anew. He thunked down another plank and turned back to his work.

"You seem rather aggressive in your work, my son," Memsy observed, appearing beside him unnoticed.

The look of genuine concern on her face did little to placate his mood. He was still mad at her, and even though it was childish, he didn't want to talk to her.

He yanked up the door and moved it into place.

She rested her hand on his arm. "I'm sorry if—" she began, but Kendrick didn't want to hear it.

"I'm fine!" He cut her off before she could get started. The thick twine ripped into his skin at the sharp movements in which he tethered the new door in place.

All was silent from the sorci, until she sighed. "All right." She turned and walked away.

The forlorn tone of her voice pricked at Kendrick's conscience, but watching her retreating back, he squelched it before it could grow. The sorci approached Adianna and that infuriating leech which stayed close by her side.

With a growl, he went back to tying up the door. He heard Memsy tell his wife she would be heading to the next street over to see if Argon and Gaidish needed any help.

Good! Let her leave.

He opened and closed the new door to test the twine hinges, but his mind was not on the task. Instead, it went back to his conversation with the sorci just after the pious elf arrived. With that arrogant oaf's hands *and mouth* all over Adianna, Kendrick had instantly accused Memsy of the deception in which she was caught, because obviously some members of the male gender could touch his wife without hurting her. His blood still boiled at the memory of learning the elf species were ineffective in providing the searing touch to a ganji, along with any other non-human species.

Despite Adianna's introduction of him being a dear friend, Tarron obviously felt more involved than mere friendship. She actually seemed oblivious to the elf's true feelings, yet she was highly receptive to his flirting. His continuous and pointed flirting.

Testing the bolt on the inside of the cottage door, Kendrick locked and unlocked it into place.

"There you go, madam," he said, turning a slight bow to the lady of the house, who was sweeping the broken debris from the floor of her main room. A couple of young girls darted about righting stools, stripping bedding, and gathering clothing from the pile their mother was making.

"Thank you, Master Kendrick," the woman said, nearly gushing with appreciation.

Despite the war going on inside him, it made him smile to be helpful and appreciated.

"I'll just get started on the shutters now." He opened the door and stepped into the lane.

His smile faded at the sight of Tarron with his arm draped across Adianna's shoulder. The two were with a few of the directing elders of Fal Dura, and they were all looking at the roof of the house adjacent to the forge directly across from where Kendrick was working. They all stared, not saying a word.

Kendrick strode over, coming up directly behind his wife. He leaned in close to her ear and rested his hand on the shining cloak over her arm. "What's going on?"

Adianna started, her hand coming to her chest as she turned to him, and the elf's hand slipped from her shoulder. Kendrick was pleased he was no longer touching her.

"Kendrick." The surprise fluttered her breathing. "We were…"

His gaze warmed at the color brightening her cheeks.

"Just… trying to decide what needs to be done with the roof of the blacksmith's home."

Her gaze dipped from his as the rosy color of her cheeks deepened under his stare. Then she turned, pointing to the building in question. Kendrick pulled his gaze away from her lovely face and glanced at the thin ribbons of gray smoke rising from several smoldering black patches along the surface of the roof. A tell-tale torch hung precariously over a gaping hole. Another hole at the other end of the roof showed where the fire inside had spread to the walls before being put out.

"Simple. Those planks and shingles must come off and new ones put in." Kendrick wondered why they hadn't deduced the obvious.

"Yes, we know this." Tarron gave him a condescending look, which made his blood boil anew. "We were simply deciding how best to do that."

Kendrick's jaw clenched, and he forced his hard gaze back to the building. When he felt his voice would not give away the contempt welling inside him, he stated, "Simply get a couple of the lads from the village up there to pull off the burned planks. Then the men can safely manage the replacement."

His stare was hard with challenge on the disgruntled elf. Tarron looked irked enough to give some sort of retort when a burst of air escaped the woman between them in a wide-mouthed sigh.

She patted his chest, her face beaming, before she turned her attention up the lane.

"Thomas!" she called, snagging her skirts in her hand and scampering toward the boy in question just up the road.

"Yes, Miss Annie?"

"Will you come and help me for a minute, sweetie?" Adianna took hold of his arm and pulled him over to the group of men staring after her.

"You bet, Miss Annie!" the boy responded with more eagerness than was necessary.

The corners of Kendrick's mouth dug into his cheeks, and he begrudgingly pursed his lips. *Is every male in sight fawning for my wife?*

He tried not to dwell on that thought but watched Adianna. She was scanning the lane from one side to the other, her lips pressed together in concentration. Finally, she spotted what she wanted.

Patting Thomas on the shoulder, she directed, "Will you get that ladder and place it against Val and Dar's cottage, please?"

The boy eagerly ran forth to do her bidding. In the meantime, she went striding up the lane toward the square, removing her gloves as she went.

Kendrick crossed his arms in front of him and queried after her, "What do you think you're doing?"

"I'm going to pull the shingles." She scoffed at him as if it were the most obvious thing in the world.

Kendrick was instantly shaking his head, but she was not looking at him.

"Is this your pack, Tarron?" she asked, swinging her cloak off and draping it over her arm. She continued to the satchel in question.

"Yeah," the elf answered, sounding befuddled.

"All set, Miss Annie," Thomas called from behind Kendrick.

He turned to the boy then back to the woman when she called, distractedly, while rummaging through the pack, "Thank you, Thomas. I'll be right there."

Again, Kendrick was shaking his head till he hovered over Adianna.

"No way!"

"'No way,' what?" A line creased between her brows as she stood, pulling something from the bag. But then she called out, "Tarron, can I borrow these?"

She dangled a pair of green breeches from her hand, waiting expectantly.

"Yeah, I guess," was the uncertain reply from behind him.

"Thanks." And she pulled them on under her dress.

"No way are you going up on that roof." Kendrick laid down the law with his arms folded for authority.

"Why not?" she asked, perplexed. Her skirt bunched on the sides and draped down in front as she pulled the pants over her hips.

"Because it is too dangerous," he chided, flinging a hand at the charred remnant.

Adianna scoffed at him, puffing a burst of air between her lips, and tied the breeches into place.

"Just look at it!" He tried again to convince her, his voice raising. "Those planks could give way at any moment."

Instead of seeing reason, she bent over and rolled up the pant legs several times.

Kendrick let out a growl and looked around for help to convince her. Strangely enough, it was Tarron who stepped forward.

"He's got a point, Annie," the elf said. "Why don't you let us do it?"

But Adianna rolled her eyes. She heaved a sigh and proceeded to pull her dress up around her chest.

"You know very well that roof won't hold you. Either of you," she accused, tugging her white undershirt down over the pants so it wouldn't come off with the dress.

The slim line of her thighs and the gentle curve of her hips were revealed, sheathed in the thin fabric now covering them. Kendrick felt his throat constrict, blocking off the passage of air. Coughing sharply to gain use of his voice, he struggled to remember his argument. He pulled his gaze away from the tantalizing vision in pants and looked to the sky.

"That's beside the point." He cleared his throat when it cracked on the last word. "You can't go up there…"

His voice trailed off, falling under the sirens' call. He could watch that figure all day. The elf still seemed to be backing his side but sounded just as inarticulate as he. Kendrick didn't need to turn to know what held the elf's attention.

Still Adianna was oblivious to the show she was putting on. She pulled the dress over her head, and he heard her muffled voice. The words were mostly indistinct, but the fact she was cussing men in general was apparent. Finally freeing her head from the yards of fabric, mounds of wavy hair spilled forth around her shoulders and framed her face.

"But you can't—" both men tried again at once.

"Oh, for heaven's sake!" Adianna declared bluntly. She flung the dress to the ground in a heap, then grabbed the excess fabric of her shirt and tied it in a knot at her waist. "You two are being ridiculous!"

Cinching the material sharply, she flung her hands akimbo. "If you are so worried about it, why don't you go grab me a cat."

Kendrick's brows jutted down over his eyes. The elf wasn't any help as to discerning her meaning. She strode up to them. With her arms now folded in front of her, he tried not to notice how her chest strained against the white fabric.

She leaned in for just the two of them to hear. "Then, if I fall, at least you'll know I'll land on my feet."

Kendrick's mouth dropped open. She gave him a mischievous smirk before flicking her hands at him and Tarron, motioning for them to part.

"Now if you boys will excuse me, I have work to do."

Kendrick fell back a few steps, as did the elf. Adianna stepped past them, hollering at Thomas to grab a hammer and get up on the roof.

Kendrick stared, unabashedly, at the retreating form of his wife. With the material of her shirt pulled tight, the entire, curvy length of her was framed to perfection. The span of her ribs was encased in thin white material slimming down to at least an inch of exposed, creamy flesh at her waist. Her waist, so slender Kendrick imagined he could span it with his hands and still have his fingers touch, then flared out to the soft bend of her hips.

He felt Tarron's approach, but he did not look away. Indeed, he feasted on the sight of her while she waited for the lad to top the ladder.

"Umm, mmm!" the elf hummed quietly.

It was obvious to what Tarron was referring, but Kendrick was too engrossed to respond. Still, the elf added in a low appreciative tone, "I must say. My breeches have never looked so good."

Kendrick was about to give him a tongue-lashing, but then Adianna started her climb up the ladder. The home-spun fabric stretched tight across her lean derrière. All thoughts of rebuke evaporated, and he found himself straining to concentrate. A knot tightened in the pit of his stomach.

"Indeed," was all he could articulate with Adianna stretching to step onto the roof.

Once on the roof, she motioned for Thomas to get started at the far end. She gingerly walked the slope of the roof. Then bending over, she proceeded to pull up a board.

"Mmm, mmm, mmm," Kendrick hummed, staring at her back end admiringly, like an art lover revering the lines of an exquisite painting.

Adianna pulled the first plank, then flung it to the ground below. In the process, she caught sight of the two men ogling her. She gave them a smile and a reassuring thumbs-up.

Kendrick self-consciously cleared his throat, looking down at the ground, abashed at being caught gawking. Quickly, he turned to Tarron. The elf was still smiling hungrily at Adianna.

"Alright. Get back to work!" he ordered, with a shove.

Tarron obliged. At least he wandered back in that direction, but since he had been working at the forge right next to where Adianna now was, Kendrick blistered on seeing the elf keep his smile on her the whole way.

With a snort, Kendrick ambled backward to his work on the shutters, most of the while glaring at his blond adversary, who continued ogling the slender form on the roof. Then with a final appreciative glance at his wife, he turned back to the job at hand.

Kendrick grabbed a tied fardel of boards to use on the shutters. He meticulously untied them and laid them in place, reconstructing a shutter on his make-shift table. The roof of the building opposite him regularly drew his attention.

He had to admit, if only to himself, she was doing a good job and making good time of it. They would be done pulling the ruined planks in no time.

As if hearing his compliment, Adianna looked his way, finding his gaze on her. Her cheeks were flushed from leaning over and from the effort she was putting into her work. Still, she smiled shyly and wiggled her fingers at him in a wave.

He smiled in return, and they resumed their work.

Hammering the wooden wedges into the boards, he noticed how the blond peacock had shifted his work so as to get a better view of the roof. With an irritated huff, he added more force to the swing of his hammer. He left repeated divots in the wood while he contemplated an adequate means of eliminating the competition in a manner most fitting.

"Whoa, whoa. Thomas, hold up, lad," the elf presently called out.

Kendrick looked to Tarron, then to the roof. The boy, Thomas, had worked around to the top of the roof, and was pulling with all his might at a particularly pesky plank. The cause for alarm came in the form of Adianna working just below the boy. Neither one was facing the other, and both were totally oblivious to their proximity.

Suddenly the board gave way, and Thomas was propelled backward.

"Adianna! Look out!"

Kendrick cried out the warning, but it was too late. The lad bumped into the unsuspecting woman, and she went careening over the edge. Her startled scream split the air.

Kendrick lurched forward, but Tarron was closer and nimbly positioned himself to catch the falling maiden. Hands flailing, Adianna plunged into the waiting arms of the elf. The gravitational force in which she hit into him, sent him toppling over backward, and they crashed to the ground.

Kendrick halted mid-stride a few yards from them, less from the urgency being abated and more from the alarming sight of his wife straddling the blond peacock. She lay on top of him, her forehead pressing into the ground, her body limp against his. Their deep breathing mingled with each other's, and they struggled to catch their breath.

Tarron brushed his hands along her slender and barely covered back, then turned his lips to her ear.

"You good?" he breathed.

She pressed one hand against the elf's chest, lifting herself to survey the damage. Glancing around, she took quick inventory, before Kendrick heard her affirmative answer.

Relief was stabbed mercilessly by jealousy at the radiant smile Adianna then gave Tarron.

The elf didn't miss the humor in her smile.

"What?" he asked, his hands slowly caressing her sides.

She pushed off his chest, sitting perpendicular to his prostrate form. Her eyes danced with mirth as she declared, "I may not have landed on my feet, but at least I landed on top."

"Oh, yeah!" Adianna's laughter rang out as Tarron began tickling mercilessly at her ribs. An angry knot contracted in Kendrick's chest. This burst into a blazing inferno, as the elf rolled his wife over and pinned her to the ground. With her legs still around the braggart, it was more than the irate man could stand.

Kendrick went to them in an instant. Reaching down, he grabbed the elf by the collar.

"That's enough," he growled, and he yanked Tarron off the laughing woman on the ground. In his inflamed state, Kendrick flung the fellow backward a few paces and pinned him with his glare. The elf snickered unrepentantly.

The laughter died quickly at the sudden removal of the culprit. Adianna's wide-eyed surprise was trained on him, despite the gentle smile still playing on her lips. Kendrick was pricked with the realization his rash behavior might be a tad over-protective, but with the anger still churning within him, he knew it couldn't be helped. Still, he was a gentleman.

"If you are indeed well, I will help you return to your task, m'lady."

Kendrick offered his hand, hoping his voice didn't sound as strained as it did to himself.

Adianna's gaze darted to Tarron apprehensively before resting on him. She reached for him instinctively, but stopped short, recoiling slightly. He could detect a longing in her eyes, but she held back.

With an exasperated huff, the elf stepped forward, petulantly. Thrusting forth his hand, Tarron said, pointedly, "Here, Annie. Let *me* help you up."

Adianna debated over the proffered hands. Then Kendrick became keenly aware of the gaffe he had made and was not surprised when she unobtrusively took the elf's assistance.

The apologetic look she gave him while she was hauled off the ground did little to placate the man's mood. Kendrick looked at his hand. The sudden urge to scream and to lash out irrationally took hold of him. He constricted his hand into a tight fist. Glaring at it, he set his jaw menacingly.

Without a word, Kendrick stalked off. When it became apparent he was not returning to his previous work, he heard Adianna call out to him. He was aware of the concern in her voice, but the boiling of his blood drove him on, down the lane and to the opposite side of the village.

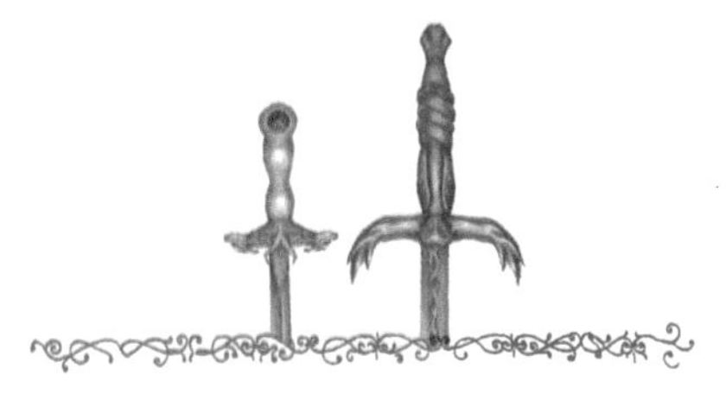

FIRE TOUCH

Adianna did not see Kendrick again until supper. As a result, her mood quailed. Even Gaidish, with his ever-jovial personality, could do little to liven it.

At supper, Kendrick was urbane in manner but remained aloof.

They were staying at the Duck and Goose, as it was the only hostry in Fal Dura. The common room on the main floor of the three story building served as dining hall, head office, and pub, so the noise grew steadily with more villagers relinquishing the repairs for the day.

At their table, Adianna sat with her back to the corner, flanked by Argon and Tarron. Gaidish pressed in closely on the other side of Tarron, not wanting to miss anything. Memsy sat beyond Argon. The healer completed the round, so to speak, but sat in a lone chair beyond their semi-circle.

For the first time, Adianna wished her friends weren't so chummy. She watched her alliance companion as closely as she could without giving it away. He sat opposite from her, which made it easier to observe him, but placed him so far from her she could feel the separation. He ate little, and she marveled he could eat anything at all with how stiff and rigid he kept his jaw. He held his attention averted from the happenings of their table except for an occasional glare at one or the other of the elves.

But she was starkly aware he never looked at her. This fact left her hollow and empty inside. Pondering more and more on the meaning of her reaction, she became steadily more reclusive, despite her friends' many attempts at reminiscing the good times. Of course, the good times that were shared were all about her and none too flattering.

"And do you remember the day you went running buck naked through Tymalia? Now that was a riot!"

Tarron's hand descending upon her shoulder made her jump, and for the first time that night, she was pinned by Kendrick's intense stare.

Adianna felt a mingling boil in her inner cauldron as humiliation and irritation converged. Her jaw tightened.

"I was *six* at the time," she said through clenched teeth, picking up one of Tarron's appendages from her shoulder with the tips of her fingers, as if it were a gross bug she needed to flick away. She thought she heard a dismissive snort from the man sitting across from her, but she dared not look his way, so she continued her defense. "And it was Gaidish who took my clothes in the first place."

She pinned the guilty party with an accusatory glare, but Gaidish merely hooted with laughter. She felt the need to sink further into her seat as the three male elves chortled at her expense.

Gaidish pointed at her, laughing. "You decided to strip down to go catching fish in Shulna's large fish tank and came out not only drenched but also covered with greenery! You looked like the Loch Shiley monster. It was so funny."

"Ha ha ha!" Adianna countered with a mock laugh. She crossed her arms in front of her, sinking sulkily into her seat. Her gaze darted to Kendrick, afraid to find him staring at her aghast. But he wasn't. In fact, he was staring at Tarron, hard and cold.

Tarron on the other hand was totally unaware. "What about the time two years ago when you took part in the choifell races? You fell off your choifell right at the finish line and not only lost the race but also most of your top as well. I thought I was gonna die!"

Unfortunately, you didn't, Adianna thought as she felt her supper threaten to rise.

"Tarron," Memsy said softly, but there was a subtle warning in her voice.

Adianna glanced at her mother. Memsy watched her closely. She could always tell what Adianna was feeling, even without probing her mind for answers, and now was no different. But Tarron was oblivious to the mortification his comments were inflicting and plunged on.

"Oh, and when you had that crush on Zeffner, so you sang a love song for him at the bonfire, right in front of his newly betrothed. Now that was hilarious!"

Around the table, the sound of laughter erupted again.

Adianna pulled the inner edge of her bottom lip between her teeth; her brows drew together slowly. The thought of the healer listening to all this made the matter worse. She tried not to, but she couldn't help peeking at him to see his reaction.

There he was, watching her. No laughter, no sense of revulsion. He merely looked at her, all emotion masked. But still that was enough.

She closed her eyes, closing the floodgates before the waters could flow. She bit down on both lips at once, willing herself to push it all away, wishing she could just run from the room.

Tarron's arm wrapped around her shoulders, and he gave her a little shake. "Ah, Annie, you were always good for a laugh!" He followed that with a mighty guffaw right next to her face.

She turned her face from his. She wanted to scream, or hit him, or rail at him, anything but cry in front of her new husband. Still, a tear squeezed through her lashes to skid slowly down her cheek.

Just then an icy voice cut through the laughter. "Is this how you treat your women in Tymalia?"

Silence blanketed the air around the table, and all eyes fell on Kendrick. His face was hard and menacing. His eyes swept over the men, repulsed, before pinning Tarron with a deadly stare. "With public humiliation and ridicule?"

The man's jaw tightened, and his nostrils flared as he seemed to struggle to suppress a boiling rage.

Adianna swiped her hand across her cheek, wiping away the tell-tale signs of her disgrace. Biting down harder now, she closed her eyes again and stifled a sob, wishing she could hide.

"Adianna?" Tarron's voice was apprehensive and full of concern. "I… Are you…?"

A trembling breath escaped her, and her chest shuddered from compressed emotion. Adianna looked into Tarron's face. But it was too much for her. A strangled sob tore from her throat, and she pushed back her chair in an attempt to flee.

Tarron's arm clamped around her waist, and he caught hold of her hand to restrain her.

"No, wait! Please, Annie. I'm sorry! Please." He pulled at her, not letting her leave. "Please! Don't go."

He came to his feet and pulled her around to face him. He tilted her chin, and he looked deep into her wet eyes.

"I am so sorry, Adianna," he said, softly. "I never meant to hurt you. Please? Please, don't go?"

The beseeching nature of his gaze, coupled with the slow, gentle stroke of his thumb along her jawline did her in. She could never seem to stay mad at Tarron, even when he deserved it. One side of Adianna's mouth dipped back deeply in an attempt to smile. She swallowed hard and swiped at the moisture around her eyes.

She pinned him with an apprehensive, but quirky, look. "Alright. But," she challenged, "no more shameful stories about me!"

She gave his shoulder a whack to express the abated annoyance at him and reluctantly resumed her seat.

"Fair enough," he said, his face lighting up as he sat back beside her again.

"Let's see," he continued thoughtfully. "What can we talk about, then?"

Adianna clenched her teeth together, watching him nervously as she sat, nearly afraid of what the big oaf would say next.

"I've got it!" he finally declared, poking the air with his finger. "We can talk about our first kiss!"

The air escaped Adianna's lungs in a disbelieving chuckle. She leaned forward, bracing her elbow on the table in front of her, and buried her face in her hand. Her chuckle died in a tired groan, and she shook her head from side to side. She slowly pulled her palm across her face, plastering the hand over her mouth and barely letting the air slip past as she looked at her mother. Memsy sat there with her mouth open, a mixture of surprise and censure on her face, while she looked from Adianna to Tarron and back again. The other elves chimed in with a chorus of whoops.

"What?" Tarron asked, all too innocently.

Adianna dared not look at Kendrick. She could feel his irritation from across the table like a tornado in her stomach. She swept her gaze past him to the obnoxious elf sitting next to her.

"*Our* first kiss?" she said pointedly, pinning him.

"Yep," he replied unabashed.

"If you will remember correctly, *you* kissed *me*," she accused, pointing from him to herself respectively.

"I sure did!" he declared, unashamed.

"Then I hit you for it!"

The other elves exploded with laughter. Adianna chanced a look at the man sitting across from her. Approval tugged at his lips, but his eyes were still hard, unforgiving, and directed at the elf, not her.

"Ah," Tarron countered. "But not the second time."

Adianna's mouth fell open to scoff at the overzealous buffoon. "That's because you paid for it!" She gave him a disgusted shove. "It was the Shay Day festival in Tymalia, and I was raising coin for Nalora's Sheoraen sign tutor. And *you* just kept going through the line over and over and over again."

Tarron leaned back in his chair, a huge smile splitting his face. He laced his fingers behind his head and declared, "Money well spent!"

Adianna's chest quaked with mirthless laughter. She tilted her head back, searching the ceiling in mock defeat.

"You are such an idiot," she scoffed, turning again to shake her head at him.

Abruptly, Tarron leaned forward. He braced his arm on the table, bringing his face right up into hers. Then he stated, low and suggestively, "What about our fire touch?"

Adianna's mouth fell open. She sat, stunned, staring into rich brown eyes. The air in her lungs squeezed out and struggled to return. She couldn't believe he was bringing that up here and now. Her cheeks colored at the memory.

Just then Kendrick's voice cut into the awkwardness. "What's a fire touch?"

A small, victorious smile spread across Tarron's face as he stared triumphantly over the table at the human.

"You know elves can utilize the elements," the elf stated, not questioning.

The healer nodded minutely.

"So, I'm sure you know elves can conjure individual elements."

Kendrick's jaw worked slightly, before he gave a tight affirmation.

"My family is of the fire line," Tarron continued, gesturing at his fellow comrades. "And one of the things we can do with it is what we call a Fire Touch. It is a way we can test relationships. Connections, if you will, between two individuals."

"Yeah!" Gaidish chimed in. "It is so cool!" Then he whacked Tarron on the arm. "Let's show him how it works!"

Tarron tilted his head to the side and his shoulders slumped. But finally, he rolled his eyes and turned to his cousin to demonstrate.

"Okay!" Gaidish announced. "You have to be touching on one side." He clamped his hand down on his cousin's shoulder. "Then you bring the palms of your other hands up to face each other, like so." He placed his hand out, fingers up in a relaxed spread, as if he were waiting to catch a ball.

Tarron leaned his arm against the table, then placed his hand in a similar fashion a few inches away, facing Gaidish's.

"Now, we conjure a flame." As Gaidish spoke, a small flicker ignited into a walnut-sized ball between the elves' hands.

Adianna leaned in closely to peer over Tarron's shoulder. The golden-orange sphere licked around in a perfect circle as if caught inside a glass globe. That globe glowed with a life of its own. She rested her chin on his shoulder, transfixed. She stared into the flame, letting the fireworks swirling inside her die down.

"Then," Gaidish went on, "the fire will burn brighter and hotter according to the connection, attraction, or family relationship between the pair."

As if by command, the sphere glowed brighter, changing from orange to yellow to white hot. As the flame intensified, a soft hum sounded from its apex. The light beamed intensely, and Adianna squinted, beholding its warm glow.

When Tarron crumpled his fingers, the blaze died down and, finally, snuffed out.

"Cheesy parlor tricks for elves," Adianna said, dismissively. She leaned back into her chair, folding her arms in front of her.

Tarron turned to her, arching an eyebrow.

"Maybe," he shrugged. He brought up his finger to wag in her face. "But very, very accurate."

His deep mocha eyes bore into hers, challenging her to disagree. His finger dropped to gently caress the edge of her hand. His voice was husky. "Our fire touch was one of the brightest I've ever seen."

"Don't be absurd!" Again, Adianna scoffed in his face and drew her hand away. "The ones between Memsy or Daerlot and I have been nearly blue! Besides," she poked him hard in the shoulder with her finger, "it probably was intensified by my absorption of your powers."

Before she could withdraw her hand, he claimed it in his.

"Maybe," he stated. Then he paused, watching his thumb draw slow circles over her skin. It was then Adianna perceived a side of Tarron she had not been aware of before. His eyes were sincere and hopeful as they met hers. "Maybe not."

For the first time, she saw he wanted more than a best friend or a little sister, and she was stupefied. Her brow furrowed, and her mouth lagged open. *How can this be? When did this happen?* His loving eyes searched hers. She was speechless, baffled... dumbfounded.

Just then Memsy's voice cut through the silence. "Why don't we see the fire touch between Adianna and Kendrick, here?"

The air left Adianna's lungs in a whoosh. Her mouth dropped open. Turning to her mother, her eyebrows jutting to her hairline, she couldn't believe what the woman was saying, and that she was saying it now, of all times. Tarron balked as well, and Adianna's hand fell limp at her side.

Her gaze then fell on the man in question. Kendrick had been sitting, glaring at the metal spoon he was strangling in his hand. His jaw was set so tight it looked nearly twice as wide as his face. But even his head had came up at the sorci's stark change in subject. Slight lines creased around the edges of his eyes as if trying to decipher a problem. Then his gaze met Adianna's.

"They can't!" Tarron piped in first.

"Why not?" Memsy countered and folded her arms challengingly, though her eyes never left Kendrick's.

"I'm sure she has absorbed more than enough of your abilities to do the job," the sorci countered pointedly.

She's right, Adianna rationalized. *It would be possible, expect—*

"But he can't touch her!" Tarron barked out, voicing her next point before she could form it herself.

Still from him, it sounded more of a threat, and it made Kendrick bristle. Adianna turned an accusatory glare on the elf, which made him catch his blunder.

"Not without hurting her, that is," he stammered doggedly, ducking his head so he couldn't meet her gaze.

Adianna looked back at Memsy. *He's right.*

"I don't know," Memsy said, her sorci emblem gleaming. She tilted her head, eyeing Adianna with a soft calculating, yet knowing, observance.

Then the sorci turned to Kendrick. "Healers have an overly powerful aura, as do ganjies, for that matter," she said, gesturing at the man, then, with a sweep of her hand, indicated Adianna.

Memsy's eyebrow arched high, turning back to Kendrick, her head nodding continuously. "I'll bet if you both concentrated, you could create enough contact, without touching, to make it work."

Slowly Kendrick returned Adianna's questioning gaze. They stared at one another, both seemingly unsure of what to do.

It was Gaidish who broke the spell and decided the next step. He slapped his big hand onto Kendrick's back, knocking him slightly off balance in the process, and declared, "Give it a go, old man! This will be fascinating!" The rowdy, red-haired elf turned his jovial countenance on Adianna and boomed, "Come on, Annie! Get on over here! You can do it!"

"Yeah, Annie!" Argon piped in with his brother for the first time. "Show us what you can do!"

She gave the enthusiastic pair an uncertain smile. Then, raising a questioning brow to Kendrick, she rubbed her hands awkwardly on her thighs. The man gave her a crooked smile in return, dipping his head a couple times. His hand left the bent spoon on the table and gestured for her to come over.

Adianna took a shaky breath and let it out slowly. She turned sluggishly, shooting a quick glance to Memsy. The sorci was all smiles and encouragement. But Adianna didn't feel so certain while she walked apprehensively around the table.

Her approach slowed further when she rounded her mother and Kendrick stood to face her. He watched her closely, but his expression was unreadable. She stopped about a foot away from him and timidly looked up. He was searching her face.

Adianna felt the color creeping along her neck and rising to her cheeks. A gentle smile touched his lips as he watched this transformation. Instinctively, her head dipped to hide her blush.

"Now what?" he asked softly, the smile apparent in his voice.

"Okay," Memsy said from behind Adianna. "Both of you get your hands in position for the fire touch like you saw Tarron and Gaidish demonstrate."

Adianna thrust out her hand self-consciously. But when Kendrick was bringing his hand up, Argon interjected, "No, use the other hand or we won't be able to see the flame."

Adianna dropped her hand and flung up her right one, keeping her eyes glued on her mother's face for more direction.

"Good." Memsy nodded. "Now, Adianna, honey, you were leaning against Tarron during their fire touch, so you felt the connection and how they did it, right?"

Adianna peeked hastily over at Tarron before answering. To anyone else, his face would be merely that of a passive observer, but she knew better. The tightness around those chocolate eyes could not lie to her. He was tense with a pent-up emotion that was barely containable.

She looked quickly back to her mother and gave a sharp nod. Then she focused on the space between her hand and the one facing it. She felt a ripple of heat trickle from somewhere in her mind, down along her arm, and press intently against the inside of her palm. The pressure built more and more, her arm trembling at the strength of it, until finally it burst through. Once freed, her body relaxed, and she felt the energy spring from her palm to Kendrick's, causing his fingers to twitch slightly. When it bounced back, a light sprang to life in glowing flame, a licking, dancing whirlpool within a small sphere. A slow smile of accomplishment settled on her lips.

"She did it!" Gaidish cheered in his gruff but likable voice.

Adianna beamed at him. Then she watched the flame play between their hands.

"Very good, my love," Memsy's congratulated, with a proud smile shining on her face.

Adianna giggled like a schoolgirl granted an invitation to her first Shay Day dance.

"Alright, now you have to put your other hand over Kendrick's shoulder and just skim above till you feel the same type of connection the boys had," Memsy said, nodding to the cousins across the table.

"Alright." Adianna smiled.

She lifted her hand so it just hovered over Kendrick's shoulder.

"Now, Kendrick," Memsy instructed. "You need to focus on pushing that inner fire, if you will, out to her so she can feel you there without her having to actually touch you. Can you do that?"

"I think so." The healer nodded briskly. He shifted into a more relaxed stance. In so doing, he bumped into Adianna's raised hand. A skiff of pain shot up her arm, making her flinch. But she moved her hand back into place and began her focused search.

Skimming her hand less than an inch over his shoulder, she moved slowly and methodically, seeking the warming pull she remembered feeling between Tarron and Gaidish. As her hand came down over the front of his shoulder, she felt a tingle of warmth. Her focus narrowed in on her hand, she tried to pull at that tingle. But just then, he drew down his shoulders, and it was gone.

"Hold still!" she hissed, playfully.

"Yes, mum," he whispered. A quirky smile streaked across his face, but he straightened his head to appear less of a wayward child.

Adianna chuckled softly but went back to her search for the elusive connection. Unable to find what she was looking for, she moved her hand over along his collarbone to the center of his chest, then, bringing it down an inch or two, skimmed slowly back. The material of his shirt tickled her fingers and palm as they brushed over it.

At first, she could hear the sound of the socializing patrons at the far end of the common room, but turning inward to find what she sought, the only sounds became her breathing mingling in rhythm with his.

On the return sweep, she became aware of the tingle she had felt earlier. She paused, her hand hovering above the slow rise and fall of his chest. She began to pull at that flicker of heat, slowly at first, but steadily increasing as the flame in her other hand swelled slightly.

She shifted her eyes back and forth from the flame to her other hand and pulled harder and harder with her mind. But it didn't seem to do anything. Annoyance rose within her, and her face crumpled.

"Here," Kendrick whispered. "Try this."

He raised his other hand until it lingered over hers. His aura engulfed her hand and, instantly, Adianna felt a flood of warmth through her mental pull.

Their touch of fire bloomed in size and color, the light flooding past their hands and washing over the now-squinting onlookers. Adianna repressed some of the mental draw, allowing the flame to reduce to a gentle glow of yellow, rimmed with orange.

"Well, I'll be a drainal rat," Argon said in hushed tones.

Adianna looked at her friend, where he was standing now just beyond a very delighted Memsy. Argon turned his lopsided grin on Tarron, then his brother.

"They did it!" Argon declared, amazement written on his face. He quickly grabbed his mug from off the table and held it aloft in grand salute. "You did it!"

Adianna beamed, her gaze moving around the table. Gaidish sprang up, anxious to toast any occasion. Tarron was slower to stand, looking less enthusiastic. He never took his eyes off the burning fire. Still, he raised his tankard high.

Looking back at the flaming sphere, a thrill of accomplishment flew throughout her body.

"We did it," she said softly. She watched the blaze swirl and spin a moment before turning her face to the healer.

His eyes were upon her, captivated.

"We did it," he said. A gentle smile played across his lips.

Despite the tender grin, his gaze held such immense power she could not look away. Then his eyes began to roam over every part of her face, a slow hungry search. *What was he searching for?*

Adianna stood, held captive by his alluring exploration. But when his eyes fell upon her lips, her breath caught in her throat. He looked into her eyes then back to her mouth. Involuntarily, her lips parted to let in the much-needed oxygen, though none entered.

The soft heat of his hand hovering over hers slowly descended to her wrist and along her forearm in a gentle caress. She could feel it as surely as if he were touching her skin, the intensity of his aura on hers that palpable. That real. She longed to feel more.

Oblivious to what was going on around her, Adianna's gaze moved to the siren's call, until it fell upon his mouth. His lips, full and inviting, were parted and enticing her, drawing her closer.

Would the burning really be that bad? she wondered, never looking away. *Is he coming nearer? Maybe it would be worth it, just to feel his lips on mine? What could it hurt?*

"By the gryphons!"

The exclamation barely worked into Adianna's consciousness, but finally the astonishment in Gaidish's voice broke through. Realization dawned upon her awareness. Her cheeks flamed as she comprehended just how close Kendrick's face had grown to hers. Her mouth bobbed open as if to speak, but unable to find the words, she merely took in a much-needed lung-full of air.

Disappointment was clearly evident on the healer's face, and the tug at Adianna's heart mirrored his shattered hopes. *Could he really want it as much as I do?* The thought sent a blazing heat through her entire being.

Shaking those thoughts aside, she turned her attention to Gaidish, but her eyes never got that far. For there, along the path, was the fire touch. The sound of it alone was enough to draw attention to it, for it hummed and whooshed like a blazing torch. But it was the flame itself which captivated her. Only now did the vast heat of it register in her awareness. The fire shone forth with such an intense white blue it was difficult to keep one's eyes on the tiny inferno.

Somehow her eyes widened yet squinted at the same time. Her jaw went slack. She had never, in all her time living among the elves, seen such an intense flame; the brightness and brilliance were awe-inspiring.

Her eyes had to adjust to peer beyond at the elves around the table. The look on each face bespoke the astonishment they were feeling, though Memsy's expression held an air of smugness, as if this merely confirmed something she had already known.

Tarron appeared torn between surprise and something else. Something dark and stormy that Adianna could not decipher or comprehend at the moment.

But this could not detract from the soaring feeling spiraling within her. Adianna once again looked at Kendrick.

He had been observing the flame but turned to meet her gaze. His eyes were as heated as the flame in her hand. Unbidden, her breathing increased, and her temperature rose. She could feel the intensity of his stare. He looked deep in her eyes, inviting her to who knew where. She didn't care where. At that precise moment, she would go anywhere, as long as it meant she was with him.

"Adianna, I…" he began but seemed unable to formulate the words that would communicate his desires.

Oblivious to all else save him, she felt her body get warm and malleable, as if she could melt into the palm of his hand to be molded like potter's clay. Her limbs grew heavy. Still Adianna was drawn deeper into the lucid desire of his gaze.

But when her hand accidently dropped upon his chest, the pain that shot through her senses broke the spell, making her flinch. Her fingers crumpled around the flame. The blue blaze flickered and went out.

Despite the pain, Adianna searched Kendrick's face, nearly scared at what she might see. *Is he upset? Disappointed? Relieved?*

She pulled her hands away, and the healer's expression turned to one of sadness. His lips parted as if to say something, but all that came out was a defeated sigh as he closed his eyes. He lulled his head forward, overcome by some emotion indiscernible to her, and his hands fell to his side. She watched him. Watched his jaw work minutely. Watched him draw in a slow, calming breath, until finally his voice came soft and low.

"I think it is time to turn in for the night."

He opened his eyes to look at her, a gentle caress of a gaze. Slowly but deliberately, he ran his hands along her arms just barely beyond the material of her blouse. He never touched her flesh, but the tenderness of the caress she felt was unmistakable. Unhurriedly, his hands moved up and down above her skin. The warmth of it was only surpassed by the heat she felt growing in her belly.

She drew her bottom lip between her teeth, which drew his attention back to her mouth. She inhaled, anticipating a renewal of the previous episode.

Unfortunately, he closed his eyes and smiled slowly. "It has been a very long day."

She agreed but felt the lack of his warmth as soon as it was gone.

UNEXPECTED

After spending all morning and a good part of the afternoon avoiding his wife, he could do it no longer. The village elders had sent him in search of her, for they desired to discuss with her her preference of the order for the celebration that evening. He had been all over the village. He had found Memsy. He had found the blowhard twins. He had even found the adorable, little deaf girl who still insisted on a dance with him, but he could not find Adianna. Nor Tarron.

That thought made his every muscle tighten of their own accord, and a boiling sensation bubbled up inside him even as he leapt onto the porch of the inn. Lifting the latch, he pushed the door open and strode into the dim interior. His eyes slowly adjusted to the lack of light. He was aware of the elf twins dogging his heels, but he turned to the quiet hum of voices coming from the vicinity of the bar.

There, Kendrick could make out outlines of the patrons, including a lanky blond elf stretched out with his feet on the chair opposite him. His fingers knit behind his head, Tarron looked the epitome of happy contentment, and he continued talking jovially with the men near him.

Seeing no sign of Adianna, the perturbed healer marched over to his lounging foe.

Upon seeing them approach, Tarron purposefully looked past Kendrick, stretching his hands wide in greeting.

"Fabulous!" he boomed at his cousins. "You're just in time!" Then he looked at the man standing ominously in front of him, a quirk of a smile pulling at the corner of his mouth. "Care to join us for a drink, old man?"

Kendrick locked his fists, trying desperately to control himself.

"Where is Adianna?" he asked through clenched teeth.

Not missing the menacing stance nor tone, the elf slowly lowered his feet to the floor. Stretching himself up, Tarron stood toe-to-toe with the irate human before answering. The equality in height was not unnoticed to either of them as they pushed the bounds of personal space.

Kendrick was aware of the silence that fell over the room as well as the two bulky forms pressing in behind him, but he kept his focus on Tarron. The tawny-haired elf calculated his adversary calmly, then slowly a smile of challenge split his face.

"If you mean, *Miss Annie*," Tarron said pointedly, referencing the name the village knew her by for her own protection, which galled Kendrick as well as chastened him. Then the elf jutted his jaw toward the back of the building. "I think she's still in the room off the back of the kitchen."

Without another thought, Kendrick turned in that direction but was stopped by Tarron's hand on his arm.

"Wait!" the elf warned. "You don't want to go back there."

"The vairn I don't!" Kendrick yanked his arm from Tarron's grasp. He shoved past Argon and stalked off to the kitchen.

The kitchen was all abuzz with preparations for the festivities that night. People darted here and there. Every flat surface was filled, and the air permeated with the tantalizing scents of meats roasting, bread baking, and sweet, decadent fare of every kind.

Standing in the doorway, Kendrick surveyed the scene before him. The clamor did nothing to ward him off, and he searched for a door that wouldn't lead him outside. Finding it, he launched himself toward where the miscreant had directed him. The oven fires blazed, but the heat of them barely rivaled the rage boiling inside him. He threaded purposefully through the hubbub.

Even amid all the hustle and bustle going on within the kitchen, someone still took notice of him, and when his hand descended upon the bright red scarf covering the door handle to the adjoining room, a voice sounded for him not to enter. But inflamed by all those insisting on keeping him and his wife apart, the indignant healer plunged through the obstructing door.

Despite his barging entrance, Kendrick halted just past the threshold. The sound of trickling water was drowned out of his consciousness by the scene before him.

There, in the center of the large room, stood an accordion-like screen stretching out parallel to the great hearth in the far-right hand corner to catch its warmth. Situated between the two sat a sizable metal tub partly obscured by the screen, and within it sat the person whom he sought. He stood transfixed at the sight of her. With a twist of wet hair pulled over her far shoulder, a luxurious plane of creamy exposed skin stretched before his view, sudsy water streaming down it in rivulets. Standing over Adianna with a bucket, the innkeeper's wife gently poured the steamy water.

Kendrick's mouth fell open. A new heat knotted in the pit of his stomach, and he could not look away. The smooth line of her back shone in beautiful detail down past a tantalizingly slender waist before it disappeared within the tub. A small voice in the back of his mind screamed at him of the impropriety of standing there gawking, but the tightening in his midsection rooted him there, uncaring. Unbidden, his thinking wandered to imagining how that luxurious skin might feel beneath his touch.

But it did not last long, for as the last droplets of water left the bucket, it unceremoniously fell to the floor. A startled gasp grabbed the man's attention. The standing woman pinned him with an accusatory gaze, her arms thrown akimbo.

"What are you doing in here?" she demanded, snatching up a large towel that sat folded on the table nearby. "Didn't you see the scarf?"

The nubile woman in the water shot a wide-eyed glance over her shoulder. When her eyes fell upon him, and recognition dawned, the lovely orbs bulged still further.

Her embarrassment evident, Kendrick instinctively flicked the door closed, blocking the bathing woman from anyone's sight… but his. He took a tentative step forward, but when he tried to formulate words of explanation, nothing came. He brought his hand up placatingly to ward off any attack that might be forthcoming. His mouth merely bobbed open and closed like a newly landed fish.

The older woman draped open the towel as a curtain obscuring his view, but he could see the top of Adianna's head duck behind the screen. The sound of cascading water could then be heard behind the partition.

The thought invaded Kendrick's thinking of water slipping over narrow hips and sliding down her lean legs to pool around creamy calves. Disgusted with himself, he clenched his eyes shut, averting his face from trying to make anything out of the silhouetted shadow on the screen. He clamped his jaw shut and pursed his lips tightly.

"Was there something you wanted, healer?" came Adianna's voice, with a slight bewilderment to it, from behind the partition.

"I…ah," Kendrick began. Trying to process her question, he glanced over. There, he beheld the silhouette of his wife, her tantalizing curves outlined to perfection before she draped the towel around them. He quickly lost all coherent reason.

"Definitely," he breathed, without thinking.

Adianna poked her head around the edge of the screen and pinned him with her gaze, an eyebrow arched questioningly.

"I mean…" He ducked his gaze sheepishly, scrambling to focus. He tried to remember what he had come in for. A swish of water bespoke her movement, and he chanced a glance.

Adianna now stood by the edge of the partition. Her wet tresses had been brushed from her shoulder to ripple down her back out of sight. The breadth of luxurious skin stretching from creamy shoulder to creamy shoulder called to him as it disappeared beneath the fuzzy material. The khaki cloth hung from there to sway tantalizingly against smooth thighs a few inches above her knees.

Kendrick peeled his gaze away from her to try to uncloud his head. He noticed the innkeeper's wife had resumed her stance with arms akimbo, glaring at him. He nervously cleared his throat.

"I...uh." He tried again, looking anxiously at the younger woman. Her hands clutched the edge of her towel, and her head was tilted, a more quizzical look on her face than before.

"I was... sent to find you. I looked everywhere... for you, and... uh... that buffoon, Tarron, said you were in here, and that I didn't want to come in, which I obviously did... I mean, I was trying to find you." He gestured in her direction. "And I didn't know you were in here like that. I mean, if I had, I would have been quieter. I mean..."

Oh, that sounded awful! He squinted at her, appalled at the blundering his babbling ensued.

The older woman's lips were pursed so tightly they were white. Her arms folded knowingly in front of her.

"More discrete. I mean..."

Adianna placed one hand obstinately on her hip. The durity of her stare told him she was unimpressed with his floundering.

He felt totally flustered with himself and somewhat helpless to correct it. A low growl rumbled in his throat. "What I mean is." He looked at her pointedly, his hands slicing the air in an attempt to focus himself. "I would not have barged in. If... I had known... you were in here like this."

He gestured again at her present state. But as the innkeeper's wife began tapping impatiently with her toe, and the corners of Adianna's mouth dipped deeper into her cheeks, he knew his excuse was as feeble as it sounded.

Kendrick flapped his hands against his legs, defeated. "I'm just gonna..." He thrust his thumb over his shoulder, and he turned slightly. "I'm sorry... for the disturbance. I'm—I'll—"

Not finding the words, he turned to the door.

"Master Kendrick," Adianna called out.

Kendrick turned back, hoping for a reprieve.

"Yes, m'lad—" His response was cut short when a large soggy sponge pelted him square in the face. It bounced off his forehead and landed with a heavy splat on the floor.

Eyes shut, Kendrick blew at the water trickling down his face and off his hair. He peeked through the stream and saw Adianna, a challenging look on her face. The older woman's mouth hung open, disbelieving.

"That," Adianna said pointedly, "is so you do not forget in the future."

Kendrick blew again, propelling droplets from the tip of his nose. Then he bowed to her, stiffly. "Yes, m'lady."

Coming up from his bow, he could see the mirth tugging at his wife's mouth and eyes. She struggled unsuccessfully for several seconds while he stood admiring her.

Then a smile of his own pulled at his mouth, so he turned to the door to hide it. Stopping on the threshold, his hand poised on the handle, he looked back at the young woman of his dreams and gave her a devilish grin. "Until next time, m'lady."

Her mouth popped open with a gasp at his cavalier wink.

Then Kendrick quickly jerked the door closed, seeing her leg swing forward haughtily. The sound of water splashing across the floor and pelting the door was muffled by his hearty chuckle.

He turned to see the kitchen workers all staring at him, and he cleared his throat. Kendrick struggled to stifle his smile, his gaze faltering under their curious stare. But when he promptly stalked to the hallway leading to the front of the inn, the sounds of the kitchen commenced.

His stride slowed after leaving the view of onlookers, and he thought again of the beautiful lady he just left. A sweet longing tightened inside him and warmed him from head to foot. But the rosy feeling dissipated quickly when he stepped into the common room and was greeted with snorts and snickering. Irritation engulfed Kendrick, seeing the source was the elves.

Tarron was seated near the end of the bar closest to the hall, the other two at a table behind him. After muffling another chuckle into his hand, Tarron stood and sauntered closer to the wet, approaching Kendrick. The cocky elf tried unsuccessfully to wipe the smile from his face.

"I told you, human." Tarron's suppressed laugh came out as a snort. "You didn't want to go in there."

Fury flamed inside Kendrick, but he tried to walk calmly past the infuriating scoundrel. That was, until the oaf could contain it no more and laughed right in his face. Then Kendrick snapped. His left fist flew out, catching the elf across the cheekbone with such force Tarron spun nearly a complete circle before crumpling to the ground.

Leaving the blackguard where he lay, the healer stalked right for the door. All concern of retaliation dissipated when the room erupted in hearty laughter from the two remaining elves.

Kendrick huffed out a mirthless chuckle, glancing back at the twins pointing and jeering at their comrade still sprawled across the floor before he slammed the door.

GATHERING CELEBRATION

The square of Fal Dura was abuzz. All around, there were people running to and fro. Some scrambled with last minute assignments. Many milled about, gathering and greeting new arrivals.

Adianna was with a group of villagers when she caught sight of Kendrick. He stepped out from behind the inn, wearing a fresh white shirt with gathered cuffs and a starched collar. His breeches were snug, showing off every muscle to perfection. His hair was wet and freshly combed, reminding her of their last encounter. Her cheeks flamed at the memory.

Their eyes met. His approving smile sent the butterflies in her stomach leaping into a dancing frenzy. Absently, she fingered the collar of her borrowed dress. She knew it was a bit too big, and she had cinched the double sash as best she could. Still, she had gone for the flattering burgundy color. Yet now she felt rather frumpy with the gown dragging on the ground.

That changed when she saw his gaze intensify, though she was unsure whether her increased blushing was the result or the cause. All she knew was she loved it when he looked at her that way. It made her feel desired and beautiful.

Then suddenly, Kendrick's face contorted into something harsh. Adianna wondered at the cause of such an abrupt change, but before she could inquire, someone slipped an arm around her waist and spun her around.

"Gotcha," came a voice, playful and low.

Startled, she looked into the face of her assailant. Tarron grinned down at her, playfully.

Adianna fought the urge to pull away. By choosing Tarron's hand over Kendrick's the day before, things had felt awkward having him so close. Then, when she realized Tarron had deeper feelings and wanted more from their relationship than she, she now felt any closeness would be leading him on. Especially when her husband was around, watching. And he was usually watching.

She felt the need to glance over to him now to see if he was indeed observing them. She knew he would be, but when she started to turn, something stopped her. Looking back at Tarron's face, she grabbed his chin and jerked it to the side. Above his right cheek, where it hollowed out to form his eye, was a deep, ugly purple. The nasty bruise started about mid-eye and spread, curving up and around to the tip of his eyebrow. It then lightened into a grotesque green that brushed his low arching brow.

"What on Sheorae happened!?" she asked.

Argon and Gaidish, who had just stepped up behind him, snickered into their hands. The noise seemed to make Tarron's back stiffen.

Pulling his face away from her grasp, his jaw tightened. "Yeah. I…"

She watched his eyes closely, seeking truth. They never met her gaze. Then they darted past her, over the top of her head. One nostril flawed before he said, "I wasn't watching, and I… walked into something this afternoon."

Another volley of barely contained snickering pelted him from behind, and Tarron stiffened even more. Adianna knew there was something more he wasn't telling her. She was about to press the matter further, but she felt something brush the back of her cloak.

The clearing of a throat told her someone was close behind her, but she kept her eyes on Tarron's rigid demeanor.

Still, when Kendrick's velvety voice washed over her, she was instantly distracted. Actually, distraction was an understatement for it pulled her toward him. She felt the heat of him through her cloak with every fiber of her being. She didn't even have to look to know it was him.

"Shall we, my love?" His hot breath stirred the tendrils of hair by her ear. She was taken aback by such an intimate endearment; she couldn't help twisting to look up at him. An excited thrill shot through her at the warm smile greeting her.

She stared spellbound, waiting, willing her lungs to pull air in and push it out. Slowly, he brought his hand along the side of her cheek. There it hovered, warm and intense, like his gaze, just above her skin. His gaze dipped. She could feel the heat radiating from his hand moving slowly along her jawline, slipping along her throat. Wisps of hair tickled her neck while his fingers brushed past on their slow descent. Her eyelids dipped, and she shuddered. Her chest quivered, pulling in air but refusing to let it out. His hand lingered along her collar bone. Her mouth drifted open struggling to pull in the much-needed oxygen. *How could she feel him so distinctly without him even touching her skin?*

The spell subsided when he gently placed his hand on her arm to turn her. The constricted air flooded out of her lungs, and she gawked, wondering what just happened. Her ribs heaved, straining for their natural rhythm. When she could finally look up, something in his eyes looked mischievously pleased.

"Come." He brushed the tip of his nose briefly against hers. The burning contact was surprisingly minimal and actually felt less intense than what he had just done without touching her at all. He smiled invitingly.

"Memsy and Shin are waiting for us at the head table."

Kendrick brought his arm fully around her waist, drawing her along beside him toward the river end of the square.

"Elf." The healer nodded pointedly.

Adianna had completely forgotten about Tarron until Kendrick made the acknowledgement.

"Oh, yes. We'll talk later," she said over her shoulder, gliding along where she was directed.

They settled in at a long table set up on a dais, the river to their backs. Several other tables were arranged on the ground following the same half-circle as the square. In the center of this half-moon was the salvaged wood piled high, ready for lighting.

Tolshin, the chief village elder, sat at the middle of their table. The healer was directed to sit at his right, Memsy on his left. Memsy motioned for Adianna to join her, but Kendrick directed her to the seat alongside him. Memsy didn't look too upset, and Adianna was surprised she wasn't either. In fact, Adianna felt certain she'd be delighted to spend the entire evening by his side, never to leave it.

Also at their table was Tolshin's family, three generations. His children were on Adianna's right, with their many girls finishing out the table and coming around the front a number of settings. The look on their faces was all it took to grasp their excitement. Yet their antsy fidgeting also hinted the fact.

Looking out over the crowd milling around the various tables, Adianna noted that laughter and gaiety abounded everywhere. Even the ladies, who were hustling to and fro setting out the last of the steaming hot platters of food on the tables, were joyfully conversing with neighbors and friends. The jovial attitude was infectious, and she reveled in it.

As she took another sweep over the merriment, something caught her gaze. Nalora was waving exuberantly, her pale blond hair bobbing with each excited swing of her hands. Eagerly, Adianna's hands began flying, communicating her greeting and enthusiasm for the celebration, too. The woman loved this about signing, being able to talk across an expanse without shouting above the clamor.

While talking with the child, Adianna felt Kendrick's eyes on her, but she tried to focus on her conversation. Though when he placed his arm around the back of her chair and leaned in close, it became nearly impossible.

"What is she saying?"

A tantalizing tremor ran down Adianna's spine, whether from the tickle of his breath on her ear or from having him so near, she was uncertain.

She looked back to the child before answering and caught the final statement, which made her bubble over with laughter.

"She says to tell you, you had better not forget the dance you promised, because she stole the ribbon from her new Rest Day dress just for the occasion," Adianna said happily near Kendrick's ear.

He let out a hearty guffaw. His eyes sparkled. He brought his arm around her shoulders, while leaning in again to respond.

"Tell her I am looking forward to it and wouldn't miss it for the world." He pulled back slightly, but returned to add, "And tell her she looks very lovely tonight."

Adianna shot him a glance, trying to make it as accusatory as she could, but her smile was too big. She ran quickly through the signs, ending with her hand sweeping a circle in front of her face. The little girl was bouncing excitedly, and at the end, she demurely swayed from side to side. With a shyness that was not in her next statement, the girl replied.

Adianna laughed aloud, but she signed a happy 'see you later' to the girl.

"Well?"

Kendrick draped his other arm along the table in front of her, pinning his full attention on her as surely as his body enfolded around her.

Her eyes danced merrily. "Nalora says she can't wait. And…" she added pointedly, "she says you are 'so very beautiful.'" She clutched her hands together to the side of her chin in mock adoration and gave a dreamy sigh.

His delighted laughter rang out above the crowd.

"You are a shameless flirt!" she accused. "And you have her eating out of your hand."

Kendrick chuckled, lifting his hand from the table to pretend to straighten a cravat that didn't exist. "What do you expect? Six-year-olds are helpless to my many charms."

Adianna chuckled, smiling at him merrily despite her sidelong glance. With a slow shake of her head, she replied, "You ought to be locked up!"

Another laugh rumbled from deep within his chest, but his next words were low and persuasive. "Is that an invitation?"

She looked at him abruptly, unsure of how to respond. His eyes were direct, boring into hers, and her heart skipped a beat. Then with a playful rise and fall of his eyebrows, she saw he was toying with her. She let out a derisive laugh, though the butterflies returned with a vengeance.

She placed her open palm on his face to give it a playful shove.

"You are hopeless," she chuckled.

But when she would have moved away, his hand came down over hers. Gently he pressed her fingertips against his lips. His eyes were intense and held her gaze, his warm breath seeping through the shimmering mail of her gloves.

He enfolded her hand in his. Turning it over so her palm was facing up, he placed a kiss into the hollow of it.

"No," he said, bringing their entwined fingers to rest against his chest. She could feel the brushing of his fingers along her back. "I'd say the word is 'hope-FUL.'"

Again, his gaze bore into hers with an intensity which made her blush. Just then Tolshin drew Kendrick's attention away, and the enchantment was broken. Adianna focused to restore her breathing and composure. Unbidden, a joyous smile spread across her face, and her eyes swept the crowd.

The jovial atmosphere buzzing before her was pierced when she caught sight of her friend. Tarron was staring at her, a look of venom on his face. The intensity of his scowl was like a slap in the face, and instinctively she signed, "What's wrong?"

She knew he could understand her. He had been coming to Fal Dura with her practically her whole life. He couldn't help but pick up some of it. But he made no answer. His gaze merely shifted to the man sitting next to her. If it were possible, the irate elf's gaze became more agitated. Then he quickly looked back at her for a brief moment before he turned and stalked to the apex of the square. When he finally settled into a seat at the table there beyond the pyramid of wood, she could just see the top of his head and, for a minute, his burning eyes. She knew when the bonfire started she would not see him at all.

Adianna leaned forward to catch Memsy's attention. When she locked eyes with her mother, the intuitive woman quickly interpreted the look on her face. Adianna immediately recognized the feeling of the sorci pressing into her mind searching for the question lying there waiting for her. The older woman looked out over the crowd, finding Tarron in an instant.

Adianna watched the sorci quickly probe the mind of the elf in question. Perplexed at the sad smile spreading her mother's face, Adianna waited impatiently. Memsy turned that knowing smile to the fidgeting woman, where it compressed, her lips pursing into more of a look of pity.

Adianna's eyebrows rose as she grew more and more concerned. But Memsy merely mouthed the words, 'All is well,' and turned away.

Adianna's mouth fell open with more questions, but a young, excited voice broke through Adianna's puzzling.

"Miss Annie? Oh, Miss Annie?"

Adianna turned to the other end of the table, finding Embrie and Teshlyn, two of Tolshin's granddaughters, bouncing in their seats at the far corner, waving madly.

"Yes, Em?" Adianna answered slowly, still rather befuddled.

"Miss Annie! You're going to be telling the Legend tonight, aren't you?"

The teenager's words nearly stumbled over each other in her excitement to get them out.

Adianna couldn't help returning a smile to the young girl. At fourteen, Embrie was well on her way to being a woman as far as social standings were concerned, but she still retained that natural excitement for life, which always showed through in all she did.

"Of course," Adianna teasingly scoffed.

The squeal she received in return signaled the younger girl's elation, followed by a quick clapping of her hands.

"Do you think we will get many fire fairies this time?" Embrie leaned forward, enthralled.

"Well, I..." Adianna began uncertainly, but she was cut off by the rich voice close behind her.

"You can summon fire fairies?" Kendrick had apparently finished his conversation with the village elder and had turned back, his arms draped around the confines of her seat as they had before, nearly encircling her in their embrace. Leaning in close, he sounded genuinely interested, though his eyes were teasing.

Adianna was unsure how best to answer, but Embrie saved her the hassle.

"Of course!" she declared, demanding the man's attention with her loud but enthusiastic voice. "Miss Annie always gets fire fairies. We usually get one or two around here when the Old Stories are spun. I think they like it here. But no one can call forth as many as Miss Annie. Especially when she tells the Great Legend."

Adianna was used to the girl's bragging, but she was seldom at the center of it, and never with such a highly attractive man eating up every word. She shifted uneasily under the man's scrutiny and wished the girl would channel her enthusiasm to a different topic.

It was not meant to be. With one abrupt motion, Embrie slapped her palms on the table, startling Adianna. "Last time—" the girl paused for dramatic effect, pinning the interested man with her gaze, "—there were thirteen!"

Just then a couple of Embrie's friends approached, distracting the girl from her tale and before anything more was said on the subject, the three teenagers ran off together, giggling.

Adianna couldn't help smiling at the departing trio. She envied their naivety but took comfort in seeing it second hand. Still, she was keenly aware they had not left her alone, and her senses zeroed in on her companion.

"I'm impressed," Kendrick murmured. "Thirteen is… amazing."

His breath brushed across her skin, stirring wisps of hair along her neck. The tickling sensation sent a tremor rippling through her body, stifling the flow of air to her lungs.

Adianna's eyes drifted shut. She struggled to resume breathing before turning to stare into eyes that were bluer than a cloudless sky.

Kendrick stared back at her, but with that quirky air of mischievousness that was endearing him to her.

Willing her voice to stay light, she countered flippantly, "Then you are easily impressed."

A slow smile parted his face, but his eyes still toyed with her. "On the contrary," he said, raising her hand, slow and deliberately, to press a leisurely kiss on the back of it. Lifting his gaze again to hers, he stared deeply into her eyes. "It takes much to impress me. And thirteen? I have never heard of thirteen fire fairies coming to anyone."

The truthfulness of his compliment did not escape her, even though her breathing did, and she felt a thrill shoot through her.

But Kendrick broke the spell by leaning back in his seat, his hand leaving hers before plopping his fingers against the top of the table in front of them.

"The most I've ever heard of appearing for a story was seven. And that—" he jutted his finger at her before dropping his hand to his thigh, "—was for an ancient, wandering, she-dwarf storyteller decades ago. Probably the last one."

He watched her closely, his eyes seeming to trace every inch of her face. Adianna felt the color rise in her cheeks under his scrutiny. Through the shamere cloak, she felt his thumb caress the back of her shoulder.

"You must be very special."

The surety in his voice made it more of a conviction than a statement. It warmed Adianna to her very soul. She felt adored with his blue eyes washing over her, a feeling she'd never experienced before. A feeling she could get used to.

Presently, Kendrick's face turned sheepish. Before she could wonder why, he offered, "I'd like to apologize again for earlier."

Adianna blushed at the memory.

"I really didn't mean to intrude on your bath." His smile at her blush twisted mischievously again before he looked away. "But I guess, yet again, it makes us even."

"Even?" She was lost to his meaning.

"Now, I suppose—" he quirked an eyebrow at her, "—we both have seen each other in a state of relative undress."

She balked. She felt the urge to take a whack at him. But then she noticed his now penitent expression.

"I suppose so," she said, looking down her nose before she turned away stiffly, still keeping her eyes on him. She delighted in seeing him squirm even a little bit.

"But," she added finally, "as before—they were both *your* fault."

FIRE & LEGENDS

Kendrick couldn't stop smiling. The festivities had been positively delightful thus far. The meal was wonderful. The company exquisite. And now they were just finishing the games. He had chased, teased, and flirted with the young ones of the village so long his sides hurt from laughing so much. He had many opportunities amid the frivolities to pull a certain beautiful maiden into his arms. The fact she came willingly each and every time made it all the more delightful. Of course, as an added bonus, one elf in particular remained alone and livid all evening.

Now everyone was gathering for storytelling and the lighting of the bonfire. The tables had been stowed long ago, except for a few long tables brandishing leftover vittles.

Kendrick presently sat cross-legged in the square near the still-unlit pile of debris, in full view of the small platform. He had desired to stay with Adianna until her turn for the storytelling began, but he had been swarmed by the children. Thus, flooded with invitations to sit among them, he could not possibly have said no. So, there he sat, amid the giggles and enthusiastic 'oohs' and 'ahs' that accompanied each spinner's tale.

Several storytellers had performed, including young Thomas, who had been quite talented. For one so young, he was well on his way of turning his gift into an art. And it was a good thing he was so young, for Kendrick might've been pricked a little by how much Adianna fawned over his attempts. As it was, he grinned widely at the young lad glowing under the attention.

The sun sank low on the horizon. The moon, Syron, arced overhead. As Adianna was now sitting on the sidelines of the platform, Kendrick wondered if the great moon, Dryden, would be rising at just the right moment to create a stunning backdrop for her performance. Kendrick also wondered why none of the elves were grouped together. They were all spread out around the square.

Then he wondered if Adianna was nervous when she signaled Memsy over. Upon removing her gloves, she sat on the edge of the platform, holding Memsy's hand. The motherly elf stroked her daughter's hair and often rested her cheek against the young woman's head. It wasn't until Adianna began her performance that Kendrick understood the tender exchange.

A hush fell over the audience when Adianna took the stand. Next to him, Nalora snatched his hand, shaking it vigorously. The great grin on her face showed the barely contained excitement exuding off her little frame. This eager anticipation radiated from not only the children surrounding him but was palpable throughout the entire square.

Adianna closed her eyes, lowered her head, and, as if turning within herself, took a deep, calming breath. All eyes in the village were upon her. Kendrick was mesmerized. *They are all in awe of her. As am I.*

Just then, a smile crept across her angelic face, and for a moment, he wondered if she heard his thoughts. Her smile broadened.

On her next exhale, Adianna opened her eyes. Without raising her head, she began her tale.

"Since the dawn of time, the inhabitants of Sheorae lived in peace and harmony." Her voice was low and melodious, yet it carried throughout the hushed square. Adianna raised her head and her arms in unison. "Humans, elves, goblins, animalia, dwarves, ogres, and dragons—the species of the

Seven Nations ruled together in unity. All things were common. All creatures accepted. All prospered and lived after the manner of happiness.

"Until… the fairies came."

At that instant, tiny flames leapt from each of her hands and shot toward the large pile of debris. In unison, Memsy and each of her kin did the same. Instantly, the entire mountain of rubble ignited. Flames leaped three feet above it into the sky. Screams and squeals erupted throughout the square. Kendrick had little ones clambering all over him. Shrieks turned quickly into laughter though, and the crowd applauded.

Adianna's face shone unearthly from the blaze and Dryden silhouetting her burnish waves. Her voice, carried with mesmerizing inflection, intoned every note as she continued her tale.

"We know not from where they came nor to where they went. All we know is what they left behind. The fairies brought with them magic beyond the elemental manipulation we then possessed. They brought unicorns and merriment. They brought frolicking and play.

"The fairies delighted in the unity of our nations. They marveled in the charity and compassion displayed by all. They especially esteemed the living consecration they found among us.

"They were so delighted in the peaceful tranquility exhibited in our world, they wished to reward us with gifts. Gifts that brought as much disruption as they brought good.

"To the elves they gifted heightened intuition. To the ogres—their rock-like skin, to the animalia—heightened physical power, to the dragons—their beloved fire breath. To the goblins—their stealth. To the dwarves—the ability to conjure spells into their forged work. And to the humans—lines of healers to rejuvenate their frail bodies."

Adianna graced Kendrick with a brilliant smile before continuing, her voice low, "But before they could see the fruits of their unfortunate gifts, the fairies left."

At that moment, Nalora tapped Kendrick on the knee. When he glanced down, he could see her staring intently into the bonfire. She met his gaze, then pointed into the embers. There, peeking out from behind a blazing cinder, peered a tiny cherub face. The soft, round cheeks and playful eyes were somewhat difficult to detect at first, as its coloring blended with the flames around it, but once found, its angelic smile was infectious.

The tiny thing waved, causing Kendrick and his little companion to wave back. Gingerly, she stepped slender, miniature legs out from behind the blazing timber. Her clothes, hair, and wings appeared as the flames themselves. Her body looked that of a six-inch elf, complete with pointy ears. Her skin was a pale yellow. Upon an inflection of the storyteller's voice, the tiny thing fluttered into the air. Easily noticeable against the darkened sky, her three-piece wings were defined amid the yellow-orange glow she emitted. The small fire fairy pointed her toes and gave a little curtsy before flitting over in the direction of the storyteller.

Presently, more and more of the delicate little creatures fluttered out from the flames and behind the embers of the blazing bonfire. Seven, eight, ten, fourteen… soon the air was filled. Several of these overgrown fireflies flew among the 'oohs' and 'ahs' of the crowd. Many dipped down to pat the cheeks of the young girls and the heads of the young boys, thus sending giggles into the night.

Adianna paused in her storytelling long enough to hail a small group that flitted forth to greet her. Salutations given and received, two fairies, a male and a female, bowed low then fluttered forward, each bestowing an honored kiss to Adianna's cheeks. The woman shined under the attention before the little band returned to the fire light to dance with the others.

With a giggle, Adianna struggled to control her features enough to continue her tale from where she was interrupted.

"Thus, the Nations refused to work together any longer. The pressure for segregation mounted. Compassion dwindled, dwindled.

"After centuries of turmoil, a young, well-meaning elf, with knowledge of the dwarven skill, pledged to find a way to unite the nations once again. Through much work and study and many failed attempts, young Drokmar—"

The crowd hissed at the name.

"Stumbled upon mystic incantations and conjurings, which would finally save our world from the pride and apathy that enveloped the land.

"He worked painstakingly, day and night, toiling nonstop for those he loved.

"But the spells, magic, and power proved too much for Drokmar. A new greed and power-lust consumed him, until his altered intentions could no longer be hidden. Elvin guards crashed into his hidden forge, bound the villain, and stripped the powerful Blades from his grasp.

"Knowing the Blades could not be destroyed without releasing all that power and magic haphazardly on their world, the elves cast one final spell upon the Blades. They conjured that the Blades would retain their goodness, never return to the elves, and thus find one pure of heart and intention to form a True Alliance—an eternal union founded on truth and love for the good of all Sheorae."

In that moment, Kendrick felt the truthfulness of her words pound home in his very being. A single tear twinkled on Adianna's cheek. He could see the love she held for her world, and he knew all he had seen in connection with the Blades had never been this of which she spoke, had never been truth and hope and love of this magnitude. He could see this gentle creature, whom he cherished so profoundly, would willingly do anything required to save the people and world she loved so dearly.

He glanced over to Memsy and found tears streaming down her face. Not one. Not a few. But many tears cascaded from this mother's heart. A burnish-skinned fire fairy, blazing yellow, nearly white, flitted closer in to console the dear elvish woman.

"And from the time the elves plunged the Blades into the Tyronda Sea, animalia, humans, ogres, goblins, and dragons have sought after the mighty Blades. With the dwarves gone and the elves out of the running, the five remaining nations have attempted, in vain, to form the union that would return peace and harmony to our world."

Adianna sought Kendrick's gaze. "For centuries now, using the Blades for personal agendas of pride and greed has caused nearly as much devastation on the people as Drokmar's ruthless horde, whom he sends out seeking the Blades to reap revenge on the unforgiving populace.

"But the Blades, too, continued seeking," she intoned. "With a will of their own, they continue even now to find those who love their people, their world, and each other more than themselves."

Kendrick's mouth sagged open, but nothing could get past the lump in his throat, nor the boulder in his chest. Adianna swiped quickly at the few tears trickling down her cheeks while she turned back to the crowd.

Suddenly, a fire fairy flitted past Kendrick's view. It caught his attention, for the tiny thing's body, wings, and aura flamed a brilliant white-blue.

Kendrick quickly glanced around, taking in the other fairies about the fire. Their numbers had grown to nearly thirty, each and every one blazing the same white-blue. Kendrick knew fire fairies flame grew brighter celebrating the truthfulness of the stories told. Transfixed, Kendrick followed Adianna's next words.

"The wonderful Blades with their resounding beacon have been silent for over a decade. But now we hear from them again. In a way never seen before. For all those who love the people in their lives, let this be a symbol of hope. A hope for peace. Hope for harmony. Hope to make our world magnificent yet again."

Upon Adianna's final words, the square erupted with cheers. Men, women, and children all leapt to their feet. Kendrick lost sight of his wife amid the jumping and cheering children around him. Even Nalora, who had been watching her mother's translation of the storytelling, was bouncing up and down, enthusiasm shining on her face.

Kendrick, unsure of what he was feeling at that moment, rose slowly to his feet. He joined in the smiles and clapping of the children. But his eyes were riveted on the beautiful storyteller.

Before he could gather his wits, he felt a tiny tap on his shoulder. He glanced around to find a male fire fairy. But unlike the other fire fairies mingling amid the merriment, this fairy wore regimental emblems and hovered in the air with his sword drawn. With a sharp click of his heels, the fairy bowed before him.

"Master Healer and protector of the Durluki," the fire fairy saluted, speaking to his mind as Kendrick was accustomed to receiving from dragons. "I've come to report—a goblin hunting party approaches from the south and should be in the vicinity by tomorrow evening."

"A hunting party?" Kendrick tensed.

"Yes, sir." The fairy flicked his tiny sword up then down to emphasize his statement.

Kendrick's mind suddenly reeled with strategy. "How many in the party?"

"Fifteen to twenty, sir," came the response. "Though they may divide into two parties when they near the village."

"Thank you, captain." Kendrick nodded, noting the little man's insignia. "The information is well received."

The fairy flicked his sword high again. "Anything to help the Durluki and her protector. The fire fairies grieve the destruction our kind have caused to your beautiful world. We cherish its inhabitants greatly, or we wouldn't have stayed."

Kendrick nodded absently in response, but when the captain turned to leave, the man called out. "Wait!"

The fairy returned, but Kendrick motioned, backed up, and glanced around to see no one could hear. He leaned in and queried, "Protector?"

He chuckled, almost self-consciously, before whispering, "Am I not the Mentaloss?"

The captain's eyebrows came down and his nose wrinkled. He shook his head, responding, "No, sir. Without the emblem, you merely protect the Durluki on her journey."

Kendrick's heart sank. "Thank you, captain."

The fairy flew off, leaving a devastated Kendrick behind. *I'm not the Mentaloss? How could it not be me? There was the beacon and the sirens and...*

He peered over to Adianna. Tarron was swinging her down from the stage, his hands wrapped around her waist beneath her cloak. Kendrick's teeth clenched.

I'm not really part of her destiny?

Tarron snaked his arms low around her waist. Then the elf leaned down and nuzzled her ear, smiling. A knot churned in Kendrick's stomach. The fact he saw Adianna whack the elf for his efforts and push her way out of his arms did little to elevate his mood. The minstrels were assembling and tuning on stage. Tarron took the opportunity to pull the young woman in and dance happily beyond the bonfire and out of sight.

Kendrick growled, his eyes flashing around. *I'm not even a part of this! I can't even touch her. What am I even doing here? And that elf!*

Kendrick's jaw clenched so hard he could hear and feel the cartilage pop by his right ear. *She has plenty of buffoons around her now for protection. I should just get out while I can*!

Just then, he heard Adianna's laughter above the din. His whole body tensed, and he could feel molten hot anger churn through his stomach. He turned a death glare in the direction of her joviality. His fists clenched, preparing for battle.

But instead of finding that insufferable elf, he found his wife helping an elderly woman to the sidelines. Kendrick's demeanor slackened as he watched his beautiful bride maneuver the hunched ancient to a chair where she might enjoy the festivities. Once settled, Adianna knelt at the aged woman's feet. Kendrick watched the years melt away and the wrinkles disappear into smiles under the younger woman's ministerings.

Presently, a tug on his hand drew his attention. Nalora had come, all smiles and excitement, the ends of a satin ribbon in each hand. With his attention on her, the small child turned her two fingers over her other hand and swung them back and forth like legs dancing. Kendrick smiled at the young girl, remembering his promise.

He looked back to Adianna. With the sounds of fiddles beginning a warell, he watched Adianna pull an ancient gentleman toward the bonfire, encouraging him to dance with her. *She really does love these people.*

Just then, she found him watching her, and she gave him a radiant smile. His heart and his hopes swelled. Just looking upon her made him want to be a better person. He continuously marveled at her goodness. It was because of her example he had spent all day helping and healing these people. He had not had such a fulfilling day in a very long time.

Resolutely, he nodded. He wanted to be with her in whatever capacity allotted to him. And he knew if he could only be her protector, no one desired to protect her more than he. This is where he would stay, by her side, until the Mentaloss claimed her. Then he would follow her into battle. He would follow her anywhere.

The excited child still hopped near him, vying for his attention, and he reached for her ribbon. Once he got the other end of the long ribbon tied around the six-year old's wrist, he noticed a whole gaggle of young ladies, ranging in age from just younger than Nalora up to several teenagers, including Shin's granddaughter and her friends, all pressing in close with ribbons and expectant grins.

Kendrick felt his eyebrows arch high on his forehead, amazement settling in. Then when an old, withered lady also joined the group of hopeful dancers, he could not help but chuckle.

He looked down at his first partner, smiling.

"I guess we had better start dancing."

DANCING

Adianna beamed as she clapped, cheering the minstrels, her elderly partner, and the frivolity in general. She untied her extra sash from Rattabnor's wrist, then looked around for Kendrick. The older gentleman hobbled back to his seat just when she caught sight of her husband bowing low before a delighted little girl. Nalora curtsied and came up bouncing and clapping.

Adianna began making her way through the crowd in their direction, but before she got very far, another adoring girl bounded forward to cinch her ribbon around his wrist. Thus, cut off, she watched from afar while he moved through the steps of the trusle with a beaming ten-year old.

Gaidish swooped her up into the lively dance, but she kept her eye on the mismatched couple. She chuckled at the healer's antics: swooping over backward for his underarm turn, going down on one knee for her little dip, and the girl's squeals when he swung her feet wide on the quick pivots.

As Gaidish was considered a relative, she was not slowed at the end of the dance by the untying of her sash. Still, Adianna found she was again too late to claim her husband as a partner. When another eager young girl shot forth, she became aware of the gathered crowd hovering close on the sidelines. At least a dozen girls of various ages, from preschoolers to a few quite withered in age—and all single, she noticed—stood ready and willing to fill any vacancy in his dance lineup.

Her mouth twitched to the side, watching even Embrie and her friends giggling nearby, their heads close together. With them eyeing her new husband like the best item at a banquet, Adianna, unintentionally, felt her eyes narrow. It didn't help that a much slower drell began playing.

Fortunately, with ribbons, the uneven couple was technically unable to move closer than was customary, though their palms touched between them.

Adianna turned to a tap on her shoulder. She graciously extended the end of her sash to a young villager. Just as she stepped into position for the dance, Kendrick met her eyes.

She saw his gaze dart to her partner then back. Without a moment's hesitation, he winked. She found she could not restrain her smile at the unexpected gesture. He grinned back heartily, then moved into the slow turn of the dance.

Throughout the evening, she laughed and danced with villagers of all ages, biding her time, only minimally annoyed. But when his horde of admirers started rallying for a second lineup, Adianna had had enough. She thanked Thomas for their dance, then tromped quickly over to cut off the advancing party.

"Sorry, girls," she interjected, "but it's my turn." She then presented her back to all the groans and complaints to face her husband's growing smirk. She made a show of tying her sash back around her waist. Then she extended her hands and asked, "Care for a dance without ribbons?"

The healer glanced at the firelight twinkling off her begloved hand. Warmly, his eyes met hers.

The first notes of a connette began, one of her favorite dances. That wonderful mischievous smile quirked across his face. Moving the slashes of her cloak higher up on her arms, she tried not to blush as she stepped into his arms. His scent enveloped her.

His smile broadened, and one eyebrow rose. "Are you ready?"

Adianna grinned at him but pulled a little of her bottom lip between her teeth. Her eyebrows went up, and they were off.

They skipped a few steps to one side, then skipped a few steps back. Around they went in a circle. Then clap, clap, clap. Up Adianna went into the air with a whoop. Then down she came into his arms. Around and round they spun. Up and down she went. The lively tune had her gleeful. Her man's eyes danced right along with their feet. She could not remember having a greater time in this dance.

When the song twanged to an end, they were both laughing.

The joviality was only stunted slightly, when yet another hopeful girl stepped to their side. Still giggling, Adianna shook her head. "I'm sorry, Shayleen. But I finally got him. I think I'm going to keep him for a while."

Interestingly enough, Adianna did not feel the least saddened for crushing her young friend's hopes. Instead, she smiled at her good fortune that another drell began.

She pressed one palm to his and stepped in. The fronts of their bodies did not touch, but she could feel the heat radiating from him. Their breath still came in short pants from their previous dance. She expected her pulse to slow with the less active dance, until she looked into his eyes.

His gaze traversed every inch of her face. He sought there another several counts of music. His lead was unbroken, their movements effortless. But he was intent on her. When a twinkle played across his face, he spoke.

"So, you *finally* got me? Been trying long?"

"Yes, actually," she countered, raising her chin, pretending to be miffed. "It took forever to get through your gaggle of adoring fans."

"Oh, jealous, are we?"

At first, Adianna scoffed at him. But, with barely a smile, his mischievous eyes coaxed the truth from her.

"Maybe..." She glanced away, then back and away again.

Instinctually, she felt him draw her a little closer. His tantalizing scent tickled her senses. Ever so slowly, he leaned nearer to her ear.

"You don't have to be, you know?"

His enticing voice sent shivers through her body, and she nearly missed a step. To cover up, she overemphasized, "I know, I know. Because they are all children and spinsters."

He took her hand which pressed to his and used it to raise her chin. Staring deeply into her eyes, he whispered, "No, that's not it."

She peered at him, transfixed. His burning eyes heated her to her very core. She felt beautiful and desired in his sight. She smiled ever so softly to let him know she understood.

Slowly, she could feel his body pressing in nearer to hers. He placed her gloved hand, which he held high against his chest, then pulled her upper body closer to him. She accepted his coaxing and gingerly rested her cheek against her own hand. Margin by margin she relaxed and closed her eyes, allowing him to pull her in even closer. Cocooned in her shamere cloak, she found herself pressing into the length of his firm body.

Now they merely swayed to the music, no longer adhering to the steps. She marveled at how her pulse could quicken and yet calm at the same time. She breathed in the heady scent of him. Her exhales fluttered the folds of his shirt.

When she finally opened her eyes, she caught sight of Kendrick's swarm of admirers now dispersing, looking dejected. She really did feel sorry for them, but not enough to let go of this beautiful moment.

"You know, you were quite perfect with them."

"With whom?" he questioned, pulling back slightly.

She looked at him and smiled. "With the children and spinsters."

She felt his chuckling response more than she heard it. He pulled her back to him, and she pressed in willingly. They swayed and swayed.

Consumed by the feeling growing within her, she reached up with her other hand and ran the cool finger of her glove over his skin just within the neckline of his shirt. His subtle intake of breath bumped his chest against her chin accidentally. The brief contact singed only slightly. She watched the twinkling metal caress the smooth skin, wishing the touch could be felt more fully.

Eyeing her small tracing pattern, she inferred absently, "You really are wonderful, you know?"

His mouth moved into a small smile, drawing her attention. With his head lowered to hear her, his chin was just within reach. She was unwilling to withstand any longer. Gradually, she stretched up and ever so lightly she ran the very tip of her nose along the hollow under his chin. He froze at the contact. But her senses came alive. The tingling sizzle at the tip of her nose. The intake of breath. The swirl of energy and light within her. Most of all the longing which boiled in her belly.

He pulled back softly and gazed into her eyes. The longing was so consuming within her, she knew it had to be evident in her eyes. He searched and searched. All she desired was for him to press his lips to hers. He lowered his mouth ever so slowly, and she willingly turned hers up to receive him. He hovered infinitesimally out of reach. His breath was hot on her lips, and her eyes fluttered closed.

She sucked in air at the first singeing brush of his lips against hers. Still, he hovered, unsure. She longed to close the distance but dared not.

Suddenly, a hand came down hard on Kendrick's shoulder giving them both a start.

"Dance is over, old man," Tarron demanded at the healer's elbow. "My turn to cut in."

Adianna could feel Kendrick's body tense under her hands, and he turned to glare at the intruding elf.

Through clenched teeth, he growled low, "Go away!"

But Tarron would have none of it. "No way. You've had the prettiest girl in the village long enough."

He reached in to pull on Adianna's arm, but Kendrick blocked it.

"As is my right." With that, the healer swiveled their position, so he was now between Adianna and the elf. "I am her husband."

Tarron's eyes narrowed, and he sized up his opponent. "Yeah. But not really."

Adianna's mouth fell open, disbelieving.

"It's not like you have a real marriage," the insufferable elf continued. "I mean, look at this. She is all trussed up in layers of metal on a warm evening, by a bonfire. All because you can't touch her."

To emphasize his point, Tarron pulled Adianna out of Kendrick's arms and began peeling away her gloves, then her cloak. The cool breeze came rushing over her skin making her shiver.

"You forget your place, elf," her husband growled through clenched teeth. His glare shot daggers, and Adianna wondered what kept Tarron from shriveling under the weight of it.

But Tarron sauntered up until he was toe to toe with him. "That sounds like either a pompous nobleman or an enslaving overseer. And *neither* have any place here!"

He gave the man a poke in the shoulder. Kendrick instantly slapped it away.

Tarron's mouth quirked on one side, giving his face a cocky, conceited air. Without ceremony, he flung the shamere items into the man's face. The healer reflectively swooped them out of his line of sight, snatching them up before anything hit the ground.

"Take care of those, won't you?" Tarron egged. "We won't be needing them."

At that, he scooped his arm around Adianna's waist, pulling her away with him. Adianna was dumbfounded. She had never known Tarron to behave like this. Before he had dragged her much distance, she planted her feet and pushed away his arms.

"What is wrong with you?" she scolded, glaring.

She turned back to Kendrick, but he was not looking at her. Instead, he stared unseeing at the ground, jaw tense, nostrils flared. In that instant, she saw many dark emotions wash over his face, before settling on something sinister, yet pained.

The healer glared at Tarron, flicked his gaze at her, then spun on his heels. He crumpled the lightweight metal up aggressively while storming off. Tromping past Argon, he hurled the mass of metallic clothing into that elf's astonished face.

"Kendrick, wait!" Adianna called.

She attempted to follow him, but Tarron caught her arm. She scrutinized her oldest and dearest friend as if she had never seen him before. He peered back at her, his mouth hard. In that moment, so much, and yet so little, passed between them. All she could do was shake her head—though in disbelief or disapproval, she was not sure.

Pinning him with a challenge, she ripped her arm free. His mouth set in a hard line, and his nose flared, but he did not try to stop her.

She spun back to her husband, calling out his name. Yet Kendrick's outline did not pause as he disappeared into the darkness, stalking in the direction of the Duck and Goose.

EVIL LURKING

Adianna started bolt upright in bed. Sweat streamed down her face and along her neck. Even upon waking, the green-fringed blackness encroached on her tense body. Panting rapidly, she surveyed the room to gain her bearings.

Memsy slept soundly next to her in the small bed. Bright moonlight flooded the tiny, rented room. Yet darkness continued its attempts to impinge her vision. Unfortunately, she was still able to detect the mat by the door was empty.

Adianna turned instantly to Memsy to shake her awake.

"Mems!" she hissed.

In a heartbeat, Memsy clambered up, wiping at her eyes. Seeing her mother's sorci emblem swirling, Adianna opened her mind to replay her dream. The blond dalphene. The healer writhing in pain. Her own inability to reach him in time. And the green-hued darkness.

"It's more than a dream," Adianna insisted. "The darkness won't dissipate. She's got to be near."

Memsy looked toward the door. "Where is he?"

"I have no idea." Her voice cracked as she struggled not to let the fear consume her.

She remembered seeing him at the bar in the common room when they came in to retire from the festivities. He sat there scowling, brooding over his tankard. She had gone to talk to him, but he hadn't moved when she called his name. He barely tilted his head her way when she skimmed her fingers along his back. The burning of her fingertips could not compete with the rejection she felt when he merely turned back to his ale without further acknowledgment.

Memsy was still staring into her face. Without a word, her mother took her hand. Her understanding smile and slow nod brought Adianna back to the present situation.

"We have to find him before she does!"

Resolutely, Adianna flung back the covers and scrambled out of bed. Memsy followed, snatching up their clothes. But Adianna was already at the door.

"There's no time for that. We have to find him."

Flinging the door wide, she dashed out into the corridor, her white nightshirt fluttering in her wake. Instantly, the evil darkness again assailed her. She groped to push it back as she ran down the hall, feeling the well-worn planks beneath her bare feet.

The common room, two stories below, sounded like a tavern. Raucous voices and loud laughter echoed up the stairs when she reached them. At the bottom of the first flight, she detected a female voice among the din. Panic cinched her insides like a corset.

Adianna hoped and prayed to find Kendrick well and clambered down the last flight. She slowed on the last few steps, allowing her eyes to adjust to the light. She glanced about the room in her final dissent. Men at the bar pounded congratulations on each other's back. At various tables, others sat playing a variety of gambling games. But what her gaze finally landed on made her halt and her blood boil.

There, not fifty feet in front of her, sat the object of all her worrying, sloshing ale and laughing with a scantily clad tavern wench perched on his lap. Arms draped across his shoulders, the buxom brunette cackled, then leaned forward to whisper in and nibble at his ear. At this, Kendrick laughed uproariously, slammed his tankard down on the table, and wrapped his arms around the tramp.

"Oh, my!" Memsy stated, after nearly colliding with Adianna.

A hush fell over the remainder of the common room, making Adianna's humiliation complete.

When his laughter echoed singularly through the somewhat crowded room, Kendrick felt an eerie prickle on the back of his neck. He pushed the tavern wench's hands away from his face to scan the room. The once boisterous commons now teemed with hushed voices, its occupants all gawking at the stairway. A half smile still on his face, the healer swiveled to see what drew everyone's attention.

There, looking angelic in her billowing nightgown and halo of auburn waves, stood Adianna. Memsy, similarly dressed, stood just behind her. Both women stared at him, shock evident on their faces.

Guilt flooded through him. He sprang to his feet, unceremoniously dumping the woman off his lap to the ground. The quick change in elevation sent his head spinning. The woman at his feet complained loudly of her mistreatment. There were snickers from various onlookers, but Kendrick strained to keep his unsteady focus on his bride.

When she finally did come into focus, she was storming toward him. Instinctively, he raised his hands to defend himself. "Adianna, I can explain…"

"Save it!" Adianna cut him off, halting a few feet away.

The tavern maid—*What was her name?*—tried scrambling to her feet in those tight quarters, whacking her head against the table in the process. But Adianna's incensed glare was trained on him.

Kendrick's mind reeled, wondering what she might have seen and heard. How long had she been standing there? And how could she be this beautiful while so enraged?

The wench was quick to assess the situation. With poor judgment, she stepped up to Adianna. "'Ere, miss. There ain't no 'arm done. We was just having a bit'a sport, we was."

Kendrick scrunched his face, watching Adianna's response. Her teeth clenched. Her nostrils flared. When her death glare landed on the other woman, it should have withered her where she stood. Memsy tried a calming hand on her daughter's shoulder, but Kendrick knew it was too late.

"Leave now. While you still can." Adianna's voice was menacing.

The next moments happened so quickly it was all Kendrick's swirling consciousness could do to keep up. Adianna shoved the woman yet flinched back from the contact. The wench stumbled and spun out of the way. Adianna's face scrunched, and she blinked rapidly. The other woman came to a stop, facing him. The smile on her face belied the severity of the situation. She raised her arm toward him with a little wiggle of her fingers. At that second, Adianna grabbed the woman's arm and wrenched it behind her. Before he could react, Adianna swiped his knife from his belt and had it at the woman's throat.

"Don't even bat an eyelash, hag!" Adianna threatened between clenched teeth.

Shock nearly slapped him sober. Kendrick stammered to calm someone down, though he was not sure which woman needed it more. With outstretched hands, he coaxed, "Okay. You're upset. It's understandable. Let's just put the knife down and talk about this."

Adianna did not turn or even look at him. Her eyes were trained on her captive, and she settled in closer, threateningly.

He tried again. "It's okay, love. Nothing happened."

The wench's eyes were wide, her face masked in terror. Her mouth turned down in a plea for help.

Kendrick's fuzzy mind reeled and tried to make sense of it all. "I don't see what you are all upset about. It was just harmless fun. Even for jealousy, this is a tad extreme."

He hadn't realized he had said that out loud until he saw Adianna sneer and the blade tighten against the woman's throat. The wench gasped. An infinitesimal dot of blood pooled at the edge of the blade.

Alarmed at both his own stupidity and his wife's reaction to it, he barked out his mounting frustration. "Oh, come on, Adianna! Calm down!"

The haggard captive's eyes turned wide on him, then narrowed. But he continued unheeding, defeat and drunkenness mingling with angst. "Even if something had happened, what does it matter? It's not like we have a real marriage!"

Before Adianna could turn to him, he saw the once frightened tavern maid's dread turn to a sinister smile. Kendrick's mouth fell open, perplexed. Adianna swung her glare and the tip of her knife to dangle it in his face.

At that moment, the captive broke free. Adianna groped for her in vain. The once harmless serving wench crumpled into a cloud of neon smoke. In her place, the drac-form of the dalphene shot toward the front door, which at that moment was opened by an unknowing villager. Adianna slammed her wrists together dalphene-style sending a pulse blast careening after the creature. But the flying lizard dipped toward the floor, untouched by the flash, then shot past the startled villager to vanish into the night sky.

Kendrick was stunned. Staring dumbfounded out the door, all the pieces fell into place even in his hazy brain. The only thing to cut through his self-chastisements was Adianna's growl. She turned slowly toward him. His brain and his mouth floundered for something, anything, he could say.

Adianna stepped closer, and he steeled himself for the tongue-lashing he so greatly deserved.

She said nothing, just glowered at him. Her gaze left his. She swallowed hard and scooped up the knife, which had fallen during the scuffle. When she came up nibbling her bottom lip, Kendrick could see her battling with more vulnerable emotions, and he longed to pull her into his arms.

Leaning one hand on the table, he reached for her. "Adianna, I'm so sorry..."

Before he could get out anymore, she hurled the knife at his hand on the table. The point thunked deep in the wood, quivering between his second and third fingers with nary two preshuns to spare. He flinched back but instinctively knew she didn't have to miss. He faced her, trying again to find the words. She didn't give him a chance. The slap came hard and fast and deserved.

His heart sank. His jaw lagged. His body gave up its tension. Somehow, he had to meet her gaze. He peered at her, flicked away, then back again.

When finally their eyes locked, it was like a knife in the gut. Accusation had melted away. Only pain remained. Her bottom lip trembled. Her throat worked, as if it struggled to swallow or even breathe. Her eyes glistened, but before a tear could fall, she turned and ran up the stairs.

"Adianna." He stumbled after her, but Memsy's hand restrained him.

Adianna's sobs echoed down the staircase. They tore at his heart like a shredding trowel.

He turned, overcome, to Memsy. Sorrow, disappointment, yet empathy swirled in her eyes like the symbol swirling on her forehead. He searched for something to say. Upon finding nothing more than a stammered apology, he lowered his head, defeated.

Memsy patted his shoulder, followed by a stroke or two on his arm. "I know, son. I know."

She looked over to the innkeeper standing dumbfounded near the bar. To him, she directed, "Someone should make sure the real serving girl is safe."

With one final pat, she moved to the stairs. She glanced over her shoulder and with a tired smile, muttered, "We'll see you in the morning."

Kendrick collapsed into his chair. The other patrons began slowly to mill about. Yet the healer's slumped body felt lifeless. He buried his face in his hand.

He had no idea how he had gotten himself into such a terrible mess, and he had no idea how he could possibly get out. He heard the patrons dispersing to their various sleeping quarters. But Kendrick knew he would not go to his room. He doubted they would let him in if he did. Besides, with all he had done, there would be no sleeping tonight.

Seymira brushed past the sentry and through the doors to the throne room. Her excitement sent her skipping across the checkerboard floor. "Your Grace, you will be so delighted with me."

Drokmar turned at her voice. His eyes narrowed slightly, but there was no other reaction to her words.

"I have such exciting news."

She had just come within reach and barely got the last word out, when Drokmar's hand shot out and clamped around her throat.

"I warned you, my sweet."

Seymira was terrified by the sudden attack. Eyes wide, she searched frantically through her mind for what he might possibly be talking about. The only warning he had given her recently had been about using his powers for petty grievances. She knew she had not possibly... then she remembered. She grasped at his arm of iron.

"It wasn't me." Her voice sounded low and squished like a toad's.

Instantly, the vice tightened. "You can't lie to me." His voice was like venom. "I felt it was you."

"My news," she squeaked. "Just... let me share..."

He squeezed off any further attempts. She groped for air. She struggled against his hand, tried peeling his fingers away for relief. Black pressed in around the edges of her vision. She feared the last thing she would ever see was Drokmar's determined face.

Yet just as suddenly as he had grabbed her, she was freed. Seymira gasped hard and crumpled to the floor.

"Very well," he cooed, turning from her. "Tell me your exciting news."

He sat with flair upon the larger of the ornately carved dual-thrones, in curtsy-fashion.

Still a heap on the floor, Seymira gasped cool, precious air.

"A ganji," she choked out between gasps, her lungs burning. Hard, heaving pants that stung as much as brought relief.

"What did you say?" Drokmar came slowly to his feet, his eyes trained on her.

"I... found a... ganji, my lord."

His face contorted into a pleased, yet sinister, expression. "Where?"

Seymira took his outstretched hand, puffing unceremoniously to her feet. "In Fal Dura, my lord," she panted. "A woman traveling to Ooflic in the company of a man and an elf."

She watched the pleasure stretch further and further into his expression, so she added the final dollop for his delight. "And I know her name."

His eyes snapped to hers. "Excellent!"

He turned and went briskly to the side door, calling to a lingering rector. "Has Vo Shen returned from Tymalia yet?"

"Yes, my lord. Only just."

"Good! Send for him!" Then turning back to Seymira, he instructed, "You will give the information to Vo Shen so he may take the message to Mendrake."

"But, Your Grace," she protested, more than slightly miffed. "I thought I would be the one—"

But Drokmar's hand came up, cutting her off. He shook his head. "No, my dear. When you need something stolen, you don't send a spy." He rubbed his hands together, looking off into the night sky. "You send a thief."

MORNING AFTER

Kendrick was out on the porch of the inn before dawn. He sat on the edge, his feet on the ground, hunched over and moping. He did not know how long he stayed there. All he knew was the sun had fully risen in the western sky, and he had not moved.

He felt Memsy behind him before he heard anything. She brushed her fingertips over his shoulder when she passed. Without a word, she came to sit on the edge of the planks by him, her feet dangling. There the two sat for several moments in silence.

Finally, he could take it no longer and had to ask, "Are you going to say anything?"

The sorci half-smiled but continued gazing out over the square. Her emblem was not shining, and she shrugged. "What do you want me to say?"

He heaved a heavy sigh. Keeping his arms propped on his knees, he flapped his hands out and then back in to steeple his fingers. "I don't know. Tell me what an idiot I was, and I made an unholy mess of things."

Memsy gave him a sympathetic smile. "You've been doing that all night. Why waste my breath?"

"Because I deserve it!"

Still grinning at him, she tipped her head to the side. "Maybe. But why don't you tell me what actually happened to bring this all about."

Kendrick huffed an exasperated sigh. "What for? You already know what happened. I've felt you in my head the last twenty minutes." He twirled the ring on his finger, absently. "Why talk about it?"

Around and round, the ring went. Presently, he felt her hand on his arm. He tried but couldn't keep her gaze.

"Because talking will help," she said.

"Don't want to talk." *Was he pouting?*

From the change in her voice, he could tell Memsy's smile had broadened, and she patted his arm. "Humor me."

He felt his nose scrunch. Finally, he took a deep breath, sitting straight and tall, but then schlumped down with the exhale. His stomach clenched as he tried to form the words. He twirled and twirled his ring. He opened his mouth a number of times before he could finally get it out.

"It's not me."

He paused, but Memsy said nothing, so he continued. "The fairies said… I'm not the Mentaloss, since I don't have the emblem…"

"And…?"

It was so obvious, Kendrick looked at her dumbfounded. "*And* that means someone else is! Someone else will be coming along. Someone who has the emblem. Someone to stand beside her against Drokmar and his forces. Someone who can take her to fulfill her destiny. Someone with 'purer motives.'"

He sneered the quote, scowling at the ground, and leaned forward again. "Someone better than me."

All the guilt and shame of his past came forth to batter him over the head. Before he could tumble too far down the ravine of self-pity, he shoved it aside, grasping at his good intentions.

"But if I was only to be her protector, I resolved no one could do it better than me… her husband." He envisioned Adianna dancing in his arms the night before. How right it had been.

She had felt so good in his arms. She had called him wonderful. He smiled, reliving the sensations of her words, her fingers running along his skin, her nearness. Then when her actual skin intentionally brushed along his—he was sure it seared him as much as it had her. Yet all he had seen in her eyes was desire, need, longing. It had nearly been his undoing. Still, he had hung back, her safety in mind. Just the slightest brush against her lips had tested positive for scorching. He had felt her reaction. Felt her intake of breath. Felt her steel herself for more. Her breath had been so warm and sweet on his mouth…

Then that infernal elf! Kendrick's hands curled into fists.

"Then your nephew showed up." It came out in a growl. "He continuously flaunts his ability to touch *my* wife. He's always pulling her into his arms. He nuzzled her neck. He takes off her protective clothing, just to throw it in my face that he can touch her, and I can't!"

He slumped back on his propped arms, dejectedly. "He's always calling me 'old man.' I'm not really that much older than her."

He pushed one arm straight to swivel his gaze to Memsy to see how she would take his justification. Her face was unexpressive, but her eyes danced merrily back at him. So, he plopped back into his slumped position.

"Then he accused me of…"

Kendrick's hands clenched so tightly that when he curled the claws into tight fists several of his knuckles popped.

"So instead of hitting him… again," Memsy offered, leaning her head knowingly toward him. "You decided to bury your burdens in booze."

Kendrick leaned back, eyeing her questioningly. "You knew that shiner of his was mine?"

She grinned. "I didn't even have to go searching. I knew with all of his shenanigans it was just a matter of time."

They shared a chuckle and a sigh.

Then Kendrick's expression sobered. "Honestly. I had no idea that woman was a dalphene intent on killing me."

"But you knew she was a woman," Memsy returned pointedly. "One who didn't care you were married."

Kendrick couldn't keep level with her gaze, though he tried. So, he went back to his hunched position, and finally muttered, "Yes. A woman I can touch."

Memsy whacked her fingertips against his shoulder.

"Adianna's claimed your heart, boy," Memsy pointed out, exasperated. "Shouldn't she have claim to the rest of you as well?"

Kendrick knew she was right. He had chastened himself all night because he knew she was right. Still, he hedged, grasping at straws.

"But what about *her* body? I didn't do anything last night that Tarron hasn't been doing to her every day since he arrived. If she cares for me as you say she does, shouldn't she be batting away that elf's advances?"

"She does! You're just too busy brooding about what he can do that you can't to see it!"

He couldn't argue. He had seen it. Still, he didn't want to admit she was right. Then he felt her hand on his shoulder.

"Nothing will ever happen between Adianna and Tarron."

"How can you be so sure?" He knew *he* wasn't sure.

"Because it never has." Memsy stated matter-of-factly. "Because he's eighty years older than her. *And* because she's in love with you. That's why last night hurt her so."

She sat in silence, letting that sink in. Then finally, she beseeched, "Kendrick. For so long you've been running from who you really are, trying so desperately to prove you don't care."

She took his chin and gently turned his face to hers. "She brings out the best in you. The true Kendrick. Kendrick, the man. Her prince. The king of her heart. And quite possibly the love of her life."

He flinched slightly at her words. Their eyes locked. "You both deserve the best in you."

Just then the inn door opened. They both turned in unison to see Adianna halt in the doorway. She wouldn't meet his gaze. Her once brilliant eyes were red and swollen. She looked haggard. She pulled her lips between her teeth. Then she dropped the packs by Memsy and stepped off the porch without saying a word.

Adianna stepped out into the sun. She wandered over to the remains of the bonfire, avoiding the eyes on her back. But the bonfire reminded her of last night and of being in his arms. So, she moved on to stare down the steep bank into the river.

She had hoped to feel numb after a night of crying but seeing him brought it all back. She wrapped her arms around herself. But neither that nor the sun warming her cloak could penetrate the chill within her. Watching the shimmering water rush by, she urged herself not to think. She didn't want to think anymore. She didn't want to cry or feel or care anymore. She was done, all emotions spent.

The world weighed heavy on her shoulders. Made heavier by slinging the Blades on again. Hidden beneath the mattress in their rented room, she had been able to pretend the last few days that she was just like everyone else. That the fate of everyone she loved was not on her. Yet that responsibility doubled, quadrupled, with the events of last evening—she longed to throw her cares into the river and never think of quests or unions, duty or love ever again.

Oblivious to the world, she was startled when a hand came down on her shoulder. Spinning around she found Tarron looking forlorn and consoling. "I heard what happened."

"Tarron, I'm not in the mood for your nonsense right now." She backed away, shooting a glance to where she had left Kendrick and Memsy. Kendrick's eyes were indeed on her, but he sadly looked away.

"No, Scrod," Tarron said, using the childhood name he'd used whenever she had come to him with a booboo. "No nonsense."

His open arms and sincere look undid her, and she willingly stepped into his embrace. Tarron rested his chin atop her head as she settled in against his chest. His genuine concern warmed her when nothing else had.

She stood there, finally consoled, listening to the soft rush of water. The rising sun sparkled off the ripples. She could hear the rhythmic double thump of his heart.

He softly stroked her hair. "It will be okay, sweetheart," he soothed. "Don't worry about a thing."

She smiled at that. He pressed a kiss on the top of her head, just like he had when she was young, when he'd always make things all better.

"We'll just gather up your stuff," he went on, so sure he could help, and she clung to that, certain he could. "And we'll take you back home with us."

"What?!" She shoved out of his arms. All night she had been hurt, apprehensive, remorseful even, lamenting what this journey held next for her. But not once had she thought of quitting.

"Yeah. Gaidish, Argon, and I will take you back with us. You won't have to see that miserable slug ever again."

He tugged on her arm to pull her back into his arms. She stiff-armed her hand against his chest.

"But what about the quest? I've got to go on."

"Don't worry about that." He pushed down at the crook of her arm to bend it and pulled her in. "We'll go back home and wait for someone more worthy to come."

At first, Adianna was so stunned by even the thought, she didn't resist being pulled back into his arms. When he brought her head back to rest on his chest, her mind reeled. Eyes wide, she stared blankly at the ground trying to zero in on a thought which made sense.

"And don't worry," Tarron assured her again. "We'll find something to do about the whole marriage thing, too. We won't let you stay shackled to a monster."

At that, she shoved him away hard. "Monster!" she repeated, disbelieving. "Marriage thing? He's not a monster!" she snapped. "He's a man. A man you taunted and tormented every chance you got."

"Now hold on, Annie." He took hold of her arm, but she yanked free.

"My name is not Annie." She gave him a hard look. "You just couldn't stop, could you? You had to keep poking and needling, didn't you? A nuzzle here. Pull off the shamere there. Just had to keep pushing." She shoved hard at his chest. "Well, are you happy now? Humiliating me with your stupid stories wasn't enough. You had to thrust me into this… And why? Because you weren't getting your precious way?"

"But he—" Tarron gestured to Kendrick, who sat patiently waiting, beyond earshot.

"*He*," she cut in, "is a better man than you'll ever be."

He bristled, glowering down at her. "I'm not a man."

"No," she countered. "You're just an arrogant, self-absorbed elf who has no part in the direction my life must go!"

He couldn't have been more stunned than if she had slapped him. "You can't mean—"

"You could've come with us," she pointed out, softening. "You could've been there beside me… helping me, as the cherished friend you are. But you had to ruin it."

"Adianna," he urged. "Don't do this."

She turned toward the river so she couldn't be swayed by the devastation she saw in his eyes. She hugged herself to hold in her courage.

"Please," he pleaded.

At the touch of his fingers skimming her arm, she pinned him with a glare. "Go home, Tarron!"

He just stared back at her, disbelieving. "But—"

"Augh!" She stalked off across the square.

She caught sight of Kendrick still sitting on the edge of the porch, arms propped, fingers pressed together, staring at the ground. *Insufferable man! He insults and humiliates me, and yet I defend him!*

Sitting beside him, Memsy stared at her, eyebrows so high they scrunched up her shimmering sorci symbol. Adianna glared her venom at her. Memsy's emblem stilled, and she threw her hands up in submission.

At her movement, it alerted Kendrick to Adianna's approach. Seeing her coming, he jumped up. She stepped past him without meeting his surprised gaze. She scooped up her pack. "Let's go."

Without waiting, she tromped off in the direction of the bridge. She tried swinging her pack onto her back, but her cloak made it difficult. She was having just as much difficulty with her emotions. She tried as hard as she could not to look at that intolerable elf. But the fact she had left him by the river, and she was now walking straight toward the river, it was nigh on impossible. She felt like an eight-year-old shunning a friend with the silent treatment because he'd let her pet spider escape.

But when she did succeed in ignoring him, he left without trying to sway her further. Relief battled with devastation.

Her feet hit the planks of the ancient arch over the river. Wide enough to afford a stream of wagons and pedestrians simultaneously, the bridge was supported by giant logs posted deep in the riverbed to withstand the continuous rush of water assaulting them. The timbers spanning the river were worn from centuries of use. Adianna watched the flow of sparkling water hurrying past beneath her feet and wished the current could wash away the tumult she felt.

At the first sound of heavy boots on the bridge, Adianna's anger kindled once again. She spun quickly, intent on giving Kendrick a piece of her mind. She turned so abruptly without warning that, in rushing to catch up, he plowed right into her.

Her smaller frame was no match for his muscular body, especially at the velocity of his approach. Adianna went careening backward. The weight of her pack made it even harder to gain her footing. Just when she thought she would sprawl backward across the bridge, strong hands grabbed her.

Kendrick caught her flailing arms and yanked her back toward him. The sudden shift in equilibrium sent her bowling the other direction. Out of control, she stumbled right into him. His arms clamped around her to steady her, solid and sure.

When she looked up irritated, his face was just inches from hers, and she lost all train of thought. *What was I going to say? It had something to do with...* something.

"You good?" he questioned, over the din of the current.

Her gaze went of their own accord to his mouth. Though he had spoken it fairly loudly to be heard over the rushing water, at this close proximity, it felt like a caress, and Adianna underwent a pause in her breathing as well as her thinking.

Adianna moved her mouth, but nothing came out. With him so near, the current beneath them was drowned out by the rushing of her pulse.

Just then Memsy stepped up next to them, all smiles, her emblem rippling to a stop. "I'd say she is. And you are, too. Good save, my man." Then she gave him a hearty pat on the back.

Jostled back to the moment, Adianna remembered she was not presently happy with this man. She shoved out of his arms, even though she truly wanted to stay.

"Yes, well," she fumbled, adjusting her pack. "He's very adept. Thank you for plowing into me, then saving me."

Kendrick's mouth quirked in that annoyingly adorable half smile of his, but she wouldn't be swayed this time. Before he could say anything, she turned to Memsy. "It seems he can't go even a day without some woman in his arms."

Memsy scrunched her face and closed her eyes, telling Adianna her snide comment hit home. Spinning on her heels without looking at the man, she tromped over the bridge. When her feet touched the road on the other side, she tried to focus on the mountains ahead and not the heartache trailing her.

BROUGHT LOW

The day had been long and an uphill climb, in more ways than one. They had left the road just out of sight of Fal Dura, veering north, but keeping a westerly direction. They stayed in the thicker parts of Kyren Forest as it encroached on the Garren Hills. The oaks and sycamores gave way to heartier pines and quakies with the steady increase in elevation.

As the environment changed, so did its inhabitants. More dovlins and bluebirds than jays and kestrels. And occasionally, the quiet of the forest was shattered by the piercing scream of a warvel.

Those tree-traveling rodents with monstrous lungs, had the bloodcurdling cry of one being murdered. One of the many reasons travelers clung to the roads, if they traveled in dreaded Kyren at all. But, though startling, the warvels were merely claiming territory and were relatively harmless.

The trio had tramped through several warvel territories that day. Which meant, by nightfall, they barely flinched at the outbursts at all.

Kendrick had said little throughout the day. Neither did his companions. Memsy would try to engage one or the other of them into conversation. But without exception, Adianna would respond with some poisonous retort or other, always aimed at him. Stung sharply, Kendrick stayed silent. Memsy's disapproving glares at her daughter couldn't diminish the fact he deserved it. He'd hurt Adianna greatly. He knew that. She needed to vent that anguish. He knew in responding he would only fan the flames and make things worse. So, he took it. All day, he took it.

When they stopped for the night at a short encroachment of rocks making a thumbnail clearing in the thick trees, no one spoke more than was absolutely necessary. To Kendrick, the silence between them was painful. When he stacked the pans from dinner aside to cool, the noise was enough to make one flinch in the stillness.

Sitting cross-legged, he stole a glance at Adianna. She sat rigidly across the fire, scowling over a map. Kendrick watched the low flames dance.

Finally, Memsy let out a heavy, sad sigh. She looked helplessly from Adianna to Kendrick and back again. "I guess we had better call it a night."

The women spread out their bedrolls opposite him, across the fire in the curve of the short stone wall. Kendrick hadn't moved while the women prepared for sleep. He watched the flames dance across Adianna's lovely features. She remained jerky and clipped in her movements, struggling for a comfortable position on the hard ground.

I have to do something. I can't just let her go to sleep hurt and angry another night because of my stupidity.

"Adianna."

Memsy opened her eyes and looked at him, but Adianna didn't move.

"Adianna," he tried again a little louder.

Memsy rose on one arm peering over at her daughter. Still, the young woman did not open her eyes, even though he could see her nostrils flaring. She was ignoring him on purpose.

"Adianna!" He hollered it this time, not intending to be quite so harsh.

But she sprang up, her eyes flashing. "What!?"

He looked at his hands to get out what he wanted to say.

"I'm sorry. I never meant to hurt you. I was trying to punish myself, not you. Never you. I hope you can forgive me."

When he had the courage to look at her, he saw her anger had been doused. A pinched, thoughtful expression had taken its place. He couldn't tell *what* she was thinking, but he could tell her thoughts were hard at work. Without another word, he prepared his bed.

Memsy relaxed back to her prostrate position. The contented smile on her face gave Kendrick a spark of hope. Still, he noticed Adianna stared into the flames of the dying fire for quite some time before finally nodding off to sleep.

Satisfied it was a start, Kendrick, too, settled down to sleep. He was even able to let his thoughts drift to their journey tomorrow before sleep overtook him.

Kendrick woke with a start. Across the dying embers of their fire, Adianna was coming to her feet, Lorooki Blade in hand, against three goblins. Instantly, he grabbed his sword and leapt to her aid but was assailed by four more. A quick glance to Memsy showed she also fought off a few of her own.

Kendrick slashed through one greenish-black goblin. It cried out, dissolving into the ground like oozing, black crude. The healer continued to slash and parry his steel against the enemies' jaggedly forged stalactites.

A cry behind him caused him to flick a look in Adianna's direction. *She got one!* This was soon followed by Memsy taking one down as well.

"This must be the goblin squad the fire fairy told me about!" he hollered to his comrades.

"You knew they were coming?!" Adianna responded, in disbelief. "You are such a moron!"

"Can't hear you, peach." He dismissed the insult and pushed hard at the pressing foe. "Besides, I was distracted."

"Yes!" Adianna emphasized, sticking her sword through a goblin skull. "And if I ever get my hands on that distraction again," she sliced through another goblin's gullet, "I will take off her head!"

"That's not what I'm talking about!" Kendrick elbowed an assailant behind him in the face, then punched another in front of him, breaking that one's nose. Angry, pained cries filled the air. "I meant that blasted elf who kept muscling in on my marriage and wouldn't keep his hands off my wife."

He saw her glare at him, then she quickly spun away from a goblin lunge. She grabbed a knife from its sheath and kicked it in the rear, sending it sprawling. Kendrick's attention was drawn back, but he again marveled at her prowess in battle. That was until he flinched sideways to avoid an assault and felt the hilt of her stolen knife ping the side of his ear. The knife continued past him to embed itself in the eye of the goblin he fought. He then ended the goblin's agony.

Kendrick turned to glare at Adianna, dabbing at the drop of blood on his ear. She scrunched up her face at him.

"It's not like it's a real marriage."

She turned back to an attacking foe, but her snarky retort, using his very words from the night before, hit their mark.

"Touché, m'lady!" He sneered, striking out at his assailants with new vengeance.

Just when Kendrick began to think they might win out, a large, heavily armored goblin stepped into view at the edge of the trees. Moonlight gleamed through the trees and reflected off the metal encasing its spindly arms, legs, and bulbous belly. Putrid green ooze spewed from its jagged teeth and gleamed on its paper-thin lips when it yelled, "Get the elf and those two mongrels, you dogs! Bring me those Blades, or I'll feed you to a greon!"

Three armed goblins appeared behind their commander. They entered the fray while four more came over the wall behind the women. Adianna and Memsy twirled opposite directions, out of reach.

Kendrick plunged his steel into an attacking enemy. The goblins he fought were so clustered together the weapon of that assailant wounded a comrade on its way to the ground. With black ooze spurting from the gash in its spindly arm, this goblin was distracted enough for Kendrick to stick his blade deep on its round stomach.

Frantically, Kendrick searched for the leader. When he finally found him, he was creeping along the four-foot wall of rock behind Memsy, out of reach of the fray.

"Mems, behind you," he warned.

She glanced over her shoulder, spotting the danger. She pivoted to keep an eye on this new threat but was soon turned around again by her attackers.

Kendrick ducked a high arching swing. Out the corner of his eye, he saw one of Memsy's assailants bump into one of Adianna's and decide to join the fight against her. *There is no way she can fight off that many alone!*

He blocked to his right, then ducked and spun to his left, slashing an attacker across the gut as he went. Maneuvered to the outskirts of Adianna's fray, he plunged his blade into the back of the nearest one of her assailants. The goblin crumpled between them.

For just a moment, their eyes met, and Adianna smiled her gratitude.

Just then, in unison, they both cried out, pointing, "Look out!"

He spun back just in time to ward off a strike.

The assault continued, swing and block after swing and block. His upper muscles were inflamed, and his legs ached. They were still way outnumbered. One of Adianna's attackers had joined his. Which left two for each of the women and three for him. But he was wearing out quickly after a long day of hiking and no sleep the night before. He saw signs of fatigue in the others as well. And he couldn't see where the goblins' leader had gone. Mild panic creeped up his spine. Kendrick simply couldn't see a way out of this one.

Just then, the last embers of their campfire blazed to life. The blast startled the opponent Memsy had backed up against it. Thus distracted, she easily sent it crumpling to a screeching glob in the dirt.

"Annie!" she called out.

From Kendrick's vantage point, he saw Memsy throw down her sword, kick her last assailant to send it sprawling, and rush to Adianna's side.

Adianna slashed through an opponent just as Memsy grabbed her hand. The young woman held on to her mother's hand while fending off her last assailant as best she could. The sorci, in the meantime, muttered an inaudible incantation. The air grew thick and tingly while she reached her free hand skyward.

High over the fire, a single light grew in intensity. Memsy released Adianna's hand. The girl kept an eye on the light and Memsy resumed her original location, kicking the grounded goblin away.

"Now!" Memsy yelled suddenly.

Instantly, Adianna dropped her sword, raised both hands to the light and yelled, "*Sho lest ri umm!*"

In that instant, the light exploded, beaming brighter than the sun. All around them, the goblins' ear-splitting screeches shattered the air.

"Yes!" Kendrick cheered. He punched the air, watching the nocturnal creatures disintegrate one by one in the brightness of the light. His sore muscles and burning lungs were forgotten, seeing their adversary shrivel in the dust.

He shielded his eyes to make sure Adianna was safe before turning back to Memsy. The last goblin dissolved at her feet.

Memsy smiled. She dipped one eye into a wink, making him chuckle with relief. She lowered her arms, and the light slowly began to dwindle.

Still shielding his eyes, he glanced from one smiling woman to the other, so relieved they were safe. Adianna beamed. Memsy sighed her relief and laughed.

Suddenly, a jagged weapon plunged through the front of Memsy's stomach. Her laugh died. Her face contorted.

"Memsy!" Adianna's scream deafened the night sky.

The wretched stalactite then ripped from the ancient's body, sending her helpless form crumpling to the ground. The goblin leader who had stayed in her shadow was now exposed to the fading brightness of the spell. His screeching ashes crumpled into oblivion. But the damage had been done.

Adianna and Kendrick rushed to Memsy's side. As gently as possible, they straightened her tattered body to lie flat, and he assessed the damage. A sickening ache engulfed him at what he saw. The plunge of the goblin's sword had severed Memsy's spine completely. There was nothing left.

Fighting the bile struggling to come forth, Kendrick jumped when Adianna grabbed his arm in a desperate grip. Her breath caught with the intensity of the contact, but when she could speak, she cried frantically, "Quick! We have to work fast to heal her!"

The healer put his other hand piteously on hers. "Adianna," he choked out the word.

But she cut him off. "You have to heal her, now!" she demanded.

"It won't..." he began. "The wound is too severe, Adianna. It won't work."

Nearing hysterics, she ripped her hand free and hit him. His jaw exploded with the impact. Saddened, he just shook it off and turned back to face her wrath.

"Even with your help, there is nothing we can do. Don't you see!" He directed her eyes to the gaping wound. "Half of her middle is missing! It is gone!" She nearly crumpled under the anguishing reality. "We can't rebuild it in time, Adianna," he whispered. "All we can do is say good-bye."

"Noooo!" she screamed. She peeled her eyes away from her beloved mother to pummel him with her fists.

Kendrick closed his eyes, tipping his head to the side, and let her hit away.

"Adianna," the word was shallow and throaty—hardly audible.

The young woman stilled. They both turned to Memsy, who watched them with hooded lids. Adianna stroked her mother's brow, "It will be okay, Mems. We can fix this. You'll be fine..."

But Memsy was already tipping her head side to side. "Shh," she breathed.

"No, Mems!" Adianna cried before tears choked her voice. She brought the injured woman's hand up to press against her cheek. "I am so sorry. I should have seen—"

"Shh, my love," Memsy soothed with much difficulty. Every breath was labor, but she had something to say.

"Adianna, I want you to remember who you are." She paused as a cough racked her body. "What you must do to save our world."

Memsy withdrew an amulet that had been tucked into the front of her dress. "You must take this."

She pulled at the cord, which held the metal heart round her neck, until it came loose. She tucked it into Adianna's hand. "It will protect you from your enemy."

Memsy stretched her hand to Kendrick. He moved to take it in his. She continued, looking back into the face of the daughter of her heart. "You must learn to trust Kendrick."

Memsy halted for another string of body-racking coughs, and the younger woman sobbed. Memsy's breath came convulsively in a series of intakes as if her lungs couldn't manage an exhale.

When it settled, Kendrick felt the slightest squeeze of his hand. This gallant sorci gazed at both of her onlookers in turn, tears spilling down her cheeks, and pleaded, "Take care… of each other's hearts… Your lives are… one now."

Kendrick held on when Memsy's weak hand would have slipped from his. The meaning of her words washed over him. He vowed then and there to do all he was able to protect his wife's heart, as well as her quest. He vowed to be his best self for her from now on.

With the last of her strength, the matriarch smiled at her devastated child. Memsy's eyelashes fluttered. "My beautiful angel… I love you so."

"I love you, Mother," Adianna sobbed, clinging to her mother's hand. "Please, please don't go. Please, don't leave me."

"Shh," was all Memsy could say. As if connected to the air leaving her body, the socri's eyelashes drifted shut, and her head sagged to her chest.

Adianna's pleading grew intense. Her voice grew louder, her crying more pronounced.

Before their eyes, their beloved mother and friend started to fade. Her whole body diminished into a gentle mist that spread out across the ground all around them. Without speaking, Memsy's final words hung in the air around them. "I will always be with you."

Then she was gone. The mist settled, and she was gone.

The forest reacted to the elf's passing as mournfully as her daughter. The wind whipped up a woeful cry. The trees groaned their pain, and silent drops began to drizzle over the sad scene.

Kendrick felt a stinging behind his eyes, and his sight hazed. It took him several moments to clear his vision enough to focus on Adianna.

Crumpled under the weight of her sorrow, silent cries now racked her body. Her shoulders shivered and quaked with each sob. When finally sound returned, the intensity of it ripped at his very soul.

Instinctively, he reached for her, but just as quickly, she shrank from his touch, her cries even louder. He pulled back, cursing his stupidity.

Frantically, he looked around. The dying light of the fire sparkled off stalactite and steel scattered around the clearing. Finally, his gaze fell on what he sought.

He scrambled to his feet. He scooped up the bejeweled blade Adianna had wielded in the fight on his way to her trampled bedroll. He ignored the sudden jolt of power that emanated through his hand from the sword. He simply tossed it out of sight under the soiled blanket with the other sword and scooped up the shamere bundle.

He rummaged through the bundle on his return trip, separating gloves from cloak. He stuffed his hands into the slender gloves but found the broadness of his hand only made it halfway in. The gloves barely covered his palms, but he'd have to make it work.

He found Adianna curled up, knees to chest, rocking back and forth. "Mother, please don't leave me here alone," she sobbed again and again to the darkness, with rain dripping down her face.

It took him a few attempts of fumbling with the slick, thumbless mittens, but he was finally able to drape the cloak around the devastated woman. At first, she reacted like a feral cat trapped in a net, but he used his strength to his advantage. Soon he was leaning against the rock wall with her bundled and seated on his lap.

Through the drizzly night, he soothed and comforted. When finally, the rain and her hysterics subsided, he stroked her hair and held her while she cried until dawn.

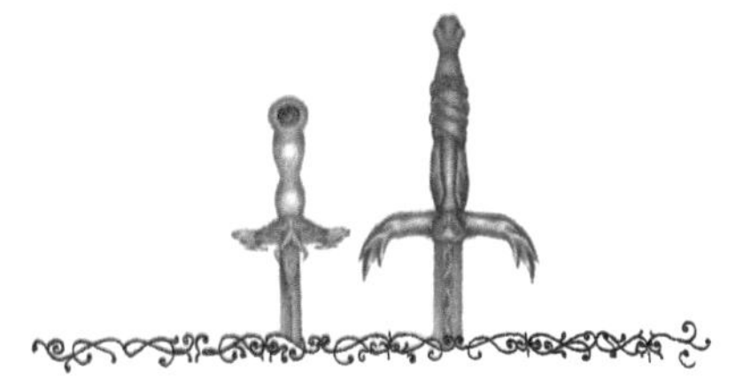

NOT OUT OF THE WOODS

Kendrick started awake. Instantly, pain shot through his neck and exploded inside his skull. He flinched and groaned and brought his hand up to his aching brain. But when he did, the end of the glove he semi-wore smacked him in the face. He grimaced, cussing under his breath. He squinted open his eyes against the pain and the light.

He was surprised to find the sun high overhead. A warm vapor of moisture hung in the air from its heat drying out the forest from the night's rain.

Still squinting, he examined the culprit of what smacked him in the face. He observed his hands, crammed like sausages into the tight casings of Adianna's shamere gloves. He also caught sight of Adianna sleeping with her head in his lap, her body perpendicular to his outstretched legs. Her cloak was wrapped around her and tucked up under her head across his thigh. One hand was tucked under her cheek. The other arm was outstretched along the ground.

He couldn't help but smile. She looked like an angel with her auburn hair fanned wide around her sleeping face. Even with his mail-encased hands, he longed to stroke once more at that soft hair, but he dared not rouse her. She'd had such a long, agonizing night, he wanted to grant her as much sleep as possible.

Distracted again by the throbbing in his head, Kendrick reached his healing hands to his pounding skull. It didn't take long for him to note that the added healing powers of his hands would not go through the restricting metal.

Carefully, he tugged the shamere from his hands. He set the gloves aside and nimbly placed his fingers along the base of his skull. With a cleansing breath, he focused his attention on the apex of the pain. Cooling relief came flooding from his fingertips, washing the pain away. Within seconds, he could see and think clearly.

Kendrick softly rested his hand on Adianna's ribs just below her shoulder. Ignoring his numb backside, he settled in to give her all the rest she required.

Several pools of black ooze and abandoned stalactite swords scattering the ground drew Kendrick's attention to the tragic battle of the night before. He blamed himself for not heeding the fire fairy's warning. He could've done something. He should have protected them better. And now Memsy was gone.

What would they do now without her? She was pretty much the only thing that had kept them from killing each other.

He looked down at his sleeping bride. Her cheeks were stained with tears. And even in sleep, her eyes were rimmed a sorrowful red. He remembered the way he had held her through the night like a little child after a terrible nightmare. He had felt so helpless. Other than consoling her in his arms, there had been nothing he could do. On top of it all, he condemned himself for not preventing it. So, the night had been horrible for them both. Still, he longed to pull her back into his arms.

It was another hour or so before Kendrick noted a change in Adianna's breathing. She drew in a slow, deep breath and let it go just as slowly. Her eyes blinked open, then drifted back closed. The fingers of her extended hand curled up. She gradually drew that arm in. She tucked one hand under her chin and cupped her cheek with the other. Snuggling into his thigh, she released a little groan.

Kendrick grinned. He gave her ribs a soft stroke back and forth through the shamere cloak.

Adianna smiled. With another sigh, her thick eyelashes fluttered against her cheek. Slowly she leaned back, tilting her face up to see him. She looked at peace and dreamy when their eyes met.

"Good morning," she sighed.

He returned it with comical inflection. "Good afternoon."

Somewhat surprised, she raised her eyebrows, and moving only her eyes, surveyed the scene around them. She conceded with a shrug and a sigh.

Slowly the sadness crept back into her face. She looked at him. Searching for some shred of hope, she asked, "Did last night really happen?"

A lump filled his throat. How he wished he could deny it. He swallowed hard and answered, "I'm afraid so."

Her expression crumpled. He caught a slight tremor in her chin before she turned away from him. Instinctively, her body curled up into itself.

"I had hoped it had been just another one of those nightmares that are always plaguing me." Her voice cracked, and she sniffed involuntarily.

"So did I." He began stroking her back again. "So did I."

By the time they had gotten up and gathered everything, it was well into the afternoon. They set off without eating, grief stealing away all hunger. The progress was slow and mechanical. Down one mountain and up another.

On the next descent, Kendrick muttered, "We'll be out of the forest soon."

Adianna looked at him. He nodded in the direction they headed. "The forest ends just over the ravine."

Adianna stared off into the distance. So, he continued. "At the base of that hill, Tranquility Meadow begins. Across the meadow, at the base of the Tamerik Mountains, lies Ooflic."

Adianna looked at him. He could tell something was working on her mind. She pulled both lips between her teeth and shook her head stiffly. It was several more paces before she said anything, but finally she muttered, "I thank you, Kendrick, for bringing me this far. What will you do…? After we reach Ooflic?"

"What do you mean?" Kendrick got a sinking feeling when she wouldn't meet his gaze.

She swallowed hard. "After Ooflic, I must continue on to Dorincia Castle, but you are under no obligation past Ooflic."

Kendrick stopped in his tracks. He felt like he had been slapped. "Obligation?"

Adianna stopped when he did, but she looked everywhere but at him. He waited, not wanting to think of that to which she was alluding. She nibbled at her bottom lip and scrunched up her nose. When she finally spoke, her voice was unsteady. "Yes, obligation. Despite all my mother and uncle heaped upon you, you only agreed to take me safely to Ooflic. I hold you under no further obligation than that which you agreed to."

Her voice cracked on the last line, and her chin quivered.

Kendrick was floored. How could she be saying this? She spun away to continue their trek before he could ask.

His hand closed around her arm, but with her metal cloak, she pulled free easily.

"Adianna," he called after her. "What are you saying?"

"You didn't want this," she retorted, not looking back. She trudged on without stopping. "Any of this."

"Adianna."

She continued as if he hadn't spoken.

"You didn't want the Blades. You didn't want this marriage. You didn't even want me. I'm not going to hold you to any of it."

"Adianna," he tried again, but she continued with her rant.

"I get it! You never wanted this! You wanted nothing to do with this quest, with the Blades. And now people are dying, just like you said. And I can't hold you to this. I'm not going to make you go with me and risk your life for something you never believed in to begin with!"

"Adianna, I—" He tried to stall her again, but she jerked free.

"No! I'm not going to force you into a life you never wanted. After Ooflic, you're free!"

At that, she ran up ahead. Kendrick was so baffled he didn't know what to do but call after her. Then he sprinted forward, calling her name. He paused when he noticed her pace quickened.

"Adianna, please."

Soon the trees invaded his view of her. Alarm pressed in on him. He took off running, still calling out to her. Sounds of the forest mingled with her departure. Unseen critters scurried about the forest, hastening a retreat from their intrusion. The continuous movements made it difficult to detect the direction Adianna had gone. Occasionally, he would see her pack or the reflection off her cloak to indicate her direction. But she was moving so quickly.

"Adianna!" he called out, again and again.

He chased her, called out to her, for what seemed like forever.

Finally, he caught sight of her at the far edge of a small glade. She had stopped, giving him time to catch up. Once he reached the glade, he could see why she had halted, and he ran to her side.

Leaning against a tree in front of her was a bald man, heavily tattooed, wearing a tattered shirt, tight pants, metal studded boots, and he twirled a dagger before her. As Kendrick stepped forward, two more sinister-looking cohorts, one with multiple piercings in his ears, nose, and lip, the other nearly twice the size, bare chested to show off his vast array of muscles, stepped out from behind the flanking trees.

"'Ere now, missy." The bald man's thin mustache and pointy little beard quivered when he spoke. "We are in a bit of a luck, ain't we, fellas? Here we was, sent out on special assignment by Drokmar, himself. And low and behold, this here gent be calling out your name. The very name of them what we was sent to find."

His flanking comrades gave a mirthless chuckle. The man in charge tossed his dagger into the air and grabbed it by the hilt on the way down. Pushing off the tree, he strutted into the glade. "Now ain't that lucky, boys?"

Adianna backed away until she was pressed against Kendrick. She took his hand.

The bald man's eyes raked over Adianna, setting Kendrick's teeth on edge.

Baldy's hungry leer never left Adianna. "Yet no one told us this catch would be so fine. Did they, boys?"

His men sniggered, falling into step behind their comrade. Kendrick slowly pulled Adianna around so he was between her and the approaching danger.

Several paces away, old Baldy looked at Kendrick for the first time. "And looky here. You must be the husband we was told about. So, where's the elf?" He raised his hand casually into the air, pointing a finger skyward, and twirling it around in circles, before leaning forward to ask, "You eat it for breakfast?"

Cackles emitted behind them. Kendrick instantly pivoted his body, moving Adianna again behind him. Three more assailants stepped out of the trees. A woman and two men. One of the men had chains hanging from manacles around each wrist as well as from a gauge in one of his ears. The other man approached, slapping a club against his palm. The woman leered at Kendrick, two katanas strapped to her back.

Kendrick's hand went instinctively to his sword.

"Ah, ah!" the leader said, shaking his head. "We don't want this to get messy."

He looked pointedly at Kendrick's hand, then smiled knowingly at Adianna. Kendrick's jaw tensed. Slowly, he took his hand away from his sword, point taken. If he withdrew his sword, Adianna would be hurt. That promise was in the bald man's eyes.

The six intruders fanned out in a half circle around them. The man with the piercings asked, "How do you want to play this, Mendrake?"

Never taking his eyes off Kendrick, their leader replied, nonchalantly, "Taji will get the girl. The rest of you can handle that bloke while I call the horses."

Mendrake fell back, and the others spread further, closing in. Kendrick looked around behind them, trying to find some vantage from where he could keep them from getting surrounded completely. But he found nothing but trees.

He maneuvered around so they were backed up to the widest tree he could find. Soon there was no means of escape. Kendrick's body tensed, preparing for battle. He didn't know which one was Taji, so he was unsure from whom he needed to protect Adianna. The rest would be gunning for him.

Just then, Mendrake let out a high-pitched whistle. Kendrick's attention shifted to him. In that instant, Mendrake winked, and his men attacked.

All five converged at once. Kendrick made contact with the clubbed man with a kick to the groin. The woman grasped at his raised left arm, so he pulled it back in an elbow to her face. Looking back, Adianna right crossed the chained man. Kendrick spun to see the other side. He instantly squat kicked the muscular guy in the knee, who was coming at Adianna's back. Next Kendrick deflected a head block with a reverse punch to his attacker's piercings.

Chain guy was rushing in again when Kendrick spun the other direction. The healer moved in front of Adianna with a knifehand head block. But instead of a reverse uppercut, Kendrick yanked the chain with its gauge from the man's ear.

A screech drowned out the pain-filled yells and groans. The woman, blood pouring from her broken nose, ran at Kendrick. She launched at his face, claws bared. Kendrick caught her arms midair, inches from his face. But instantly her legs clamped around his midsection. Like a boa, she constricted the breath out of him.

He released the woman's arms with the intent to punch her. But once freed, the woman propelled her upper body backward. Her core tightened to bring her lower body with it. The momentum sent Kendrick flying forward over her and landing in a heap on the ground.

"Kendrick!" Adianna yelled.

Prostrate on his back, Kendrick looked to Adianna just as a boot landed in his side. He reflectively curled up. But when the boot came again, Kendrick wrapped his arms around it. Coming to his knees, he pushed the leg and sent his attacker sprawling.

Suddenly, Adianna's scream pierced the glade. Kendrick saw the mammoth-sized man with his steel band arms clamped around her, hoisting Adianna off her feet.

Kendrick poised to charge them but was tackled to the ground. Body after body pounded on top of him. He scrambled and struggled as much as he saw Adianna kick and fight. But they both were overpowered.

Soon Kendrick was yanked to his knees, each arm pinioned by an assailant and a whip strung tight around his throat. A bloodied piercings guy with two newly missing teeth landed a punch to his ribs. All air left him in a rush.

Then the glade was filled with the sound of stampeding horses. Before any came into sight, a brilliant white unicorn magically appeared at Mendrake's side. A bright yellow ring was clamped in its soft, pinkish nose.

Adianna still screamed, thrashing her body around and flailing her attacker's shins with her feet. But the massive Taji walked over to his master as if she were sitting calmly in his arms.

Mendrake mounted the magnificent animal with the golden horn. Once settled, he motioned Taji forward.

The giant lumbered over to the unicorn. With one arm still clamped around hers, he used his other hand to toss Adianna's leg over the beast's back in front of Mendrake. Then he shoved her body up into place. Adianna screamed out anew when Mendrake's hands assaulted her skin.

Kendrick thrashed again against his captors, but the more he struggled the tighter the whip became around his neck. Suddenly another punch clipped him in the belly. He recoiled, putting even more strain on the leather at his throat, leaving him struggling for oxygen.

"We don't need him," Mendrake yelled to the others. "Mount up, and let's take our prize to Drokmar."

Gasping for breath, Kendrick watched that human snake run his tongue along the side of Adianna's face. Her scream cut through Kendrick like a knife.

Just then the tether around his neck released. Taking only a moment to suck in much-needed air, Kendrick moved to take advantage of the slackening grip on his arms. But something came crashing down on his skull, sending all into blackness.

ESCAPE

Breathe! Adianna told herself. *Just breathe.* But it was so hard to block out the burning.

Mendrake groped at the neckline of her dress. She bit her lip to keep from crying out. He dug his nose in her hair and around her ear, making her stomach lurch.

They topped the crest of the final ridge of the Garren Hills. Tranquility Meadow waved and rippled like a yellow-green sea. It was a beautiful site—one she had only seen once or twice in her life.

Yet the slobbering of her captor's tongue running along her neck killed it. It felt like burning acid.

Just a little bit longer, she told herself, sinking her fingers into the silky mane of the magnificent creature beneath her.

She closed her eyes and tried to focus on the beautiful energy show coming up through her legs into her core. The unicorn mare's essence danced and swirled like rainbow fireworks caught in a tornado. It spiraled in her belly, in her chest, in her mind.

Adianna struggled to breathe. She squeezed her eyes shut tight, but the tears still welled through.

Just then, the magical dance within her erupted, sending electric shards of energy to every inch of her body. The unicorn bobbed her head up and down. Adianna stretched her fingers over the beautiful creature's neck, leaning forward as far as she was able.

"Come with me," she pleaded to the beast.

Her groping captor yanked her back hard against his body, and asked, "Where will we go?"

But Adianna watched the unicorn. The magical creature shook her head aggressively. Then she flung her nose high in the air, nearly stumbling in the process. It was then that Adianna saw the glaymot ring pinned in the unicorn's nose. It shown a brilliant yellow, telling Adianna the beautiful beast was imprisoned by Mendrake to forever do his bidding. To leave her master with that ring still in place would mean death.

Adianna knew the cutoff spell, but she had to be touching the ring.

She wiggled one arm free, which was easier than she thought since he'd rather grope at her body than her arm. She bit down hard against this new area of pain. She leaned forward, stretching her hand out as far as she could reach. But with her captor's grip around her waist, she could barely manage past the unicorn's eye.

Yet once her hand moved into the mare's line of sight, she bumped at Adianna's hand with her head.

"What have we here?" Mendrake moaned suggestively into her ear, making her skin crawl beneath the burn.

But she flinched back, realizing he pulled at the hidden Blades beneath her cloak. She struggled and squirmed against his hold.

Again, the unicorn shook her head to the affirmative.

"I will find you!" she promised into the unicorn's ear, then disappeared.

Kendrick roused slowly, face down in the dirt. A quick appraisal told him his stomach was bruised, as well as his throat. His head pounded, and his lungs burned. But his arms still worked, so he pushed his face off the ground to roll to his side.

Squinting against the pain in his head, he assessed his surroundings. Small glade. In the forest. A sloped hill. All alone.

Adianna!

He pushed himself up immediately. Everything spun. Aching pulsed in the back of his head.

"Adianna!" he yelled. Pain exploded in his head.

He gingerly felt through moist, gooey hair. Feeling a gash several inches long, he brought up his other hand and focused his mind intensely. Within seconds, he felt the gash begin to close.

Keeping one hand on his head to speed the healing, Kendrick hobble-crawled to the nearest tree. When his world stopped spinning, he tried again. "Adianna!"

The explosion of pain was more bearable, but still his call went unanswered.

When his vision cleared again, Kendrick searched the ground for signs. His heart sank when he saw the hoof prints. *Horses? There is no way I can catch them on horses.*

He tried to get up, using the tree for support. Still, fireworks of pain exploded before his eyes, and he sank back to his knees. He pressed his forehead onto the back of his hand resting against the tree. Anger and helplessness welled within him. Balling his hand into a fist, he pounded the tree.

"Adianna." It escaped his throat in a pleading, strangled whisper.

Then suddenly, she was there! He felt her sink down beside him, her arms going around his shoulders.

"I'm here," he heard her voice, soft and gentle near his ear.

He turned, not daring to hope, certain it was only a dream. Some hallucination caused by his head injury. But there she was. He stared at her, disbelieving.

He reached out his hand, still uncertain. She tipped her head slightly away from his touch. *No, not a dream. In my dreams, I'd be able to touch her,* he thought. Still, he took a soft tendril of hair and ran it over his fingers to be sure she wasn't an illusion.

"But how?" he queried.

"The unicorn," she smiled at him, out of breath. "She let me use her magic."

Instantly, she searched the glade. She looked back at him, concerned. "Quickly!" She grabbed his arm. "We have to leave—now."

But instead of helping him to his feet, Kendrick was surprised when she pulled him into her arms where she knelt and closed her eyes.

Ribbons of light suddenly rippled around them. Multiple rainbows of color danced everywhere, obscuring the view of the forest, like they were trapped inside a giant prism. A slight tremor flowed through their bodies. But just as quickly as it began, the effect faded. The colors dissipated. The ribbons of light dissolved, leaving only a view of the forest. Except, the forest had changed.

When Adianna released him, Kendrick gawked around. They were now in an entirely different part of the forest.

Adianna raised her hand to her heaving chest. He stared at her, struggling to regain her breath, transfixed. Awed, he blurted out, "You are a wonder."

She giggled, leaning back on her heels. "I don't know about that," she panted.

He looked at her beautiful face, emotions flooding over him. A jumble of loss and relief. He blinked hard.

"I thought I had lost you." His voice choked.

Their eyes met. She pursed her lips in a smile, then said, "It's okay. I'm fine. I don't know what Drokmar wants with me, but they didn't even know I had the Blades. They're safe."

She then reached forward, looking at his wounded head. He grabbed her wrists midair.

"No!"

He gave her arms a frustrated little shake, growling through clenched teeth. He looked intently into her eyes, and with emphasis said, "I thought I had lost *you.*"

He held her gaze for several moments. A blush crept up her cheeks, and he was sure she was the most beautiful thing he had ever seen.

Her eyes grew watery. She blinked rapidly until she could no longer keep his gaze. She glanced at her hands, but he continued to look at her.

She pulled the pack off her shoulders. It was when she carefully set it aside that he saw the scorch marks across her skin. *All* across her skin.

He grabbed her by the shoulders. She flinched at the sudden movement and eyed him warily. He moved her by her shoulders, twisted her this way and that. What he saw made his anger flame anew.

Seared, red flesh covered her one ear, ran all over the side of her neck, and disappeared below her neckline. Kendrick's teeth clenched so tightly, he felt his jaw tick. When he finally looked her in the eye, she pulled away from his anger.

But his steely eyes bore into hers, and when he spoke, his voice was hard. "Did he do this?"

At first, she didn't seem to understand to what he was referring. So, he grabbed the corner of her cloak and nudged her chin to the side.

"This!" He dabbed the metal mail slightly against her burned flesh. Her sudden seethe of breath told him she now understood what he meant. She delicately touched her scorched skin, then nodded to the affirmative.

Gingerly, so as not to touch her, he pulled the material of her dress aside. All across her shoulder and much farther down then he dared move her clothing for modesty's sake, the red, angry flesh stared back at him. His lips curled into a hard line. Then he carefully drew the material back into place.

"Anywhere else?" He nodded to her.

When she drew her bottom lip between her teeth, he knew. He looked away, fury brimming past the boiling point, and he wished with every fiber of his being he could rip Mendrake to shreds with his bare hands. His nostrils flared. He tried to cool his temper enough to speak. Finally, he had to get it out through clenched teeth.

"Is there anything besides burns?"

"No," she offered, tentatively. "Nothing, other than a splitting headache."

He huffed a sigh. The intensity of his anger was making the throbbing in his head more pronounced. With a smirk, he agreed, "Me, too."

Adianna looked at his head, undoubtedly seeing the blood-matted hair. She probably even saw the gash that literally split his head, for she began to chuckle softly.

He smiled back at her, his half-cocked smile, which made her mirth deepen. This, in turn, made him snicker as well. Before long, their little part of the woods rang with laughter.

The location Adianna had moved them to was several miles to the south, clear on the other side of the forest road. Due to the circumstances of the day, they decided to stay put. They needed time to rest. They needed time to heal. And being so far from where they had been originally, this was as good a place as any.

Kendrick had fussed and argued with Adianna repeatedly when it came time to tend to wounds. She insisted on helping him heal his injuries more quickly. He knew she could not do so without touching him with her flesh, and he refused to inflict any further injury on her. But he wanted desperately to increase her healing, for he said the angry welts called out to him every time he looked her way. Which also caused his temper to flare. Yet, he was in the same predicament. He knew he could not relieve her pain without inflicting more.

Finally, she cornered him into an impasse. He relented when she presented her plan. He would touch a single spot on her head, above her hairline, where he would not see the burn, and hold his finger there long enough for her to absorb his power. Upon the relief of her pain, he would then allow her to rest just the tippy top of her fingertips upon his head to accelerate his own healing.

Once their session was complete, Adianna was beaming. She skipped merrily about, gathering kindling and firewood. She sang softly as she went. Occasionally, she caught Kendrick smiling at her, which lit her up anew.

They built a small fire and prepared the meal in a hollowed-out thicket, which a braidoc had burrowed into. They kept their fire low, their conversations lower, and used the thicket as a barrier of protection. Yet as darkness approached, Kendrick grew more and more nervous about something. Adianna could tell he had something he needed to say, so she waited for him to say it.

Finally, as she began preparing for bed, Kendrick blurted out, "Will you please sleep by me tonight?"

Startled by his outburst and surprised by his request, Adianna just stared at him.

He ducked his gaze away, sheepishly. "I just mean that… Well, I… I can't protect you when you are across the fire from me. I'll be awake much of the night anyway because I can't bank the fire too high up here. Even in the trees, it could be noticeable."

She continued to look at him, mainly because he looked like an adorable little schoolboy asking for his first kiss. She nibbled her bottom lip, trying not to smile, for fear he would think she was laughing at him.

Still, when he glanced back at her, he reacted by bringing up his hands in defense. "I promise I won't try anything. You can keep your cloak about you. It's a cool night anyway. I won't… I just… I have to keep you safe!"

Kendrick ducked his head, waiting. Waiting for what, she wasn't sure—her scorn? Her laughter? She wasn't sure what she should say. So instead of saying anything, she quietly gathered up her bedding.

He didn't look at her until her skirt brushed against his knee. She smiled at him, her arms wrapped around her blankets, and waited. When he didn't say anything, nor did he move aside to make room for her, she eyed him questioningly.

Finally, he got the point. He scooted back, pulling his bedroll with him. She spread out her blankets, and he adjusted his. Since there was nothing left to do or say, she bedded down for the night.

The shamere, draped over her like a blanket, pulled in the heat from the fire. Yet she was also distinctly aware of a heat emanating from just behind her as well. She closed her eyes and tried to keep her breathing slow and regular. If she hadn't been so exhausted, it could have proven to be a long night.

Kendrick had his shoulders propped against a pair of aspens that grew together. His lower body stretched out along the ground. He was propped high enough to see the dying embers beyond the figure curled up next to him. He had meant to be watching the fire, but he spent most of his time watching her.

Her breathing had found the deep regularity of sleep. Still, he watched. He noted she curled up tighter and tighter around the fire the more the flames dimmed.

Kendrick sat to grab another log for the fire. He propped one hand on the ground, close to his sleeping wife, then reached across to stoke the embers to life.

With the flames igniting low once again, he stared at its dance instead of lying back down. As the fire licked higher, the blaze grew warmer. Kendrick watched Adianna uncurl when the heat enveloped her.

Presently, she released a sigh, and with it, she rolled onto her back. He slid his hand away while she moved. She came to rest and moaned contentedly, bringing her arm above her head.

She now pressed into his side, with just shamere for protection. He looked at her upturned face. The flames danced shadows across her lovely features. Longing grew anew. He wished; wanted. *If only.* He watched her lips part and longed for a taste. He watched her face come slowly closer.

It wasn't until he propped his hand on the ground on the other side of her that he realized he was the one moving closer to her.

What could it hurt? he thought. *Here in the dark. She's asleep. She won't even know.*

Desire pulled him closer and closer. There he hovered, feeling her breath mingled with his. He closed his eyes, breathing in the tantalizing scent of her.

Just a little bit more. She'll never know.

His body poised above her. Her mouth just within reach. He knew she would taste so good if he could just…

He dipped his head, and his mouth came in contact with her soft, full lips. He tasted of their sweetness for just a moment. But her sharp intake of breath yanked him back to reality. Her eyes fluttered, and he pulled away instantly. He pushed off the ground and flopped back, banging his head on the tree. He winced, cursing himself. His low growl drowned out her responsive sigh of contentment.

PEACE

Warmth. An all-encompassing warmth. Not heat. That wasn't it. There was light, too. A soft light like the gentle glow of a fire on the hearth. But the warmth didn't come from the light. It was within. A peace. That was it. A nice, cozy peace. Adianna had never felt that before, not for as long as she could remember.

Slowly, into her consciousness, she became aware she had her body wrapped around something. Was that it? No. It was just a log or tree root of some sort, for it was firm and it was larger where her arm draped it, yet smaller under her leg. And it was hollow for she could hear a breeze flowing through it.

Strange. An animal must be within somewhere, Adianna thought, for she heard a rhythmic thumping as her face lay against some material spread over her log.

Not wanting to open her eyes and possibly have this delicious peace escape her, Adianna merely spread out her hand to feel the bark, trying to determine the kind of tree she cuddled. Extending her fingers wide, she could feel the uncommon smoothness of the bark, as well as a strange series of ripples under the material. She then closed her hand up onto her fingertips, her nails skimming the surface. The thumping increased minutely.

Adianna nuzzled in closer to hear the rhythmic sound. *This is so peculiar, yet so wonderful. So soft, yet hard. Too smooth, even for birch, and that sound? It seems so close now.*

She draped her arm around her log. With a pleased moan, she snuggled in still closer, so content. The thudding increased still more but slowed back to a rhythmic pace the longer she held still to listen.

Adianna matched her breathing to that rhythmic sound and reveled in the peace that enfolded her. She was aware there were no lingering nightmares from her sleep. No encroaching restlessness or concerns. Just peace.

This blissful peace mingled with a heavenly aroma. She couldn't quite put her finger on it, but she knew it. It was so familiar. So inviting.

She longed to know more but refused to break the spell by opening her eyes. So again, she let her hand do the exploring. She brushed it upward. She felt the ripples, each expanding and retracting with the flow of the breeze. Above them came a larger mound.

Just as her hand extended over this larger mound with the hard, teeny twig protruding, she heard a sharp intake of breath. Suddenly a hand closed over hers.

"Easy now, love."

Adianna's eyes flew open at the sound of Kendrick's voice so nearby.

"Let's not go playing with fire now that the coals are out."

Without lifting her head, she looked up and came face to face with his wonderful smile. *Oh, my!*

"Not until we know they're out for good, at least," he drawled.

She felt his other hand brush tenderly up her back.

Panic, surprise, and embarrassment flooded over Adianna, and she shoved herself upright. The sudden shift onto Kendrick's midsection knocked the air from his lungs with a groan. He flinched, reflectively curling his free leg into the air. When it came down, it pinned her leg in place. Which meant when she sat up, she was straddling his other leg.

The warm peace she had experienced left her as soon as she left his side. Her body yearned to reclaim it, but there she was perched on his knee, and all she could do was stare at him, wide-eyed.

He gazed back at her with quite a bit of delight on his face from his reclined position against a twined pair of aspen trees. His gaze explored every inch of her face, her hair. The more he looked at her the more merriment filled his expression.

"I…" Adianna struggled to find words. "How…? I mean…." She trailed off, the entirety of what had transpired finally hitting her.

"Maybe we shouldn't ask questions and just enjoy it while we can." Kendrick smirked. Then, without warning, he brought up his knee beneath her which sent her flopping headlong over him. She let out a startled squeak. Her hands flailed to catch her. When she came to a stop, she was stretched out on top of him, her face just inches from his. He grinned even wider. Before she could form a coherent thought, he waggled one eyebrow.

"Really?" she accused, suddenly exasperated. "You pick now to be a buffoon?"

Instantly, Kendrick wrapped his arms around her, then rolled them both over. She reacted with another squeak. Now he was on top of her, pinning her with his tantalizing warmth. He shifted one arm up to prop himself so as not to crush her. With the other, he ran his hand temptingly along her waist.

"I just don't believe in passing up a golden opportunity." He looked at her, still quite amused.

She rolled her eyes at him, trying to ignore the glow flooding her body again at his nearness. "Aren't you the least bit curious why, all of a sudden, you *can* sprawl all over me and I not be screaming in pain?"

He smirked again, that wonderfully, mischievous smile, and quipped, "For the record, you were the first to do any sprawling. And I've had the past hour to consider what might have created the sudden change."

He's had an hour of me sprawling all over him? Adianna felt her face and neck burn, but from embarrassment, not contact.

Kendrick's expression became much more serious. "Now, none of that, my dear, or I might not be able to contain myself."

He ran his finger along her jawline. The caress so tender. So inviting. Adianna found it difficult to think straight. Or to breathe.

"What did…" she tried, finding her voice thick and cracking. "Did you come up… with?"

She couldn't focus. His eyes followed his finger tracing a trail down her neck, over her collarbone and along the neckline of her dress.

"I thought perhaps it had something to do with the unicorn…"

He dipped his head and placed the softest of kisses against her collar bone. Her mouth fell open, attempting to pull in much needed air. Her eyes drifted closed while his mouth hovered just above her skin.

"Or maybe from using her magic…"

He nudged her head to the side with his nose. His hot breath caressing her neck sent a shiver through her. His lips took a little nip against the side of her neck. Her breath came out in a soft moan.

Then he pulled up slightly. His fingers blazed a tantalizing trail from where his lips had set her on fire, up to just below her ear, along her jaw, over her chin, and drifted along the edge of her bottom lip. In a dreamy state, her eyelashes fluttered. His face was so near. His gaze hovered on her parted lips while he finished, "Or possibly from me kissing you last night."

Adianna's eyes flew open. Kendrick was dipping in to kiss her, but she shoved him back.

"You did what last night?"

He arched an eyebrow. "I kissed you." He leaned in for another attempt.

She pushed harder at him and inched away, using her shoulder blades across the ground. "When?"

Kendrick's head was still tilted in the position he had been in while trying—yet again—to kiss her, his brows furrowed.

"Last night, while you were sleeping," he said matter-of-factly.

"While I was sleeping!" This time she shoved against him hard enough he pushed off the ground, and he sat back on his heels.

"Is that a problem?" His expression narrowed.

"Of course, it's a problem! I—" Adianna responded, reflectively, but she cut it off and flamed uncontrollably. She couldn't tell him of the agony she felt at that moment. All this time she had longed and dreamed of kissing this incredible man and now that it had finally happened—she'd been asleep through the whole thing! Augh!

But Kendrick turned irate. He tried to jump up, but his foot was caught in her skirt. He kicked out in his frustration and sent a rock careening into the brush. Suddenly some grouse flew up from the disturbed undergrowth.

They both jumped at the sound. Kendrick glared at the bird's ascent. But Adianna reached out to him.

"No, Kendrick. That wasn't what I meant." Her hand closed around his fingers, but he didn't respond. He just looked into the thicket wall.

"It's just I had wanted… had hoped…" But she couldn't finish. She felt too vulnerable. Her hand slipped off his, and she fell silent.

When she looked back at Kendrick, he had receded out of reach. He stared at nothing in particular as he slowly balled his hands into fists. His jaw tensed. His fists clenching and unclenching, he ducked through the opening of the thicket.

"Kendrick," Adianna called before he could disappear.

He turned back to her. She didn't know what to say. All she could do was look pleadingly at him, hoping somehow, he would know what she meant to say. But he barely looked at her. His face was chiseled with pent up emotion. His jaw worked a bit before, finally, he said flatly, "I'll be back."

Without another glance, he left.

When he returned, he found Adianna had moved everything out of the thicket and was pulling things out for breakfast. His short walk had not really done anything for his mood, but it had informed him nothing of danger was about.

He went about making a new fire, his actions sharp and clipped. The silence was almost painful between them. *And why can't I get this blasted fire to start?*

Just then he felt Adianna close beside him. He tried to focus on building the fire, but she placed her hand on his shoulder. He paused but didn't look up. When she said nothing, he finally swallowed his emotions enough to look at her.

Her watery eyes didn't meet his but stared at his chin. Her teeth gnawed at her bottom lip a moment before she attempted to speak. "I didn't mean to…"

Her face crumpled a little, and her lip went back between her teeth. How could he feel so hurt by her yet in the same moment want so badly to console her? In the end, she sighed heavily, and met his gaze. "I just wished I had been awake for our first kiss."

Before he could speak, she bent down, kissed him on his forehead, then ran off beyond the thicket.

Breakfast was a quiet affair, both lost in their own thoughts. Kendrick wasn't sure what to think of her pained revelation, but from her shy smiles throughout the thrown-together meal, he dared hope. That hope carried them on their journey.

They crested the hill long before noon. Tranquility Meadow stretched out before them, rippling and waving in the climbing sunshine. And at the far side of the grassland to the north, nestled at the base of the Tamerik Mountains, they could just barely make out the outline of the village, Ooflic.

"If we make good time—" Kendrick pointed "—we should be there by nightfall tomorrow."

He was pleased to see another smile and a nod. He observed her take in the beauty of the vast field of blowing grasses and rich heather. She turned slowly away from him, taking in the splendor all around. The view was magnificent. From where they stood, they could see the plains and mountains where they were headed but also the hills and forest from which they had come.

Presently, she touched his arm.

"Kendrick, look." Her voice was full of sadness and concern.

His thoughts of joy at her casual touch were dashed when he perceived what had drawn her attention. There, a few hundred yards northeast of where they stood, the base of the hill was strung with the remains of some recent battle. The ground was littered with abandoned weapons, scorch marks, and bodies.

Kendrick tried to slow Adianna's pace, for safety's sake, but she wouldn't stop. Headlong, she ran into the thick of the wreckage. She did not stop until she was square in the middle of it, then she could do naught but stare in horror at the carnage around her. When he finally reached her, tears were running down her face, and her hand pressed over her mouth and nose keeping out the smell.

As a warrior, Kendrick was used to this visage. He had seen too many battlefields littered with the remains of the hate and pride of the world in all its forms and species. But this must all be new and horrible for her. This fair creature with beauty enough on the inside to match her outward appearance. This great Durluki! This keeper of the Blades and fighter for the peace of Sheorae was now face to face with the reality of the state this land was in.

He could not help but pull her into his arms to somehow shelter her. She buried her face in his chest and sobbed.

Looking over her head, Kendrick surveyed the area more closely. The scorch marks told of striders. There was a large dent in the slope of the hill and the crushed foliage and snapped trees below where a dragon must have been taken down, then had rolled before being absorbed into the earth upon its death. Its rider's body pressed into the ground just below the place where it landed.

Bodies and feathers of hawkmen dotted the area. Trenches from wooden wheels of portable trebuchets and war machines cut grid lines through the soil. Traces of goblins feasting on the remains of battle were visible from the ripped flesh and severed or missing limbs. And everywhere were flies and the smell of rotting death.

"Come," Kendrick said to Adianna, rubbing vigorously on her back. He did not wait for her to respond. He took her hand, and, scooping up the large shield of a nearby fallen hawkman, he pulled her after him back up the hill.

Kendrick gathered up the packs they had dropped along the way. She was still sniffling when they again reached the crest of the ridge. He dropped the shield at their feet and quickly pulled on his pack.

"Get on," he urged.

"What?" she replied, like she hadn't quite heard him right.

"Go on." He motioned to the shield. "Get on it, close to the front."

When she still looked unsure, he took her arm and led her to the front of the shield, then pressed on her shoulders to get her to sit. He plopped her pack gently onto her lap, then went around to the back.

"You'll want to gather in your skirts and not let them drag," he said, moving the six-foot shield over about a foot or two to the left.

Realization dawned on Adianna's face, as Kendrick settled himself behind her, tucking in his legs on either side of the shield.

"You have got to be kidding!" she exclaimed, trying to turn to look him in the face.

"Not at all!" he grinned back. Then without further word, he bumped them off.

Adianna cried out as the shield became a sled and they went swooshing down the hill. She wasn't sure what to hold on to—the stuff in her lap or the sides of the shield, so Kendrick slipped one arm around her waist as he held tightly to the handle of the shield.

"Relax," he encouraged over the breeze whipping past them.

He felt her body melt by degrees into his. Seeing a rock approaching fast in their path, Kendrick called out, "Lean to the right!"

As one they leaned, causing the shield to veer from the previous path, and they zoomed past the rock without harm.

They hit a patch of bumpy terrain toward the middle of the slope, and Kendrick laughed out loud when he heard Adianna's voice intentionally vibrating their way over the jarring ground. Soon her merriment mingled with his.

He stopped laughing though when he saw the bottom fast approaching. He hadn't expected the flat to angle off so abruptly. They were going to hit, and at the rate they were going, none too softly.

He dragged one hand along, trying to slow them down a bit and grasping at the sawd to turn them sideways. The shield turned right before impact. They both went flying sideways, tumbling across the ground.

When he finally came to a stop, Kendrick quickly scrambled over to Adianna's side to make sure she was unharmed. She had stopped face-down a few feet farther than where he had landed. He reached to roll her over, worried at her stillness. But as he pulled on her shoulder, she swung herself about, sprawling across the ground, laughing.

Her eyes sparkled, her cheeks all rosy. She looked up into Kendrick's face and declared, "That was great!"

Oh, how I love this woman! The thought came unbidden and shook Kendrick's soul. But before he could gather his senses, she sprang to her feet, looking first up the great hill, and then back at him.

Her eyes dancing with mischief, she asked, "Can we do it again?"

He laughed despite himself.

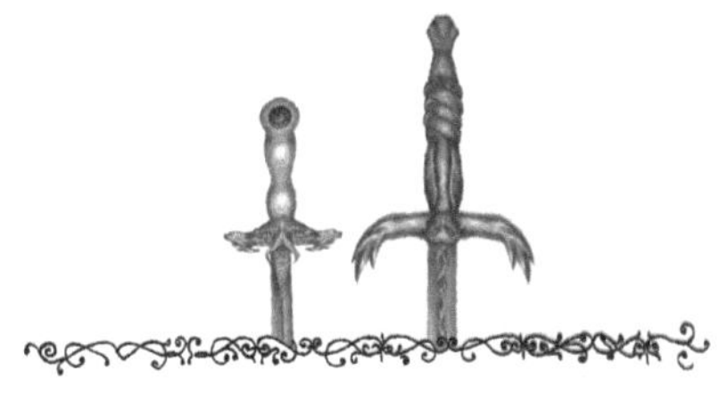

TRANQUILITY MEADOW

The grasses waved against their knees. The arching sun beat down on their heads. Though he kept stealing glances at his wife, he had to keep his attention on the uneven ground. The lovely grasses may have made it look like rolling terrain, but in truth it was pockmarked with gopher burrows, snake holes, and hoof divots.

By midday, he noticed the grasses growing taller. This perplexed him until he realized they were actually moving downhill toward a small stream. They heard the water long before they saw it. By the time they reached its banks, the grasses were neck-high on him. He had to keep an eye on Adianna for they nearly buried her completely.

The two dipped their faces to the cool stream. Kendrick splashed water playfully in Adianna's direction while they filled their waterskins.

Suddenly, the ground began to rumble beneath them. The two instinctively crouched together. Tension built inside Kendrick as the sound of pounding hooves and whinnies drew closer. The sound grew louder and louder, and the earth trembled around them. At just the moment it felt like all the heavens themselves would tumble down around them, the descending herd stopped.

Horses snorted and tromped nearby, so Kendrick sneaked a peek. He uncurled himself from around Adianna where he had pulled her close for protection and peered through the grasses.

An immense herd of fire mares milled around, drinking peacefully at the stream. Reds, bays, paints—all colors possible were gathered, pressing down the meadow with their eagerness to drink.

Kendrick strode tentatively to the edge of the water. In so doing, a massive, black unicorn stallion stepped forward to intercept. Kendrick was in awe. He had never been this close to a unicorn before. He inched his way still closer.

The stallion snorted, eyeing him intently. It pawed at the ground once, then twice.

"Kendrick," Adianna warned in hushed tones.

He motioned for her to stay where she was and to stay quiet. Kendrick then outstretched his hand.

"Hey there, fella," he coaxed softly.

The stallion threw back its big, black head and shook it aggressively.

"He wants you to stop," Adianna hissed low behind him.

But Kendrick took another step forward.

It was then that the stallion lowered his head, his ears flattened, and he pressed the tip of his golden horn right to the center of Kendrick's chest. Kendrick stopped short. He lifted his hands in submission as the piercing tip pressed against his flesh. Trying to fathom what to do next, the healer held his breath. *Should I back away? Should I go down on one knee?*

Presently, he heard a gentle voice behind him. "*Naa nuw tat tu lacmare.*"

The unicorn pricked his ears to listen. He raised his head and looked beyond the mortal standing in front of him.

Kendrick released his breath and turned his head slightly to Adianna.

"*Tat tu lacmare majaic ta.*" Adianna stepped forward, bowing her head to the mighty beast before them.

The stallion nickered a response; the woman answered in elvish.

Once again in awe, Kendrick marveled in the presence of this exchange.

The woman offered her hand for the colossal creature's inspection. Then, when the unicorn nodded, she stroked his massive neck. Pretty soon all the horses were pressing in around them.

Adianna glanced at Kendrick then spoke something in elvish to the stallion. He could have sworn the great beast laughed. It neighed heartily, nodding his head vigorously, prancing his front hooves side to side. Many of the mares surrounding them nickered as well.

"What did you say to him?" Kendrick had to ask.

Smirking, Adianna replied, "I asked him to forgive you, for as all studs do, you were merely showing off for a mare."

She didn't hold back her laughter any longer, and the mighty horse joined in.

Kendrick tried to be reproachful but couldn't help snickering a little himself. Especially since he knew it was true.

Adianna motioned him forward. He eyed the stallion warily but approached. Stroking the velvety muzzle, Kendrick stood amazed—by both creatures before him.

"He is the last full-blood male of his kind," Adianna stated, patting the strong neck, and staring up into the stallion's eye. "Most of the unicorns were eaten by the gryphons before they were sent into asylum until a True Alliance is formed. The remaining have been hunted or captured, like that beautiful creature yesterday."

Her face contorted in memory. "I wish I could have released her before escaping."

She sounded so forlorn Kendrick had to reach out to her. He was so grateful now he actually could. He took her hand in his, drawing her sad gaze. "Maybe we shall see her again."

"I hope so." She smiled gloomily. "For I promised her I would set her free."

Kendrick thought over the events of the day before. The back of his head still tingled from healing the gash the kidnappers had left behind. Flashes of possibilities flooded his mind of what could have happened to his precious wife had she not been able to escape. The vile things that could have transpired at the hands of those scoundrels or their merciless master. His jaw tightened, and his back expanded involuntarily. *I hope we see them again, too!*

Adianna pulled him from his fuming thoughts. She gestured to a pair of foals standing nearby. "Aren't they adorable?"

Staring at the tiny pair, his spirits couldn't help but shift to higher ground. One foal was pure black, signifying her sire, while the other was splotchy white and gray, similar to the mare by which he stood. The painted colt bore a golden star on its forehead with a short nub protruding.

Kendrick gazed around the meadow. He figured there were well over a hundred horses in the herd. There were several other foals and numerous yearlings. There were stallions and mares of all colors. There were even some who had seen many, many years. But even though there were several with stubs like the painted colt, he could not find any that appeared to be full-blooded unicorns.

This drew the man's attention to the stud. Sleek coat, silky mane, pure black in color, and golden horn—he was indeed magnificent. *Could he really be the last?*

Then he remembered the mare unicorn from the day before. She too had been full-blooded. But Adianna said she was trapped by some ring or spell or something. There and then, Kendrick added his vow to hers. They would find her, that magical unicorn who had aided his wife in her escape, and set her free to unite her with this stallion. Then with that rescue, they would not only grant the beautiful creature liberty but sponsor the continuance of their magical species.

Just then, he heard Adianna giggle. He came around the big black to see Adianna dash among the grazing equines. The gray and white colt galloped by and nipped at her skirt before dodging away. The laughing woman darted to the black filly.

"Gotcha!" She tagged it.

The little one neighed her glee, pranced her front hooves, and scampered after them. Kendrick laughed aloud. The black unicorn came towering next to him and added his neighs to the merriment.

Soon the grazers moved aside as more of the foals and even a few of the younger yearlings had all joined in the fun. Adianna's giggles mingled with the whinnies. Kendrick watched the gaiety with pleasure.

Just then Adianna toppled over the uneven ground, landing flat on her face. Kendrick guffawed heartily, but when she didn't move presently, he meandered over.

"You alright?" Merriment was still in his voice, and he nudged her with the toe of his boot. Adianna flopped over onto her back with peals of laughter escaping her in hearty gasps.

"Those little rascals have far more energy than me. I'm exhausted!"

She lay there breathing heavily. Still chuckling, Kendrick squatted beside her.

"At least you didn't land on any steaming piles."

She swatted at him with her fingertips but plopped her arm down on her belly. Her mirth continued between heavy pants.

The black filly wandered over, nosing up close to Adianna's head.

"I'm all right, girl. Go play." The woman petted the soft black muzzle, her chest heaving a little less.

The foal's lips parted over Adianna's face, covering it with a nibbley kiss before galloping off.

"Oooooo!" she groaned.

Kendrick laughed again with gusto. Then he gazed at the sky and the sun arching overhead.

"We really should get going," he offered.

"Noooo," she moaned.

"Come on." He nudged her ribs with his fingers. "I'll help you up."

With a huge sigh and exaggerated efforts, Adianna flung both arms into the air. Kendrick snickered and hauled her up with very little help from her.

Once upright, she groaned loudly and flopped forward against him. There she was, eyes closed, face smeared against his chest looking like an exhausted child avoiding an early rising. Her arms dangled in the air between them.

Kendrick chuckled at her antics and pulled her into his arms. Adianna smiled and sighed. He liked that she would come so easily into his embrace.

He gazed out over the meadow and couldn't even see Ooflic from his vantage point. He took in the herd milling about. At the stallion grazing nearby, he smiled.

"I've got an idea."

He slipped his arm under hers. Her inquiry hooted out in a whoop when he scooped her into his arms. Kendrick walked purposefully to the big stallion, Adianna's sheath and cloak banging against his leg with each step.

Then he smirked at her. "Ask him if he's up for a run."

Her face scrunched for a moment until understanding dawned.

Quickly, approval was obtained, and Kendrick slung Adianna over the stallion's back. Then he gathered up their things and placed her pack in her lap before swinging himself astride the unicorn behind her.

He took his pack and slung it over his shoulder, then settled in for a good ride.

The unicorn gave out a loud neigh to his herd, then was off. Once they topped the rise that descended to the stream, the powerful beast gained speed.

Kendrick curled his fingers into the silky mane, keeping both arms snuggly around his wife.

The herd kept abreast with their leader, spreading out across the open grass. With the accelerating speed, flames ignited beneath the horses' hooves. The non-consuming fire exploded with each contact of hoof to earth, giving the Fire Mares their name. How the blazing trails didn't engulf the entire meadow in flames was unfathomable to him, and he marveled at the incredible sight.

Kendrick leaned forward to revel in the wind sweeping past. In doing so, he caught a glimpse of his wife's face. She was beaming.

Her smile broadened upon finding him looking at her. Then with eyes dancing, she leaned forward, patting the mighty stallion, and muttered something in Elvish to him. The steed's ear crooked back, listening. The galloping mount let out a mighty neigh and nodded his great head.

Adianna's sweet laughter carried away on the breeze. She eyed Kendrick quickly over her shoulder, patted the steed's neck, then disappeared.

Instantly, Kendrick slipped forward into the hollow of the unicorn's back. He clutched at the mane to stay on the animal. Frantically, he examined the ground behind them. *She couldn't have fallen!*

The ground was speckled with flames for leagues behind them, but no Adianna.

Seriously worried now, he searched around, only to discover her astride a bay mare running alongside him. Her exhilaration made her radiant, and his heart swelled with pride at this magnificent woman. Laughing together, they urged their mounts forward. The race was on across the vast grassland.

Miles flew by quickly. Never had Kendrick ridden such a swift land animal in his life. Even with the sun at their backs, he knew they'd reach Ooflic long before dark. But there was one problem. Adianna was breaking into the lead.

Kendrick urged his mount on, but still she gained.

Come on! You're supposed to be this great, magical creature! Why can't you go faster? He grumbled to himself, even though he knew fire mares were inherently swifter.

But the stallion seemed just as frustrated if his snorts and sudden head shakes were any indication.

Opting for a different tactic, Kendrick called out to Adianna. When she glanced back, he made a quick gesture with his arm indicating her need to slow down.

But instead of slowing, she merely smiled. Then with a quick sticking out of her tongue, she urged her mount faster.

Despite himself, Kendrick grinned wide. He would never admit it, but he just might adore her more now. Yet, there was still the dilemma of her winning.

Soon the dot of Ooflic took shape, and the Tamerik Mountains loomed before them. The glistening sun was vibrant. The breeze was refreshing and the view awe-inspiring. The pace was simply exhilarating! But all he could think about was the growing space between him and the mare.

The village was now only a few leagues away, and Adianna was over halfway there. She would reach Ooflic in two minutes tops. Seeing the futility of the situation, Kendrick patted his mount's heaving side and released his tense posture.

But the stallion snorted and gave a great shake of his head. Suddenly ribbons of color rippled around them. Multiple rainbows invaded his vision, obscuring the scene from view. A slight tremor swelled through them, and suddenly they were skidding to a halt on the outskirts of Ooflic.

Once Kendrick realized what had happened, he patted the steed and chuckled, "Good boy!"

He slid to the ground just as Adianna's mare plowed to a standstill next to where he landed. He had to grin at the great look of surprise on his wife's face.

"A cheat!" Adianna grinned, still catching her breath. "That's what you are. An indescribable cheat!"

"It was all his idea," Kendrick hedged, thumbing over his shoulder at the unicorn, who whinnied shamelessly.

"Sure, it was," she scoffed.

She kicked her leg over the mare's back, but Kendrick encircled her waist with his hands before she could slide off. He pulled her close against his chest and held her at eye level. She kicked her dangling feet several inches above the ground.

"You going to put me down?" she queried, her eyebrows arching high.

He smirked. "Probably not."

At her laughter, he hooked his arm around her without letting her slide, and there he held her fast. She looped her arms around his neck, settling in for the time being. Her eyes danced merrily with his. He stood, delighted to have her in his arms.

Then he leaned in to nibble her neck just below her earlobe. The way she shivered against him made him smile.

Pulling back, he quipped, "Still think I'm a cheat?"

Her eyes drifted dreamily back open, and she countered, "Undoubtedly!"

He guffawed loudly, her laughter mingling with his. He was just about to claim her mouth when the bay mare let out a neigh. They looked over just in time to see her nip the black stallion lightly on the flank, then take off.

Instantly, the whole herd was on the move. Kendrick let Adianna slide to the ground. Once freed, she waved and yelled after them, "Thank you!"

Together they watched the flaming herd race out again across the lush grassland.

But out of nowhere, Kendrick was nearly knocked over by something hitting him. Stunned, he quickly examined what it was and found it to be Adianna's pack hitting the ground at his feet with several items falling out.

When he met her gaze, he found a mischievous gleam in her eye. She ran her teeth over her bottom lip, then grinned beautifully. "Race you to the Cone and Dragon."

She gave him no time to respond before running off, her laughter tinkling its way back to him. He quickly scrambled to gather up the items that had fallen from her pack, all the while shouting out, "Who's the cheat now?"

Her response was a peal of laughter as she rounded the corner and disappeared into the town.

OOFLIC

Laughing and out of breath, Adianna slammed into the door of the Cone and Dragon a split second before Kendrick. She reveled at the look he gave her. She thoroughly enjoyed the playfulness they shared, but she delighted even more in this new comfortable unity which settled between them.

"They do say cheaters never prosper— or is it... they gain twinkle staff?" he said through haggard breath. He had both packs slung over one shoulder, and he held his side with the other hand. But the smile continued to play happily on his face.

"I learned... from the best!" she panted, gesturing at him. Then she leaned forward, propping her hands on her knees, pulling in much-needed air.

Just then the door opened. Adianna and Kendrick stepped aside to allow the patrons of the Cone and Dragon to exit. It was the only public establishment in the small village and thus carried a continual stream of activity. The leaving customers, all men, eyed the couple curiously. Adianna smiled in return but settled her cloak more demurely around her shoulders and pulled her gloves from her belt.

Once she slid her gloves on, Kendrick stepped in close. He settled his free hand upon her hip and pressed her back against the wall of the establishment.

"So, I've delivered you safely to Ooflic." He grinned at her. He slid his hand around behind her, coming in closer. "Might I be granted permission to continue this journey with you, m'lady?"

Adianna smiled, pulling her bottom lip between her teeth. She slid her hands up to encircle his neck. "I think that would be delightful, *kind* sir."

They smiled at each other, and she watched his mouth descend toward hers.

Just then, a new patron cleared his throat as he and his companions stepped around the intimate couple. Kendrick sighed heavily, raising his head. Adianna snickered but pressed her reddening face against his chest. Still, she didn't miss the smiles they received from the men now entering the inn.

"Come." Kendrick kissed the top of her head. "Let's get a meal and a room for the night. We can continue this later."

With that, he released her. Yet before she took a step to the door, he swatted her lightly across the rump. Her mouth fell open, but upon finding him unrepentant and smiling at her, she wasn't quite sure how to respond. Then he winked at her and gestured to the door.

"Shall we?"

She tried to tame her smile. She tucked her hair behind her ear while she stepped past him in an attempt to hide her burning cheeks. But a warm excited feeling spread through her belly. As it grew, so did her smile, and it continued while her eyes adjusted to the dimly lit room.

The first thing Adianna registered was a wide bar directly in front of her. A number of guests, including the three men who interrupted them, were propped against the bar talking with the innkeeper, who they seemed to know quite well. Tables of various shapes and sizes littered the wide room on either side of the door with mismatched chairs scattered here, there, and everywhere. To one side of the bar was a wide set of stairs leading to rooms above. Off the other side ran a hallway, from which the clatter of a kitchen could be heard. A number of windows across the front and sides of the wide rectangular room let in the light, giving it an inviting feel.

Adianna noticed a dozen or more soldiers conjugated at tables in the far-right corner under the front windows, talking happily. Then she heard Kendrick hiss softly behind her. When she looked at him, he had shifted so his back was toward the soldiers. He then quickly ushered her toward a table on the opposite side of the extra-wide room. He gestured to the man behind the bar before helping her take a seat. The table he chose was a small, secluded thing nestled between two windows. The light streaming in brightened the room but left that corner table shrouded in shadow.

Once settled, Adianna observed her husband. He had taken the seat directly in the corner, and even from where she sat, she noted his features were more obscure in the shaded light. While he gave the request for a meal and a room to the innkeeper's wife, she took the opportunity to peer over her shoulder at the group of soldiers.

They seemed a jovial band, laughing and carousing as soldiers often did when off duty. She didn't notice anything untoward or particular about their appearance. None of them even seemed to be familiar—at least to her.

Then her eyes fell upon the dark skin and features of one who did seem familiar. He sat under a side window with his back to the wall, emanating an air of command. He observed his comrades, ever watchful and present in their camaraderie, but seldom actually participating. Adianna searched for insignia to match his air of authority, but still it was his face that seemed familiar.

"So, what will be our next move?" Kendrick asked, drawing back her attention.

Lost in thought, she stared at him, confused. "Next move for what?"

"For our journey, of course." Kendrick smirked, his gaze roaming over her face.

Journey? Journey. What journey? "Oh, yes! Our journey." She blushed at having been so fully distracted.

She leaned forward, resting her arms on the table, and tried to refocus. "I thought we would need to continue into the mountains to the north."

Kendrick rested his arm across the back of her chair and let his thumb run lightly along her back. "That sounds like a plan."

"And we'll have to find some way to get out to Balcore Island."

"Of course." He smiled an agreement. The whole time he drew circles along her ribs with his fingertips.

Her body responded, fully aware, but unsure whether it was more a tickle or a tingle. She cleared her throat and tried to focus on the conversation. "Do you happen to know how to sail a boat?"

"No." He now shifted his gaze to watch his fingers continue to wreak havoc on her senses. "I always found flying much more fun than sailing."

"Oh." Her eyes drifted shut, taking in the sensation of his fingers drawing up her back to her shoulders, then along the side of her neck. She swallowed with difficulty. "And is it?"

Kendrick leaned toward her. "Is it what?"

The warmth of his arm encircled her more. She gulped some much-needed air and tried to stay focused on what she was saying. "More fun?"

He arched his eyebrows questioningly over those heavenly blue eyes. "What, flying?"

She nodded, lost in a sea of blue.

"Most definitely!" He smiled and brushed her hair over her shoulder, following the trail of it all the way down her back. "Haven't you ever flown before?"

"Not much..." Her eyes were again drifting closed at the feel of his touch. She jerked herself back to the conversation with a shake of her head and took another gulp of air. "Not much opportunity. What was I to ride? Puffin?"

They shared a chuckle. Yet his mischievous look was intent on watching the hair he tucked behind her ear. The slow, deliberate movement felt far more like a caress than a gesture.

"We will have to fix that."

Each whisper, each glance, each caress felt like seduction. Adianna was afraid it would take all her concentration to make it through dinner and to their awaiting room. A luscious heat spread throughout her body at just the thought of sleeping yet again in his arms. But they had to wait a little longer.

With difficulty, she turned to search the room for a distraction. There was the sound of approaching horses outside, and the camaraderie of several men at the bar. Reminiscing and laughter came from the soldiers in the far corner. Then she saw the dark eyes of the commanding officer glance their way.

She turned back to Kendrick. He was still looking at her tenderly with a smile on his face. She easily returned his smile. He ran his knuckles softly along her cheek. She turned into it, welcoming his touch. Then she wrapped her fingers around his hand. She brought his palm to her lips. He drew in a deep breath in response to her kiss.

She smiled, realizing he was not the only one who could be distracting. She tucked his hand between both of hers and placed them in her lap. Then she nodded across the room.

"Who is that soldier over there?" she asked.

The smile slowly left his face, but he said nothing.

She attempted again. "The commanding officer by the—"

Before she could finish, heavy footsteps pounded on the porch outside, followed by the crash of the door opening.

"Rum!" was shouted by a man being all but dragged into the room by none other than the massive Taji!

Adianna felt Kendrick's hand constrict, and she flinched, moving her fingers out of the pressure, but still held on.

The huge kidnapper was hauling the man with the piercings. This lethargic man no longer wore the post in his swollen mouth nor his two front teeth. The post was missing from his inflamed nose as well, which still showed signs of occasional bleedings. The deep, purple bruising around the nose and mouth made the poor man look as if he were turning into a dreffelig, if that were possible. He held his stomach like he would lose its content at any moment. The wretched man's large supporter heaved him to the bar with a decided limp.

Right behind them, another man entered, and Adianna cringed at the raw, mangled mess of his ear. Seeing the cuffs and chains at his wrists, she realized it was the man Kendrick had relieved of his gauge.

Then in waltzed the bald Mendrake with his arm draped across the shoulders of the woman who sported the katanas. She also wore two black eyes, a taped nose, and a menacing glare.

At the rear hobbled a very bow-legged man who no longer carried his club.

Beside her, Adianna could feel the anger ripple off Kendrick's body in waves. She wasn't sure whether the trepidation growing within her was from the new arrivals or from him.

The poor pierced man slapped his hand down on the counter once he was propped there, and again demanded rum.

"And ale for you?" the innkeeper nervously asked the others as they reached the bar.

"Rum!" the mangled ear man roared.

Eyes wide, the innkeeper turned his question to the odd couple approaching, but the declubbed man pushed through. "Rum, rum, rum!"

"Very good, sir," the owner burbled, handing the first his glass.

The man clung to the bar for support and downed the liquid in one motion but cried out when it stung the gaping wound where his teeth used to be.

The previous patrons originally occupying the bar backed away from the howling man pounding his fist against the counter. Yet his comrades ignored him, impatient for their own respite.

The innkeeper lined the glasses before them, then stopped the bottle. Taji yanked the bottle from the man's hand. Biting the cork from the bottle, he repoured his buddy's glass, which was downed again with more yowling.

Mendrake's pointed beard and mustache quivered with laughter as he plunked a coin down. He leaned in to give the woman a nip on the neck, but she stood rigidly beside him. He sneered at his mates. With great ceremony, he pulled a hefty gold piece from his pocket.

"'Ere, Innkeepa,'" he summoned, dangling the coin in his sight. "There be a pair coming this way. A man and woman. This woman. Bout yay high. Long reddish-colored hair. Green eyes. Wears a metal cloak. Kinda woman what makes you want to bed her soon as see her."

Adianna jerked on Kendrick's arm to keep him seated. She gripped tightly, but she knew even using *his* strength he merely allowed her to hold on.

"If you see the woman," Mendrake elaborated further. "And tell me—immediately—this here coin'll be fur you."

"Yes, sir," the innkeeper muttered. Fortunately, he waited for them all to turn toward each other in conversation before he glanced Adianna's and Kendrick's direction. With a minute shake of the head, he let the couple know there was nothing to fear.

Adianna didn't realize she had been holding her breath until that gesture made her relax. She looked to Kendrick to ask how he wanted to slip out without being seen, but the rage on his face made her pause. She had seen him angry in the past. That was nothing like this. He was beyond livid.

His body was rigid. His jaw tensed. His glare was deadly. It sent a fear through her, and it wasn't even directed at her. Then he started to rise.

"No, please!" she pleaded under her breath, clawing at his arm to keep a hold. It was no use. This time he would not be held.

"Kendrick, please, wait—let's just go. Please!"

He pressed her back into her seat.

"Stay here." His voice was hard, leaving no room for argument.

She froze.

Yet she instinctively looked to the officer on the other side of the room. He was no longer lounging. His gaze was trained on Kendrick; his finger ticked on the hilt of his sword. He was at the ready but made no move to intercept.

The kidnappers were still cloistered at the bar. Taji dabbed at the gaugeless ear with an alcohol-soaked rag. Mendrake was now the closest to them, save the poor piercings wretch. None of them were at a vantage to see Kendrick's approach.

He stepped across the floor stealthily. The few patrons he passed eyed him warily but remained still. No one of the offending party were even aware of his coming. He was nearly upon them.

Adianna could stay in her seat no longer. She darted in their direction but skidded to a halt when Kendrick stepped past the piercings wretch and tapped Mendrake on the shoulder.

The bald man turned mid-sentence. Before Mendrake realized who he'd encountered, Kendrick headbutted the man in the face. Stunned, the kidnapper grabbed his nose, which now bled profusely. He backed up, bumping into his comrades, who were trying to get around him to aid his defense.

Adianna stepped forward, pulling her dagger from its sheath. The wretched man at the bar behind Kendrick stared wide-eyed at her approach. Quickly, he downed any and all rum within reach, then lumbered briskly from the room, leaving the fight behind him.

With no adversary behind them, Adianna flanked Kendrick and prepared for battle.

Despite their larger number, the remaining four seemed furious, yet not in the least anxious to engage. Taji hobbled, spreading out to Adianna's side. The man with the mangled ear followed him, sneering his displeasure, yet got into position. The woman glared at Adianna nearly as much as she glared at Mendrake. The last man, the bowlegged one, eyed them so warily that before long he turned back to the bar to down another shot.

Mendrake staggered himself upright. He yelled his fury in Kendrick's direction, spewing blood that streamed into his mouth.

Then he pointed menacingly. "Ye're dead where ya stand, and ya don't even knows it."

Kendrick never took his eyes from the tattooed man before him. "They may take me down, but *you* will never touch her again!"

For an instant, Adianna saw fear flit through Mendrake's eyes. His frame tilted slightly. But he flared his nostrils and glared past the fear, before saying, "Get 'im."

THE GENERAL

Taji grabbed for Adianna, and she sliced her dagger at him. The gang shifted forward.

"Hold!"

Everyone froze where they were, sneers still in place. Adianna's gaze darted from Taji to the man who had spoken. The dark commanding officer strode toward them. His men fanned out around the battle zone.

Kendrick's gaze never left Mendrake. He returned the glare while his band apprised the situation with growing trepidation. Their man closest to the bar again reached for more rum.

The officer stepped up behind the bleeding Mendrake, though his gaze was trained on Kendrick. Despite the gravity of the situation, he quipped, "Having a bit of trouble, are we?"

Kendrick smirked, though he still stared down his foe. With a nod, he charged, "Major-General, I want these men arrested for assault and kidnapping."

At the bald man's scoff, Kendrick added, "And anything else you can find against them."

Baffled, Adianna stared wide-eyed as the commanding officer snapped to attention and saluted. Instantly, the remaining soldiers were on their feet saluting.

"At your service, commander!"

Adianna was dumbfounded.

With that, the Major-General ordered his men to take the five into custody. The disbelief of the gang members was comical. Their leader glared hatefully at Kendrick until the soldiers dragged him off to the garrison on the southern edge of the village.

"As I live and breathe!" Laughter rent the air, and the major-general clasped Kendrick's hand in a stout shake, followed by a hearty clap on the shoulder.

The remaining soldiers gathered around their officer. They, like Adianna, must desire an explanation for what had just transpired.

"I wasn't sure I'd ever see the likes of you again, lad!"

The general slid his arm over Kendrick's shoulders and announced, "Look sharp, men! For you are in the presence of none other than—"

The general's announcement was paused by an elbow to his ribs. The healer coughed, shifting his stance and staggering to cover it up. The two made eye contact, then Kendrick turned to the gathering crowd.

With his hand on his offended ribs, the general attempted again. "None other than the Guardian!"

The soldiers cheered, but Adianna was pretty sure they had no idea what they were cheering. To her, the exchange had been obvious, and the title a cover-up, which only made her more curious.

The general pivoted toward her, his hold on Kendrick becoming more of a headlock.

"Oh, the outlandish stories I could tell about this ragamuffin you choose to travel with, m'lady."

Kendrick feigned to struggle. The general laughed and glanced at Adianna, then took a double take. Recognition showed on his face. "The maid from the woods!"

He smiled back at Kendrick. "I should've known it was you. Who else could have made old Tylin turn that young whelp on his duff?"

The pair shared another laugh. The general's gaze shifted to the door. He eyed the healer again. "So that band took you on, did they? And the little lady?" He gestured to her, then stroked his chin.

At Kendrick's nod, he looked back to the door, pondering.

"Six against two—you sure haven't lost your touch, Guardian. That's for sure!"

Several of the surrounding soldiers made shoves and remarks of admiration. Kendrick half-smiled, shaking his head.

"You old scoundrel. I'd like to say it was all me, but the lady here can hold her own."

The general reached over to shake her hand. It was then she realized she still held her dagger. She sheathed it while Kendrick continued.

"My dear, to answer your earlier question—this is Kytus. The craziest, most foolhardy, conceited major-general in all of His Majesty's Dragon Fleet!"

Their handshake paused midair as the general scoffed, "*His* Majesty's… That regent has made a fine mess of things, he has! After you left, there was no one to catch my swings at the poppin-dove, so I had to tour out more often to save his face and my neck. That's what!

"As for the rest…" He eyed Kendrick pointedly. "I learned from the best—on all accounts!"

Kendrick clapped the older man on his back, laughing heartily. Then giving his comrade a shake, he turned to Adianna, smiling.

"Kytus is the dearest, truest friend a man could have. He never backs down in a fight. And would give you the shirt off his back."

He leaned toward her with a conspiratorial air. "You just don't trust him with your alcohol or your women!"

Kytus's smile dropped. "Here now!"

"Deny it." Kendrick cut him off, pointing him square in the face.

The general squared his shoulders, and he lifted his chin a notch. "I would." He turned to Adianna with a twinkle in his eye. "But I'm a truthful friend as well."

The inn erupted in mighty guffaws from all the men in the room, soldier and patron alike. Adianna laughed right along with them. She observed Kendrick, trying to fit these new pieces into the puzzle. She wasn't sure where they fit, but she enjoyed seeing him this jovial.

When the merriment died down, Kytus reached for her hand again. "Now for the introduction of this lovely specimen."

Kendrick clapped Kytus on the shoulder. "Kytus, this is Adianna." He stared at her with great admiration and added, "My wife."

Kytus had been bowing over her hand to kiss her glove, but at this last admission he stopped. He turned his head to Kendrick. Then he stood straight and stared at Adianna amazed.

"Then, m'lady—" he bowed even lower over her hand, kissing the shamere, "—it is indeed a great pleasure."

Kytus stood before her, pulling her hand between both of his. Adianna was unsure what the total admiration on his face meant, but she smiled back at him.

At this he patted her hand. Turning to the bar, he hollered, "Innkeeper! Your best wine for the Guardian and his exquisite spouse!" He then hooked his arm around both of their waists and dragged them with him to the counter.

The innkeeper disappeared into the back room. When he emerged, he held a delicate, dust-covered bottle.

Kytus clapped his hands and rubbed them together. He pulled a coin from his pocket and held it up. The gold twinkled in the light of day.

Suddenly, Adianna remembered the unicorn with a gasp. Kendrick came to her, Kytus ducking out of his way.

The excitement must've shown on her face for Kendrick's brow quirked in question.

"Mendrake's mare!" she beamed.

Kendrick grinned and scooped up her hands. "She should be right outside with their horses!"

She giggled up at him. "We can set her free."

"Come!" Taking her hand firmly in his, he turned to race from the room.

Kytus protested immediately. "Whoa! Where are you going?"

Adianna pulled on Kendrick's arm until he halted. "No, Kendrick, wait."

He eyed her questioningly.

"You stay here and enjoy your friends." She interlaced her hands upon one of his shoulders, and reaching up on tiptoe, kissed him tenderly on the cheek.

That adorable half smile reappeared on his face. He looped an arm around her waist, pulling her gently to his side. She smiled at him, and he ran a finger along her jawline. His gaze played over her mouth, making her blush and nibble at her lip. She was beginning to like the idea she could distract him so easily.

"I can take care of the mare. It won't take long, and I'll be back before you know it."

He smiled his agreement then he closed in to kiss her, but she didn't want their first true kiss to have such an audience. So, she interceded by turning her head into his shoulder before he reached her. She tangled her fingers in his hair at the back of his neck and pressed in close.

They stayed in this intimate embrace for a few moments. Adianna couldn't stop smiling. She pressed her cheek lovingly against his and inhaled the wonderful scent of him. She reveled in his warmth. She savored every facet of being in his arms. Then someone cleared their throat, and the spell was broken.

She grinned broadly to hide her embarrassment, settling back on her feet. But Kendrick followed her down. He nuzzled his nose along her ear and breathed deeply.

"Hurry back," he sighed.

"I will," she whispered. Then she turned her smile to Kytus and pointed. "But there's to be no sharing of anything embarrassing until I return."

Kytus's smile split open, shining white against his dark face. "I wouldn't dream of it, m'lady."

Adianna giggled and turned to leave. Kendrick's hand trailed along her arm as she left until they held on by just the fingertips. When she stepped out of reach, she tucked her hair behind her ear and bit down on the very edge of her lip.

Just before the door latched shut, she heard Kytus ask, "So it's Kendrick, is it?"

The sound of a slap on the back could be heard before he finished, saying, "Then Kendrick it shall be."

GUARDIAN'S PRAISE

Adianna felt quite gratified. After pronouncing the cutoff spell for the glaymot ring, she had shared with the unicorn where to find her family. She had barely suppressed tears when the beautiful white mare pressed her muzzle against her face. The gratitude expressed in the moment touched her heart deeply. The next minute, the beautiful creature was gone.

Now as she stepped foot onto the veranda of the Cone and Dragon, tucking the glaymot ring into her pocket, her tummy rumbled. Though the sounds of it were drowned out by the merriment inside the tavern, the hunger pains were harder to ignore. Needless to say, she was grateful to be back where she could get something to eat and hoped their meal was ready.

But when she stepped through the door, she was stunned by what she saw.

Kendrick stood sheepishly at the bar, Kytus still close at hand in animated dialogue. Every soldier in the place, including new arrivals, had gathered around. A few of the patrons even leaned in from their respective locations to hear the officer's engaging tale.

"And, I kid you not," Kytus said. "The young dolt sneaked into that goblin horde right smack in the middle of their sacrificial chanting, snatched that tiger cub from off the shrine of Greidruth, and dashed out."

Kytus slapped his hands together, then shot one off for effect. Next, he brought both hands up around his head to mimic an explosion. "The goblins went nuts. They were jumping up, cussing up a storm and charging after him. Kendrick, here—" he pointed to the one in question, who stood with face lowered yet looked sidelong at the storyteller with raised eyebrows, "—was dodging trees this way, evading arrows that, shouting for his mount. The whole while, that pesky tiger was scratching the vairn out of him!"

"I still have a dozen scars to prove it, the ungrateful thing." Kendrick scoffed, pulling aside his collar and shoving up a sleeve. The tell-tale lines rose white against his tanned skin across his collarbone and forearms. For a healer to have scars, they had to have been extensive.

The group of soldiers guffawed heartily. But Kendrick lowered his head.

"Anyway," Kytus continued. "He goes running for the cliff. And when he gets there, he doesn't even slow down! He runs right off the edge of Gristen Ravine!"

"No way!" several of the men bellowed, totally enthralled with the story.

"The tiger cub goes ballistic. They plummet hundreds of feet—nothing but rocks below. And Kendrick yells out one more time, 'Tyyyyyyliiiiiiiin.'"

Nearly all of the villagers were getting into the officer's well-spun tale now.

"At the very last minute, his dragon swooped in under him—the beast's belly bending the tops of the trees before they climbed back up into the night sky. But Ken's clinging on with just his one hand grasping the halter band. His dragon gives him and that rascal cat a shoulder bump, then tilts, and he goes flying up. And kid you not, he lands square in the saddle like it's just another day of training. Free as you please."

Adianna's merry laughter mingled gaily with that which flooded the room. Kendrick must have heard her voice among the men, for his eyes found hers. A warm smile spread across his face, which warmed her as well. He gestured for her to come join him.

Just then, she felt someone brush her arm.

"Beggin' your pardon, mum," the innkeeper's wife said, bobbing her head. "Your vittles be ready."

She motioned to a table just behind Adianna on the edge of the dining area laden with steaming dishes. The succulent aroma set the maiden's tummy to rumbling again.

"And I moved your things to this 'ere table, as your mister instructed, as well, mum."

Adianna smiled appreciatively at the middle-aged woman and touched her on the arm. "Thank you so very much. You have perfect timing. I am famished, and it smells heavenly."

The older woman gave a wide, toothy grin in response to the praise. She nodded a number of times and bobbed a couple of awkward curtsies before rushing off to the kitchen.

Kytus had only gained a sliver of Kendrick's attention back, for Adianna saw him looking at her through the corner of his eye. But when she turned back to him, he averted his full attention to her.

She pointed to herself, then ran an open, cupped hand from her throat down to her belly. Knowing he wouldn't know the sign, she mouthed the word hungry, then pointed to the table.

He nodded with a smile but didn't turn away quite yet, even though Kytus was beginning another story. The commander slapped Kendrick on the back. "Then there was that time outside Rumati, remember?" he boomed.

Kendrick turned to his friend with a half-smile to cut in. "You mean the night you were so intoxicated you decided to show off for that tavern wench by catching a wild tenshi off the back of your dragon and landed headfirst in six feet of snow?"

The men broke out in uproarious laughter, taking the elusive opportunity to point and jeer at their commanding officer. But Kytus's sarcastic laughter cut through the merriment.

"Ha ha, ha ha… No," he said pointedly, then smiled. "I was referring to the time you took off to the sound of a maiden screaming, and by the time I caught up with you, you had taken out four of her would-be ravishers and barely shared the remaining two with me."

Kytus beamed with pride, but Kendrick responded charily. The men rejoined with enthusiasm, yet he ducked his head in the face of all the praising.

He shrugged. "I guess I was just never good at sharing."

Guffaws erupted again. Kendrick flicked his gaze toward Adianna but barely made eye contact before looking away. Kytus shook his shoulder to gain his attention. The older man drew the younger's gaze and voiced softly, "She was extremely grateful."

When Kendrick would have shrugged him off, he pressed, "And so was her family when we got her home. They declared you their hero and professed their undying devotion."

Kendrick gazed at the ring he twirled on his middle finger. Adianna was touched by his humility.

"Many people pledged their devotion to you," Kytus muttered.

The room grew still. Apparently, the others wondered as Adianna did at this cryptic conversation.

She watched her husband very closely. What she had taken as humility, she now detected from his demeanor seemed more like he was ashamed of the esteem his old friend was pouring out upon him. Despite his unpretentious exterior, she could see an inner battle raging, and her heart was pricked for him, though she did not know the reason for his suffering.

The silence bred awkwardness, and the men started to fidget. One, standing on the fringe of the group of soldiers, piped up, sneering, "If you're so stinking good at fighting, why do you quit?"

Both friends responded as if they've been slapped. Kendrick flinched inwardly, while Kytus straightened and tensed. He pinned the subordinate with a steely glare. Kendrick did not look up from his hands. His face looked tortured, then contorted into a strained mask.

His voice was tight when he finally spoke. "I left when the king died."

Kendrick tightened his fist to tap, then pound against his open palm. He pulled abruptly away from the bar and moved to push his way through the crowd.

Before he could get far, Kytus caught hold of his arm. "Hold there, my friend. Let's take a minute and speak privately."

The commander gestured toward the window where Adianna had first seen him sitting. The chairs were all in disarray among the tables there.

Kendrick eyed his friend, deliberating. Finally, he consented but pointed in the opposite direction.

As the two men approached, Adianna scrambled to pile food on the empty trencher, knowing her husband would be hungry. He stepped to the table, and she gave him her brightest smile, hoping to eliminate some of the stress etched on his face.

His responding smile was so sad. Looking up at him, she wanted so much to say something, anything to take away the hurt she saw in his eyes. She didn't know what to say. She knew not from where the pain originated. She knew not what lurked in his past. For the first time, she truly realized how little she knew about this man she had married.

He paused but a moment, before looking back at Kytus. To her, he offered a short thank you. Then, without stopping, he scooped up the trencher and ambled back to the dark corner they had previously occupied. The aged officer acknowledged her with a nod and a tight smile but continued to stare at the back of the man he followed.

Adianna watched. She didn't know how to process this. She didn't know what to think. She shifted her chair around the table so as to better view their conversation. With the waning light outside, the corner had darkened considerably. She could barely make out the trencher Kendrick flopped on the table, let alone him seated stiffly behind it.

Kytus leaned in to speak as soon as he was seated, and how Adianna wished she could hear what he whispered.

THE TIDE SHIFTS

Moments passed. Adianna pushed the food around on her trencher, straining to hear something, anything. But try as she might, she could not make anything out other than a word here or a word there. Once, she was able to hear the tense strain of Kendrick's voice dispute something Kytus had said. When she glanced over, the intense lines of her husband's expression were hard to miss. As was the pleading attitude of his friend.

Their speaking grew quiet again, giving no indication of the topic. Adianna gazed absently out the front window she now faced. Her mind tried to pull in everything she ever remembered Kendrick mention about his life before they met. But there was so little. So, what did she know?

She could testify he was a superb warrior. She had marveled at his abilities from the very beginning. She knew he was a healer and thereby could hear dragon speech. Apparently, he had worked with dragons and trained as a strider. She knew he hated the Blades with a passion. That passion stemmed from the loss of his father, which was evident by how he had talked about his mother and marriage. Now she had learned he was a protector and guardian of the weak. He charged in to save being and creature alike. This she could testify to as well.

He said he had left the military life when the old king had died. From what she understood from her limited interaction with the human nation, when the old was killed, the new, rightful king had deserted the throne four years prior, leaving his half-brother to rule as Regent in a reportedly tyrannical manner. So that would mean Kendrick had left four years ago as well.

She calculated in her mind that she would have been about fourteen at that time. And where Kendrick was only four, maybe five years older than she, he would have been about her age when he left. *How could he have been so young, yet so experienced and high ranking with the dragon strider forces?*

All these questions just created more questions in her mind.

Presently, she became aware of someone standing by her. She looked up to find the soldier who had previously scoffed at Kendrick and questioned his loyalty now smiling down at her.

"I haven't seen you around these parts before. May I join you?"

Before Adianna could answer, the young man pulled out a chair and sidled in close. A little too close for Adianna, considering they hadn't yet been introduced. But he soon took care of that.

"Hi. The name's Marius. I'm a dragon strider."

The soldier's demeanor—from his arched eyebrow to his lopsided smirk and the way he propped himself against the table to lean in—denoted he expected a reaction.

Adianna stared back at him, somewhat amused. Though not for the reason he thought, of course. The man was young, blond, and attractive—but he knew it. No, she sat bemused at the thought of women actually falling for his tactics.

He proceeded to talk, mostly about himself, and Adianna marveled at how so much arrogance could be stuffed into one so young.

Lanterns and candles were lit around the room in the approaching dusk. Now she could see her husband more clearly. And he did not look happy. But instead of his displeasure being focused upon Kytus as she expected, she was surprised to see it focused upon herself.

Her thoughts again returned to the two in the corner, yet she was at a loss to discern how their conversation could have included her or how she could have gained his displeasure from it. For about the hundredth time, Adianna wished she were over there to hear what they were saying.

Just then, the young Marius draped his arm over the back of her chair and leaned in close. Surprised at his nearness, Adianna flinched back, nearly falling from the chair. She righted herself, yet still had to lean precariously to the side to maintain her personal space.

"You're really beautiful, you know."

Adianna could hear the slight slur in his speech. She eyed him askance, for she knew if she turned her head their noses would touch.

"Thank you," she said sedately.

He chuckled, and Adianna could smell the ale on his breath. She felt him draw her hair away from her ear with his finger. She tried to pull away more but found she was as far as she could go without toppling from her chair. Instead, she pulled her head back so she could face him fully. She opened her mouth to speak, but he spoke first.

"And we both know how beautiful I am."

"Yes, well," Despite his hungry leer, Adianna could see shadows of pain and horrors lurking in the depths of the young man's eyes. Though she thought him a dolt, she perceived his manner for the shield it was. She wondered at the extent of fighting seen by one so young. Just as acutely, she wondered how long it would be before those same horrors would be hidden behind her own eyes.

Suddenly, pain shot through her leg. A small cry escaped her before she realized the cause of the piercing agony. But just as quickly, swirling energy joined the burning. The young man's touch sent fear and insecurity mingled with arrogance as a murky spiral sloshing into her awareness.

Yet before she could remove Marius's hand from her knee, he was gone. Relief flooded through her, and she took a deep breath, eyes wide, to clear her senses. It was then she recognized Kendrick standing near, holding the young soldier by the scruff of the neck like a wayward pup. Adianna nearly laughed at the surprised look on Marius's face—until she saw the venomous expression on Kendrick's.

He was positively seething, staring at the startled man's face. She could see her husband's mind work through courses of action, none of which seemed pleasant.

Marius took a feeble swing at Kendrick. He reacted by dropping the young cub to the ground, only to clamp his hand around the other man's throat. The soldier's eyes bugged, and his face quickly turned red.

Stunned, Adianna jumped up to wrap her hands around Kendrick's arm. He did not respond. The flesh felt like a band of iron as he tightened his grip. Marius gasped weakly for air.

"Kendrick, please." Her voice was soft and pleading.

Somehow, it penetrated. The ice melted from his veins, reducing the tension in his arm. But Kendrick's eyes were still hard as steel when he pulled the gasping man's face in close. Not a single occupant of the room breathed, so his deadly whisper was heard by all.

"Don't you ever—" he gave his victim's head a slight shake for emphasis, "—ever touch my wife again!"

Then Kendrick released the whelp as quickly as he had swooped in. The young man crumpled to the floor in a gasping heap. Kendrick then gave the young pup a contemptuous shove with the toe of his boot.

The soldier's comrades, who had risen from their seats when one of their own had been put upon, now reached for their swords. Kendrick pivoted so Adianna was squarely behind him and drew his first.

Adianna could see the surprise in the younger of the troops' reaction to her husband's speed and agility. The more seasoned men simply glowered.

"Hold!"

Kendrick did not relieve his stance nor move his eyes from the threat.

Adianna watched Kytus approach. The commanding officer put his hand on his young friend's back, then stared down his own men.

"Return to your ale and your reveling!" The command in his voice was indisputable.

The men who had previously cheered and praised him now resisted conceding to the young healer. Yet, in the end, they did as they were commanded, begrudgingly returning to their seats. Two stepped forward to collect Marius from the floor, who was still nursing his reddened throat.

Kendrick relaxed his stance only minimally until the last one was seated. His feral reaction to Kytus's slap on the back denoted the tension had not subsided.

But Kytus brushed it aside. "Come, my friend. Let us return to our table as well. Joined by your lovely wife, of course."

Kytus nodded to her, and Adianna released a breath she did not know she had been holding. Still, she watched Kendrick very closely.

He took his time to deposit his sword into its sheath. With his shoulders slightly hunched, he turned mechanically. He would not meet her gaze. Nor would he meet his comrade's. She could see his jaw working, could almost hear the gears churning in his mind.

But Kytus took it all to mean consent. "Good!" he declared, rubbing his hands together. "Innkeeper! Bring ale! And wine for the lady."

At that, Kendrick halted, his head snapping to attention. His eyes pierced Kytus.

"We're not staying." It came out as frigid as his stare.

Kendrick motioned to her, though he did not take his eyes off Kytus. "Get our things," he told her, his voice still hard.

Adianna's mouth bobbed, but she moved to his bidding. Her hand barely closed around the straps of their packs when Kendrick's hand closed around her upper arm. He flung a couple coins on the table next to the half-eaten food and guided her to the door.

"Come on, Ken," Kytus sputtered. "We can work this out. It can all be made right after a few drinks. Let's talk this through."

The guiding hand left Adianna's arm abruptly when Kendrick snatched Kytus's hand from his shoulder.

He spun sharply. "No, Squawk!"

Kytus's eyebrows arched high in response, looking dazed. Kendrick heaved a breath. The exhale left his shoulders drooping.

He let go of his friend's wrist, his own falling limp at his side. Kendrick's voice was softer but still determined. "It didn't work last time, and definitely not like this."

He tipped his head toward the men still eyeing him disgruntledly. Adianna was about to say something, but Kendrick ushered her through the door of the Cone and Dragon.

"Please, my lord," Kytus pleaded. "Don't leave again."

Kendrick paused, his hand poised on the door handle. Adianna, though oblivious to what was happening, could not deny the battle raging inside the man whom she loved. Though his jaw was set and determined, he couldn't hide the pain evident around his eyes. On his brow. She wanted so much to console him, to bolster him, to shield him. Whatever it was he needed right now. She wanted to spare him this turmoil with which he struggled. But she didn't know how.

She heard the door click shut. When she stepped from the veranda, Kytus's growl came from inside the lodge, followed by the crash of furniture upending.

She paused, but Kendrick scooped up her arm as he swooped past. Tugging her gently but purposefully along, he strode through the small village to the mountains beyond.

At the edge of the village, he halted, releasing her, and took both packs from her hand. Without a word, he turned and headed up the trail.

UNITED AT LAST

His pace was fast, and Adianna had difficulty keeping up. The coolness of the late evening air was refreshing after such an intense situation. Yet Adianna longed to comfort the man tromping up the trail before her.

"Kendrick," she called, but other than a slight hitch in how he held his shoulders, he made no response.

"Kendrick, please," she tried again. "If I did anything to upset you, I am sorry."

At that, Kendrick halted, turning to her. She nearly ran into him in her struggle to keep up. The expression on his face showed definite surprise.

"You have nothing for which to apologize for, Fair One. You are all goodness and generosity. It is no wonder people are drawn to you."

Kendrick's eyes grew stormy, and he stared off into space, reliving something hidden.

"But—"

Kendrick cut her off by turning back to the path. "No. You have nothing to be sorry for." He growled back over his shoulder. "As I said before, I'm not good at sharing!"

And that was it. He stormed along the trail, and Adianna was once again scrambling after him. She was grateful he had taken the packs, for she would never have been able to keep up with him if he hadn't. His pace was one of heightened emotion and determination.

But Adianna felt lost. She so longed to help him, but she had no idea what the problem was. *Why is he so upset? Why is he refusing to stay and talk further with Kytus? Why did Kytus call him 'my lord?'* So many questions swirled around in her mind. She searched desperately for answers, so she'd know how to help. But nothing was forthcoming.

Determined to try again, she sprinted forward and took hold of his arm. He paused but did not turn toward her. She placed her hand to his cheek, so he'd look at her. He did not resist, nor did he meet her gaze.

"Please, Kendrick, let me help you."

A war of emotions raged across his face, and his jaw tightened. She again tried to get him to look at her, but he closed his eyes. She brought her other hand up to cradle his face in an attempt to grant him a peace he desperately needed. His body was so tense, his expression so tortured. His energy so pained. She longed to give him what peace she could.

But he would have none of it. He turned once more to tromp up the path.

Adianna sighed in frustration. She didn't know what else she could do but follow him.

Twilight conceded its grasp and gave way to night. The bright moons cast shadows across the forest floor and lit the way over the winding switchbacks leading into the heart of the Tamerik Mountains. Stars glistened above them. Crickets chirped merrily in the brush along the trail. All seemed peaceful and serene, belying the tension churning within the man she loved.

Before long, Adianna's calves protested the uphill climb. Her lungs strained. She had to pause long enough to catch her breath. The terrain was steeper now, the forest more rocky than grassy on this side of the mountain range. The ridgepole pines were sparse yet brushed the sky.

Turning back the way they had come, she could make out the lights of the village below. Even though they had walked quite a distance, due to the switchbacks, they were still within a couple miles of Ooflic.

She turned back to the trail, only to find her husband had disappeared around the bend. She scrambled to catch up, skidding on the loose rocks covering the ground as she rounded the corner. Gravel toppled over the edge, upsetting the mellow noises of the night.

Adianna hugged the mountain face more tightly, though the trail was wide enough for two to walk abreast.

The mountain now blocked the village, as well as Syron, the smaller moon. Only Dryden lit their way. Yet, at its fullest, it cast dazzling silver light over all. Still, Kendrick had gained much ground during her dalliance. The distance between them made Adianna's body slump in defeat. She sighed, then bit down hard.

"Enough!" she exploded, her voice echoing off their rocky surroundings.

But Kendrick did not stop. He continued stomping purposefully up the mountain. He would soon reach another bend in the road, and she would lose sight of him completely.

Adianna's anger flared. Flinging off her cloak, she withdrew her bow, strung it, and nocked an arrow before he had gone two more of his hasty paces. Without a second thought, she let the arrow loose. *Thunk!* It embedded in the rocky face less than a foot in front of her husband.

Kendrick's reaction was quick and intense. He spun instantly with sword drawn. But upon seeing her standing solitarily, the tension he had bottled up exploded.

"What are you thinking, woman!" he roared, before sheathing his sword and storming back down the trail.

Adianna slipped her bow back into place, then scooped up her cloak before answering. "What am *I* thinking? I think you're behaving irrationally!"

She stomped up the trail to meet him. When they were nose to nose, she ranted on.

"I *think* something has greatly disturbed you from your past. I *think* I don't know what it is, and you won't let me in! I *think* you were glaring at me when that drunken sot was clamoring for my attention, and I don't know what I did wrong! And I *think* you're tramping around in the dark at a breakneck speed, and it simply cannot continue!"

Kendrick's nostrils flared, and his nose crinkled. His lips curled around clenched teeth. He glared down at her, but she refused to relent. She was going to get to the bottom of this or maim him trying.

His jaw clenched, unclenched, then contracted again. Finally, with a ferocious growl, he snatched a chunk of rock from the mountain face and flung it over the edge of the trail to clamor down the ravine to the valley floor some thirty feet below.

"I just want to put as much distance between us and Ooflic as possible!" He emphasized this by kicking more rocks to tumble down the steep hill.

Adianna's eyes narrowed. "Fine!"

Without taking her eyes off his irate face, she dug into her pocket. She withdrew what she sought, and shook her fist clenched around the glaymot ring at his confused though still fuming face. With a huff, she turned, letting her eyes scour the terrain around them. Mountain, trench, forest, mountain. Finally, she found what she sought—a meadow far in the distance, topping a ridge. It was a good fifty miles away straight through, and more than two week's walk.

She glowered back at her husband then turned to face the moon. She held the six-inch metal ring up so she could see Dryden through the center, and chanted, "*Ta lu layt sher, merane shou bek.*"

The glaymot ring illuminated, turning from steely gray to brilliant silver. The etchings on its surface glowed iridescent blue. Purposefully, Adianna moved the ring, her arm outstretched, until the distant meadow could be seen within its round.

"*Voo blain to vee shent lay troe nesh.*"

Suddenly, a swirling vortex of air whirled before them.

Kendrick backed away from the ten-foot whirlpool of air. "What in the blazes are you about, woman?"

Adianna stuffed the ring back into her pocket. "You wanted to get away fast. Here you go!"

She gestured for him to proceed through. With brow furrowed, he stepped tentatively forward, eyeing her and the vortex intermittently. He approached the edge but hesitated.

Adianna rolled her eyes. "Just go through it so we can get on with this!"

And without any more warning, she shoved him over the edge. Kendrick's yowl faded quickly once he toppled through the whirlpool and disappeared.

Adianna smiled despite herself. *That actually felt kind of good!*

Without another moment's hesitation, she pulled the edge of her cloak around her and jumped. A gust of air whirled through her hair and whooshed against her skin and clothing. Yet a mere second later, she tumbled into the ankle-high grasses of the meadow and rolled to a stop against her husband's side.

Kendrick propped himself to look around mystified. "Where are we?"

Adianna knelt and faced him. "We're in Thalandrell's Meadow, well over fifty miles from Ooflic. *Now* will you stop tromping around and tell me what is wrong?"

Kendrick stared at her. She could see his mind working. Presently, he released a breath, and his shoulders slumped. He pulled his knees up and draped his arms across them. He stared at the grass for several long moments until Adianna was afraid he wouldn't answer her at all.

But finally, he stammered, "I'm... I'm afraid I just wasn't... able to handle... it all at once."

His voice was so meek he sounded like a child trying to share his nightmare. Instinctively, Adianna reached for him.

"All of what? The memories?"

Kendrick gave a minuscule shrug. Then he snatched up a blade of grass and proceeded to pull it apart strip by strip. "The memories. My past. What I left behind. And why. And then Kytus comes with all his stories, making me out to be some kind of hero." He shook his head. "I'm no hero."

He plucked up a couple more blades, but instead of stripping them, he tore them into pieces. "I'm a deserter... and a disappointment... and I do not deserve the honors I have been given."

He looked at her then, tracing the lines of her face into memory. His eyes became glossy, and he shook his head sadly. "Especially not of you."

He went back to watching his decimation of grass. He plucked and shredded. Then plucked and shredded again.

Adianna pondered his tortured revelation. She had not needed Kytus's stories to believe Kendrick a hero. She had known the first time he spoke to her he was worthy of that title. And over the last few weeks, she had come to know him and to love him in a way she couldn't explain. He was the most honorable, valiant, and decent man she had ever met. He was considerate and kind. He was a hard worker and a skilled fighter. He valued others freely and protected them boldly. He was everything she had ever dreamed of finding, both in a husband and an alliance. And here he was, deeming himself unworthy.

Adianna's throat constricted, and she felt a tight prickling at the end of her nose. She had to blink rapidly to keep him in focus.

Just then, Kendrick tore a whole clump of grass in half. "And then that maggot thought he could lay hands on you."

He glanced at her but quickly looked away. He clasped one hand tightly over his other fist. The muscles in his arms constricted.

"I didn't want him touching you. I didn't want him, or any of his co-horts, or even Kytus touching you. I didn't want anyone touching you… especially if I couldn't."

Adianna closed one hand over his tense fingers and pressed her other palm to the side of his face until he looked at her. "But you can touch me. Remember?"

Kendrick squeezed her fingers, then clasped her wrist to press her hand more closely to his face. He swiveled toward her and pulled her palm against his lips. He closed his eyes and breathed in the scent of her.

Adianna tingled at the feel of his kiss in her hand. That same warming peace she had come to crave from his touch spiraled within her. She felt the essence of him permeate her body, but best of all, she felt hope spring forth. She simply had to ask.

"Kendrick, do you love me?"

He opened his eyes to stare at her. She held her breath as he searched her face. The more he deliberated, the more doubt began to creep in.

Slowly, he drew their hands away from his face. He pressed the back of her hand against his other cheek and slipped his fingers through hers.

Closing his eyes, he took a deep breath. A timid fear settled in Adianna's chest until he finally spoke.

"Uncontrollably." His eyes sought hers. "And with all my heart!"

The breath Adianna had been holding punched out like a sob. Adianna crumpled into a mess of tears. Disbelief collided with inexpressible joy. She could hardly believe her ears.

Kendrick faced her, cupping her hands between them as if to plead with her.

"Adianna, would you ever—*could* you ever—grow to love me and want me for your husband, even if we never find a wielder for the Blades?"

Adianna sobbed again, and Kendrick looked apprehensive. But she smiled through her tears. She laughed and gasped and laughed again, trying to compose herself enough to speak.

"Oh, my darling, Kendrick, I already do."

Kendrick grinned, elated, then laughed and reached for her. He pressed his palm to the side of her face, and she snuggled into it. His thumb brushed along her cheek, and his face mirrored the longing she felt kindling in her belly. That longing erupted into a giddy excitement when his eyes sought her lips.

At last, she thought as her breath left in a rush.

He drew nearer and her lashes drifted low. But inches away, he paused. She found him searching her face, hesitantly.

"May I kiss you?" he whispered.

Taken aback by the question, she drew away to apprise him.

"I mean, I vowed upon leaving Fal Dura to strive to always be worthy of your trust. I vowed to be your protector and never be a rogue with you or your heart again."

Adianna bowed her head and bit back her smile. Purposefully, she looped her fingers around the fabric of his shirt to pull him closer.

"Oh, my love," she said, "I've known from the beginning you were a bit of both."

His responsive laughter filled the meadow. When the merriment settled into his chest, his eyes danced above that mischievous grin she loved. Then his hands laced around her hips, and she was airborne.

She squealed until she realized he was lifting her to straddle his lap. Once landed, she settled in, pressing her hands to either side of his face.

"Besides, you are my husband." She smiled, a mere breath away from his lips. "All I am is yours—now and forever."

Then her mouth met his. The irruption of energetic colors igniting within her was as spectacular as the tantalizing feeling flooding through her body. His hands crept up her back to press her closer and deepen the kiss. Her fingers moved up to lace through his hair. She clung to him wanting—needing—more.

His mouth moved over hers until she was breathless. She turned her face to gasp for air, but his lips left a fiery trail down her neck. He slid his hand along her side down to her hip, pulling gently to compress the heat building between them.

Her moan was echoed by his own when she arched her body into his. He pivoted, bringing her around to lay on the soft grass. She reveled in the press of his body more fully on hers.

His hand traced the line of her body, igniting senses she never knew she had, from her thigh, up over her hip, along her waist, brushing her ribcage. Her breath caught when his fingers feathered over her chest and along her collarbone.

Then he lifted his head, and she stared dreamily into his sapphire eyes.

"My exquisite Adianna. I love you so. With my whole heart, I love you. And I will—now and forever."

She rewarded him by pulling him down for another kiss. Their bodies entwined into breathless bliss, and all of her hungered for his touch.

She sighed in his arms. Heaven would be attained this night. No more wondering. No more coaxing. He was hers, and she was his. Now. And forever.

So captivated in the joy between them, the two lovers paid no heed to the explosive beacon shooting skyward from their intertwined bodies, illuminating the night like day. They, too, were oblivious to the blast of trumpets sounding, which shook the hilltops. They were wrapped up within a cocoon of protective energy; nothing could penetrate their bliss.

Dragons roared. Lightning flashed. The earth quaked and shook its elation. All of Sheorae was apprised of a new, unmistakable union.

Then the beacon pulsed and went out. The moon was cloaked, and the world was plunged into darkness. The only light throughout all of Sheorae came from two legendary swords within a sheath, strewn aside and forgotten by an enraptured couple now fated to save their world.

FINALLY

Seymira stepped out onto the balcony and looked out over the empire. The moons slipped behind clouds, leaving the stars to bathe her view in semi-darkness. Faint lights dotted here and there, depicting villages. A fire crackled in the hearth of the throne room behind her.

She contemplated what was to come. Soon they would find the Blades, all resistance would be crushed, and the world would be theirs. A cool smile crossed her face.

And I will rule. Just as I was always meant to.

Her smile broadened. But slowly, another thought stole in—a sad, forlorn thought. She looked at the moon, Dryden, peeking out from behind the cloud to spread its light on all below.

If only...

She choked down the thought and the emotion that clung to it. It didn't matter now. She'd left that palace, the regent, and her heart back there long ago. Without a heart to feel, she was free to rule at Drokmar's side.

Suddenly a beacon of light shot skyward above the Tamerik Mountains. The enormous pillar touched the heavens and spread out like a giant mushroom, sending a brilliance of light everywhere. Seymira was dazzled by the brilliant brightness, and before she could react, the night's silence was split asunder by a deafening chorus of trumpets.

Frantically, she covered her ears to stifle the noise, but it was as if the sound came from everywhere at once, including inside her head. Her next impulse was to flee—flee the light, flee the sound.

Just as she was about to run, the balcony beneath her feet began to tremble. The blinding light, the deafening noise and the instability of the ground were too much. Seymira crumpled to the floor. She clamped her eyes shut, covering her ears again to block it all out with little success.

Through the din, the roars of dragons sounded, loud and glorious, coming from everywhere at once.

Seymira's heart pounded at the sheer velocity of the clamor.

When finally, the noise abated some, she peeked to find feet before her. There stood Drokmar, his intense gaze riveted on the beacon. She struggled quickly to her feet.

But just as she gained her footing, Seymira was thrown to the floor again. A bolt of lightning shot from the pillar to hit her master square in the chest. The power surge instantly snaked around him, encompassing his entire body. The pulsing electricity coursed so rapidly it began to lift Drokmar from the ground.

Seymira looked on, horrified. But Drokmar's face showed neither fear nor pain. His features mirrored those of an unresisting saint peacefully praising heaven. Yet an ominous smile played on his lips.

When Drokmar's feet touched down again, the beacon pulsed and retracted its energy. Drokmar gazed around with an intensity that startled the maiden at his feet. A menacing grin rearranged his face.

Seymira followed his gaze. The beacon sank to a soft glow back where it originated, among the Tamerik Mountains. But what became startlingly apparent was as the beacon receded, it took all other light with it.

The countryside once dotted with life was now blanketed in darkness. Even the sky was snuffed.

In every direction—nothing. The fire was gone from the hearth. The Burning Plains to the north—pitch black. Nothing could be seen anywhere.

Even the distant glow from the beacon was snuffed out, like a blanket was thrown over the pair who finally formed the True Alliance.

Seymira felt panic creep up to choke her. She frantically peered about, the darkness stealing in on her. Yet everywhere she turned it was black.

Suddenly her eyes grabbed hold of two pale green sparks of light. She watched them closely, yet the relief she expected to feel never came. Slowly, those pinpoints of light backed away from her and started to blaze. Through the blackness, she could hear breathing from the direction of the duo-blaze, deep and intense, causing vapors all around her. The hair on her arms stood on end, raising goosebumps across her body.

Then without warning, two new spheres of light appeared, orange and spinning. These were lower than the first and much farther apart. As the orbs grew in intensity, she could make out the form of her master. The pulsating spheres undulated within the palms of his hands. His eyes were the other points of light, glowing a menacing green in the surrounding blackness.

The sound of his breath deepened to a low rumble. Growing and growing, it finally bellowed forth into a mighty roar that he sent heavenward. At the thundering of his cry, his body transformed.

Seymira skittered back, bracing herself against the balustrade of the balcony. She shielded her gaze from the great flashes of light but could not pull it free of her master. He grew and grew, his features shifting. Each pulse of light showed her a new change. His skin turned scaly; his eyes were slivers of light. His body stretched, and his limbs turned to great and powerful claws.

When finally the flashing stopped, darkness enveloped her again. Yet through it all, there was still the rumble of breath. It grew gruffer, deeper, more savage, until… it again erupted into a mighty roar, piercing and primal. With it came yet another pulsing blaze.

Bone-chilling fear gripped Seymira at what it illuminated. There, standing before her, was the most massive and most frightening dragon she had ever set eyes upon.

Slowly, the roar of the dragon abated, and the flame diminished with it. Soon darkness gripped her again, leaving only the gleam from the creature's eyes. She could see them watching her. Try as she might, she could not look away.

While she observed, those eyes became smaller and slowly descended from their great height until they were yet again the height of an elf's.

Those pinpoints of light came slowly toward her. Seymira stifled a scream as they loomed above her. She could not breathe nor swallow. She felt a hand grip her arm that pulled her to a standing position. Panic flooded through her, yet she could do nothing but stare into those points of green flame—the only sparks of light to be seen in all of Sheorae.

"Seymira."

A fleeting sense of relief washed over her upon hearing Drokmar's voice. She reached out to him, clinging to his constancy to calm herself.

"At first light, send out the gibblings and the tarapins. It is finally time to crush the enemy and take Sheorae for my own."

Seymira felt his arm encircle her shoulders. He turned her to look out over what she believed to be the edge of the balcony. Of course, there was nothing to see. Nothing was visible. No light. No fires. No moons. Not even stars showed in the blackness of the sky.

"Out there…"

She felt his hot breath against her neck. His tone was deadly.

"Is the only real threat to my empire. If you want to stay by my side, get me those Blades before they reach Balcore Island. Is that clear?"

"Yes, master," Seymira croaked, yet the darkness stole her words.

"Good," Drokmar cooed.

He turned, taking with him the only points of light. Frantically, she reached out. She could feel nothing. She could not even see her own hand in front of her.

"Master!" she cried. "I'm afraid."

Again, the lights appeared, bringing with them a respite to her panic.

"Do not worry, my sweet." One gleaming eye disappeared and reappeared. Then they both narrowed menacingly. Despite his words, fear gripped her, choking the air from her lungs.

"The only thing to fear… is *me*."

If you enjoyed this book, I would sincerely appreciate it
if you would leave a review on Amazon, Goodreads,
and wherever you made your purchase.
It would mean so very much to me! Thank you!

Do you want more?

Can't get enough of Adianna and Kendrick?
Don't want to wait for or miss out on the next book?

Sign up now to be first in line for

Coming Spring 2024

and get the first chapter to *Wielding the Blades* for Free
www.tygerprice.com/Wielding-the-Blades

Also you can check out the world of Sheorae
on Tyger's Pinterest Boards at

www.pinterest.com/tygerprice/

ABOUT THE AUTHOR

Tyger Price is a native of the land of dreams and imagination where they do happy your way, and though her background is in children's literature, she just liked kissing books too much. Now she specializes in steamy-clean fantasy smattered with more than enough romance, adventure, and mystery to keep the pages turning. Along with her husband and ten children, they currently terrorize the Rocky Mountains of Idaho, where they savor delicious food, speak sarcasm and quotes, laugh till their sides hurt, build trebuchets in the back yard, and watch Skittles melt on Jell-O - just for the joy of it.

Tyger loves to hear from fans of her work.
So, visit with her on the Web at
www.tygerprice.com

Facebook https://www.facebook.com/TygerPriceAuthor
Instagram www.instagram.com/tyger.price/
Pinterest www.pinterest.com/tygerprice/

More by Tyger Price

The Blades of Sheorae:

Awaiting the Blades novella
An introduction to the world of Sheorae

Get your Free copy here
www.tygerprice.com

ACKNOWLEDGEMENTS

My Team—I have dreamed for so long of having a team as amazing as this! I'm so excited to thank all the wonderful people at MindStir Media, 100Covers, and Lincoln Writes. A warm thank you to Mariel Hemingway for taking the time on my book. I am so very grateful. Thanks to J.J. Hebert as well for endorsing my work. Thank you to Claire Ashgrove and Nicholas D. Goudsmit for helping to make my words and my world harmonize. Diana Estrada and Janet Hagan are amazing for all they do in keeping my social media humming so that all I have to do is mingle. Also, a great shout-out to Brittany Weese and the Best Page Forward team for such a winning description.

My Sister, Beth—This story could not have been realized without its humble beginnings. I'm not sure it would have developed the way it had had it not been for the accountability and joy of meeting weekly with my sister at the park to share our developing worlds with each other. Those were fun times! Thank you.

My Treasures—I am so grateful to all my kids, not simply for all the hours you tended yourselves while I wrote, edited, and prepped this book, but also the soundboarding, the drawings, the beta-reading, the feedback, and the encouragement you all provided, enabling me to turn this project into a dream come true. You truly are my treasures.

My Love—So much love and gratitude goes out to my amazing husband. You kept me going when I wanted to quit. The hours you put in listening to my woes, hashing plot points, enacting scenes, holding down the fort, and comforting me through meltdowns could be nothing but a true labor of love. I cannot thank you enough.

My God—An enormous amount of gratitude goes to Him for strengthening me, keeping me, for inspiring this instrument, for leading the way, and for making my beautiful life possible. Thank you for teaching me that dreams are for creating, not just imagining. I am so blessed.

Lastly MY AWESOME READERS—Holy Hannah! The success of this book would be piddling if it weren't for You. For that reason, I would like to offer a special Thank You to you.

Go to www.tygerprice.com/thank-you/
for a
FREE GIFT

www.ingramcontent.com/pod-product-compliance
Lightning Source LLC
Chambersburg PA
CBHW030419310726
48979CB00009B/1525/J

* 9 7 9 8 9 8 6 4 6 9 6 0 7 *